Daelan The Damned

By James Clay

Cover art by Michael Gladigau
Developmental Editing by Joel Brigham

Acknowledgements

I owe thanks to Ben Price, Nathan Hacking, Lorraine Peters, Brian Masteller, and Aaron Ihnen for reading an earlier version of the book and providing invaluable feedback. Thank you, guys!

I also want to acknowledge the contributions of my wife, Merilee. She read more than one version of the book (a sign of love as great as any I've ever heard of) and offered an encouraging word whenever one was needed. Thanks, honey.

Chapter 1

"Are you ready to head out, Jen?"

"Almost."

Joseph stopped by her room to see what she was doing. He surveyed the room quickly. There were clothes on the floor, but fewer than usual.

Maybe the talks are getting through to her.

Posters of Suga and Cristiano Ronaldo adorned the walls, and plushies from her favorite animes were on the windowsill. Imogen was lying on the bed, face up, staring at her phone, finger flying around and tapping on the screen.

Texting. Of course. Joseph sighed, regretting giving his eleven-year-old daughter a phone, but she and his wife had ganged up to convince him that her social life would be non-existent without it. He did have to admit that her gaggle of friends all had them.

He decided not to give her a hard time. This was supposed to be a good day, so he just continued packing the fishing gear in the SUV. Jen showed up in the garage a few minutes later.

"Okay, I'm ready."

"Could you grab the sandwiches that Mom made and put them in the cooler?"

"Sure."

"Thanks."

Before leaving they said goodbye to Anna. Jen just gave a quick "Bye, Mom," while Joseph gave her a kiss and a quick squeeze of her bottom that, judging by Jen's eye-roll, was not as discreet as he had thought.

Joseph smiled with embarrassment at his wife in mute apology.

She shook her head and smiled. It was her way of saying "You dummy" and "I forgive you" at the same time.

"Have fun."

"You too."

He wasn't sure what Anna would do, but when she had the chance she usually got together with one or more of her friends. Though Joseph knew she loved them, he also knew she looked forward to days like this.

The drive to his favorite fishing hole was quiet. He liked to talk with his daughter at times like this, but their relationship had become awkward over the last year. He used to go camping with her, but she wasn't as interested these days. He regretted that they seemed to have less in common all the time. He wasn't sure what to do about it. If the fishing trip didn't go well, he might break down and let her paint his nails or something.

"How are your friends doing?"

"Fine."

"Are you guys going to do something tomorrow?"

"Probably."

"Have you watched any good anime lately?" Joseph didn't know much about anime, but he knew Jen and her friends enjoyed it.

"Not really."

He sighed quietly. Jen clearly wasn't in the mood to talk, so he let it be. When they got to the stream, he handed her his fishing pole and the fly she had made in the last few days. While it wasn't as neat and tight as store-bought or the ones he made, it wasn't bad for a first try.

Besides, there's nothing like catching a fish with a fly you made.

After they put on their waders they went out into the gentle stream. They walked out to Joseph's favorite spot, where he demonstrated how to flick the flexible rod back and forth so the fly would land in the water and then flick back out, mimicking the movements of one of the fishes' favorite foods. Afterwards, he encouraged her to try.

Jen's casts were awkward at first, but with some guidance she became smoother. Joseph knew that coaching her longer would be counterproductive. At some point you have to do it yourself and figure it out, so he moved to a different area, leaving the prime fishing spot to her.

They fished for the next couple of hours, occasionally moving to different areas. Joseph loved fishing. He loved being out in nature, seeing the sunlight glinting off the ripples in the water, hearing the insects and birds.

I could do without the gnats, but nothing's perfect.

He was pleased that Jen caught a couple of trout. They released one because it was too small, but the other was a pretty good size. When they decided to call it quits they had four fish in the water-filled bucket.

"Are you ready to gut the fish?"

"Ugh. I guess."

Once she started, Jen got over the grossness and did a good job. The scales on the fish were small enough that they didn't have to be removed, but Joseph used the opportunity to teach her how to do it anyway. When they were done they rinsed their hands, pulled the sandwiches out of the ice-filled cooler, and put the fish in.

"Dad?"

"Yeah?"

"Can I ask you something?"

"Of course. What's up?"

"What do you do when you mess up?"

Joseph looked over at her. Jen looked uncomfortable, her hands clasped between her knees, eyes downward.

"That depends on the mess up. What happened?"

She told him a convoluted tale that, to his amusement, boiled down to her and one of her friends liking the same boy, who probably hadn't even been through puberty yet. In her social maneuverings Jen started a rumor that her friend, Madison, was just using Liam to get to his friend, Brian.

When Joseph sorted it out, he chuckled.

Imogen glared at him. She was too full of righteous wrath at the moment to be just "Jen".

"It's not funny, Dad!"

"Sorry, sorry," he said as he held up his hands placatingly. "I wasn't laughing at you. I was laughing at how much more complicated your relationships are than mine."

She muttered, "I knew I should have asked Mom..."

"Hey, hold on. Asking Mom is a good idea, but I might be able to help too."

She looked at him skeptically, but still asked, "So what do you think I should do?"

"What do *you* think you should do?"

Jen rolled her eyes. "If I knew that, I wouldn't have asked."

Joseph just gave her his own skeptical look, only his was the cocked-head version that said, "C'mon, really?"

Jen frowned and looked down. "I-I don't want to."

He thought about how to approach this. After a few moments, he said, "There are two kinds of people in the world, Jen."

When she saw that he wasn't going to continue until she said something, she rolled her eyes. "Let me guess, people that screw up, and people like you who don't?"

He shook his head, smiling. "No, though I'm flattered you think that, even if you were joking. No, everyone screws up. The two kinds of people are: those who do what they can to fix it, and those who pretend they didn't screw up. Your mistake bothers you, like a sliver. It hurts. You can ignore it, but it's always there, and the annoying pain reminds you of that. The best thing to do is get it out as soon as you can. If you wait, you'll still have to get it out eventually, and it will just keep hurting in the meantime."

Jen chewed on her lip.

"What happens if you ignore it? Does it eventually stop hurting?"

He shook his head again. "Not really. It still hurts; you just get better at ignoring it. You just keep getting more and more slivers until you become one big ball of pus."

Jen laughed at the unexpected image. Afterward she nodded and said, "Yeah, I get it."

"Good." He ruffled her hair, which she pretended to hate.

"Gross! Your hands smell like fish, Dad!"

Okay, maybe she actually hated it. Joseph turned to her with a bright smile. "See? I screw up too. I'll fix it by washing your hair. C'mere, and I'll give you a patented river hair wash."

She rolled her eyes.

How many times can that girl roll her eyes in one day?

"Let's just go, Dad."

"Alright. Just know that if you ever want that river hair wash, I'm good for it."

4

"I'll keep that in mind."

They had finished their sandwiches while they talked, so they cleaned up and stowed everything in the car. The drive home was just as quiet as the drive to the river, but it was a comfortable kind of quiet.

When they arrived home they parked the car and opened the back of the SUV to pull out their gear and cooler. Anna came out while they put away the rods and tackle box.

"How was the fishing?"

Joseph grinned. "Good! Jen caught two, only one of them was even smaller than her, so we had to let it go."

Jen stuck her tongue out at him. "I think we could have caught all of the fish in the river, and even combined they wouldn't have weighed as much as you, Dad."

Joseph mock-frowned and said, "Now you're just being mean."

Sensing that she had him on the ropes, Jen grinned. "It only hurts because it's true."

He turned to his wife. "Do you hear this daughter of yours?"

Anna nodded with a gentle smile. "I do. Unfortunately, someone has taught her how to be sarcastic since she was in the cradle."

"I wonder who that could be?"

"Yes," she said as she rolled her eyes. "I wonder."

Joseph pointed at her in accusation. "There! You see! She learned the eye-rolling from you!"

Anna shook her head with the corners of her lips curled up and started to roll her eyes again but, when she realized what she was doing, forced herself to stop.

He was about to crow in victory when he heard steps coming up the driveway.

"Joseph Santos?"

"Yes?" he responded while turning around.

He saw a man wearing sunglasses and a beanie lift a gun and point it at his chest.

What the...?! "Imogen, Anna, run!"

He pushed his daughter to the side and started to lurch towards the gunman. Before he even finished the first step, he heard the roar of the gun and felt the impact of the bullet.

Though he was shocked, his other selves had been through enough physical trauma and danger to fill twenty lifetimes, so he pushed through it. When the man saw him continue to stagger forward, he shot twice more, dropping Joseph to the ground. Despite the roar in his ears, he heard his wife and daughter screaming.

Run, you fools! he thought while desperately looking for them through his blurry tears. He saw Anna run towards him. He wasn't sure whether she was coming to help him or attack the gunman. Either way, the gun roared again and opened a red bloom on her chest.

Oh, no. No, no, no… Imogen… please, run…

He looked for her, but everything became fuzzy, muddled, and, all too soon… quiet.

**

Fifty-three beings on different worlds felt the loss of Joseph. None of them had been experiencing him when he died, so no one was alarmed. Sometimes one of them died. It happened.

When the second one died seconds later, though, they all reacted. It was possible that it was a coincidence, but…

When the third died, they knew. Someone was hunting them.

Some of them were powerful, and some were not. Regardless of their abilities and actions, their lives continued to be snuffed out. A sea elf in an underwater city. A dwarf in a mountain fortress. A human on an expedition in a jungle. An elven woman caring for her baby. All dead.

**

Darius, the God-King of Sicanthus, broke out of his meditation and looked at his surroundings, though his attention was not on the spartan but expensive decor. He hadn't experienced anything like this in his 108,000 years of life. Thirty-two of his avatars had been killed so far, and the number was still rising. Whoever had done this had obviously put forth enormous effort and had detailed knowledge about his avatars. They had been on fifty-three different planets, after all. Well, fifty-two planets and *that* place. Setting up a hit like this must have taken decades, at least, and a vast amount of resources.

It didn't take a genius to figure out that it had to involve people very close to him.

As he pondered which of his confidantes it could be, the door to his bedroom opened. In walked his second wife, Helen. She was beautiful as always, but her malicious smile ruined the effect. She had always been ambitious. That part of her had appealed to him tens of thousands of years ago, but he had changed. Now, she just seemed shallow.

Helen had been his top suspect, so it was not a great surprise that she was here. What did surprise him was that his younger brother, Tyrus, and his friend and general, Lysander, followed her. His eyes narrowed as he took them in.

With a negligible effort that was as natural to him as breathing, Darius opened his third eye to take in the people before him. He saw the karma that hung heavy upon them. They carried the stink of betrayal and blood.

And... lust?

Darius laughed bitterly when he realized his betrayal was as base and banal as what happened daily to the lowliest street sweepers and beggars in his empire.

I am cuckolded. How droll.

There was a mystery still. How did they have the courage to do this? As strong as they were, he was stronger by far.

Helen bowed. "Lord Darius, greetings."

Darius snorted. "What have you done, Helen?"

"It is not what we have done, my lord, but what we are doing."

"And what is that?"

"Killing you."

Angry at their betrayal and brazenness, Darius cycled his energy to literally crush them where they stood. His energy, normally so quick to respond to his desires, moved like molasses. Like tar in his veins. He looked at his hands and body in shock.

He reached out to the energy in the air. He knew it should be plentiful—he had created the mana-gathering arrays himself, after all—but he felt nothing. After millennia of god-like power, he felt like a cripple.

Helen laughed, and his brother and erstwhile friend smirked. "You feel it, don't you? How dead your energy is. We have been administering a subtle poison to you for the last thirty years. You have no idea how much we've done to make this moment possible. The years of planning, gathering resources, finding allies and agents, coordinating it all, and solving problems along the way.

Darius looked at the threads of fate into the past to get a feel for what they had done. He saw a few of the "problems" Helen mentioned—loyal subjects who discovered a part of the plot and were killed. Even in the midst of his troubles, Darius mourned them.

I'm sorry that I wasn't a better king for you. Rest in peace.

Darius looked at the three of them and asked, "Why?"

Lysander stepped forward and gestured at him and the mat that Darius was kneeling on. "Because this is all you do! You stay in here for years, and decades, and *centuries*, contemplating your damn navel. You pay no attention to your empire!"

There was an "or us" that was heard, but not spoken, at the end of his complaint.

Has it been so long?

Darius had spent tens of thousands of years building his power and his empire. After he had laid all his enemies low and achieved everything he had set out to do, he was unsatisfied. He was bored. He could have invaded more planets, but that just felt like it would be more of the same. He wanted something *more*. Something meaningful.

Darius started what he called "The Sum of All Men" project. He created avatars of himself by creating bodies and implanting a piece of his soul in them. He sent the avatars far and wide to experience the universe so he could learn and—hopefully—grow. The early avatars were all extremely powerful. Although they did not often use their power, they always knew it was there if needed. Darius eventually realized that his avatars were not experiencing the same kind of life their fellows were, because they never risked anything. They were never in danger. They never lacked money. They could usually solve their problems as easily as snapping their fingers.

He started sending out avatars that were mere mortals. Men, women, elves, humans, dwarves, gnomes, orcs, and beasts of various kinds. Some were beautiful, and some were ugly. Some started with a multitude of gifts, while others began with just the rags on their backs. He sent them to all of the known inhabited planets so they could live, experience, and comprehend.

Comprehend what? Darius wasn't entirely sure, but he felt like there was *something* he was grasping at. During this process that took millenia, he came to think of the avatars as his children—sons and daughters with whom he shared the most intimate of connections, being able to see what they saw, feel what they felt, and hear what they thought.

As his mind returned to his beloved and hated enemies, he felt pain. He had experienced enough through his sons and daughters to have a broader sense of self than most. While he was angry and wanted to deny his friend's accusation, he knew in his heart it was true.

The fact that they got this far without me detecting the plot is the strongest proof of my negligence.

Darius sighed. He had screwed up badly, but that didn't make their betrayal acceptable. He rode the threads of fate to see how he could defeat his enemies with his paralyzed powers. His expression grew ever dimmer as every thread he followed ended in his death. The closest he came to success was feigning an attack and then running away to buy time to clear the poison from his body. Though he never entirely regained his powers, he was able to kill his brother and wound Helen and Lysander. But he still lost.

Worse, their fighting devastated his empire, and his home, the planet of Sicanthus, most of all. Billions of people died, and significant portions of the planet turned to magma.

Though he would dearly love to kill his traitorous brother and give grievous wounds to his wife and friend, he wasn't willing to do it at the price of so many.

I am sorry, my people. I hope they are better rulers than I was.

Darius returned his attention to where it had started—his avatars. He mourned that they were all dead except for one, Daelan the Damned, as his sibling-avatars had come to call him.

Poor Daelan.

A thousand years ago Darius discovered, for the first time, an alternate plane of existence. It was an exciting discovery that was quickly dampened by the nature of the place. Though he had long since given up believing in gods or goddesses, the plane bore an uncanny resemblance to how various religions described the state and suffering of sinners after death. The avatars started calling the plane "Hell".

Darius believed that experiencing suffering could be enlightening, so he asked for volunteers. No one wanted to go. He could have forced one of his avatars, but that would have been wrong. No one volunteered until he created Daelan. "Send me," he said.

For the last 20 of his years, Daelan had suffered. Darius noticed that, unique among the avatars, none of them experienced Daelan. Ever.

Darius did, but it was, well… painful. Now Daelan was the only one left. Apparently his enemies had not learned about Hell.

While talking with them, Darius gathered information that Daelan would need to grow stronger. He had long since mastered dividing his consciousness to execute multiple tasks simultaneously. It was child's play compared to creating an avatar.

He had to be selective about what he sent. Daelan simply did not have the capacity to remember everything that Darius knew, so he picked possible cultivation paths for him and sent everything he would need.

He thought about transmitting a piece of his consciousness. It was sorely tempting, in part because he did not want to leave his son alone in such an awful place. He knew, in his heart of hearts, though, that part of his motivation was that he didn't want to die.

Darius shook his head. He had strived and failed. It was his son's time, not his, so he used all of the capacity to give Daelan information he would need. It would have to be enough.

Task finished, he made peace with his ending. It was time to die.

Chapter 2

Daelan

"You know I only do this because I love you and want you to be the best man you can be, right?" Daelan's wife asked as she finished securing his legs to the chair. His arms were already tied to the armrests by leather straps.

"Yes, dear, so you keep telling me," Daelan said dryly. "Truly, your love knows no bounds."

She eyed him suspiciously, as if to determine if he was mocking her.

Yes, he said with his eyes, *I absolutely am.*

Her nose flared with anger, but she ignored him and continued with her soliloquy. "Many wives," she said as she grabbed a shiny pair of pliers and held it up to the light, inspecting it for who-knew-what, "would feed their husband dinner, snuggle with him, and tell him how wonderful he is, but not me."

"Not you," Daelan agreed.

"Those wives want their husbands to be *soft* and *weak*. I want better for you. I'm helping you strive for perfection!"

Seeing what the night was going to bring, he did his best to stifle a shudder and said, "I take it my nails are imperfect and thus need to be removed?"

She narrowed her eyes again and pointed the pliers at him. "You are obstinate and defiant, with a weak, flippant manner. I mean to cure you of those flaws."

Contrary to her accusation of flippancy, Daelan took his "wife" as seriously as a heart attack. How could he not, when she tortured him every night? Choking, burning, electrocuting, beating, skinning. Sometimes she mixed it up with the psychological variety, forcing him to watch other men pleasure her, often his boss, who mocked him with every thrust.

Daelan didn't mind those nights. It helped that he knew his "wife" was an ugly male demon with scabrous skin and a club

11

foot, and his boss was an even uglier one with three legs and four arms, the extras pointing in the wrong directions. He wasn't honestly sure what sex the boss was, but it didn't matter. No actual sex took place, thank goodness. He had zero interest in having that image in his brain.

And then of course his mind, being the perverse thing it was, created the image.

Damn it. I so did not need that.

The demons were masters of illusion, creating new identities and scenarios at will. The illusions went so far as to affect the mind, making him believe—if he let them—that the demon was indeed his wife. Fortunately, Daelan could use the true sight of his third, inner eye, to see the truth of things.

"I have an idea. I hate surprises, which seems like a weakness to me. Why don't you surprise me by being nice to me tonight?"

She sneered. "You'd like that, wouldn't you? No, my dear, someone as recalcitrant as you requires special measures."

Daelan frowned. It was better than weeping and begging for mercy, for there was none to be found here. It was going to be a long, painful night.

**

Daelan's "wife" was working on the nail on his right ring finger—the fourth of the night—when he felt one of his avatar-siblings die.

He wondered who it had been while he futilely tried to wipe away the tears and snot, when he felt the next one's existence end.

Uh-oh.

He narrowed his eyes. This was not the first time he had felt a sibling die, but a second one in seconds? That was a first.

Then another was ended. Daelan was paying attention, so he knew who it was this time: Iliana.

Damn it.

He didn't want any of his siblings to die, but Iliana and her young son, Colin, a rambunctious three-year-old, were a couple of his favorites. He would miss the tender moments between them. Experiencing their love made living in Hell a little more bearable. He sincerely hoped Colin was okay.

One by one, more siblings died. He knew, from dropping in to experience them, what the survivors were feeling: fear and horror. Daelan felt the same, only there was a great deal of anger and bitterness too.

He didn't mind the thought of dying—he was, after all, in Hell—but he couldn't bear the thought of everything he'd done, everything he'd suffered, to be… meaningless.

He wept angry tears as he watched more and more of his fellow avatars die violent deaths.

Daelan wasn't afraid to die. Hell, he welcomed it. He didn't want his avatar-siblings to die, though, because he was a believer. He believed in Darius' project, "The Sum of All Men". It was part of why he had volunteered for this place. It gave his suffering meaning.

"No, no, no…" he cried out as he felt the violent passing of more siblings. As his family dwindled moment by moment, he contemplated his own approaching death. He looked around through blurry tears.

So this is how it ends. Tied to a chair, my "wife" ripping the nails off my fingers before she bangs the demonic pool boy. How pathetic.

The tension was so thick that the demon stopped torturing him. She looked at him strangely. Daelan hardly noticed.

"Come on, already! Kill me if you're going to do it!"

There were only six avatars left. Daelan didn't experience them because he wanted to at least see his end coming.

Five. Four. A full minute went by with no deaths, giving him some hope that a few would survive.

Three… two… one…

Daelan couldn't help it at that point. He dived into the consciousness of the only other avatar: Matias, a mighty serpent mage on the planet Nyoka. He was slithering through murky swamp water, reeds, mud, and patches of land. He was in pain, bleeding from grievous wounds that penetrated deep into his body.

Matias created shields as he slipped through the landscape, but they were torn down just as quickly by attacks from multiple directions. Daelan sensed his sibling's frenzied thoughts as he desperately sought a path to survival. Flight? He would take more attacks without cover. Teleportation? Not enough time to cast.

His hopes grew as he neared a deeper swamp that had many hiding places. His pursuers were human and not well adapted to a watery swamp, which should give him enough time to escape, heal, and prepare to destroy them.

As he slithered over one of the last patches of land, he felt a mana buildup that started to lift him into the air. He tore it apart, releasing him onto the ground, but the second of delay was enough for a mage in a mud-stained gi to land heavily next to him, causing mud to splash ten meters in all directions. He was already sweeping his bloody saber down with unstoppable speed as he landed.

The last thing Daelan experienced was Matias mentally screaming '*NO!*' before all went dark and he was forced back into his own perspective.

I'm the last avatar.

At least his Father was still alive. Though he could not step into his Father's thoughts and senses like he did—had done, he thought with a fresh pang of grief—with his siblings, he would know if he died.

As long as Darius survives, it will all be worth it. I'll be remembered.

Those thoughts consoled him, and were why he broke when he felt his Father die.

Nooooo!

Daelan didn't remember much about the next few hours. It was a straight-up mental breakdown—a new low that not even the demons had driven him to before.

He gradually "woke up" from his depressed stupor. The demon was long gone, and he still had four of his fingernails. Daelan smiled, but could not summon the energy to chuckle. He wondered if it was the first time that a demon had seen pain that even it couldn't bear to watch.

He knew that was just his ego talking though. The universe had seen far more pain than what he was feeling. No, the demon

14

probably left because it didn't like him not responding to her efforts.

Whatever the reason, he was glad she was gone.

He started working on freeing himself from the restraints. He'd found, from past experience, that lubrication was needed to loosen them. Usually he struggled to produce enough spit to get the job done, water being scarce in this arid land. Tonight, though, his tears would more than suffice.

**

When Daelan was free and far from any demons, he lay down in the dust and looked up at the drab sky.

What now? Is there any point to going on?

He didn't know. It wasn't in his nature to end himself, but there was no way in Hell he was going to let himself be tortured now.

Daelan started coming up with ways to kill himself. It wasn't easy when you had virtually no resources and a body with superhuman regenerative abilities. He was pretty sure bashing his head with a rock wouldn't work. He wasn't strong enough to cave it in in one shot, and anything less than that would just make him unconscious, which he would recover from. The dominant plant life in Hell was dry, tough vines with wickedly sharp thorns up to five inches long. Though he could reach his heart with that, he wasn't sure that would be enough.

No, the only way he could guarantee death was by finding a good, long thorn and burying it in his eye.

Maybe even swirl it around a bit if I can.

In the middle of his dark thoughts, a burst of mana broke into his head. It started creating spellforms that targeted certain portions of his brain, particularly the hippocampus and neocortex.

His memories and knowledge were being expanded.

In the middle of his shock, he heard a voice.

'Daelan,

I have failed. By the time you get this, I and all of your siblings will be dead. I was betrayed by people close to me. It doesn't matter who—they are far beyond your ability to harm.

15

I have seen that you will be tempted to kill yourself. I value free choice, so I won't coerce you to choose one way or the other, but I hope you will choose to live. Your siblings left loved ones behind. If you need a new cause, let them be your cause.

I am sorry, my son. You were my most devoted avatar. You have suffered much. I hope you can find just as much happiness.

Darius'

Daelan was a maelstrom of emotions. Elation at the attention and appreciation of his Father. Despair at his death. Hopeful about the new knowledge and memories. Terror of living the rest of his life in Hell.

Death would be easy. Right now, in the middle of his pain, it was appealing. Like undisturbed sleep, untroubled by cares.

It would be so damn nice to not be in pain all the time. And yet... if I die, everything dies with me.

He shook his head in refusal. He couldn't allow that to happen. He would do as his Father bade and help the families of his siblings. That was the least he could do for the God-King, his final act of piety.

After that, he would do as he wished, no matter how dark the road or tangled the path, even if it went against the God-King's implied command.

He would do as he wanted, and what he wanted was revenge. He wanted to kill everyone that destroyed everything good in his life. He wanted to destroy root and branch, tear it from the soil, and salt the earth.

And then he could rest.

Chapter 3

It did not, unfortunately, take Daelan long to come down from his emotion-driven cocktail of hormones. As the horror, anger, and fear cooled, the pain returned to fill up every nook and cranny they had abandoned.

Gods, how he was tired of pain.

He wasn't sure what the motivation for the demons' sadism was, at least in his case. He thought he understood why they tortured the damned souls that came here. The pitiful spirits descended from the sky at random times and were seized upon by the demons. They seemed to be able to physically interact with the incorporeal spirits. How, he didn't know.

The damned spirits were flayed, ripped, or otherwise dismantled, which released their core, their *anima*, to leave Hell and, presumably, move on to reincarnation, leaving the demons to consume their cast-off spirits.

It filled Daelan with helpless rage and frustration whenever he considered his situation, because he suspected that the demons tortured him for no other reason than habit, given that he provided them with no sustenance.

Tortured because that's the demon way to say "hello", he thought bitterly. *At least she doesn't lick my tears anymore.*

Early on, he had thought it was another way to humiliate and traumatize him, but he eventually realized that she was hoping it was pieces of his spirit. He chuckled darkly and thought, *Worst marriage ever. Neither one of us getting what we want.*

Daelan trotted off through the sharp and dusty rocks to get some distance. He needed time. Time to grieve and see what knowledge his Father had sent. And, once he knew what he had, he would need time to plan, because he had no intention of staying in Hell forever.

And if he didn't see a way to make that happen, he would find the longest thorn he could and end things, regardless of what Father wanted.

**

Daelan spent the next few hours poring through the information the God-King sent. Much of it was about how to use mana, the primal catalyst of the universe, to alter reality, but Daelan skipped that part. Hell had no mana.

The God-King knew that, so Daelan desperately hoped he had sent a solution.

A primer on the sciences... Pass. A rocket is not going to get me out of this dimension. Sympathetic magic? Also not helpful. Voodoo dolls are not going to help me.

He knew that sympathetic magic involved much more than "voodoo dolls", but in his worried and agitated state, he had no time for generosity.

It took two days for Daelan to survey the various paths of power that Darius had sent. Almost all of them required mana, which was both infuriating and unsurprising. Darius was, after all, a master of mana who believed it to be the ultimate source of power.

There were two sources of magic, though, that didn't rely on mana and seemed potentially useful: contracts with supernatural beings and runic magic.

The contracts were interesting because Darius had the true names of several powerful beings who, since they had contracted with him, were now unbound. There were two problems though: he didn't have much to offer them, and all but two of them were from Darius' plane of existence. Daelan had no idea if the others were capable of extending their power to other planes or not.

The two that were left—a malevolent being that craved death, and an emotionless being of pure logic—could cross planes, but he didn't like the sound of either of them. Daelan wasn't convinced the creature of logic would be useful, and he just didn't like the sound of the other one. It didn't seem much better than the demons themselves.

Daelan also didn't know if they could extend themselves to Hell. Darius had never figured out where their planes were, so they may have been farther away from Hell than his native plane.

Daelan shrugged. Whether they were or weren't, there was nothing he could do about it. If it worked, it worked. If it didn't, there was always the fallback plan of runic magic.

18

Runic magic looked very interesting. It used written language to guide energy and create magical effects. What was interesting about it was that it sounded like the runes could use pretty much any form of energy. Even, in theory, fire or electricity.

Or souls.

And Darius had included the runes for "Consume" and "Soul". Daelan didn't know if a runic phrase that simple would work or not, and what would happen if he consumed the soul… There were questions that needed to be answered, but it was promising enough to give Daelan hope.

**

Daelan's first step was to get a weapon. He couldn't do anything if he couldn't even harm the demons.

He wanted to get a mystical weapon through a contract. There were a number of beings in Darius' list of names that would fit the bill, but Daelan narrowed it down to two: Tor'elanoth'darnish'tysan'gehelt, and Quoz'zethrien'allanit'yuribaal'felanit'non. He wanted to make a deal with Tor because it had above-average power, hated evil, and was relatively benign, as these things go. He figured that it wouldn't be hard to convince Tor to make a deal, given that he was trying to kill demons. The problem was that Tor was from Darius' plane. He wasn't sure if he would, or even could, extend himself to Hell.

Quoz was not benign. He was very powerful, but the kind of powerful that was a double-edged sword. Daelan hoped to make a deal with Tor and avoid dealing with Quoz altogether.

Daelan looked at the hard, two inch long thorn in his hands. It was still attached to a rope-like piece of vine. The tough plant was his only source of sustenance. His jaw muscles had become exceptionally strong from having to grind down the tough and fibrous plants.

His "wife" came by with his "boss" while he was working to free the thorn. They taunted him about his uselessness and how he was going to take care of her like she needed. Daelan just waved them off as he chewed without even looking at them. A couple of hours later, through sheer dogged persistence, he had the wickedly sharp spike.

The ground acted like hard, baked clay that resisted all attempts at digging. Daelan found that he could, when armed with the thorn, scratch shapes into the hard-as-nails dirt. He spent a few hours laboriously scratching mini-trenches in an intricate pattern. Thankfully, no demons approached. He didn't want to push his luck, though, so he continued digging with the less-than-ideal tool even when he grew tired. He made the pattern neater and deeper. The summoning ceremony was too costly to allow mistakes.

At last, when it was nearing time for his sleep, he decided the pattern was ready. An imp had disturbed him towards the end, but he drove away the vile creature by stabbing it a few times.

Afraid that more demons would come, he thought about doing the ceremony right then.

No. I have to be patient. If a demon interrupts the ceremony, it would be disastrous.

He hunkered down and waited to see if more demons came. None did, but sleep crept past his careful guard and invaded his tired mind.

**

Daelan dreamed. It was not an elaborate dream. Much like someone exhausted from a long hike who would like nothing better than somewhere to sit, Daelan didn't want much. Just kindness and compassion. Somewhere to go that was a respite from the rest of the world, where he could be with people he loved, and who loved him.

His wife—a woman who had a nebulous, dream-like attractiveness—looked over her shoulder at Daelan.

"Would you like to have a drink, honey?"

"Yes, please."

She brought him freshly squeezed juice with ice. The cold glass felt good on his warm hand.

"Thank you."

She sat on the couch and turned to lean on the armrest. She swung her legs over Daelan's lap and smiled, wiggling her toes.

"You're welcome. You know how you could pay me back, right?"

Daelan chuckled. She loved having her feet rubbed. He knew how to press into the arches of her feet just enough to release tension without causing her pain. She sighed with pleasure as he started working on her feet in between sips of juice.

While he had the glass upended, trying to get the delicious pulp, he heard loud scratching. He put the glass down and saw his wife casually scratching the oak hardwood floor. Her thick nails dug in and created deep scratches. His confusion became an uneasy feeling.

"What are you doing, honey?"

She smiled at him.

"Don't mind me. I just felt like redecorating. These floors are so passé, don't you think?"

Everything felt surreal and ominous, but he didn't want to push her away, so he just sat there, rubbing her feet, though he no longer concentrated on the task.

"There. That's better."

She brought her heavy, hairy hand up to her face and inspected it. She pulled out an emery board and started idly roughing the talons.

"Honey…?"

She looked at him questioningly. "What, sweetie?"

"W-what happened to your hand?"

His wife looked puzzled. "What's wrong with it?" She turned the hand back and forth, looking for problems. Daelan saw the rough, manly skin, the hairy knuckles, and the thick, knobby nails, and shuddered.

Apparently finding no issues with the hand, his wife turned to him with a playful smile. "Oh, you're just teasing me, aren't you?" She smiled sweetly as she put her feet down and scooted over next to Daelan. He shuddered as she put the hand on his chest. As much as he adored his wife and thought she was beautiful, his entire focus was on the hand. It made his skin crawl, and he unconsciously distanced himself from his wife in an attempt to get away from it, but she simply got closer.

She raised the hand so only the index and middle fingers were touching him, and then started to "walk" the hand downwards as she spoke, one word per step.

"I. Know. How. My. Hand. Can. Make. You. Feel. Nice."

When she said the last word, the hand was above his groin. When Daelan realized what she intended, he jumped up and moved away, unable to contain his disgust and fear.

The shock brought him to a state of semi-consciousness, and he felt a warm body next to him. It took Daelan only a moment to realize what that meant, even with his sleep-addled brain. When he did, he once again jumped up and saw a monstrosity that had been embracing him just a moment before.

The demon looked like its flesh had melted down its body, creating folds of flesh. Its two octopus-like limbs were covered by suckers and ended in large talons. When Daelan looked down, he saw that his skin had round abrasions—the same size as the demon's suckers—that bled profusely.

The worst thing about the demon was its pinkish flesh-colored hue. Even with all of its grotesqueness, it made him wonder, just for a moment, if it was actually a hideous person, and it wasn't much of a step to connect it to his dream wife.

"Aagh!" he screamed as he stabbed the monstrosity over and over with his thorn. It was awkward with it being only a couple of inches long, but he didn't notice or care. All he cared about was making the hideous thing go away. Whether that meant causing it to flee or tearing it into shreds, he didn't care. He just wanted it gone.

As Daelan tore into its skin, it made unhappy noises and started shambling off. Daelan thought about chasing the creature and trying to kill it, but decided he just wanted to be away from the damnable thing, so he threw the thorn down and shuddered.

After a few minutes, he wiped his eyes and nose and stood up. He was more than ready to do the ceremony because he wanted nothing more than to kill his tormentors.

He sagged, though, when he saw the summoning circle he had spent the day before on. It was ruined, with deep scratches running across it. He sank back down to the ground and covered his head with his hands. His eyes, which had been dry for just a moment, became wet again.

Damn it.

**

It took a few days for Daelan to prepare the summoning ceremony. He had to find a small, hidden cave in a rock that he couldn't even fully sit up in, let alone stand. It was dark, which made it challenging to ensure the pattern was correct. He used the ever-present dim light and his sense of touch to do his best. It would have to do.

On the morning he intended to perform the ceremony, Daelan chewed on another vine. He ate to alleviate his ever-present hunger and distract himself from his fears. Fear of failure. Fear of being stuck here. He had mixed feelings about death. As the only thing left of the God-King—other than his descendants, but they weren't him like Daelan was—Daelan didn't want to die, because that would mean he was totally and irrevocably gone.

On the other hand, he longed for release.

If "release" meant escape from Hell, he would jump on it. If it meant death, he would still take it. Anything to end this.

He sighed and spit out the unconsumed parts of the vine.

Time to do this.

He crawled over to the summoning circle and blew on it to get rid of any dust or missed bits of dirt. He avoided touching it even though he knew he couldn't scratch the baked dirt with his bare hands even if he tried.

There could be no mistakes.

When he finished blowing on it, he hesitated. As much as he wanted release, he was still scared to die. Steeling himself, he pulled out a new, unused thorn that was as sharp as the finest dagger.

As thin as he was, it was easy to find prominent veins all over his body. He remembered how his avatar-sibling Joseph had donated blood from a vein in the crook of his arm, so Daelan stabbed the needle into the same vein. He pulled the thorn out and watched the blood spurt out in synchronization with his heartbeat. It intermittently shot out like a stream of water from a fountain. Between spurts it dribbled like a drooling baby.

23

The blood made a right mess. Daelan used his hands to push the blood into the lines of the summoning circle.

Damn it! How did I not realize this was going to make a mess?

He was kicking himself as he did his best to squeegee the blood off the hard dirt and into the pattern. He knew it was far from ideal, but he had to move forward while the blood was still fresh.

Once there was enough blood, he clamped the self-inflicted wound with his hand and awkwardly used the other one to continue getting as much of the blood into the pattern as he could.

Daelan was freaking out, but his personality was based on a man who had been through numerous life-and-death experiences, and made it through them all.

Well, almost all of them.

The "freaking out" part of his mind receded to the background, while he quickly went over his options.

I can go forward as-is. Not ideal, but it could still work. I could try to clean it up some more. I don't think I'm making any progress at the moment, but the small amounts of blood on the dirt should dry up faster than the blood in the pattern. I could give it a couple of minutes, let it dry out, and then sweep it.

What if my blood attracts demons, though?

He went back and forth on what gave him the best odds of success. He would have just retreated and tried again another day if he could simply regenerate and be back to square one, but he couldn't do that. He could make new blood, given his body's healing powers, but he couldn't replace the lost life force because of the paucity of mana in Hell. The life force was what really mattered in the summoning ceremony.

He decided to try cleaning up the blood on the dirt after he thought about how he was the odd duck in Hell. The demons were used to spirits, not mortals. They would not have had any reason to evolve the ability to smell blood.

He wasn't 100% confident in his reasoning, but decided to push forward anyway. With his body's more-than-natural healing ability, it didn't take long for his arm to stop bleeding, allowing him to work faster with both hands.

He felt the coagulated and dried blood roll into balls as he slowly swept his hand across the raised portions of the summoning circle. He swept it all into the pattern lines, hoping that the dried blood and detritus would not cause any problems.

Here goes nothing.

He crouched over the summoning circle and used the words the God King had sent him. He was careful with each word, particularly the entity's name, and envisioned reaching out and calling his desired partner.

"Tor'elanoth'darnish'tysan'gehelt, I summon thee. I call to thee from a dark and beknighted world, so thou canst enact justice and slay the wicked. I request that thou comest unto me to protect the innocent and rid the world of evil. I invite thee to be my companion and helpmeet. Tor'elanoth'darnish'tysan'gehelt, I summon thee!"

He felt tendrils of energy spread forth into unknown places, seeking Tor'elanoth'darnish'tysan'gehelt. Daelan was elated that the ceremony had worked, but as the seconds and minutes passed without response and the tendrils of energy faded away, he bowed his head in despair. He had failed.

**

It wasn't in Daelan's nature to wallow in self-pity for long. Within an hour he started cleaning the pattern, and it was ready later that day.

Unlike the first attempt at summoning, he didn't hesitate. He had adopted a fatalistic attitude. Either it would work or it wouldn't. If it didn't, he would try runic magic.

If *that* didn't work… well, not even his healing powers would survive slashing both of his carotid arteries with his reduced lifeforce. Especially if he kept ripping at them while they bled.

One way or another, things were going to change.

Daelan used the same needle and the same vein. Though it hadn't been ideal, it had worked well enough. Though he had not summoned the entity he wanted, the tendrils of power had searched. Daelan had felt it.

The main reason for doing it the same way was that Daelan didn't have any better ideas. It wasn't like he had a funnel or something. He could use a smaller vein, which would spurt less, allowing him to carefully direct the blood into the pattern. Unfortunately, a lot of blood was required. He was afraid that if it didn't come fast, some of the blood would dry up and go bad before he was done.

Besides, the entity I'm calling probably won't mind a little messy blood, he thought grimly.

Quoz'zethrien'allanit'yuribaal'felanit'non could hardly be more different from the first entity. Where the first sought justice and the eradication of evil, Quoz wanted death. Death, havoc, and, according to the God King's notes, travel. Mostly so it could kill new things.

Daelan had really wanted the first summon to work, but it hadn't. Given that each summons used a non-easily-renewable resource, his lifeforce, he couldn't afford to mess around. The God King had only had two contracted entities from a different plane than his own, and of the two, Daelan believed Quoz was the only useful one.

So, one serial killing entity of power, coming up, he thought sarcastically.

Daelan cleared his mind and started the incantation.

"Quoz'zethrien'allanit'yuribaal'felanit'non, I summon thee. I call to thee from a world full of creatures I wish to destroy, a world where literally every creature is fair game. I request that thou comest unto me to rend and slay. I invite thee to be my companion and helpmeet.
Quoz'zethrien'allanit'yuribaal'felanit'non, I summon thee!"

Daelan once again felt the tendrils of power spread and seek, through what medium—space, time, or the planes of existence—he couldn't have said, but they spread far and wide.

They found nothing at first, causing Daelan to bow his head in despair again, but as they started to fade, something touched one of the tendrils and injected a bit of its energy, solidifying the connection between them. It felt like death and revelry in destruction. When Daelan opened his eyes, he saw that the cave had become even darker, and the smell of blood had become even stronger.

'What seekest thou?'

26

The whisper in his mind caused Daelan to jump. It was soft, but pierced him to the soul. It felt… tainting to be so intimately touched by something so bloody. Still, despite his fear and disgust, he felt excited. This was his opportunity.

'I seek the destruction of my enemies, and power.'

The entity felt satisfied. *'It is well. What dost thou offer me?'*

'Your meat and milk—death and destruction—and I will share the resulting energy with you.'

'Thou art familiar to me... Ah, thou art Darius, and yet not Darius. How curious. No doubt this is how thou knowest me so well. I will help thee, Not-Darius, if I get 90%, and thou 10%.'

'90%! That's unreasonable!'

Quoz'zethrien'allanit'yuribaal'felanit'non laughed. *'Darius was strong, but thou art not. Thou hast nothing. Thou canst barely even hurt thy enemies while they torture thee. Thou needest me far more than I need thee.'*

Daelan wanted to grind his teeth, but forced himself to slow down and think about it.

The whole "you need me" schtick is just his way of saying that he can walk away from the negotiation, and I can't. He doesn't know that I am willing to walk away if I have to. Time to make that clear.

The two went back and forth for a couple of hours. A significant amount of brinkmanship was involved, with both sides threatening to abandon the negotiations. The longer they haggled, though, the more confident Daelan was that the entity really wanted into Hell. He felt it put power into their connection to keep it going while they negotiated.

It took far longer than he would have liked, and he was often scared that the entity would leave, but at last they hammered out a deal that they were both satisfied with: 60% of the mutually useful energy went to Quoz'zethrien'allanit'yuribaal'felanit'non, and 40% to Daelan. 100% of the energy that Daelan could not use went to the entity. In return, it would take the shape of any weapon that Daelan desired, and could be stored in a proto-space when not needed.

Daelan nodded, relieved. *'It's a deal.'*

'Then let our covenant be witnessed, sealed, and executed.'

Daelan felt a massive influx of energy that burned every part of him, body and soul. For a moment he tried to resist the pain, but it was too much. Blackness took him.

Chapter 4

Daelan woke up in pain. Everything ached, and he had the mother of all migraines.

"Oooh…" he moaned. He opened his crusted eyes, which brought new stabs of pain, surprisingly, since there wasn't much light in the cave.

'*Wilt thou sleep forever?*'

Daelan's eyes shot open, regardless of the pain, when he heard the entity's voice.

'*Quoz?*'

He could almost hear the eye roll as the entity responded, '*Who else wouldst it be? Wilt thou always be this stupid, or can I expect more from thee in the future? Oh, and I do not like being called "Quoz". My name is Quoz'zethrien'allanit'yuribaal'felanit'non.*'

'*I don't want to take five seconds every time I say your name, so it's going to be "Quoz".*'

'*Hmph. I shall allow it for another 1% of our enemies' energy.*'

'*Seriously? Fine, whatever.*'

Daelan knew it wasn't smart to negotiate when he was feeling like crap, but whatever. One percent wasn't going to make or break him.

'*Deal! How can Quoz help thee?*' it asked in a mocking tone.

'*Ugh. Give me a minute.*'

He slowly rose to his hands and knees. He saw the summoning circle below him, completely blood-free.

That's not creepy at all.

He crawled backwards out of the small cave, ignoring the pain of rocks digging into his hands and knees. After he got out he stood up and looked for demons out of habit. A humanoid demon with three arms and two heads was cutting off the arm of an imp in the distance while it squealed. Other than that, it was nothing but dry, dusty land, painted by the ever-present dim red light.

Let's see what I got out of this deal.

Daelan held out his hand and thought, '*Quoz, come out.*'

A black stiletto dagger appeared in his hand, slim and menacing. It felt like it could pierce anything.

In the fuller groove in the middle of the blade there was a set of small, very finely-worked runes in silver metal.

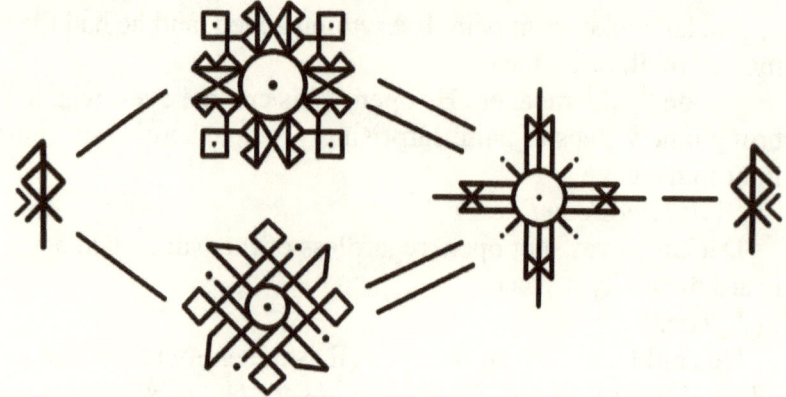

Those look familiar.

They looked like the runes that Darius had sent him. He looked through his list of runes and found them.

There's a connection between "Consume" and "Body" and "Consume" and "Soul". Consume body and soul? The thought made him uncomfortable. Though Darius had done many terrible things in his quest for power, he had considered such magics to be beyond the pale. Daelan knew that if he wanted to get out of Hell, he couldn't afford such qualms.

'*What are the last two runes? "Mana"... and... "Create". "Consume body and soul, create mana"?*'

'*In this context it maketh more sense to translate it as "Consume life and soul, create mana",*' Quoz said, '*but thou hadst it more-or-less right.*'

'*You can eat souls, Quoz?*'

'*Of course. And I shall give 39% of it to thee.*'

Daelan shivered. Quoz scared him, but he would need it to get out of here.

'*Turn into a longsword.*'

The weapon quickly and smoothly flowed into the desired shape, forming a blade a little over a meter long, and enough hilt for two hands. It was double-edged, and though the blade was dark as night, Daelan could see that the fuller groove ran the length of the blade.

He made a few tentative swings with the blade. It was an unfamiliar weapon to him even though his Father was a renowned swordsman and Daelan had some of his memories. Nevertheless, it felt good. The sword was lighter than he thought it would be, but his forearm still tired after a few minutes. He switched to using two hands, which made it easier.

Daelan had Quoz change to several different forms so he could try them out. Occasionally he asked for changes in size, shape, or weight, but not too often, since it was clear that Quoz knew far more about weapons than he did.

Given Daelan's inexperience with weapons, he was surprised to find that he was drawn to one in particular: a war scythe. Though he would need to get used to its length and balance, the weapon felt familiar.

After moving around with the polearm and shadow fighting with it in a way that he hoped wasn't too awkward, he decided to see if Darius had sent him anything that would help him to use a war scythe. He wasn't that hopeful, since he knew the weapon was unusual.

Let's see... war scythes, war scythes... he thought to himself as he searched through the information. He was shocked to find that there was a great deal, including an entire style that focused on war scythes and the falx, a sword that, like the war scythe, had an inwardly curved blade.

'*Wherefore art thou surprised?*' Quoz rasped. '*Didst thou think thou wert so different from Darius?*'

'*He used a war scythe?*'

'*Yes. Together, we reaped many lives in this form. It feeleth good to return to it.*'

Daelan wasn't sure how he felt about that. Quoz's bloodthirsty nostalgia made him uncomfortable, but he was glad to have a connection to his Father.

'*Tell me if any demons approach.*'

Quoz snorted mentally in a way that suggested disdain, but he didn't refuse, so Daelan sat and immersed himself in the technique.

**

31

'Get up, fool.'

Daelan startled out of his study of the style Darius had given him. He had become entranced by the beauty of it. He found the flowing attacks, footwork, and defense mesmerizing. He couldn't wait to try it out.

His happiness curdled, though, when he saw what had made Quoz wake him up. A demon approached. And not just any demon, it was his "wife".

The corners of his lips crept up into a malicious smile.

I'm going to enjoy this.

He put Quoz away and walked up to the demon. "How are you, dear?"

She narrowed her eyes at him. "Why do you look happy? Have you been naughty?"

Daelan nodded his head. "Very naughty."

Her eyes narrowed into slits as she glared at him. "Then you shall be punished. I haven't peeled your skin in a while. Perhaps it's time to…"

"I don't think so," Daelan said with a sense of finality that caused the demon to stop. "How long have we been together?"

Looking uncertain at what was going on, she said, "We have been together for years."

"You have been an excellent teacher during that time. I think tonight, as a demonstration of gratitude, I'll show you what I've learned," he said as he caused Quoz to appear as a dagger.

"What are you doing?" she asked nervously.

"Shh. Just sit down and relax."

He enjoyed seeing her nervous indecision, but was surprised when pain erupted from his stomach. He looked down and saw a line of blood seeping from a wound in his belly. Realizing he'd been tricked, he scrambled backwards and opened his third eye.

His "wife" disappeared, and the scabrous demon was moving towards him, licking the blood off its talons.

Sensing his desire, Quoz reshaped itself into a war scythe.

"That was a mistake, dear one," Daelan said.

The demon rasped in a sound that he had long since realized passed for laughter. "I…"

Daelan would never know what the demon was going to say, because it started screaming when he cut off the demon's feet

32

with a sweep of the war scythe. He calmly gathered the vines the demon had brought and proceeded to tie it up, thorns digging into its flesh.

Daelan wore a grim smile the entire time, pleased that his revenge would start here.

When Quoz came back out in the form of a scalpel, he spoke to Daelan. '*Much as I'm pleased to see thee enjoying thyself, I have bad news.*'

Daelan paused, worried. '*What is it?*'

'*The demon's body is pathetically low on energy, and it hast not a soul. There is almost no energy we can easily take from it.*'

Daelan thought through the extra-planar being's statement.

'*Are you implying that there is energy to take, it just won't be easy?*'

'*Correct. I'm glad to see thou art not a complete fool. Whilst the demon hath not a soul, it hath anima.*'

'*The core of the soul that gets reincarnated? What good does that do me? Anima can't be harmed.*'

'*Ah,*' Quoz laughed wickedly, '*That is true, unless it chooseth to be harmed.*'

Daelan was confused. '*Why would it do that?*'

'*Make oblivion more attractive than continuing to exist. Make the demons yearn for death so keenly that they will do anything to have it. Make them long for annihilation. And then give it to them.*'

As Daelan considered Quoz's words, an evil smile slowly grew. It appeared that the only way for him to escape Hell wasn't to merely kill demons, but to torture them like they had tortured him and the countless souls that were doomed to this place.

He watched the scabrous demon try to crawl away as it mewled, ichor leaking onto the dry and dusty ground, and remembered the many times it had taken pleasure in his pain.

'*Thank you, Quoz.*'

'*For what?*'

'*For giving me a reason to break it.*'

Quoz laughed, but said nothing.

The next day and a half was filled with screams, sobs, and ragged breathing when the demon didn't have enough strength to cry out. Finally, silence reigned.

Daelan stared at Quoz in shock. It had changed form without his permission, elongating from the scalpel it had been until, like a burrowing worm, it dove into the demon's body.

"What the hell are you do…?" Daelan shouted, afraid of what Quoz's rebellion meant, until he felt the rush of mana coming from it. He was transfixed by wonder and ecstasy as he felt a universe of possibilities in the churning energy. He knew that his Father would have considered this a pittance, but to him it was life, and freedom.

After a glance at the scabrous demon's dead eyes and terrified expression, he dismissed it and looked over the dry wasteland of Hell. Demons were watching him from a great distance, as if they were both curious and afraid.

Daelan smiled. Their disgusting bodies looked like priceless treasures to him now, like gleaming pearls shining in the night.

"Stay there," he breathed. "I'm coming."

Chapter 5

5 Earth years / 219 Hell years later

Russ pushed his glasses higher onto his nose as he nervously glanced over the instructions one more time. He didn't really need to. He had long since memorized each and every step, but it wasn't every day you tried to reach out to dark beings.

He knew it was bullshit, that there was no such thing as demons or devils. But still.

"Alright, let's do this," he said as much to himself as to his friend, Wyatt.

"Are you sure about this, bro? I mean, I don't know. It just…" His voice trailed off into an uncomfortable silence.

Russ grinned mockingly at him. "What? You scared?"

"No!"

Russ snorted and started lighting the candles at the points of the star. *Is it still a pentagram if it's only upside down for me?* he wondered. For Wyatt, on the opposite side, it would just be a right-side-up star in a circle.

Since he was the one executing the ceremony, he decided that only his perspective mattered. Besides, it was all drawn with blood, even if it was from his mom's ground beef.

Blood's blood, right?

He was pleased at how the pentagram looked in the glow of the candles. The reddish-brown of the dried blood in the candlelight looked hardcore.

"Do you think it matters that we watered down the blood?" Wyatt asked.

"Shut up, dumbass," Russ said, annoyed. *He just had to bring that up…* It was a sore point with him because there was only so much blood in a five-pound package of ground beef.

Shaking his friend's doubts off, mentally and physically, Russ prepared for the final part of the ceremony. As he spoke the words of power, he tried to give them the proper gravitas. He was surprised, thrilled, and frightened when he felt something happening. The words took on a deep timber and were imbued with a power not his own.

Oh crap!

Russ just about soiled his pants when he saw part of a black blade appear in midair about six feet above the pentagram, angled upward. He tried to stop the ceremony, but he couldn't. Quailing inside, he kept saying the dark words, his efforts to stop as useless as if he had tried to stop an avalanche. Though he spoke, his eyes and attention never left the midnight blade.

As he said the final phrase, the blade swept downwards, forming a slit in reality. It pulled back back and disappeared, and for the briefest moment Russ thought maybe everything would be okay, until a pair of rough hands forced the slit to open wide, and a man appeared wearing black leather clothes.

His features were not particularly notable, with his sandy-brown hair, thin lips, and brown eyes. What made him stand out was the feeling of *evil* that emanated from him. And his eye. The muddy brown eye had a flat, dead quality to it that made him look like a serial killer. The eyepatch where the other should have been did nothing to detract from the impression.

Russ let out the breath he'd been holding when the man snorted and looked elsewhere while stepping through the hole in reality he had made with Russ' help.

What was I thinking?!

He scrabbled backwards until he had pinned himself against the wall, unable to move any farther back. He could have, of course, exited the room and fled, but that would have required looking away from the demon and having some form of rational thought. It was perhaps a good sign that a small portion of his mind noticed the warm and wet feeling of his urine around his crotch, buttocks, and legs. Normally he would be ashamed, but at the moment it was just a minor distraction, an afterthought.

He kept as still as he could, millions of years of evolution having conditioned him to play dead in front of a predator.

**

Daelan was shocked at how different this place felt. It was…clean. Pure. It was like jumping into a shockingly fresh and cold lake of water. It was so vastly different from what he was used to that his senses didn't know what to make of it.

He briefly looked at the two young men who had foolishly provided him an anchor point. Though almost all of the power came from him, the minuscule amount from them was enough to establish a hold that he could, and did, build on.

He smiled sardonically. If it were anyone else from Hell that had come through the portal, the two boys would have been in for a very bad time. As it was, they would just see a little more than they were expecting.

"Um, what are you doing?" the black-haired teenager asked from behind.

Where do I know this language? Ah. Joseph. It's... English.

Daelan had to work at understanding the words. The language was one he knew, but he was very rusty. He dredged up memories of the language and haltingly put together words that had, to the boys' hearing, a harsh and unrecognizable accent.

"I taking clothes off. What look like?"

"Uh," the boy said with a quivering voice. "W-why are you doing that?"

Daelan laughed as he saw the boy's terrified look.

"Relax, boy. I no do anything to you. I want leave everything behind," he said as he tossed the shirt into the portal. It landed on a white marble floor with black and gold veins. A few feet from the shirt was a wall consisting of the same white marble and a deep black quartz. All of the stones were dressed and polished, and had not even a hint of a gap between them or mortar to hold them in place.

The sound of a door opening came through the portal, followed by the appearance of a somewhat human-looking butler. Though its uniform looked nothing like that of an English steward, it had the unassuming but dignified air of one.

Of course, its reddish skin, curved horns, and bat wings dashed any expectations of being served high tea.

It started to step through the portal, but was stopped by Daelan's outstretched arm.

Taken aback, the demon said in the language of Hell, "Sir, am I not to come with you?" Though the demon affected humility, Daelan could see its eagerness to step into the new world.

He gave it a hard-to-interpret look and said, "Not this time. Here, take my clothes." He continued to undress and handed the clothes to the demon. Last of all, he took off his leather eyepatch and threw it at the demon in a more-than-casual way, hitting it in the face. It had not seemed taken aback by his lord's nakedness, but flinched when struck by the eyepatch.

The demon recovered and asked, "What shall I do then, sir?"

Daelan tensed and said with suppressed animus—not that he thought he needed to hide his hatred any longer, but because hiding it was a habit ingrained in his psyche for over 200 years— "You can die, Briz't!"

Before the demon could react, Daelan lifted his hand, palm out, and poured out fire as if he were a flamethrower. Even though black was heavily woven into the fire, it was so bright that the two teenagers were blinded.

Daelan, however, was not. Once he had exhausted every iota of his mana, he looked at the smoking legs of his erstwhile servant that were no longer attached to a body. Behind the legs was a large, glowing hole in the stone wall. He sneered at what little remained of his servant. "Good riddance."

The portal collapsed upon itself, causing the legs and marble room to disappear.

Daelan slowly looked around and took in what he was feeling. He felt cleaner than he had in centuries, but also weak as a kitten. He was out of sorts—ecstatic at escaping hell and having endless possibilities before him, and scared about his vulnerability. He found himself nervously scanning the two boys, even though they were clearly terrified of him, to see if they had any weapons or instruments of torture on them.

I don't see any, but that doesn't mean they aren't there. Anyone who would summon a demon is crazy and can't be trusted.

The rational part of his mind knew that Earth humans were not mages or cultivators and were therefore far weaker than he, even in his current state. Rationality had little to do with how he felt at the moment, though.

Daelan frowned. He thought he was past all this. Yes, he still had to deal with nightmares sometimes, but during the day he had been the overlord demons had learned to fear and admire.

The last few decades had been, if not exactly pleasant, at least far less painful than the earlier years. Demons were not exactly good company. They weren't even good servants. Daelan had to keep them afraid of him and have eyes in the back of his head to keep uprisings and assassination attempts down. He wouldn't miss any of the bastards.

No, he wanted to leave everything from Hell behind. Clothes, demons, and even his hard-won mana. Though what he'd had left after opening the portal was a small fraction of his power, he didn't have to use it all on Briz't.

Though it was fun to see the rat sizzle.

No, he could have killed the demon while keeping most of the mana he'd had left. He'd intentionally burned it all in Hellish fire to get rid of everything with the taint of that miserable plane.

Daelan had even gone so far as to unmake the power he had built up for over 200 years. He sighed at the loss, but it was for the best. He had planned to do it from the beginning, which was why he could regress in his cultivation without crippling or killing himself. He had built up his power with that exact purpose in mind, like a tie knot that unmade itself when the ends were pulled. For him, unmaking his cultivation was painful, but not damaging.

Well, not permanently anyway, he thought as he felt the raw ache where his mana core had been. *I hope.*

He was forging new territory here, as most cultivators did not unmake their cultivation, let alone set up their foundation with that in mind.

If he had crippled himself, it would be lamentable but an acceptable loss. He would rather live out his life as a mortal than stay in Hell, even if he had carved out his own territory. He was of the firm opinion that anyone who thought it was better to rule in Hell than serve in heaven was a fool.

If he could just stop reliving his time in Hell in his dreams every night, he would consider giving up his power a more than acceptable sacrifice. He could only hope. His dreams were... unpleasant.

That wasn't to say he was okay with feeling this weak. He felt vulnerable, and it made him uneasy. If someone tried to kill him right now, all he would have was his weakened body to fight them off.

Still, just the lack of brimstone in the air made it all worth it. He looked forward to exploring this world.

Daelan looked around himself again and re-focused on the two teenagers. The fool who had performed the ceremony was in the corner, trembling from fear, sitting in a puddle of his urine.

Daelan's lips quirked up. He liked that reaction. It meant safety.

Though it doesn't look like he'll be useful for questioning anytime soon.

The other boy, the one who questioned him earlier, had also moved as far away as he could, but seemed more in possession of himself. He proved that by asking, "Who are you?" even if his voice quavered while he did it.

Daelan held his hand up, palm out, as a sort of universal sign language for "wait", but the boy shrieked in fear and made himself into a tight ball, covering his head with his arms.

Huh? What's that about? He looked at his positioning and realized it was the exact same posture he'd had when incinerating his steward with hellfire. *Oops,* he thought while chuckling.

The two boys were still cowering, so with his immediate safety mostly ensured, Daelan couldn't wait any longer. He opened his third eye to look for mana. At first he was disappointed, but then he saw it—a thin, almost completely transparent wisp of glowing blue mana that slowly slid across the room, as if blown by the gentlest of breezes, and exited through a wall.

At last! he crowed to himself. The amount of mana was pathetic. His Father would have scoffed at it and declared this land barren, but to Daelan it was a beautiful sight. It meant he could build up his power without...

Without doing what I did in Hell. He refused to acknowledge the slight tremble that accompanied the thought.

He had no illusions that any judge would ever deem his soul fit for anything but Hell when he left this mortal coil, regardless of what he did from now on, but he still wanted to make a change. He *needed* to make a change.

Shaking his head, he returned his attention to the two boys. They shrank back. They were clearly terrified of him, but fixated on his missing eye in particular. Daelan concentrated on the one that hadn't summoned him, because he hadn't peed himself.

"My name is Daelan. Where I am, boy?"

Seeing that the whatever-it-was was talking and not frying him, the boy slowly uncoiled and hesitantly asked, "Uh, what?"

"Where I am?"

"Do you mean, 'Where am I?'"

The other boy came out of his paralysis long enough to hiss, "Do you really think this is the right time to correct his grammar, Wyatt?"

When his friend stopped talking, Wyatt looked back at Daelan, terrified that he had offended him.

Daelan just said with quirked lips, "Yes, where am I?"

"S-Salem. Salem, Oregon."

Daelan combed his memories for knowledge of such a place. Seeing that he still hadn't been incinerated, Wyatt's fear turned into babbling. His voice still quavered, but the words rushed out nonetheless.

"We don't actually live here, but Russ thought it would be a good idea to do the summoning in Salem because of the name. I thought…"

"Boy," Daelan said in a commanding tone. Living amongst demons had given him lots of practice, and the young man froze comically, mid-word. "Is this… uh…" Daelan paused as he scoured his mind for the name of his dead sibling's planet. When he found it, he looked intensely into the boy's eyes. "Is this Earth?"

"Y-yes."

Joseph's family might still be alive.

Though he had been in Hell for centuries, he knew from experiencing his siblings that time was much faster in Hell than their native plane. Even though it had taken him a couple of centuries to escape, only a few years should have passed here.

Daelan decided that while he rebuilt his power, this time permanently, he would look for Joseph's family. It was the least he could do for his sibling. He started making plans, and his two goals quickly turned into layers of subgoals, eventually causing him to re-focus on the young man.

"Give me pants," he commanded, while pointing at the article of clothing.

The black-haired boy quivered in fright again. "M-mine? Why?"

"Because I naked. You keep other clothes." Daelan paused and then said with an impish grin and a nod at the other boy. "Take other boy's pants if want."

The boy got up and started taking his pants off. In his hurry his feet caught in the legs and he hopped around, trying not to fall. Unsuccessfully, as it turned out.

Once again on the floor, he removed the pants, stood up, and hesitated between approaching and tossing the article of clothing to the naked man who smelled evil.

Daelan chuckled darkly. *Probably trying to decide which is least likely to get him killed.* "Give me."

Even though a part of him was always watching for danger, Daelan had already half-forgotten the boys while he put on the ill-fitting garment. He was putting together his next steps. He had a lot to do, after all.

Chapter 6

Though Daelan was focused on revenge and finding Joseph's wife and daughter, he remembered that everything on Earth revolved around money. He needed a way to get some. The problem was, he didn't have a lot of Earth-relevant skills.

Much as he'd rather be done with the two boys, he decided to see if they could help.

"Hey," he said to the guy whose pants he was wearing. He was still in the corner of the room, afraid to move other than to sort of cover himself while pretending that wasn't what he was doing. "Are jobs where you beat people?"

The teenager gulped and became even paler. "W-why do you want to know that?"

"Money. I need money. Do you know jobs?"

"Um, I guess you could be a police officer, though they're not supposed to beat people up or kill them…"

Daelan imagined himself as a law enforcer. It was a ridiculous image, and way too confining. He shook his head and said, "No. Something else?"

"You could be a soldier!"

That was, surprisingly, from the other teenager. He was no longer functionally catatonic.

Hmm, soldier. Too much chance of actually dying in my weakened state. Still, to encourage the boy he nodded at him and asked, "What else?"

"Dude! You should enter the Kumite, like that 'Blood Sport' guy! That would be so fire! They could even make a movie about you or something!" He looked even more gleeful as he turned to his friend and said, "Wyatt, we could go with him and make a documentary!"

Daelan suppressed a chuckle as he took in the boy's enthusiasm, even though he hadn't understood everything said. *The resilience and foolishness of youth.*

They haltingly offered more ideas. Most of them were bad, but a few caught his interest: boxing, MMA, and bounty hunting. The Kumite thing turned out to be fake when they looked into it more, which Daelan considered a pity. Anything called "Blood Sport" that involved large amounts of money sounded like it was right up his alley.

"Okay, so, pros and cons of each avenue," the boy, who he had learned was named Russ, said. Once he had found his way out of his shell, he became surprisingly invested in helping Daelan. "Pro Wrestling. You can make a ton of money, and you're tailor-made to be a heel."

Daelan furrowed his brow. "What is 'heel'?"

"The bad guy. The jerk. Uh, no offense," he said with a worried look.

Daelan quirked his lips. "It okay. What are cons?"

Russ frowned. "You'd need to bulk up first. The wrestlers usually end up taking a lot of drugs. Steroids to bulk up and painkillers because of injuries. Some of them go all roid-ragey. And even though it's fake, they do get injured."

Daelan nodded. He was not too worried about injuries. Though he had vented out all of his mana, his body had soaked in it for a couple of centuries. It was tough in a way that mortal bodies simply couldn't match. He wasn't sure he liked the high profile of being on TV all the time though.

He nodded and asked, "Boxing?"

"You can make lots of money once you're a champion, but it can take a few years before you get to that level. And the bouts don't happen that often, so the money would be sporadic."

Daelan didn't know what "sporadic" meant, but he got the gist of what Russ was saying.

"Okay. MMA?"

"Same thing as boxing, really, just a different combat sport."

Daelan grimaced. If he were successful and made a lot of money, he would have just as much notoriety as a pro wrestler. So far, none of the jobs looked ideal.

"Okay. Bounty hunter?"

"There's not as much money in bounty hunting. I'm not sure how it works, but I think you get a percentage of their bail money if you catch them, or something, so the bigger the criminal, the more money you make."

"Hmm. Look at that."

Daelan crouched next to Russ while he looked up information about bounty hunting. They found a lot of information and watched a TV episode about someone named "Dog".

Wyatt asked haltingly, "By the way, uh, what happened to your eye?"

Daelan turned his head to give him the full effect of the empty socket.

"Demon eat."

Wyatt's eyes went wide and he trembled. "I'm so sorry, uh, sorry I asked. Uh, that must have really sucked."

Daelan chuckled when he noticed his friend, Russ, making shushing noises and frantically making slicing motions with his hand at his neck.

Maybe he's worried I'll cut off his friend's head?

He could, of course, and it would give him some much-needed energy, but he wanted to do things differently on Earth, so he just laughed darkly and turned back to Russ' phone.

Half a minute later Russ said, "Aw, crap. Oregon doesn't have bounty hunters."

Daelan was getting frustrated.

"I could do, uh, other place?"

"Yeah, but it looks like they're licensed by states, and can't cross state lines when chasing fugitives."

That wasn't ideal. He wanted freedom to go and earn money wherever he wanted.

"Okay, no beat people. What jobs can do anywhere?"

"You mean work remotely?" Wyatt scrunched up his nose in thought. "A lot of programmers can. I have a cousin who works wherever."

"Anything else?"

The boy shrugged his shoulders. "I dunno. You could probably look up remote jobs on the internet."

Daelan frowned. "I need phone…"

Both boys protectively pulled their phones back. Daelan rolled his eyes.

"I no take phones. Help me make plan. Never see me again."

**

Hours later, in a men's shelter that took him in, Daelan dreamed of a distant past in Hell.

He was in the dry, dusty crags that tore at his feet. Though they didn't move, Daelan would've sworn that they were maliciously trying to tear him apart, bit by bit. The windswept dust irritated his eyes, causing him to tear up.

At his feet lay a wounded demon. It, like all the demons he'd seen, was strange. It was humanoid, with two arms and legs, but the head was too big for its body, and its arms and legs were misshapen and... *pillowy*. It looked like a baby that had been scaled up to the height of a man, but with white eyes and a mosquito's proboscis instead of a mouth.

Disgusting.

The baby was missing parts of both of its legs, making its mobility lacking, though it did drag itself with its arms while mewling and dripping bile-colored ichor onto the dry ground.

Knowing it wouldn't be able to move far, Daelan went to the nearest withered vine and cut off four long thorns. Gathering them up, he slowly walked back to the demon. He grimaced as he looked at the hideous and pitiful creature.

Steeling himself, he grabbed an arm and flipped it over. The demon cried out and scratched his arm with nails that hadn't looked like much. Now they had his blood on them.

Displeased, Daelan stomped on the wrist of the offending hand. Seeing that it was immobilized, he returned his attention to the wrist he was holding. He stretched out the arm and pinned the wrist to the ground, the demon's hand palm up.

Moving as quickly as possible to get it over with, he drove one of the thorns through the hand, causing the overgrown baby to cry out again. Daelan ignored the noises and commanded Quoz to become a mallet, which he used to drive the thorn into the ground.

He moved on to the other limbs, similarly pinning them to the ground. Once he was done and looked at the mewling demon, looking for all the world like the start of the world's most disgusting butterfly collection, he went over his plan.

The first step was to prick each part of its body to see what got the biggest reaction. He wanted to break it quickly, and that meant knowing where it was most sensitive. With his wife, he didn't mind taking lots of time, because he had a lot of anger to work through.

Now he needed to be more efficient. More scientific. Frowning, he got to work.

Chapter 7

"Time to get up, everyone! Breakfast time! Up and at 'em!"

Daelan watched as his roommates slowly got up and got dressed. He mimicked them, careful to not show too much speed or grace. He didn't want to stick out, especially since he was "injured". He felt the bandage and the eyepatch they'd given him to make sure they were in place.

He felt a little off. *Must be the lack of mana.* Though he'd very intentionally structured his cultivation in Hell so he could start over from scratch after he escaped, it was inevitable that the loss of power would be felt. He would just have to deal with it for the time being.

The lack of power made him nervous though. He eyed the other men warily. Part of his plan was to pretend to have injury-induced amnesia, to explain why he didn't have an identity. He wouldn't mind if it got him some sympathy too. Not that he seemed to need any with the shelter staff. They seemed perfectly happy to take him in as long as they could talk about Jesus.

When the boys researched local shelters they found that Calvary's Hill of Salem was by far the largest and the most likely to not be full.

Daelan quirked his lips and thought, *I'm going to take a wild guess and say that all the Jesus talk has something to do with that.*

Though he wasn't looking forward to the preaching, he was kind of impressed at how they'd taken care of him medically and given him clothes. The jeans, t-shirt, underwear, sneakers, and socks were not fancy by any means. He was pretty sure the jeans and t-shirt were used, but he didn't care. He could and would get something better later, he just needed something that would let him operate in society without problems.

"Breakfast ends at 7:00 AM, everyone, so don't miss out by sleeping in! There's an optional prayer meeting at 8:30!"

The up-and-at-em guy was a man who looked like he'd been a blue-collar worker, or truck driver, or something before he found

God. His face was lined, with wrinkles on top of wrinkles, but it looked like it was more used to smiling and laughing than crying.

"Hey, Daelan, welcome to Calvary's Hill. You know where the cafeteria is?"

Daelan shrugged. "I follow everyone."

The man, whose name tag said, "Rob", clapped him on the shoulder and said, "Good man. Glad to see that head on your shoulders works." Before Daelan could respond, Rob had moved on to another resident.

Daelan was glad. He was not a cheery person at the best of times, and would much rather be silent than engage in useless talk.

He observed the other men while he waited in line for food. They were a pitiful bunch. Weak. Glassy-eyed. A third of them looked like they were either born stupid, had burned out their brains with drugs, or simply never bothered to use them in the first place. Another third looked like they were frightened of their own shadow. A few just looked plain nuts, talking to the air or making erratic movements. Everyone avoided them, even the listless dead-heads.

The breakfast was simple but filling: grits with butter and brown sugar, a hard-boiled egg, and toast with butter and jam. Daelan was grateful for the food. Though his body was far tougher than everyone else's here, it still needed sustenance.

This is pretty good.

He took another bite of the toast with butter and strawberry jam and almost moaned in pleasure. Sugar wasn't a thing in Hell. No, the diet there was a variety of questionable meats. For the demons, cannibalism was a way of life.

Daelan saw one of the few people who wasn't one of the dead-heads, scaredy-cats, or crazies approach. He thought about driving him away with a look, but sighed and refrained to avoid sticking out. It was aggravating, though, because he had been thinking about how to recover his power without becoming a serial killer again.

The twenty-something man with three-day-old whiskers and a dirty hoody sat down across from Daelan and said, "Hey, man, looks like you got a nasty knock on your noggin."

"Noggin?"

49

"Your head, man."

"Ah. Yes, the nurse help me last night."

The man nodded. "They take good care of us here. We're lucky to have 'em."

Daelan just grunted. He knew that the wound had healed already, and he would have to "reapply" it before he was called in to change the bandage if he didn't want questions.

The original injury hadn't been that serious. Russ hadn't been strong enough, and the old stairway spoke hadn't been durable enough to do much damage. Daelan chuckled softly when he remembered how he'd had to give Russ ten tries, yelling at him each time to swing harder before he finally broke the spoke.

"Something funny?"

Daelan was tempted to crush the annoying man. He didn't, of course, but it made him appreciate his demonic servitors a little more. They knew not to bother their superiors.

"Just laughing at memory."

While Daelan finished off his grits, the man said, "I'm Jackson." He had his hand out, which Daelan ignored.

"I no remember my name."

Jackson awkwardly pulled his hand back when he saw that Daelan had no intention of shaking it.

"Oh. Sorry, man. That must be rough."

Daelan just grunted again.

Jackson hesitantly asked, "So, what are you going to do?"

"Become programmer."

"Wow! Ambitious much?"

Daelan shrugged.

"Well, I can tell you've got your plan. Good luck with that." He stood up and put his hand out in a fist, thumb down. "Grind more and talk less, right?"

Daelan nodded and said, "Right," and bumped his fist.

"See you around."

Daelan nodded again.

Finally.

**

50

Daelan walked through the doors of the library at mid-morning, pleasantly surprised by the shock of cool air that greeted him. Though he was used to hotter weather than Oregon's summer, air conditioning was still a nice luxury.

A middle-aged woman at the check-out counter looked up at him over her glasses and said, "Hello! Can I help you with anything?"

He paused and said, "Yes. I need computer to research. I also like to, uh, borrow books."

"I can help you with that. Do you live in Salem?"

"Yes. I stay at Calvary's Hill shelter."

"Oh." The librarian's eyes widened momentarily, but she quickly schooled her reaction and put on a wider smile, as if to make up for her momentary faux pas. "Do you have something showing that you're staying there?"

Daelan nodded. "They said give you this." He handed her a card with his picture and the Calvary's Hill logo and address.

"John Doe?" The woman looked at him. "Is that really your name?"

Daelan grimaced. "I not sure. When I get this..." he pointed at his head, "I no remember who I am."

"Oh, dear! I'm so sorry, that must be terrible."

Daelan nodded.

"Well, don't you worry. We'll get you set up with your temporary name. After all, we don't want to get in the way of someone who's trying to get back on their feet!"

In less than half an hour he had a library card, gone through a crash course on surfing the internet on the library's computers, and had instructions on how to print out information. Thankfully he had memories of Joseph to make these tasks a little more familiar.

Daelan was pleased, and gave her a rare smile.

"Thank you."

"You're welcome, 'John'," she said with a smile and air quotes. "If you need anything, you can find me at the counter."

He nodded and turned to the computer. It was going to be a busy day. He was going to spend a couple of hours brushing up on English vocabulary, and then start learning how to program.

Though it had been a productive day at the library, Daelan wasn't happy. When he was getting ready to leave, he realized that he might be able to get information about Joseph's murder on the internet, so he searched. He'd found that his wife had died as well, leaving their daughter, Imogen, an orphan.

I hope she's okay.

He frowned, because even if he wanted to help her, there wasn't anything he could do until he had money and a way to get to Florida. It didn't change his plans, really, it just made them more urgent.

Daelan walked out of the library with books on Javascript that he would study. He left at 5:00 because he wanted to get dinner at the shelter. His stomach was growling after going without lunch.

I've grown soft.

He wasn't pleased at the thought, but shrugged his shoulders and loaded up his plate. Afterwards he moved to his shared bedroom in the shelter and sat on the scuffed linoleum floor, back against the cheerful-but-unobtrusive pale yellow wall.

Once he was in a comfortable position, he opened his third eye and *saw*. Lingering fears. Pain. Hope. Determination. Resignation. Paranoia.

It was clear that the shelter's goal was to help people get back on their feet and find Jesus. Judging by the psychic impressions he was sensing, he suspected their success rates were not good on either count.

Though I suppose it's probably the 'less than successful' people who stay the longest, so who knows?

As interesting as it was to spy on the emotional state of current and past residents, that wasn't his goal. Daelan ignored the impressions and focused on finding mana. It required a great deal of patience. An hour of waiting netted four wisps of mana that he pulled into what would become his new mana core, his center of power. Though he was glad to feel the sweet power again, even if it was mere wisps, the rate was too slow. It would take a year of cultivating like this, full-time, to produce another flame thrower like he'd made when he'd come through the portal, let alone making another portal.

Though it was a strange way to cultivate, Daelan moved to the common area and started scanning for more wisps, assuming that he would be able to find more of the slowly drifting mana in a larger space.

It worked. Over the next hour he collected ten wisps. Still far too slow, but an improvement.

The hard part was not looking like a crazy person as he walked around, ignoring the people and things around him other than avoiding bumping into them. He tried to be discreet and not make any strange movements, which was why he let two wisps get away, because he would have had to jump to get them.

Just not worth it.

Eventually he would be a mana vortex that could pull in any unbound mana near him, but he was far from that point.

Deciding that enough was enough, Daelan rested on his cot for an hour and then headed out for the evening. He walked towards the shelter exit, thinking of his next steps. He was pulled out of his ruminations when someone hailed him.

"John! How'd your day go?"

Daelan snapped out of his inner thoughts and saw Rob in front of him, smiling. Daelan found the staff's frequent smiling weird, but ignored it as he didn't want to bite the hand that was feeding him.

"Not bad."

"Good! So you're going to be a rich hacker soon?"

"I hope so. I no want to be problem for you."

Rob shook his head. "We're happy to have you. To be honest, you're the most interesting guy we've had here in a while. It's not often we have someone so smart."

Part of the reason Daelan hadn't gotten to the library until mid-morning was that the staff had Daelan take tests that indicated what occupations would be a good fit for him. He'd tried to get out of the tests by telling them he wanted to be a programmer, but it didn't work. They hadn't taken him seriously, though they'd tried to be nice about it. Once he finished the tests, they were shocked by his results.

Apparently he had an IQ that was at least 130, whatever that meant. He didn't know or care, other than being pleased that they were now okay with him going to the library and studying on his own.

Daelan nodded at Rob and said, "Please excuse me…" as he stepped past.

"Where you goin', John? We're getting ready to turn off the lights and lock up for the night."

Daelan paused. "I want to work as bouncer at bar. I need to earn money while studying." When he was tired of studying at the library, Daelan had continued to look for jobs he could do. He'd settled on bouncing because it sounded like chances were good he could get paid in cash, and his intimidation game was on point. When he saw Rob's frown, he said, "I return at night and get in like when I came here."

"We let new folks in whenever they show up, but we like to have our residents stick to the schedule."

"I need money to get apartment. Will be bouncer until I get job as programmer."

Rob chewed his lip, and then reluctantly nodded. "Okay, I'll ask the guys at the front to let you in."

"Thank you."

"No problem." A small smile returned to his face. "Good luck finding work."

Daelan nodded and walked out into a gentle rain that turned into a steady drumbeat on his head and shoulders as he walked. He didn't mind. It gave the air a clean, fresh smell.

Man, I love this world.

He quirked his lips as he saw people rush through the rain, scuttling to escape into their nooks and crannies.

Run, little bugs. The scary water comes.

When he reached downtown there were people outdoors, but they stayed under cover to smoke or vape. Their haze-veiled eyes glanced at the tall and muscular man with hair and t-shirt plastered to his body. Their attention drifted, quickly losing interest.

Smells were muted by the rain, but when he stepped into the covered area of his first target, a bar called "Sean's", he was hit by the cigarette smoke and the pungent smell of marijuana. His

Earth sibling, Joseph, had partaken in his pre-family days, and Daelan hadn't forgotten.

The glow of the neon lights cast everything in artificial monochromes that somehow made the smokers look like they were a shade of gray. Music from inside the bar with a strong, driving bass provided the tempo. Daelan saw that some of the smokers were swaying to the rhythm, as if they were under its hypnotic pull.

He stepped inside, and the rumbling music crested and was joined by a sharp melody that was loud enough to be uncomfortable. Daelan ignored it. The band was on a "stage" that was all of six inches high and right next to the crowd.

How can anyone talk in this?

Judging by how the customers shouted at each other, the answer was "not easily".

"Hey, watch it, bruh!"

Daelan looked down at a college-aged man sitting at a table with another man and two women. He looked angry, which made Daelan snort in amusement. He doubted the kid had been in a fight his whole life. While he wasn't as fat as most of the people he'd seen so far, he was still pathetically soft. His cheeks looked like a baby's, and his tight jeans were wrapped around skinny chicken legs.

"What wrong?"

"You're dripping on me!"

"So?"

Although he thought the kid was ridiculous, he honestly wondered why it was a big deal. It was just water—it would evaporate. Then he remembered one of the times he'd experienced Joseph, how the rain had been cold.

Daelan couldn't remember the last time he'd been cold.

The college kid looked surprised, and his mouth opened and closed like a fish. The amusing comparison made Daelan chuckle. He wasn't sure why, but that made the man turn pale and turn back towards his table, his shoulders hunched over as if he was trying to look smaller.

Shrugging, Daelan continued towards the bar.

An older guy and a young woman tended the bar, both of them busy taking orders and making drinks. Daelan found the variety of drinks mildly interesting, but still became impatient as the minutes rolled on. He could have stepped in and asserted himself, but he wanted to talk when things were slower and there weren't people clamoring for the bartenders' time.

Unfortunately, that meant he had to wait.

"What'll you have, hon… er, sir?" the young woman asked. She hesitated and changed her greeting when she looked into his eye.

"I look for job as bouncer."

She frowned. "That would be Rod's call," she said, nodding with her head towards the man who was pouring a beer. "But I can tell you right now that you're not going to have any luck. He uses his nephew and a friend's son, so he's not looking for anyone else."

Daelan was puzzled. "I no see bouncer when I come in."

The dark-haired woman smiled, lifted her head an inch, and puckered her lips to gesture at a big young man with broad shoulders flirting with three ladies at a table. "They're not exactly the most diligent guys in the world, but they rise to the occasion when they're needed."

Daelan nodded at her and said, "Okay, thanks."

"Good luck."

**

The decor and clientele of the bars changed, but the answers stayed the same. We're not hiring.

As he moved away from the Willamette River and downtown, the bars became farther apart and seedier. He was about ready to end the job hunt for the night when he got to "The Devil's Taint". The "T" of the neon sign was broken, so it showed as "The Devil's aint".

In front of the dive was an assortment of Harleys, old muscle cars, and cheap pieces of crap that were, as often as not, covered by more primer than paint. The ramshackle building itself was slathered in black, peeling paint that exposed the aluminum siding underneath. The air, instead of smelling fresh from the rain, stunk of piss and vomit. When Daelan looked at the ground and the walls of the building, he saw there was a reason for that.

56

The side of the building was stained yellow here and there at an appropriate height.

He shook his head and thought, *This place is giving Hell a run for its money.* Still, beggars couldn't be choosers, so he walked in.

The music hit him with an almost physical force when he opened the door. Raw, pounding sound that featured a man screaming in an unnaturally deep voice. He had no idea what the man was saying and figured he probably didn't want to.

I thought the music at Sean's was painful.

He did his best to ignore it and, like he had every time before, made his way to the bar. Given his lack of success so far he knew the approach probably wasn't ideal, but didn't have any better ideas.

As he made his way through the bikers, wannabes, and women with daddy issues, one of the men he tried to slide by backed up, inadvertently bumping into him. The man turned around and yelled, "Watch it, asshole!"

"Sorry."

The large biker who, based purely on body language, Daelan figured was a wannabe, looked surprised and then grinned.

"What a pussy. Go on, little kitty cat, go to your mama," he said while making shooing gestures.

"Beat his ass, Viper!"

"Take him down!"

Daelan's anger, always simmering, roared to life. He would have killed one of his servants for far less, but he didn't want to start a fight when applying for a job that involved stopping them, so he stifled the urge to smash the man's face in and instead rolled his eye as he turned around and started walking.

His senses were on high alert, so he heard the man move and felt the fist approaching. Incredulous at the man's stupidity, Daelan shook his head as he slipped to the side, caught the arm, and used the leverage point to get behind him and sink in a choke. He was tempted to break the idiot's arm, but limited himself to making the hold painful by twisting it hard behind his back. Between the choke hold and the arm, the biker's back was arched way back. Daelan could have dropped him to the ground simply by letting go.

"Stupid idea, *Viper*," he said, loading the words with all the derision he felt.

Viper's two friends who had been egging him on looked shocked, but, knowing their roles, shot up and moved towards Daelan.

"Sit down, or I break…" Daelan wanted to say 'neck', but knew that would be going too far, even as a threat. "…arm."

They stopped, unsure of what to do, so they looked at Viper.

"Kick his a…" he rasped until Daelan twisted the arm harder, causing Viper to arch his back even further and shout, "Okay, okay, sit down!"

Daelan waited until both men were in their seats, then he whispered into Viper's ear, "You done, *ass-wiper*?" He punctuated the man's new name with an extra twist on his arm.

"Ow! Yeah, we're good. We're good, man."

Daelan pushed him away so he collapsed onto the table his friends were sitting at. With a final glance to make sure the friends stayed seated, he turned around and walked to the bar.

The bartender was an older man who looked like he'd lived fast and planned to die young, only it didn't happen. He looked like he was seventy years old, but for all Daelan knew he might have been fifty.

"What'll you have to drink, son?"

Daelan shook his head. "No money. I here to look for job."

The man sized him up and said, "It's on the house, as a thank you for not hurting Johnny too bad or causing any damage."

"Okay. Give me… uh, whatever."

The bartender raised an eyebrow. "You don't have a preference?"

"I from long way away."

"Accent like that, I believe it. Where are you from?"

Daelan just shrugged.

The bartender poured a deep-amber colored liquid into a shot glass and said, "Can't go wrong with old Jack."

Daelan picked it up and looked at it before sipping whatever the "old Jack" was. It had a pleasant burn that was much nicer than the lousy alcohol they had in Hell.

"Thanks."

"You said you were lookin' for a job?"

Daelan nodded before taking another sip.

"Can you wait until closing time? It'll be easier to talk then."

"Yes."

The bartender smiled and went off to pour more drinks.

Chapter 8

Gabriel

Gabriel pulled up to an abandoned house that stank of mana. It wasn't often he put the words "stink" and "mana" together. He lived for magic and would give his right arm for more.

He knew something abnormal must have happened to make the magical residue feel so... ugly. He took in the house's boarded windows and decaying wood siding and wrinkled his nose. The mana wasn't the only thing that stank.

He tried the front door, and it was locked. He had ways of getting in, but decided to try the back first. The back door was unlocked, the nearest window had its plywood covering pulled off, and the window was busted.

They probably got in through the window and left through the door.

He didn't know who "they" were yet, but that was part of why he was here.

He could have done a time-scry to verify his deduction and see who entered, but that much mana was far too precious to use unless absolutely required. Instead, he walked into the house, which was pretty much like what he'd expected. Dark, filthy, and decrepit. It smelled of mildew and rot.

He examined the window sill of the uncovered window. The weather damage was minimal.

The plywood was pulled off recently.

He followed the wisps of mana to their source in the main room, where dusty and broken furniture was pushed to the side, and a faint pentagram was amateurishly drawn on the floor. Gabriel usually rolled his eyes at such things because they were much more often than not the product of edgelords and would-be satanists that had no actual power.

This, though, was different. The mana and sense of... he hated to say it, but it felt evil. He generally thought of "good" and "evil" as abstract concepts, but what he was sensing just felt *wrong*, and he couldn't think of a better term for it.

Gabriel looked around, but didn't see anything more that would help him figure out what had happened. He sighed and once again considered using his mana to time-scry what had happened.

If it turns out to be unimportant, the Society will make me work extra shifts for months to pay for more bones.

He knew it was a risk, but he also knew he had to do it. If it was important, the Society needed to know about it.

He pulled out his spellbook and turned to the time-scry spell. Though he thought he could cast it without the book to help him get the incantation right, the mana was too precious to risk.

Gabriel gingerly took out a small box made of jade so dark green that it was almost black. It was finely worked with subtle bas-relief on all sides, but the most important thing about it was that the stone box was practically airtight, to the point that it resisted being opened.

He inhaled the mana-filled air wafting from the contents, and selected the biggest bone—a metatarsal if he wasn't mistaken.

With practiced motions he started grinding the bone with his mortar and pestle. Whether due to the hurried motions or his nervousness, sweat appeared on his brow as he worked.

When Gabriel was satisfied the bone powder was fine enough, he pulled out a small straw, put it in a nostril, pinched the other, and snorted up the powder as if it were the finest cocaine. He couldn't help but moan with pleasure as the mana spread throughout his body before he pulled it into his core.

When the euphoria abated, Gabriel reluctantly returned his attention to the task at hand. After quickly reviewing the spell, he spoke the words of power and fed the mana into the chant. When he finished the last syllable, the spell snapped into place, causing a ghostly overlay of the room to appear.

He "rewound" quickly, looking for the event. He needed to be fast to avoid running out of mana.

When he got to three people, a man and two teenage boys, he slowed down but continued to rewind. His breath caught when he saw, in reverse time order, the appearance of the man through a portal.

Oh shit...

He stopped rewinding when the man disappeared and started moving the time-scry forward. When the ebon sword pierced reality, Gabriel's skin crawled. He watched the whole thing through until the three left the room.

Gabriel considered what he'd seen. There was no question that the Society needed to know about this, it was just a matter of how best to report it. He decided that it merited using the fastest manner possible.

He quickly pulled out the smaller of the two bones that were left and ground it up. Midway through inhaling the bone powder, for the first time in his life, he was tempted to stop when he knew he had enough to pass his information to the Society's regional Archmagus. Knowing it would be stupid to waste mana to save a few seconds, he inhaled every bit until the mortar was as clean as he could make it.

Finally done, he connected to the anchor that he knew so well. When the connection was established and he knew the Archmagus was listening, he hurried to get his words out.

"Dad, we've got a problem."

Chapter 9

Imogen

Imogen hated visits with her parole officer. Ms. Fennis was okay, but her visits reminded her of how she had come to be in the foster group home in the first place.

Such bullshit. If he didn't want me to threaten him with a knife, he shouldn't have tried to take advantage of me.

Hank, the dad in her last foster family, had always given her the ick. With his age, potbelly, bad breath, and how he watched porn where everyone could hear it, there was never the remotest possibility of being attracted to him, but it went way beyond that. It was the way he looked at her. She still shuddered whenever she thought about it.

He'd waited until they were alone in the house, then tried to talk her into bed. When that didn't work, he started threatening.

The way Imogen saw it, threatening him back was 100% legit. The knife was just a way to make up for her size disadvantage. And it made the threat of castrating him a whole lot more believable. The problem was, it was her word against his, and Imogen had a history of misdemeanor theft.

The lawyer said she was lucky to not go to juvie.

Because the group home is so much better, she thought bitterly.

When Imogen saw Ms. Fennis walk in, she put on her "mask". Genial, but not too happy—that would look fake. No anger. She called it her "stoned airhead" look.

"Hi, Jenny! How are you? I see you bleached your hair. It suits you."

Imogen had bleached one-tone hair in a pixie cut, sweatpants, and an open plaid button-up over a white t-shirt.

"I'm good. How are you, Ms. Fennis?"

Ms. Fennis was a slender, bottle-blonde in her late twenties. Imogen assumed she came from money or had a rich boyfriend, because her clothes were too nice for her salary.

"I'm doing well! Shall we?" she asked as she gestured towards the small conference room that was set aside for meetings like this.

"Sure."

They sat down across the table from each other, the cheap rolling chairs creaking even though neither of them weighed much. Ms. Fennis opened up her briefcase and pulled out a vial with a stopper. She handed it to Imogen and, with a sympathetic smile, said, "You know the routine."

Imogen grunted with a frown and moved to the open stall at the end of the room that was also set aside for this exact purpose. Though she had become used to the process, she was still humiliated when she pulled her pants down and peed into the vial. Getting up wasn't any better, because now she was holding a warm vial that she really didn't want to drop.

"How much longer do I have to do this?"

"Until your parole is over."

"And how long is that?"

Ms. Fennis riffled through some papers, looking for the answer. "Uh, seven months."

Damn it.

She felt her eyes start to tear up, but she forced the emotions down. She did not want to cry. Ms. Fennis took the vial and put it into a special container in the briefcase, all the while pretending to not notice Imogen's wet eyes.

"How's work going? It's at a hot dog place, right?"

"Yeah, in the mall." She worked at one of those places that made the workers wear dorky outfits that kind of made them look like hot dogs. "It's okay."

"How many hours are you working?"

"Usually fifteen to twenty a week."

Ms. Fennis wrote down some notes on a legal pad.

"How are things here in the home?"

"They're okay."

"Are you getting along with the other kids?"

Imogen shrugged. "Well enough."

64

More writing. The visit continued for another twenty minutes. Imogen focused on maintaining the mask. As shitty as this place was, if things didn't work out here the next stop was juvie. She'd never been, but she'd heard things. She didn't want to go to juvie.

You can do this, Imogen. It's only two more years, and then you're out of here. Just two more years.

She kept telling herself that while looking at Ms. Fennis through the mask, pushing the tears down so they wouldn't leak.

Chapter 10

Daelan

Between handling Johnny without too much mayhem and repeatedly losing bouncers, the Taint's owner and bartender, Gus, had been happy to hire Daelan. He started him at fifteen dollars an hour and a free pitcher of beer, which he emphasized he didn't get until the *end* of his shift.

It was good enough for Daelan. Gus paid him in cash and didn't care about ID, which was exactly what he needed.

Daelan's life fell into a routine. Breakfast at the shelter, studying at the library, dinner and nap at the shelter, and work at the Taint. His only real problem was the achiness he'd been experiencing since coming to Earth. At first he'd assumed that it was just his body feeling mana deprivation, but that it would get used to it again, just like it had in the early days in Hell. So far it hadn't gone away, though. If anything, it was getting worse. Oh, well. He'd just have to deal until it calmed down.

"Hey, Gus," Daelan asked him on a slow Wednesday. "What's up with name of bar?"

Gus grinned. "The Devil's Taint? It's our signature drink! You want to try it?"

Daelan shrugged. "Sure."

Gus raised his voice and said, "Boys and girls, I do believe we have a virgin in our midst, and he's going to pop his Taint cherry before our very eyes!"

Cheers and laughter rang out through the bar as the patrons turned to look at the pair.

"I will regret this, no?"

Gus smiled widely. "You have no idea. The Taint…" he explained as he started making the drink, "is three parts Everclear—or gasoline, whichever we have on hand—and a half part tabasco sauce. Then we light it on fire."

Daelan had no idea what tabasco sauce or Everclear were, but judging by the looks on everyone's faces and their laughter, he was pretty sure the combination wasn't good. He figured Gus had to be joking about the gasoline, though. He hoped.

In short order Gus put a red, flaming drink in a shot glass in front of Daelan. The muscle heads, bikers, and biker chicks started chanting, "Drink! Drink! Drink!"

Daelan wrinkled his nose at the acrid, noxious smell coming from the flames. He sighed and, after a last look at the evil concoction, tossed it back.

Unlike the Jack Daniels Gus had given him, this drink had a most *un*pleasant burn. While he tried to keep his eye from tearing up, the crowd cheered and laughed.

Daelan narrowed his eye at Gus and said, "That was not nice."

Gus laughed and said, "No, but now you're officially one of us. I should, uh, probably warn you that you haven't had the worst of it yet."

"No?"

Gus shook his head. "No. In a couple hours, well… let's just say someone's butt is going to be as hot as the devil's taint."

"I hate you, Gus."

**

That night, Daelan dreamed of the past, walking again with his first friend in Hell, who happened to be a human spirit. He had saved Farad by killing the demon that was torturing him, and then the spirit stayed and cackled as Daelan turned the screws on his tormenter.

'*Give it to him good! Yeah, you like that asshole? Do you?!*'

If the man had been alive, Daelan was pretty sure he'd be spraying spittle as he screamed. As it was, he was limited to howling telepathically. Though there were no words in his thoughts, Daelan could still understand the meaning in them.

He continued to inflict as much pain on the demon as he could until it believed, heart and soul, that non-existence was its best option. Once Daelan consumed its anima, Farad followed him around.

'*So how do you have a body? Are you a demon?*'

67

"No."

'Then what are you?'

"I'm like you. I just came here without dying."

'Why the hell would you come here?*'*

Daelan sighed. "Good question." After explaining his situation, he asked, "What brought you here?"

'I don't know. If you ask me, I don't deserve to be here.'

Daelan side-eyed him skeptically.

'I'm serious! Maybe everyone comes through this pit stain on their way to reincarnation.'

"Maybe."

One day when they were talking, Farad asked, *'Have I ever told you about my daughter?'*

"No. What was she like?"

'She was beautiful, just like her mother. Her mother died when she was young, and Leena, like the darling angel she was, started taking care of her father, just like her mother had. She cooked my meals, mended my clothes, and even made money by taking in laundry.'

"Did you work?"

'Yes. I worked in a mine that was as cold as death. That mine was, as far as I was concerned, a pit of hell too. Every night I was glad to escape its maws, but I would be so cold. I shivered when I was home, so Leena would fix me a hot bowl of soup. Sometimes we'd only have broth, but she tried to make sure I had a few vegetables or pieces of meat. I think sometimes she went without so I would have something. She was so frail, and so thin.'

Farad paused for a long time, until Daelan thought he was done, so he was surprised when Farad continued.

'I was so cold at night. I still shivered after eating the soup, so Leena crawled into bed with me to warm me up. I was so grateful that she took care of me, just like her mother would.'

Daelan felt uneasy. He wasn't sure he wanted to hear the end of the tale, but he asked anyway.

"What happened, Farad?"

'I'm... not sure. Why don't I remember her husband or children? I lived to be an old man. Why don't I remember?'

After a few seconds, Daelan said, "Perhaps she died."

Farad scoffed. '*You think I wouldn't remember my own daughter's death? Please.*'

"What's the last thing you remember about her?"

'*I remember her… softly singing a song. She told me that night she wanted to leave. She wanted to leave together. Why would she want to leave our home?*'

"You tell me. Why would she want to leave?"

'*She wouldn't,*' he said, looking troubled. '*Humble as it was, she put her life and soul into making our hovel a home.*'

"Something must have worried her."

'*Yes… something.*'

Later that day, when Daelan was experimenting with burning a many-limbed demon to see if that would break it faster than his usual technique of cutting and flaying, something broke in Farad.

'*Leave her alone!*'

Daelan paused. "What's wrong?"

'*Just… leave her alone… please.*'

"Leave who alone?"

'*My daughter! It's… it's not her fault…*'

"What isn't her fault?"

Farad would say no more, so Daelan continued torturing the demon. Farad just whimpered.

The next day, Farad was very quiet until, while they were walking through the dusty plains, he said, '*I do belong in Hell.*'

"Why?"

'*I let them take and burn her. They burned her because I was a coward!*'

"Who?"

'*The villagers. My daughter…*' Farad wept for a time. It was some minutes before he continued. '*My daughter was with child. Her thin, frail body could not hide that she was pregnant. I could not admit that I was the father of both her and the baby…*'

"And they burned her."

Farad just wept.

"You are lucky that I cannot torture you like I do the demons. Do better in your next life."

Daelan summoned Quoz and swept it through the spirit. Its bodily form dissipated and was drawn into the midnight blade.

All that remained was a softly glowing mist that dissipated, leaving the plane for other worlds.

Daelan didn't know if Farad would be punished further wherever he went. He just knew that he should.

**

Daelan was putting the finishing touches on his latest programming exercise—a pair of googly eyes that always looked at the mouse pointer—when a little boy who he hadn't realized was standing behind him asked, "What's on your head?"

Daelan cursed in demonic as he looked at the boy, startled. "Is eyepatch."

"What's it for?" he asked guilelessly.

"It covers hole where eye used to be."

His eyes grew wide. "Really? How did you lose it?"

"When I am your size, someone hit me on back of head and it pop out."

His eyes were now round saucers, with a tinge of fear. "Would my eyes come out if someone hit me?"

Daelan chuckled. "I not know. Should we try?"

"No!" he said, backing away a step. From his more distant vantage point, he pointed at the computer screen. "What's that?"

"Eyes I made on computer. You want to try?" He showed him how the eyes moved when he moved the mouse.

"You won't hit me on the head?"

Daelan smiled. "No."

"Promise?"

"Promise."

"Okay."

Daelan scooted his chair over and let the boy, who was holding a threadbare stuffed lion, take over the mouse. He gleefully moved it around and laughed when he saw the googly eyes swing around with his movements.

"Griffin, what are you doing, sweetie?" asked a woman from behind. Her voice was warm, but the warmth covered a note of concern.

"I'm playing with the eyes!" Griffin said unconcernedly, not bothering to look away from the computer.

Daelan nodded uncomfortably at the woman, wanting nothing more than to leave but unwilling to while he was still logged in and his latest changes were unsaved.

"Hello," she said. "I'm Griffin's mom, Jessica." She held her hand out to shake, her eyes skeptical. She had the air of a bodyguard who was assessing a potential threat.

"John."

After looking in his eye for a moment, Jessica turned to her son and said, "Let's leave the nice man alone, okay, honey?"

"Just a minute." Griffin had discovered that if he put the mouse in between the two eyes, they went cross-eyed. That started a new round of giggles.

Jessica gave him an embarrassed smile. "Sorry about this."

"It fine. I invite him to try it."

"Are you taking classes or something?"

"No. I learn how to make websites, but I do, uh, by myself."

"Oh." His answer seemed to surprise her, though he didn't know why. She turned to her son again and asked, "Are you ready to go?"

"Alright." He released the mouse and started skipping to the checkout desk.

"What do you say to the nice man, sweetie?"

"Thanks for not hitting me on the head!" he called out as he kept skipping.

Daelan chuckled. "You welcome." He dipped his head a touch towards Jessica, who looked confused after her son's comment, and said, "Take care."

"You too. Good luck with learning!"

Daelan just nodded again, eye already on the computer screen.

**

When Rob saw him at the shelter that evening, he greeted him warmly. "Hey, John!"

"Rob." Though he and Rob were as different as night and day, the man's friendliness had grown on him.

"I want to ask you something."

"Yes?"

"What would you think about teaching a class to the guys here?"

Did not expect that. Daelan furrowed his brow. "What would I teach?"

"That's what I wanted to talk with you about. It could be anything, as long as it helps them get healthy, learn a skill, have a positive attitude… whatever."

Though he didn't like the idea, he felt like he owed the people here for their help, so he tried to come up with something he could teach the other men.

What am I good at? Torturing demons? Consuming souls? Fighting with war scythes? He couldn't help but quirk his lips in a self-mocking smile. *I have such useful skills for this world.*

"I am no sure what I could teach, Rob."

"How about exercise? You're a fit guy."

Exercise? I don't think they want to get fit the way I did. Daelan grimaced and, after thinking for a few seconds, said, "I could teach how to fight."

It was Rob's turn to frown. "That, uh, isn't quite what we're looking for. As I'm sure you've noticed, not everyone here is quite *right*, if you know what I mean."

Daelan chuckled. "Yes, I know what you mean. I afraid I do no have many useful skills, but I think about it."

Rob nodded and said, "Thanks, John," as he gave him his trademark clap on the shoulder.

**

During the first couple of weeks at his job, the guys tested Daelan. After showing them that he could kick their asses if he wanted to, they backed down.

Now, apparently, the women decided it was their turn.

Brianna, a bottle-blond with cat eye makeup, leather jacket and skirt, and lacy fingerless gloves walked up to him, head tilted and smiling coyly. Daelan took her in, then continued watching the crowd.

"Hey, John."

"Hey," he said without bothering to look at her.

"Can I buy you a drink?"

72

"No."

He could hear the pout in her voice when she said, "That's kind of mean."

With a frown, Daelan looked her in the eyes. On the way he'd glanced at her boyfriend, who was seething.

"Go back to Nick, Bri, so he do no beat you too much worse than he usually do."

She did a good job of hiding it with her makeup, but he'd noticed the hints of bruises.

Her eyes became wet, and she seemed to drop the act. Of course, Daelan didn't know people well enough to know if she was being real now, or if she had just traded one act for another. He didn't care much either way.

"If you know about that, why don't you help me?"

"Why would I? You do no even help yourself."

She looked flustered, and tears started to form. "What do you mean?"

"I mean you could leave him any time."

"Maybe that's why I'm here, talking to you."

Daelan rolled his eye before going back to watching the crowd.

"I live in homeless shelter. You are no here to leave Nick."

"Then why am I here?"

"I do not know. Look like you want to get beaten." He looked down at her again and said, "Look. I do this for you. Leave him. Calvary's Hill has women's shelter, you can go there if you need. Clean yourself up. Get job, and if Nick touches you I beat the shit out of him one time. I do that for you."

Her tear-filled eyes looked at him searchingly. He wanted to roll his eye again, but refrained. He looked at her for a moment, then went back to scanning the crowd.

Without a word she slipped back to the crowd and her boyfriend, who angrily grabbed her by the wrist and pulled her out of the bar.

**

Bri was not, unfortunately, the last woman to approach him at work.

73

"Hey, John, how ya doin'?" Jasmine asked warmly.

She often came in with her boyfriend, Matt, to drink, dance, and party. Unlike Brianna's boyfriend, Matt was quite obviously not jealous. Both of them had a habit of picking up people of either gender, often more than one, and leaving with them.

Apparently it's my turn.

"Okay," Daelan said as he continued to watch the crowd.

"Hey, my eyes are down here, big boy. First time I've ever had to get a guy to look downwards," she said laughingly.

Daelan looked at her. "I am working, Jasmine. What you want?"

"I thought that was obvious. I want *you*," she said as she moved in close and slid her arm around his waist.

Daelan was annoyed and about to push her away when he realized that something about her felt… off. He opened up his third eye and didn't see anything obvious, but it did strengthen his feeling that something was wrong. His spiritual sight was affected by his weakness, and was not as discerning as it had been before he escaped Hell.

Daelan went back and forth on whether to ignore it or investigate, and finally decided to look into it.

"You want add me to, uh, harem?" he said with a quirk of his lips.

She smiled. "Something like that. Only you would have pride of place. Like your dong on a mantle or something."

Brow furrowed in disbelief and disgust, Daelan said, "Wow, that sound great."

Laughing, she playfully swatted him on the chest and left her hand there. "I'm just kidding, big guy. Just a replica, of course, for those nights when I can't have the real thing."

Ick.

Daelan didn't have a lot of experience with non-demonic women, and even he knew she was laying it on too thick.

"Come see me when bar closes."

She smiled at him as she slid her hand down to his stomach and hooked the tip of a finger into the top of his pants before releasing him. "It's a date."

No, it's not.

As far as he was concerned, she was a walking STD. If it were just of the physical variety, he would ignore her and they could go their separate ways. Live and let live.

He suspected that something supernatural was going on though, and he didn't feel right about letting that be. Especially since it could be a source of power.

Hours later, bar almost empty, Jasmine walked up to him and said, "Are you ready for the night of your life?"

Daelan stopped wiping a table with a dirty rag, looked up at her, and thought, *If that means consuming your soul to power up, yes.* Though he was a patient man, he was eager to start walking the road to power and revenge.

Daelan looked back at Gus, who was cleaning the bar and getting ready to take a tray of glasses to the back to wash. "You good, Gus?"

Gus looked at him like he was trying to decide whether to say something or not, but ended up shaking his head and said, "Yeah, I'm fine. Have a good night."

Jasmine grabbed his hand and pulled him towards the door, where Matt was talking with a man and woman. The pair said their goodbyes and left right as Jasmine and Daelan walked up.

"Just me?" Daelan asked Matt.

"Just you." Matt smiled. "Jasmine's been talking about wanting to get with you for weeks now. I think she'd be pissed if there were any distractions."

Daelan frowned. "I'm no into guys, bro."

"No worries. I'll just be a spectator tonight, then. If that's alright?" he asked, as if it just occurred to him that some people might not want to be watched.

"Whatever."

They got into a Dodge Charger that had dings and scratches on it. The interior was black, and the back was surprisingly spacious for a muscle car. Daelan looked at the upholstery skeptically. He didn't want to know what had happened in this car.

Jasmine slid into the back with him, while Matt got into the driver's seat. As he pulled away from the bar he said, "I only have one rule in the car."

"What is it?"

"No getting naked."

"Oh, shoot," Daelan said.

"Okay, it's more of a guideline really," Matt said laughingly.

Jasmine chuckled and pulled his hand to put it between her thighs.

Nope.

Daelan pulled his hand out and, not wanting to arouse her suspicions, put his hand on her knee and rubbed it. That seemed to satisfy Jasmine, who put her head on his shoulder and hugged his arm.

The ride was thankfully quiet and uneventful, other than Jasmine feeling his leg and asking, "What happened to your eye, John?"

He remembered one of Imogen's favorite Christmas movies and said, "Accident with BB gun."

Matt looked at him through the rear-view mirror and said, "You're shitting me."

"No shitting." He looked at Jasmine. "It bother you?"

"Uh uh," she said as she turned into him and nuzzled his neck. "I think it's sexy."

Matt asked, "What about your finger?"

The index finger of his left hand was missing. There were striations in the flesh, as if it had been bitten off.

"I forget to feed pet shark."

Matt laughed. "Now I know you're messing with me."

Daelan shook his head as much as he could with Jasmine at his neck.

"Sharks good pets. Unless you forget to feed."

They went through a gate with spiked ironwork and stopped at a large house in the hills to the west of town. It was a two-story colonial with lots of gables, as if it had been added to many times. A small, unattached house sat next to it.

As they walked to the mansion's front door, Daelan pointed to the smaller house and asked, "What's that?"

Jasmine said, "That's our place."

"So why we go to big house?"

After Matt opened the door and gestured for them to enter, he said with a grin, "Because this is the party place."

Daelan was looking at it with his third eye. He would not have described it as a "party place". The house felt ugly. He was sure now that something was going on.

When he and Jasmine reached the door, he gestured for her to go in. "Ladies first."

She giggled. "Been a while since someone called me that."

I bet.

He tried to not make a big deal of it, but insisted that Matt go in before him too. Though Daelan was stronger, faster, and tougher than normal humans—the achiness he 'd been feeling since coming to Earth notwithstanding—Jasmine and Matt weren't normal. Besides, he'd be damned before he'd willingly have an enemy at his back if he could help it.

He'd been backstabbed before.

Shrugging, Matt entered the house and Daelan followed.

The entry looked like it belonged in a marble palace. Two sets of gently curving marble stairs glided up to the second floor from both sides of the room, meeting at the top. A crystal chandelier softly illuminated the room, while sconces on the walls added dramatic flair.

Jasmine and Matt grinned while looking at Daelan expectantly, so he said, "Nice place."

"Right?" Jasmine said. "We've got a fully stocked kitchen on the right, the bar and dance floor on the left. Pool and jacuzzi in the back."

Daelan was, of course, looking at everything with his third eye. The entire place felt… uncomfortable, like insatiable, demented hunger. The spiritual miasma was thicker on the second floor.

The feeling in the house reminded him of Hell.

"What is upstairs?"

Jasmine laughed and patted him on the chest. "So impatient! Those are the bedrooms. Oh, and the movie room. Don't worry, big boy. There's plenty of time for that."

"I'll go make us some margaritas," Matt said before walking towards the side of the house with the bar.

With her hand on his chest, Jasmine moved in close. "So, what would you like to do first?"

Daelan wanted to go upstairs to find out what was going on, but decided to play it cool and gather information. As long as he could keep a little distance from STD-chick anyway.

"Do you have pool table?"

Jasmine's brows furrowed like she couldn't believe what she'd just heard.

"Pool? Don't you, uh, get enough of that at the bar?" The Devil's Taint had a pool table that was popular with the patrons.

Daelan shrugged. "I never get to play because I always working. Make me jealous."

"Okaaaay, if you waaaant," she said as she playfully expressed her disbelief by shaking her head. She started walking towards the back of the house and navigated them to stairs leading down. "Maybe we can make it interesting by betting on the games."

"I do no have much money. Gus is not very generous."

"Money? Money's boring. I was thinking clothes."

Daelan shook his head in disgust, glad that she was in front and couldn't see him.

I'm not sure she even has a two-dimensional personality. Can she talk about anything else?

The fact was, she didn't excite him. He'd had plenty of sex with women—well, of the demonic variety anyway—that wanted to deceive, use, or hurt him. Often it was all three. He'd had his fill and then some of that, from creatures that were hotter than Jasmine. She had less than zero appeal for him.

The only thing interesting about Jasmine was figuring out how she was trying to use him. That mystery was the only reason he was here.

Frustrated with her boring single-mindedness, he decided to mess with her a bit.

"I was thinking about songs."

She stopped and turned her head to look at him. "Songs?"

"Yeah, loser has to sing 'I'm little teapot'".

Daelan chuckled inside. It had been one of Imogen's favorite songs when she was a little girl. He cherished the memory of two-year-old Imogen singing it with all the motions. She didn't get it all right, of course, but that was part of the charm.

Hmm. Not sure I want to associate Jasmine or this place with that memory. Oh well, I doubt it will come to that anyway.

She stared at him for a moment. "Seriously? You want to sing 'I'm a little teapot'?"

"Of course not," he said as he shook his head. Her face relaxed for a moment until he said, "I want *you* to sing it."

Her jaw dropped. He waited for her to say something, but she appeared to be at a loss. Daelan filled the gap by shrugging and saying, "It is fetish," as he looked through a hallway door at the most luxurious half-bathroom he'd ever seen. He looked at her and asked, "By the way, how you feel about wearing diaper?"

"A diaper?" It took a few seconds for her to process that. She shook her head again and walked off, presumably towards the pool room. "You're not what I expected."

"I get that often."

**

Daelan, as it turned out, was a terrible pool player. He understood the geometry of it, but, never having played, knew nothing about technique, when to strike a ball hard or soft, or how to set up the next shot.

He ended up singing the first three times, which made Matt laugh uproariously, while Jasmine was mirthful while hiding her mouth with her hand, trying not to embarrass her "date" too much. Daelan, for his part, didn't care.

He barely touched his drink while he played. Ever since the assassination of his Father, he'd always been careful about what he ate and drank. There was nothing to indicate the drink was drugged, but he didn't want to chance it.

When they encouraged him to drink, he kissed a surprised but happy Jasmine and said, "I like taste of hers better," before throwing back what was left of her second margarita.

Daelan ended up winning the fourth game, but he was pretty sure it was only because Jasmine lost on purpose. She stood up straight with a laugh and started singing. Halfway into it, Daelan made the "timeout" sign and said, "Stop, stop, stop."

Jasmine frowned and said, "What's wrong?"

"You doing it all wrong."

79

"What do you mean? I'm doing it just like you did."

Matt just watched, amused and sipping his drink.

"Let me show you." Daelan went behind Jasmine and started moving her arms to form a proper teapot. "How someone going to pick up pot with weak handle like that? Firm up arm! Okay, good. Now, trick of spout is give it, uh, double curve, like snake. Better. Okay..." Daelan slid his left arm around her and put his hand on her bare midriff. Jasmine giggled, but Daelan ignored it. Touching her skin made it easier to sense her spiritual state. He got that same sense of hunger that he'd felt on the second floor. "... now we *bend*! Good, good. Okay, I think you ready to do on your own."

Jasmine pouted and said, "I think I need you to help me still."

Daelan smiled widely, which if they had known him would have set their alarm bells ringing. Daelan never smiled big. He took his position behind her, held her by the waist again and pulled her into himself. He made a spout with her, and together they sang, "I'm a little teapot, short and stout! Here is my handle, here is my spout..." When they finished, they both laughed.

Matt clapped. "Well done. Should we move on to the main event of the evening?"

Daelan nodded. "Shall we?" He asked Jasmine as he held out his hand.

She tittered and held his hand. "I never know quite what to expect with you."

That's the idea. "Lead way, Matt."

They made their way to the second floor, Jasmine telling him all the things she was going to do to him. He ignored her. His attention was on his third eye.

When they reached the upper floor, Jasmine tried to lead him into a large bedroom when he saw an oddly ornate door at the end of the hall. The door felt like it was holding back a black hole of hunger.

Daelan stopped and asked, "What is in there?"

Matt said, "That's, uh, the one place we don't go in the house. It's the owner's room."

Daelan started walking towards it, and said, "I want to meet him and say 'thank you' for letting me see home."

"That's not necessary, John. He doesn't like to be disturbed. Stop, John!" Matt became more anxious as Daelan got closer to the door, and by the time he shouted, he was actively pulling on him.

Matt was far stronger than he looked, but given the situation, Daelan was not surprised.

Jasmine had been pulling on his hand the entire time. At first, it was playfully trying to entice him into the bedroom. By the time Matt pulled on his shoulder, she was also getting serious about getting him to stop.

Daelan had lost any doubts he'd had about something sinister going on in the house, so he decided it was time to drop the act. He twisted and used his free left hand to grab a very surprised Matt by the throat and slam him into the wall.

The violent move detached an equally surprised Jasmine. Daelan used his right hand to reach into the spatial pocket for Quoz, the contracted entity that had risen in power with him in Hell. Unlike Daelan, Quoz had not released any of that power.

A long dagger with red glowing runes formed that was surrounded by a haze of shadows that dimmed the light in the hallway. Matt's and Jasmine's eyes were drawn to it as it exerted a spiritual oppression that pressed on their minds and hearts.

It only took Daelan a moment to whip it up to Jasmine's throat, causing her to go completely still with a horrified look when she felt the edge leave the slightest of cuts on her neck. A wisp of her power entered Daelan. It made him hunger for more.

'I was beginning to wonder if thou wouldst ever call on me again,' Quoz whispered in his mind. It was uncomfortable feeling the vast disparity in power between them now. Though he could tell the entity wasn't even trying to hurt him, its laughter was painful. *'I should have had faith thou wouldst find people to kill wherever thou went.'*

Daelan didn't bother to respond. Instead, he looked at Jasmine. "What is behind door?"

Terrified, she looked torn until Daelan heard the creak of the door. She looked past him and stuttered, "M-master."

Daelan turned to look at an old, weathered man whose skin looked like well-worn but sturdy leather. He was dressed in a bathrobe and fuzzy slippers, but the ridiculousness of the image

81

before him hardly even entered into Daelan's consciousness. The man exuded *power*, which made Daelan nervous.

"Well, isn't this interesting. Jasmine, dear, what's going on?"

"M-master, we brought what we thought was healthy livestock, but he s-surprised us."

The man chuckled and said, "I had no idea you had such a talent for understatement, my dear." He looked at Daelan and said, "My name is Arthur Constable. May I have the pleasure of your acquaintance?"

Still trying to assess how to handle this mess, Daelan simply said, "John. What are you, Mr. Constable?"

"Very direct, I see, John. Well, I suppose it's understandable, given the circumstances. I am a striga."

"What is striga?"

"A vampire," he said with a smile. "And you, John? What exactly are you?"

"Would you believe if I tell you 'human'?"

Arthur tilted his head as he pondered that. "No, probably not. At least not just a human. And then, of course, there's the matter of *that*."

Everyone understood what "that" was. "That" was Quoz.

"It is my secret weapon."

Arthur stared at the dagger for a few seconds. "I recognize a kindred spirit."

'*He thinketh to compare himself to me in any way, shape, or form? I demand that thou lettest me eat him!*'

Daelan struggled to not close his eye from pain. As it was, he still winced.

'*You're not making this easier for me, Quoz.*'

'*I am the only reason he isn't trying to eat you.*'

'*Probably true,*' he thought grimly.

"I'd like to make you an offer," Arthur said.

"Yes?"

"Join us. These two…" he gestured at Jasmine and Matt, "…are competent herders, but that's all they are capable of being. I want you to be my protégé. What do you think?"

"I like being human."

"Why? Do you believe all those myths about vampires? We are not dead. I assure you, I am very much alive, with sensations and emotions. There is nothing more pleasurable than feeding."

"Do you feed on them?" Daelan asked, gesturing with his head at Matt and Jasmine.

"I do. It is my right as their Master."

"So, you would feed on me?"

Arthur nodded. "I would. I don't mind giving you one of them if that would make you feel better about it."

The vampire's nonchalance about feeding on him enraged Daelan. He forced himself to not look at the missing portion of his index finger. Instead, Daelan glanced at Matt and Jasmine. Struggling to breathe, Matt was not in a good position to express his opinion about his master's proposal, but Daelan saw that Jasmine's mouth dropped open at how easily she was given away.

Daelan looked at Arthur and said, "No thanks."

He was about to make his counter-offer when Arthur said, "Pity. Kill him."

Daelan wasn't ready to go on the run from the law, so he wanted to kill Arthur without killing Jasmine and Matt—at least not yet. Still, he needed them out of the fight, so he threw Matt at Jasmine.

Or at least he tried to.

Matt grew claws and dug them into Daelan's arm, preventing Daelan from throwing him anywhere. Even worse, Daelan had released his throat, and Matt took the opportunity to bite into his wrist.

Jasmine didn't attack. Instead, she retreated to get out of the range of his dagger, which was the only good thing about the situation. Even that speck of positivity was wiped out when he felt a sledgehammer strike him in the back of the head, sending him flying down the hall.

Whether due to cat-like instincts or luck, Daelan impacted the wall on the flat of his back, upside down, having rotated 180° in the air.

Holy crap, that hurt...

He picked himself up and shook off the cobwebs. As tough as he was, that blow had him feeling punch-drunk.

83

He saw Matt whispering something to Arthur, who looked intrigued. The master vampire grabbed Matt's wrist and pulled his hand up so he could lick one of the claws that were stained with Daelan's blood.

After ingesting it, Arthur shuddered and his eyes rolled back in his head for a moment. When he came to, he looked at Daelan, eyes with a touch of red glow.

"What *are* you?"

Hurting and watching monsters consume his blood, Daelan's always simmering anger became a raging bonfire. He had no interest in talking.

Talking with them was a mistake. I should have killed the master when I saw him.

He cycled the tiny bit of mana he had to reinforce his body, become a little faster, and improve his healing.

Quoz was eight feet away. He didn't run to it—he simply willed it to come and it did, disappearing from the floor and appearing in his hand in the form of a throwing knife. Daelan threw the knife at Matt, who was still talking excitedly to his Master. He seemed to sense something at the last moment and turned his head, which meant that the blade went through his temple instead of taking him from behind.

The supernaturally sharp knife buried itself in the vampire's brain and would have kept going if it hadn't intentionally stopped to feed on Matt's body and soul.

Daelan ran towards the group of vampires without bothering to recall Quoz. It wasn't out of consideration for the entity's desires. He knew Quoz would come when he called, so it was better to do it at the last moment to surprise the vampires. It was a technique he had perfected over centuries of fighting demons.

"Slow him down!" Arthur shouted at Jasmine.

What a coward.

Whether from bravery, fear of Arthur, or because she couldn't disobey his orders, Jasmine approached, but she was clearly not a fighter. She looked terrified and held her fists up awkwardly.

Making a split-second decision, Daelan decided to not kill her. Instead, he bobbed away from a tentative punch and then decked her in the jaw. It was her turn to fly down the hallway. He wasn't sure how tough vampires were, so he split the difference between hitting her with enough strength to break the jaw of a normie human and his full power.

Hopefully she wouldn't die.

While she had technically slowed Daelan down, the results were much worse for Arthur, who had to take a precious second to extricate himself from the woman. When he was done, he angrily threw her into the bedroom door behind him.

Daelan had already moved into a thrusting attack with no weapon, which would have looked strange to an observer until he recalled Quoz, who appeared in his hand as a long dagger again. The blade punched into the vampire's chest where a human's heart would be.

Groaning, the vampire tried to grab Daelan, who released the weapon and dodged backwards out of reach. He recalled the blade into his hand and reassessed.

Though the chest wound bled, it was clearly not the killshot it would have been on a human.

'*I keep telling thee,*' Quoz said, '*When in doubt, go for the head.*'

'*Yeah, yeah.*'

Arthur, meanwhile, became blurry and turned into a dark cloud that moved towards Daelan.

'*The hell? Quoz, what is this?*'

'*It's an ability of powerful strigas. He has become a gaseous being temporarily. When he reforms he'll be healed.*'

That pissed Daelan off, but he had long since given up complaining about life being unfair, so he just tossed the feelings onto the bonfire of his rage.

When the vampire reformed, it was with both hands on Daelan's knife hand and biting down on his neck. Arthur started greedily draining his life essence and turning the knife towards Daelan's chest.

You're not the brightest bulb, are you?

Quoz disappeared and reformed in Daelan's left hand. His *free* left hand, which swiftly plunged the blade into the vampire's skull.

Arthur's body quivered and then collapsed, as if it were a puppet whose strings had been cut. Daelan released the blade so Quoz could keep feeding. He allowed himself to enjoy the rush of mana he received as a result. In seconds he received thousands of times more than what he'd slowly gathered on Earth.

Daelan enjoyed the ecstasy of the mana, but his rational side looked at the surroundings: two dead vampires, one crumpled up in the corner, a dent in the wall, and blood on the floor.

What a mess.

Chapter 11

Daelan drank a beer as he sat on the floor and leaned against the wall. He thought about what to do with Jasmine while he waited for her to wake up.

He really hoped she woke up, because he had a good thing going in Salem. If she was in a coma... well, that was going to be awkward, seeing as how multiple people saw him leave the bar with her and Matt.

Daelan breathed a sigh of relief when she stirred while he was working on his third beer.

"Morning."

"Ooh... what happened? I feel terrible..." Jasmine sat up, holding her head and her side. She looked at Daelan and her eyes went wide. "W-what...?"

She looked around in a panic. Though they were still in the hallway, Daelan had used his mana to clean up by disintegrating the bodies and the blood on the floor and walls. It drained most of his mana, but he deemed that it was necessary.

"What did you do, John?!"

"What do you mean?" he asked calmly.

"I mean, where are Matt and Master?"

She slowly and gingerly stood up and limped to the Master's room. Daelan had pretty much left it alone other than taking $8,000 in cash he'd found in the side table. He was sure that many of the items in the room, such as silver candelabras, were valuable, but he had no interest in pawning them. It wasn't worth the effort, and could only lead to trouble.

"Arthur is on trip. He always wanted to see Turkey, so he left. Matt become jealous when you decide you want me now, and not him. He is okay with sharing, but does no like being kicked out of your bed, so he left too."

"W-what are you talking about?" Jasmine asked confusedly, as she looked at the other rooms.

"Jasmine, look at me."

She did, but then she teared up and pointed at Daelan. "You killed Matt!"

"No, he left because he is jealous."

"You *killed* him!" she screamed as tears ran down her bruised and swollen face.

Daelan got up and walked over to her, angry that a stupid whore had leverage over him. She flinched and backed up awkwardly a couple of feet until she reached a door frame. She reached back to hold onto it, as if it would protect her. She looked terrified. Terrified was good. It meant safety.

Daelan put his hands on his knees so he could get on her level and look her in the eyes, from inches away.

"You have choice to make right now, Jasmine. Arthur is gone. Matt is gone. Are there other vampires?"

She shook her head jerkily.

"So you all that is left. You have two choices: you can tell my story, that Arthur is out of town and Matt left because he upset that you like me so much; or I clean up things here and leave town. Do you understand?"

Jasmine looked shell-shocked, but after a couple of moments she nodded her head.

"Do you understand what I mean by 'clean up things here', Jasmine?"

She nodded her head, glassy-eyed.

"What do I mean?"

"You'll kill me," she said in a whisper.

"That is right. So, what do you choose?"

Instead of answering, she looked at the floor again and asked, "Where are the bodies?"

"I get rid of them."

It took her half a minute, but she eventually said in a small voice, "I'll do it."

"Do what?"

"Stick to the story, and pretend I'm into you."

Daelan grabbed her by the jaw, which made her cry out in pain and look at him.

"No, Jasmine, pretend you are 'into me' is no good enough. You have to make everyone believe you like me so much that Matt left very mad. If cops look into it, I have to 'clean up things here'. Understand?"

She nodded with difficulty amid fresh tears of pain and fear.

"Good."

He released her and turned away. It was, of course, a test. One that she passed by not attacking him. That didn't mean she didn't want to kill him; it just meant she was smart enough to realize that she needed to cooperate for now.

It would have to do.

"How you become vampire?"

"Huh? Uh, Master fed me his blood."

"When Matt bite me, no cause me problems?"

"No." After a few moments she asked, "What are you?"

"You do not need to know."

Daelan could tell she didn't like that answer, but she moved on to another question.

"Can I still bring guys here to feed?"

Daelan rolled his eye. "You like me so much but bring other guys home? No."

"If I can't bring guys here, how will I feed?"

A good question. "How long can you go without?"

"About a week."

He thought about possible solutions, including letting her feed on him, but didn't like any of them.

"We figure it out, but for now, no feeding."

"Okay."

Before he reached the stairway down to the main floor and the exit, Daelan turned his head to look at her. She was a mess. "Cheer up. You just inherited 'party place'."

She narrowed her eyes at him and hissed, the tips of fangs showing.

Daelan didn't mind. He'd be more worried if she could hide the anger. Fearful and angry subordinates were something he knew how to deal with.

**

The next few days were weird for Daelan. He moved into the smaller house with Jasmine, both to support the story that they were a couple now, and so he could keep an eye on her. He didn't want an actual relationship though, so he slept on the couch.

She seemed glad that he didn't insist on sleeping in the bedroom. Neither one was comfortable with the other. He'd been worried that she wouldn't be able to pull off the deception, but the woman's acting skills were first-rate. If he hadn't known better, he would have been convinced that she lusted after him.

"Hey, baby," she said before kissing him at the Taint. For the sake of appearances he let it happen, but he still felt her insatiable hunger every time he touched her. He could handle it, having dealt with demons almost his entire life, but that didn't make it pleasant. "Did you miss me?"

Daelan grunted.

She smiled and pressed her body into his as she rose to tiptoes. Her hot breath tickled his ear as she whispered, "If you want people to believe it, you have to give me something to work with. And no eye rolling!" She took a moment to nibble on his ear lobe—no fangs involved, thankfully—and then giggled as she gave him his personal space back.

Smirking, she raised an eyebrow as if to ask what he was going to do.

Daelan smiled and said, "You can no tease me and get away so easily. Come here."

Jasmine's smile grew bigger as she approached him again.

Daelan pulled her in by the hips and started kissing her on the neck, causing Jasmine to moan softly. He moved his hands lower, grabbed her by the cheeks, and lifted her. Jasmine wrapped her legs around him, and they started kissing passionately.

Or at least, they made a good show of it. Daelan could also act when he needed to.

After a few seconds he let her back down, and when she started to saunter away he gave her a smack on the butt that was a little harder than was strictly necessary.

"She's sexy as hell, but are you sure you know what you're gettin' into, John?" Gus asked him as he poured a beer.

"Nope. Probably fun mistake."

Gus laughed. "That's a good description of my first two wives. They were a lot of fun, until they really, really weren't."

"What happened? Left you and took all your money?"

"Hell, if it was just money, I wouldn't have minded as much. Those rancid witches, they... well, it doesn't matter. I'd just watch myself with Jasmine if I were you."

Daelan turned his head to look at Gus and grinned. "I will not marry her, Gus."

"At least you're that smart."

"Can I ask you question?"

"Sure. Let me handle this order, and then we'll talk."

Once Gus had a pause, he wiped his hands with a dishcloth and asked, "So what's your question?"

"You know I have amnesia, and do not know where I am from, or name."

"Yeah...?"

From his voice and expression, Daelan didn't think that Gus bought the amnesia story, but didn't seem to be interested in calling him out on it.

"I need papers to get bank accounts, pay taxes, drive cars. Government take..." Daelan shrugged expressively, "...who know how long with amnesia. Do you know someone who can help get papers?"

Gus chuckled. "You want papers of a 'less than legit' nature that will let you, uh, what was it again? Pay taxes? Boy, I don't know who you're trying to fool, but it sure as hell isn't me!" he said with a laugh.

Daelan gave Gus an embarrassed smile. "I, uh, may have other things to do with papers."

Gus side-eyed him. "You wouldn't be trying to get another job, would you?"

"We both know this will not last forever, Gus."

"Yeah, I suppose I did, though I did my best to convince myself otherwise. Damn. That's exactly what I did with my first two wives. Here and I thought I'd gotten a little smarter after all these years..." he said as he shook his head.

"I promise to no take half your money, Gus."

He laughed. "Well, that's something anyway."

After a few seconds, when Gus still seemed wrapped up in his thoughts, Daelan said, "Gus? Papers?"

"Sorry. Um, let's see. If I had to talk to someone about getting a social security number and passport, who would I talk to?" He looked over at the bar's patrons in thought. "I think I would talk to Julio or Danny."

"Why them?"

"They're in a gang that pushes drugs and is into some other stuff." He shrugged. "It wouldn't surprise me if half the people here knew someone though."

"You say things like that, and wonder why I want new job."

Gus chuckled. "I don't want you to go, but I didn't say it was a bad idea."

Chapter 12

As it turned out, Julio did know a guy who knew a guy. It took three weeks and $6,000, but Daelan got a social security number, birth certificate, and Oregon driver's license that the fixer guaranteed were solid. Said he knew a couple of people in the government bureaucracy who entered him into the right databases.

Daelan hoped it was true, but he was going to do his best to stay under the radar and not test how good they were.

Things with Jasmine had settled down. They had an… interesting relationship. The first time she fed she coyly told him that they could do it the "fun way" instead.

"What way is that, Jasmine?"

She tilted her head, smiled, and said, "Let's just say there's more than one way to get your bodily fluids."

Hard pass.

She was offended that he didn't want to have sex with her, but he didn't care. She was a necessary evil, and nothing more.

She was still afraid of him, but when he allowed her to drink some of his blood she had an almost orgasmic reaction, much like her Master had.

Daelan didn't know why they liked it so much, but he assumed it was the mana in his flesh and blood. That, or the hellish taint.

He'd noticed that the taint was slowly diminishing over time. He had a troubling thought. *What if that's why I've been feeling like crap?* He chuckled bitterly. *What irony that would be if the place I despise so much became so much a part of me that I fall apart without it.*

He would have to look into it more when he could.

Though Daelan didn't like feeding Jasmine, he was glad that she got a rush from it. It made her desire it, and him, like a drug-addled streetwalker. Her fear of him and her longing became an almost tangible push/pull force, depending on which emotion dominated at the moment.

Fortunately for Daelan, because his blood was so potent, she didn't need very much. *Couldn't* take very much, actually, so it wasn't much of a drain on his mana. It was a good thing, because he took in so little that losing any was problematic. His drive to become more powerful was unshakeable, and Jasmine taking his mana was an annoying hindrance.

He was tempted to let her start taking her usual "livestock" somewhere to feed on them, but was still uncomfortable with the idea. It wasn't because of scruples. Sure, all things being equal, he'd rather she didn't feed on anyone at all, but if she were going to feed, he'd rather it was someone other than him. Besides, the vampires seemed to have made a point of not killing their victims. Daelan himself had seen people leave the bar with the couple and then come back a few nights later. They came back a little paler, a little feebler, but they got better over time.

No, the reason he didn't want her to feed on others was because it would mess with the story. Even if she got her victims from somewhere besides the bar, the chances were too high that the wrong people would hear about it.

When he wasn't working or dealing with Jasmine, Daelan continued to study programming. It was going well. He thought he had gotten pretty good at developing websites with JavaScript and React. He was inexperienced, of course, but he believed he had a good grasp of the framework and what was generally considered the best practices. He'd also learned enough HTML/CSS to make pages look good.

He began studying the code of some of the best-looking sites on the internet. He used the browser's developer tools to look at the pages' source code, trying to understand how they implemented the site.

The process was a chore, and there were often obstacles. Some websites, for instance, intentionally obfuscated their code using tools specifically intended for that purpose. The tools did things like put all the code on a single line, insert random comments to make it harder to read, and change variable names from something useful, like "buttonToBuyProduct", to something nonsensical, like "kdlsfls". When he found sites like that, he just skipped them and moved on to another.

All in all, Daelan felt the day was coming when he could get a remote programming job and leave Oregon.

He was a little torn. Part of him wanted to just get stronger and do whatever he wanted, go wherever he wanted, and enjoy life while he could. He didn't expect to survive his revenge, so this was the time to eat, drink, and be merry, for tomorrow he would die.

A nagging voice in the back of his head kept telling him, though, that there was a little girl out there, his niece Imogen, who had lost her dad.

Daelan sighed. *I should at least make sure she and her mom are okay.*

Then he could go wherever he wanted.

**

Over the next month, Daelan continued his studies and built up his savings. The cost of his fake documents was a major hit, so he told Jasmine to see what she could do to find more money in the house or her Master's bank accounts. She found another $500 in the house, and promised to do what she could about the bank.

Other than lining up a new job, there were only a couple of things Daelan needed to do before he could hit the road. The most important one was finding a way to build up his mana. He could, in theory, cultivate mana directly, but Earth was almost as bad as Hell in that regard. To make meaningful progress he had to find a different way.

In Hell, he consumed the souls of the damned and the anima of demons and converted the energy to mana. That was, for obvious reasons, an unacceptable solution on Earth.

It wasn't that he couldn't. Quoz would give him energy from every human it killed, but he would have to become a mass murderer to accomplish his goals.

Daelan believed there was another solution: converting electricity to mana. It was a lower-order energy source than soul essence, resulting in lower conversion efficiency. Because electricity was plentiful, though, that was okay. It would just slow things down.

The only obstacle was that he needed to set up runes to help him make the conversion.

Hmm. "Take/Store/Consume Lightning, Mana Create/Release/Emit". That should do the trick.

Part of the legacy of knowledge that his Father had given him was runes. He had not had much opportunity to use them, but this was the perfect time. He enjoyed the effort to find symmetry that perfectly described what he needed and multiplied the power of the runes.

It was much like what he enjoyed about programming. He liked finding elegant solutions to problems.

He drew the runes so he would have something visual to work from.

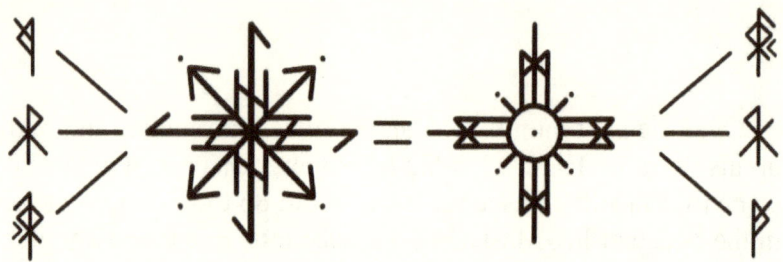

Pleased with the result, he set it aside. He would need to find a tattoo artist and prepare the materials, including platinum. He would take care of the chemicals, and Jasmine, his servant, would get him the platinum.

**

Daelan found that he enjoyed the pleasures of this world very much. Not carnal pleasures. That sort of thing was abundant in Hell, and he had partaken to the point of being tired of it. No, what he enjoyed was music. Movies. Art.

He adjusted one of his earbuds, as it had started to work itself out of his ear. The pumping bass of the heavy metal music came in clearer and stronger, which made him grin and nod his head in time with the music.

He lay down on the bench and ducked his head so he could get under the barbell without hitting it. He started banging out reps of 225 lbs. He stopped at 20, because that was a good warmup. He put another 45-lb plate on both sides and got back into position. He noticed that he was getting looks from the other gym-goers, most of them glares. He shrugged and turned the music up a little louder.

Daelan started cranking out more reps. When he reached 25 his arms were getting tired, so he stopped. After a moment to rest he started moving the plates to a squat rack. Once everything was ready, he positioned himself beneath the bar, settled it onto his shoulders, and rose to his full 6'2" height. Once he was clear of the j-hooks he started dipping down, watching himself in the mirror as he went down and up.

He noticed that he was getting more unfriendly stares.

What's the matter with them?

He was dressed a little differently from them, wearing jeans and a t-shirt. He was far from the only one in a t-shirt, but jeans appeared to be unusual.

Is it really that big of a deal?

He was starting to become concerned that the others were sensing his Hellish background somehow when he heard a loud, annoying klaxon going off. He set the bar back on the squat rack and looked around to see what was going on.

There were red flashing lights around the annoying noise maker on the wall, and above it was a large sign that read "Clunk Alarm".

The hell is a "clunk"?

Judging from how the people glaring at him were now smirking and a pudgy twenty-something with a wispy mustache and a "World Fitness" vest was walking towards him, Daelan inferred that he was himself the clunk.

When the man stopped in front of him, Daelan read his name tag. 'Hi, I'm Simon!', and beneath that, 'Assistant Manager'.

"Sir, I'm going to have to ask you to leave," Simon said with a great deal less politeness than the words implied.

"Why?"

Simon pointed to the alarm. "Someone hit the alarm. That means you've made them uncomfortable."

"I have not talked to anyone. How could I have made them uncomfortable?"

"The weights, sir. You're using too many of them."

Daelan pursed his lips in confusion. After a few seconds of going over the relevant facts, he still didn't understand what was going on.

"Is not that what this place is for?"

Simon huffed in annoyance and rolled his eyes. "Yes, sir, it is, but not when you use too many!"

"But... no one else was using them..."

"Sir! Am I going to have to call the police to get you to leave?"

"No, I will leave." Daelan didn't care. He was just trying the gym out, he hadn't become a member yet. While being escorted out of the building he saw some treats by the entrance. "Can I have one of the doughnuts?"

With a steely look and narrowed eyes, Simon growled, "No."

**

Daelan spent the next couple of weeks preparing everything for the mana conversion tattoo. Jasmine found platinum jewelry in the Master's collection that was pure enough for his purposes. Daelan procured concentrated hydrochloric acid and nitric acid.

They were both highly corrosive individually, but not enough to dissolve the "noble metals": gold and platinum. Mixed in the right proportions, however, they became *aqua regia*, "royal water", which could dissolve even the noble metals.

If only the fumes weren't so damn caustic.

Regretfully, Daelan put on a gas mask that he had found to be annoying and hot. He knew that he should be doing this work in a facility with a fume hood that could carry away and neutralize any caustic vapors, but he wasn't willing to go that far. He didn't have those kinds of resources or connections.

Anyway, the small house's garage was good enough. He wasn't planning on staying here, and didn't care what happened to the place after he left.

He looked at the two beakers of hydrochloric acid and nitric acid. He had already prepared them to be the correct ratio of 3:1 to make the strongest possible *aqua regia*. A third beaker held cut-up chunks of platinum.

Here goes nothing.

Daelan poured the hydrochloric acid into the beaker with the platinum, careful to not let the ever-present pain make his hand shake. He might as well have been pouring water, for all that the metal reacted. As soon as he poured in the nitric acid, however, things started to get interesting. The liquid turned yellow, and bubbles started to form on the platinum as it began to dissolve.

That would have been enough for gold, but with platinum, an even "nobler" metal, waiting for it to dissolve at room temperature would take days. Daelan sped things up by turning on the hot plate that the beaker sat on, and bringing the solution to a boil.

Daelan heard the door to the house creak from someone opening it.

"What are you doing?" Jasmine asked.

"Chemistry."

She looked at the fumes rising from the beaker and spreading into the garage. She coughed a couple of times and asked, "Isn't that bad for us and the house?"

Daelan wasn't personable at the best of times, and the increasing pain in his joints and bones over the last few months had made him crankier than usual. He gave her a withering look before returning to the solution. "Probably."

"You're such an asshole," she said as she hurried back into the house and slammed the door.

Ignoring her, Daelan watched the contents of the beaker as he thought about the increasing achiness in his body. He was starting to get worried about the never-ceasing pain. He thought it would be a temporary problem that would be fixed by his body adapting to Earth and being without mana, but there were no signs of that happening. He was banking on the tattoo giving him what he needed. Either the mana itself would fix things, or he would cast spells to heal himself. Either way, he should be fine as long as the tattoo worked.

With that thought, he redoubled his focus on the job at hand.

Even with the solution boiling, it took a few hours for the platinum to completely dissolve, leaving a deep orange solution. Daelan added some hydrochloric acid and boiled the entire thing down until solids began to form. Not wanting to burn the solids, he turned the burner off so the liquids could evaporate, leaving pure, solid, chloroplatinic acid.

Step one of the electricity-to-mana tattoo was complete.

**

"So let me get this straight. You want me to tattoo you with this almost colorless liquid that is an acid…"

"A very weak acid," Daelan clarified.

"… you want me to tattoo you with an almost colorless acid, and then tattoo you with another colorless liquid?" The tattoo artist with full sleeves and tattoos on his neck looked like he thought Daelan was crazy.

"That is right."

"I'm gonna take a wild guess and say that this acid hasn't been cleared by the FDA."

Daelan nodded calmly. "Probably not."

"So, when you get, like, gangrene or something, I could get in trouble."

"I supplied the ink, so I will not bother you if something goes wrong." When the tattoo artist didn't look convinced, Daelan added, "I can sign whatever, uh, waivers you want."

The tattooist took a lot of convincing, but between Daelan's promises, multiple signatures, and $2,500 up front, he was able to get him to agree to do the unusual job. Between the tattoo and the fake documents, all the money from the vampire's house was gone, leaving him with only $4,000 from his saved-up bouncer wages.

The artist drew the runic spell on Daelan's inner forearm with a sharpie pen. Daelan had him touch up a few areas and, when he was satisfied, told the man to proceed.

The first "ink" was chloroplatinic acid. It was the result of dissolving the platinum and boiling away all the aqua regia, turning it into a powder. Daelan later dissolved the powder in distilled water, resulting in the vial of yellow liquid that the tattoo artist was holding.

The artist held the jar up to the light and made a face. "Bro, are you sure you want this piss in your arm?"

Daelan quirked his lips. "I am sure."

The man sighed and shook his head. "Your funeral."

He poured the solution into the disposable ink cup and started working on Daelan's arm. It was uncomfortable, but not a big deal. He was used to far worse pain than this.

Seeing that Daelan wasn't crying out and his arm seemed okay so far, the tattooist lost his hesitancy and proceeded to create the runes and connecting lines. He finished a few hours later and, after a short break, redid the tattoo with the second, clear solution. It went a little faster because he didn't have to be precise, he just had to completely cover the tattoo. If some of the "ink" went outside the lines, that was okay.

When he was done, the artist looked at Daelan's tattoo that had turned light brown.

"I thought you said it would be platinum."

Daelan nodded. "It will be. It needs one more step."

**

The last step was going to be a pain, on multiple levels.

After the solutions reacted, millions of tiny particles of platinum had formed. The result looked brown, though, because there were unwanted side products and some of the platinum still had sulfur compounds weakly attached.

The solution to both problems was the same: heat it up and vent the gases. Actually doing it was not so simple though. Everything he'd done so far could be done by anyone on Earth who had the know-how and money. Only Daelan, or someone like him, could take the final step.

He circulated his mana and brought most of it to his arm. He focused on the end of one line in the tattoo, a square region about $\frac{1}{8}$" on each side, and started heating it up.

The heat, unpleasant at first, became downright painful. Daelan grimaced as the smell of cooked flesh and rotten eggs mixed and smoke rose into the air, but was pleased when he saw the tiny portion of tattoo turn a bright silver color.

Success.

Seeing the result, Daelan turned off the heat and let the skin start healing. While the process was painful, it wasn't much compared to what he'd experienced in the past. He'd manage.

The process was tedious, but as more and more turned into shining platinum, creating a lustrous silver-colored tattoo, Daelan became more and more excited.

It had taken time, money, pain, and mana to get here, but he could almost taste the power he was going to build soon.

It was a big step in his road to revenge, and fixing his damn body.

**

To keep his mind off the pain of the healing tattoo, Daelan kept himself busy. He decided that he had learned enough about web programming to try getting a job. He wasn't sure if it would work, but if it didn't, he could always try again later.

The main obstacle was his total and complete lack of credentials. Sure, he had a social security number now, but no college degree or job experience. He could probably earn some certificates through paid training, but his research indicated that their perceived value to employers was not great.

Even college grads complained about the difficulty of getting their first job, so he could only imagine what it would be like for him.

He could put in years to get a degree and grind until he got his first programming job, but he wasn't that patient. As far as he was concerned, as long as he could do the job, it didn't matter how he got it.

Which was how he found himself in front of Rob from the men's shelter, who was looking skeptically at his resume.

"Daelan Peregrinus? That's your name?"

Daelan quirked his lips. "It is now."

"You had a 3.31 GPA in computer science at Howard University?"

Daelan just shrugged.

"You realize Howard is a historically black college, right?"

"What does that mean?"

"It means people who know anything about the school will ask questions when they see you."

Daelan frowned. "I see. I, uh, may have exaggerated some parts of my resume."

Rob snorted. "'Exaggerated', huh? Let's see. You've been working at 'Web Presence LLC' for four years, and at 'West Coast Media, Inc' for two and a half years before that? Is any of this true, John?"

"What do I do, Rob? I need to be a productive member of society and make money. I have the skills to be a web designer, but no experience. If I can do the job, then who do I hurt?"

Daelan believed what he was saying... mostly. He didn't care about being a productive member of society, but figured that was the sort of thing Rob cared about.

Rob gave him a flat stare and sighed after a few seconds.

"I think you're going about this the wrong way, but I'll do what I can to help you. Within limits! I'm not going to lie for you."

"Thank you. I appreciate it."

Rob just nodded. "Alright, let's see what we can do then."

When they were done, Daelan had a nicely formatted, single-page resume that showed him graduating from Iowa State University of Science and Technology. His experience consisted of two small web design shops that had, conveniently, gone under since he left them. Daelan had been traveling for the past year and was ready to re-enter the workforce. He had Rob as a character reference, and he intended to talk Gus into being his work reference.

He didn't have any worries about Gus being willing. He'd probably get a good laugh out of it. Daelan's only concern was whether he could play the role of someone who knows more about websites than how to find porn.

It is what it is.

Hopefully recruiters wouldn't check his references. And if they did? It would work or it wouldn't. Either way, he would survive.

He would prefer a way to survive that was comfortable and peaceful, but if that didn't work out... there were always other options.

Chapter 13

Daelan was excited when his tattoo healed enough to try and create mana. Even better, the stun gun he'd ordered came the same day.

"Hey, Jasmine, come here for a minute!" he yelled towards her room.

"Why?" a sleepy voice answered.

"I need to test something."

She came out with tousled hair, dressed in black panties and a t-shirt that said, "Come to the dark side. We have cookies." She yawned and rubbed her eyes.

"What is it?"

Daelan walked over and tased her on the neck. Jasmine yelped and collapsed in a heap, limbs akimbo.

"A stun gun. I guess it works. Thanks!"

"You asshole! Why?!"

Daelan shrugged. "It sounded more pleasant than testing it on myself. Besides, is not 2:45 p.m. kind of late to get up?"

She hissed at him.

Chuckling to himself, he went to his bedroom and locked the door, causing Jasmine to mutter imprecations at him.

Daelan hadn't actually needed to test the device on her. He was, after all, planning on shocking himself. It was just a convenient way to remind her who was boss.

He sat on the bed cross-legged and looked at the device. Its operation was as simple as could be. Two metal studs separated by an inch and a half that sparked up when he pressed a button. He pushed the two studs into the skin of his arm around the *Take*, *Store*, and *Consume* runes that connected to the *Lightning* rune.

Daelan prepared his mind for what he was about to do. Though the runes had inherent meaning and power, they were still affected by his will. Guided by intention and insight, they would be many times more efficient than they would passively.

After taking a deep breath, he triggered the taser.

Daelan grimaced and muttered a few demonic curse words. Though he had experienced far worse, it was still unpleasant.

104

Still, he saw a steady stream of mana wisps moving up his arm that caused him to smile, to the point where he was disappointed when the stun gun stopped.

He looked at the LEDs on the device and saw that it needed time to recharge. That was okay. The tattoo worked, and that was all that mattered.

He looked at the electrical outlet and smiled. Soon he would have an inexhaustible source of mana.

**

It took a while with all the pausing to let the stun gun recharge, but Daelan eventually created and stored enough mana to cast the spell he'd been dying to use ever since he came to Earth: *Targeted Healing*. It was basically two spells in one: medical diagnosis and healing. Daelan really wanted to know what the hell was going on with his body, and he hoped that the spell could show him.

It's a shame, though. I hate to lose the mana as soon as I got it. He had missed the feeling of power. *No matter,* he thought as he looked at the electrical outlet that was more precious to him than gold. *I'll just make more.*

He concentrated on enunciating the words of power correctly, and smiled when the spell snapped into place. He looked at his arm and could see the layers of tissue: skin, fat, nerves, muscle, bone, and tendon. The spell found general degradation throughout, especially in the bones.

Alright, heal the damage. The spell refused to act. *What the hell...?*

Thinking perhaps his thoughts had not been clear enough, or his will not strong enough, he tried again. Nothing. Frowning, he checked the rest of his body and saw the same degradation throughout. It worried him that the degradation in his liver and heart was almost as bad as the bones.

Heal, damn it!

All too soon, the spell ran out. Frustrated and worried, Daelan sat down to accumulate mana again. He needed to get answers, and wouldn't stop until he got them.

After a long night, Daelan decided to take the morning off in Riverfront Park to think. Daelan found that he enjoyed watching the sunlight dance on the river's gentle ripples. He was fascinated by how the water constantly shifted from deep blue, to a reflection of the opposite shore and sky, to flashing diamonds from the sunlight. There'd been nothing like it in Hell. He was glad to see it even though being here, on Earth, meant he might die.

It turned out that the spell couldn't heal him because the problem with his body was systemic, like old age. There was nothing to heal, as far as it was concerned. That was just how he was now.

Most of the carbon and oxygen atoms in his body had been replaced with the silicon and sulfur that were so common in Hell.

I guess I'm a bunch of rotten-egg-smelling sand, now.

His body had adapted to Hell a little too well, and now that he was out… Apparently its "adapting" days were over.

The thought made him a little angry. *Did Father never intend for me to leave Hell? Is that why my body could only adapt when I was young? Was he going to let me rot there forever?*

He didn't want to believe it, but he wasn't blind to the God-King's ruthless nature. If he thought it was important, it was definitely possible he would have left Daelan there.

Of course, he could just have easily planned to remake my body when I left, or he may not have even known that it would be an issue.

Daelan would never know. Whether the God-King was a ruthless bastard or a kind-but-imperfect father didn't matter much at this point. Either way, he had a problem to solve.

"Mom! Look, it's the man with the eyes!"

Daelan saw the little boy from the library pointing at him and tugging on his mom's shirt. He let a frown touch his lips, not sure what he thought of this development. Part of him was annoyed at the distraction, and part of him welcomed the change from his morose thoughts.

106

He wasn't happy to see the woman frowning, though, in contrast to her son, who was pulling her towards Daelan. He remembered that she'd been distrustful of him at the library.

I guess I did make her kid think I could pop out one of his eyes, so... maybe not totally unjustified, he thought, chuckling at the memory.

"Hey, have you made any more games?"

Daelan looked at the little boy, but before he could reply his mom said, "Griffin, is that how you greet people?"

The boy sighed and said, a little more subdued, "Hi! I haven't seen you at the library in a while."

"I have not been in a while. I got a computer of my own, so I do not have to go anymore."

"How do you get books then?"

"I do not read books."

His eyes went wide in shock, and then they fell into a pitying look. "Do you not know how to read?"

Daelan couldn't help but laugh. "I know how to read."

Griffin looked confused, as if it didn't compute that someone could read but would choose not to.

His mom said, "Not everyone likes to read, Griffin."

"Why not?"

"They just don't."

"Huh. Hey, what's on your arm?" He darted towards him and, both gently and firmly in the way that only children can do, took hold of his arm. He looked at the platinum runes and lines with his eyes wide again in surprise and wonder.

"It's a tattoo."

"I've never seen a silver one like that before. It's so cool!"

Not sure how to get out of the situation gracefully, Daelan just said, "Thanks."

"Griffin, it's not polite to grab people."

The boy released him reluctantly and looked up into his eye. "Sorry."

"No problem."

The woman hesitantly said, "Mr. ...."

"Peregrinus. Daelan Peregrinus."

She looked flustered and her eyes narrowed in suspicion. "I thought you said your name was John."

I did tell her that at the library, didn't I? Damn it. Daelan sighed and said, "It's a long story."

"Do you mind if I look at your phone, Mr. Peregrinus?"

Now Daelan's eye narrowed. "Why?"

The woman chewed her lip, and said. "I want to see if you've taken pictures of us."

Why the hell would I take pictures of you, lady? Though she was pretty, she wasn't that pretty. *Was it about the boy? Gross.*

He thought about it for a few moments. He considered just leaving, but would rather not have her call the cops or something. He didn't have anything to hide on the phone, so, shrugging, he unlocked it and handed it over. He kicked back and watched the water, and was surprised when Griffin softly held his arm again to look at his tattoo while his mother was engrossed with the phone.

Daelan was caught between annoyance, anger, and amusement. Shaking his head in exasperation, he gently pulled his arms back and folded them.

"What does it mean?"

"What does what mean?"

"The tattoo!"

He shrugged again. "Nothing."

"Can you do a silver tattoo for me?"

Daelan chuckled. "I don't think your mother would like that." Thinking back on the final stage of the process, when he had to burn his arm, he thought, *I don't think you would like it either.*

Griffin scowled and said, "She doesn't let me do anything."

His mother raised her head and said, "So I guess taking you to the zoo last Saturday doesn't count as something?" She turned to Daelan and handed him his phone back, looking guilty. "I'm sorry. I was worried that you might be…" She paused.

"What?"

"My ex-husband doesn't know where we are, and I was afraid he had sent you. I apologize for invading your privacy, but I hope you understand why I did it."

Not really, but whatever.

"Have you eaten lunch?" she asked.

"No."

"Then please join us so I can make it up to you." She gestured to her bag which, judging by its bulges, had food in it.

"Thanks, but you do not need to. I don't eat lunch often."

"Are you sure?" She reached into the bag and pulled out some tupperware that she opened, revealing what appeared to be some sort of yellow tarts. "I made quiche!"

"Um..."

Seeing his hesitance, she smiled and pulled out a pastry in a tin. "And roasted squash and feta cheese pie."

"What is feta cheese?"

She looked scandalized. "You've never had feta cheese?"

Daelan shrugged. He had no idea.

"Then you must eat with us, if for no other reason than to expand your gastronomic experiences."

She sat down on the bench next to him and started preparing plates.

"Mom, you said we'd eat at the playground!"

"We'll eat here and go there as soon as we're done."

Griffin said, "Alright," in a dissatisfied tone.

"Really," Daelan said, "You do not have to do this."

She paused and looked at him. "I know, but I want to."

"Why?"

"You want the truth?"

Daelan rolled his eye. His avatar sibling, Joseph, had often asked that same question.

Like anyone can say 'no' to that. "Sure."

"Because I feel bad about suspecting you, and because I'm still only 99% sure you're not a bad guy."

Griffin, who'd been swinging a stick like a sword to cut down grass and weeds that had dared to grow too tall, stopped and said in a surprised voice, "You think he's a bad guy?"

She smiled at her son, "No, I don't." Turning to Daelan, she said, "I think he's... different."

Uh oh. "Different? What do you mean?"

She quirked her lips. "Well, let's see. You used to be "John", and now you're "Daelan". You don't have a single picture on your phone, except a screen capture that looks like you took on accident. You haven't sent any texts or received any except from your phone carrier. You have an exotic accent that I can't, for the life of me, place. And given my background as a linguist, that's something of a feat. You are, in other words, a mystery man."

"Maybe I'm just a boring loner."

"A loner?" She thought about that for a moment and looked him in the eye again. "Definitely. Boring? Maybe. Could I get a better look at your tattoo?"

Daelan, who really wished he'd worn a long-sleeved shirt, asked, "Why?"

"Linguist, remember? I'm curious about the runes you used."

Daelan couldn't completely hide the tattoo without looking weird and suspicious, so he frowned and said, partly out of spite and partly to even up the information imbalance, "I will if you show me your phone."

Her eyes widened in surprise and then narrowed in annoyance and suspicion.

"Why?"

"Because I do not like you knowing about me without knowing about you."

She chewed on her lip and looked at her son.

"Fine," she said with a sigh. "I suppose if my husband had sent you, you would know everything about me anyway. And I did intrude in yours. Here."

He didn't care that much about her, but he did poke around enough to get her full name, Jessica Hollis. He didn't know if that was her real name or not, given that she was hiding, but it was something at least. He did, in his fumblings with the unfamiliar phone, come upon her pictures too. They appeared to mostly be of Griffin and picturesque scenes, like sunsets over the ocean.

He returned the phone wordlessly. She seemed relieved when he gave it back, and quickly put it away in her bag. Turning back to him, she said, "So?"

"What? Oh, right."

Daelan held out his arm, palm up, so she could get a good look at the tattoo.

"Is that actual silver?"

He shook his head. "Just an unusual ink."

Jessica, like her son, held his arm gently to keep it still as she looked.

"Why not just do it in black?"

He smiled sardonically. "Women are more interested in silver."

She chuckled. "These look similar to Elder Futhark runes, but I don't recognize most of them. This one looks a lot like the rune for… what was it…?" She closed her eyes as she thought. "Lightning! It means lightning, right?"

Daelan shrugged and said, "Probably. I just told the artist to make something cool."

She looked at him intently while holding his arm as if trying to decide if she believed him.

"You are still holding my arm."

"Oh! Sorry." She released him and faced forward, her cheek slightly flushed. "Sorry," she repeated. "I find languages fascinating."

Mildly curious, Daelan asked, "Why?"

Jessica turned back to him, smiling at his question.

"They're so interesting! They give a unique insight into how people think and see the world. For those of us who think in words, language is the tool, domain, and limiter of thought."

Daelan was surprised at her enthusiasm and intrigued by the implications of what she had said.

"Limiter of thought?"

Jessica nodded. "If you don't have words for a concept, and you think in words, how do you even think of something you don't have a word for? For example, the word 'orange' didn't exist in English before the 16th century."

"How did they describe oranges?"

"They called them a hue of red, or yellow-red."

"Hmm. What is something we do not have words for now?"

"Good question. A tough one to answer, unfortunately, because English is adaptable and adopts vocabulary from other languages very easily. There are lots of words in other languages that don't have corollaries in English, but you can usually describe the concepts with multiple words, so I'm not sure that really counts.

"An example of a truly missing concept, though… hmm… I believe scientists say there might be more dimensions than just

111

the three we're aware of. We have no language for talking about experiencing or moving through those dimensions."

Daelan laughed. "That is because we cannot experience them. We are the limiting factor, not language."

"True. But at some point it becomes a 'chicken and egg' problem. Take flavor, for instance. We all know what salt tastes like, so we can say something is 'salty', but we don't have a way to talk about what dirt tastes like. If we all took to eating dirt, we'd probably invent words like 'silty' and 'clay-ey'.

"Maybe a better example is the Kuuk Thaayorre people in Australia," she continued. "They have no words for 'left' or 'right'. Instead, everything is tied to the cardinal directions: north, south, east, and west. So, they wouldn't say my 'right arm', they would say my south-west arm, if it happened to be in that direction."

"Huh. Interesting. What would they do if they didn't know which way was north?"

"They have an exceptional ability to always be oriented. We used to think only animals could do that, because of magnets in their beaks and stuff like that, but the Kuuk people are turning our assumptions on their head."

"So, they are missing the concept of, uh, relative directions?"

"You could say that, or look at it as a different way of thinking. They would probably think that directions depending on you instead of the world is an extremely egotistical way of looking at things. When westerners place pictures in chronological order, they usually do it from left to right, probably because that's the direction we write. When the Kuuk Thaayorre do it, they do it from east to west, no matter which way they're facing."

"Why east to west?"

"Probably because the sun rises in the east and sets in the west. Makes more sense for time order than left to right, right?" Jessica smiled.

"I suppose so."

Griffin, who had thrown his stick on the ground, said in an aggravated voice, "Mom, you said we would go to the playground!"

"You're right. Sorry, honey. You know how mommy gets sometimes," she said with a smile.

"It was very interesting," Daelan said. "Thank you for talking with me."

He looked down and realized he hadn't finished his food, and it was on a real plate, not disposable.

"You're welcome, and thanks for letting me talk about my favorite topic! As you can see, I can get on a roll sometimes." Seeing him looking at his plate and food, she said, "Don't worry about the plate. Keep it."

"Can I return it later?"

She chewed on her lip for a moment, then said, "No, I don't think so."

Daelan quirked his lips. "Maybe I will just clean it and take it with me everywhere I go so I can give it to you the next time we see each other."

Her look became cold. "If you're not following us, Daelan, or John, or whoever you are, there's no reason we should see each other again."

Daelan nodded in acknowledgement.

"You are right." He turned his head to Griffin and said, "Have fun at the playground."

Though he didn't feel much for people, he wished them well in his mind as they walked away. He recognized in Jessica a kindred soul who was familiar with pain.

Chapter 14

That night, in his dreams, Daelan walked with his last friend in Hell.

He'd had a few others, but all of them wanted to leave Hell, so Daelan helped them do that painlessly while collecting their soul energy and releasing their anima. He saw it as a "win-win" situation, though he regretted the crushing loneliness afterwards.

More and more he found himself wanting a companion more than he needed a small jump in power, so when Leaves-a-trail expressed a desire to "live", Daelan took him in.

If only the spirit wasn't such an asshole.

'Don't you think the demons have a pretty nice gig, Daelan?'

Daelan stared at the spirit of the giant salamander in disbelief. "You think the demons have a good life?"

'I mean, they're ugly as sin, but it seems like they have fun.'

"They torture people. What's fun about that?"

It was the spirit's turn to stare. *'Kind of a strange question from a guy who tortures people on the regular.'*

"Not because I like it," Daelan muttered. "It's the only way I can get out of here. And I only torture demons."

'You're telling me that you've never once enjoyed it?'

Daelan started to deny it, but the words choked in his throat. He hadn't ever enjoyed it for its own sake, but there were times when the vengeance had felt good. "I… guess there have been times."

They were quiet for a time, but Leaves-a-trail was never silent for long. He loved to tell stories. Many of them were funny, but they were usually dark too. Some of them made Daelan uncomfortable.

'Have I ever told you how many chicks I banged when I was alive?'

"Many times."

'Ah, but I don't think I've told you my best stories yet.'

Daelan didn't respond. Most of the giant salamander's stories revolved around mating or sadism. His favorites included both.

'There was this one chick, Glistens-out-of-water, who I'd had my eye on for years, but she kept rejecting me. Thought she was too good for me or something. Said I had bad breeding. Bad breeding! Me! I told that stuck-up waste of slime that I had the best skin-spots of anyone in the lake, but she didn't listen.

'She eventually took a mate—total loser, of course. I left her alone after that, but I still had my eye on her. I was waiting.

'Well, when the time of heat came on, she laid her fertilized eggs the next day. Her mate left to get food, and I...' his lipless grin turned evil, *'I pounced. I started stomping on the eggs while she cried and tried to stop me. The stomping wasn't working too well, and I was getting frustrated before it hit me that I was doing it all wrong! I just needed to eat them! That way I got rid of the nuisances and filled my stomach.'*

"You killed the kids?"

'They hadn't even hatched yet! You know how many eggs we lose before they hatch? Like 90% of them. Anyway, I haven't gotten to the good part yet.

'So there she was, crying about losing her eggs. Oh, how she cried! But the best part of it was...'

Daelan hadn't thought it was possible, but the salamander's smile became even more sinister.

'...even though she cried, when she saw that all of her children were gone, her body went into heat again. As the nearest male, I took care of her, mating her good and hard, while she cried and hit me with her fists, even as her body moved in rhythm with mine.'

Daelan felt sick. Even though Leaves-a-trail was talking about a salamander, he couldn't help but imagine how the creature must have felt. Not for the first time, he regretted not reaping Leaves-a-trail's soul.

Maybe tonight, he thought. Though Leaves-a-trail disgusted him, he still wavered. He'd been alone for so long. Years. As disgusting as the spirit was, Daelan wasn't sure he was worse than nothing.

Sighing, he kept walking.

"How long until we get to the demon you saw?"

'We're close. It's in the cave over there.'

As they approached the cave and went in, Daelan stepped more carefully, both to be as quiet as possible and to avoid the jagged rocks on the walls and ceiling. He had long since become used to the rotten egg smell of Hell, to the point where he no longer noticed it. What stood out, though, was a bestial stink.

Something is here.

He used a bit of mana to power a night vision spell, illuminating the cave in shades of black and white.

'*Can you see anything, Daelan? Because I can't see jack.*'

"Shut up," he hissed.

Daelan came to a fork. The passage to the left was smaller and would require him to crawl, while the one ahead would allow him to keep walking, though he did it in a crouch to keep from hitting his head.

Just to make sure, he sniffed both directions. Though he smelled something to the left, it was unclear what it was. Ahead, on the other hand, left no doubts. That was where the bestial stink came from.

Silently, he moved forward, assuming Leaves–a-trail would follow. Even if he didn't, it wouldn't matter. It's not like he ever helped him in fights.

Daelan crept around a bend and saw a cavern, and on the far side was a large feathered demon that, rather than a bird's tail, had two leathery whip-like tails that thrashed around while the demon mumbled to itself.

Seeing that the demon was turned away from him, Daelan crept forward. When he was twenty feet away, he called forth Quoz as a black war scythe with an unfathomably sharp edge. He was about to rush in and strike when he heard the demon emit a deep rumble that took him a few seconds to recognize as laughter.

The demon turned around calmly and looked at Daelan. Now that it was standing, Daelan realized it had two muscled arms and was even bigger than he'd thought. Probably ten feet tall and at least a thousand pounds.

The demon did not seem concerned about the man or his weapon. It turned to Leaves-a-trail and said in a deep mind-voice, '*Leave now.*'

'*I kept my side of the bargain, Impaler. He is alive, as promised, and thus a prize unmatched in this godforsaken world. Give me a body, like you promised!*'

While Leaves-a-trail spoke, Daelan heard sounds coming from the tunnel he'd come from.

What a fool I've been.

Three worm-like demons entered the cavern, mouths full of rows of shark teeth that looked like they could saw through rock as easily as flesh.

While he assessed the situation, the bird-demon and his traitorous friend finished their negotiations.

Daelan turned to Leaves-a-trail and said, bitterness filling every word, "I'm going to kill you, you son-of-a-bitch."

The spirit only laughed and said, '*This is perfect! Glistens-out-of-water said the same thing when I fucked her.*'

**

When Daelan woke up, he swung his feet off the bed and looked at his stomach, where the ugly circular scar showed where the damned demon's tail had pierced into his guts. He involuntarily trembled when he remembered how it had continued squirming and burrowing after he cut it off.

Damn salamander. I hope the little shit reincarnated as a dung beetle.

Now that he was out of the dream haze and was calming down, Daelan stretched and yawned. He looked at the time and frowned.

Gotta shower and shave.

He had an interview to get ready for.

Chapter 15

"So, Daelan, why do you want to work for us?"

"Money. I'm a fan of having some."

"So if someone else offered you a higher salary, you'd leave?"

"Absolutely."

"Daelan," Rob said with a disapproving sigh. "You're not taking this seriously."

"Sorry, Rob," he said, though his grin made it clear he wasn't. He wasn't sure why, but he was feeling puckish today. "I admire how Hobs, Nobs, and Bobs has played a leading role in building websites for the small business market. I love how you have used templates to drive down the number of hours required to put together a quality site, and give the buyer a competitive price while maintaining a healthy profit margin."

"Better, though you could work on your sincerity."

"You know what they say—if you can fake that, you have got it made."

"How about you try for *actual* sincerity?"

Daelan pretended to think about it for a couple of seconds. "Nah."

Apparently deciding it was a lost cause, Rob returned to his list of practice interview questions.

"Where do you see yourself in five years?"

"On a beach in Tahiti, tanned, sipping a margarita, with my pretty girlfriend on the chair next to me. I am, of course, coding up a storm for Hobs, Nobs, and Bobs with both hands. Though I have a minimal salary because I have not asked for a single raise during those five years, I've hired a local to bring the drink to my lips and fan me with palm fronds so I can dedicate myself fully to my work."

Rob looked at him with a gimlet eye before shaking his head slowly and chuckling. "I'll call the practice a success in that you clearly know what the interviewers want to hear. The only question is whether you'll give it to them or not."

Daelan looked at him with a crooked smile. "I thought that you, a man of God, would insist that I tell the truth."

"Are you trying to say that Tahiti on the beach was the truth?"

"Absolutely."

Rob laughed, stood up, and clapped Daelan on the shoulder. "Then take me with you when you go."

"Okay, but you have to get your own girlfriend."

**

When Daelan wasn't thinking about how to fix his body, he sent resumes and cover letters out to dozens of companies. He was eager to get a job that earned more money and would allow him to go find Imogen, the daughter of his avatar-sibling Joseph.

There were thousands of web programming jobs, but insisting on being able to work remotely eliminated the vast majority of them. Five responded, and four of those had asked him to take an online programming test.

He thought he had done reasonably well at all four. He'd had to look up some information, but didn't all programmers use Google and Stack Overflow? They were practically part of the tool chain at this point.

For whatever reason, after the tests and a brief phone screen only two companies wanted to schedule an interview.

Daelan had gone home, kicked his shoes off, and was in the middle of researching the two companies—Gunnarson Design and FTL Media—when he heard a knock at the door.

When he opened the door, he saw a short man with graying hair at his temples standing in front of him. He was wearing a long, cashmere overcoat in the cool air that looked like it cost as much as his monthly salary at the Taint.

"I'm looking for Arthur Constable."

Aw, crap. Daelan was especially displeased when he opened his third eye and sensed the same things he had from the other vampires. At least he knew it wasn't law enforcement. "Who are you?"

"A friend of his."

"He does not live here."

"I know he lives in the main house, but no one answered the door."

"I do not know," Daelan shrugged. He started to close the door while saying, "You should come back some other time…" but was interrupted by the man putting his foot in the doorway.

"What about Matthew Ferreli or Jasmine Cooper?"

Daelan cocked his head at the man, and acted pissed. He *was* pissed, but he was also worried. He tried not to let that part show.

"What gives you the right to question me or keep me from closing the door?"

The vampire smiled ingratiatingly, if not sincerely. "I haven't heard from a friend for a while and I'm worried about him. Surely you can understand that?"

Daelan's mind raced as he considered what to do. He thought about blowing the guy off and running after he left, but he hated to go before he was ready and have someone chasing him.

No, better to deal with the problem at hand. He opened the door wide and said, "I understand. Why don't you come in, Mr. …?"

"Nesmith. Marcus Nesmith."

Daelan moved away from the doorway and gestured for Marcus to come in. He curled his lips after the man entered calmly, allowing Daelan to stand at his back.

These vampires are so damn confident that they are the masters of their "cattle".

Daelan intended to make this particular vampire pay for his hubris.

He enhanced his speed and strength with mana, grabbed Marcus by the back of the neck, and slammed his head repeatedly into the wall. The vampire grabbed Daelan's arm, but he ignored it. He just kept making holes in the drywall until he found a wood stud. It made satisfying "thud" sounds when he pounded the head against it, until the third time when it cracked.

Crap. Outer walls are load-bearing, right?

Sensing that the vampire had gone limp, he tossed him onto the ground and looked for rope to tie him up. He had some questions for Mr. Nesmith.

**

Three hours later, the front door opened and a sweet, musical voice that sounded nervous called out, "Honey, I'm home!"

Daelan, amused, yelled out, "I am in the kitchen, schnookums!"

He could almost imagine Jasmine looking at the damaged wall and blood in fright as she set down her things. "What, uh, happened in here?"

"We have a visitor, honey."

"Why are they still here?"

"We're having a nice chat, aren't we, Marcus?"

When Jasmine walked into the kitchen and saw the vampire tied to a chair, naked and bloody, she screamed and then whispered, "Shit, shit, shit, shit…!"

Daelan looked at her and sneered. "Don't worry, honey, I'll clean up the mess." He gestured at the transparent plastic sheeting that covered everything in the room except for the people. An assortment of bloody knives sat on the plastic-covered table, along with her curling iron, needles, a damp washcloth, and a gag.

Jasmine looked around, horrified. "What are you, a freaking psycho?"

Daelan took a moment to think about that. "I don't think so? Maybe?" He was pretty sure he hadn't started out that way, but after 200 years in Hell? He shrugged.

"Do you know who this is?" she asked, still in panic mode.

"Yes. This is Marcus N…"

"I KNOW WHO HE IS! Do you know who he *works for*?!"

Daelan's anger flared. "Lower. Your. Voice." He didn't think anyone would hear her, given the distance to the nearest neighbors, but he didn't want to tempt fate.

"Sorry! I, uh…" Her frightened face twitched back and forth between Daelan and Marcus, as if she wasn't sure who she should be more afraid of.

"Hey," Daelan growled. "Get it together."

She nodded nervously and kept quiet, eyes still wide.

Seeing that she was mostly in possession of herself again, he looked at Marcus. "Yes, I know who he works for. We were just talking about that, weren't we, Marcus? It sounds like Jasmine knows your boss. Are there any statements you would like to change before I ask her the same questions? I do not think I need to tell you what will happen if your answers don't match."

The vampire, who had looked miserable, angry, and defiant, widened his eyes in panic. "Wait, wait, don't…"

"Shut up, Marcus."

The vampire immediately stopped talking and looked at Jasmine with pleading eyes. Jasmine's eyes went even wider when she saw the vampire's reaction.

"Go to your bedroom, Jasmine. I will be there in a few minutes."

"O-okay." She slowly walked to her room, wondering what she could do to give herself a slight chance of living through all this.

**

Daelan pondered what he had learned while he wiped blood off the knives. He glanced at the unconscious vampire at his feet. He'd used magic to put him to sleep. It had been trivially easy given how battered he was. His mind and body already wanted to escape the pain, so they hadn't resisted the magic at all.

Daelan sighed as he considered what to do.

He'd gotten much more than he bargained for from Marcus. He'd extracted what he wanted—information about the vampires—and so much more besides.

Not only were there vampires on Earth, there were human mages, lycanthropes, yetis, skinwalkers, the odd elf or two, faeries, deep sea monsters, and a host of other supernatural creatures.

He wasn't bothered by their presence. His Father and many of his siblings were used to that. No, the headache here was the Pact. The various groups had, over 300 years ago, signed a treaty that specified what was expected of each group. First and foremost among those things was secrecy from the non-magical populace, and the Pact made it very clear what the punishment was for spilling the secret: death. Death by hanging, immolation, drawing and quartering… The Pact breaker could choose any of several manners of execution as long as it was effective for their species, but the final result was pre-determined from the outset.

Death.

Daelan was in a delicate position. He was not a member of The Eternal Society of Noble Wizards and Magical Studies, the pompous name for the worldwide organization of human mages. It was the group with which he clearly fit best.

According to Marcus, mages from other worlds were rare and had a decidedly mixed record with the Society. The last one he knew of appeared in Spain during the Middle Ages and was the reason the Society got the Catholic Church to start burning witches when he struck out on his own.

So, if an otherworldly mage showed up on the Society's doorsteps? High likelihood of death. If he revealed the existence of magic and/or the supernatural to normies? Death. Oh, and if he practiced magic and didn't join the Society? Death.

It was enough to give Daelan a migraine. He thought he would be safe on Earth. Now he had even more threats to deal with.

He used a technique that intentionally relaxed muscles one by one. There was no great secret to it; it just required being hyper-aware of one's body. When he finished, the headache had receded, so he applied himself to the problem.

Should he join the Society? Maybe, but there was no way he was going to do it from a position of weakness, so that was out for the time being.

What should he do about the vampires? He had originally planned to kill Marcus and take out the local leadership to put them in disarray, and then get out of town. Now that the situation was more complicated, he had to update his plans.

While considering how to handle the vampires, he moved Marcus to the tub. Daelan was going to have to clean him up before he sent him back.

**

"You let him go?! Why did you let him go?" Jasmine shouted. She put her hand to her mouth and started talking to herself.

"Maybe this is a good thing. They'll kill him, and I can run away…"

Daelan's anger, always on a low burn from paranoia and tension, flared. He didn't want to have this conversation while he had 110 volts running through his arm, but he knew he couldn't afford to not gather as much mana as possible. The spells he cast on Marcus had all but wiped out what he'd had.

He gritted his teeth and said, "Sorry to disappoint you, but no one is going to kill me."

She sneered. "You think you can take on the whole Aemilianus family? You're dreaming."

"Give me a year and I will grind them under my feet. But no, I was not talking about fighting your entire 'family'. Poor Marcus seemed rather broken towards the end of our chat. He probably would not have recovered mentally, so I was kind enough to remove his memory of it," Daelan said with a sadistic smile.

"What about all his injuries? Did you heal him?"

"No. I implanted a new memory of an unfortunate run-in with a group of orcs. He killed one, but the others beat the hell out of him before he escaped."

She stared at him, then turned away with a snort. "You have a way of molding reality to be what you want."

Daelan just smiled without responding.

"Someday it's going to catch up with you and you'll be the one with an 'unfortunate run-in'," she said with a smirk as she turned away.

That little… Daelan thought in a rage. His anger, always on "simmer", flared at her insubordination.

He knew he couldn't let it go. It would have been bad enough if she had said it in such a way that she thought he wouldn't hear, but in his face like that? No, it demanded a response.

He came close to using a spell to grab her and smash her against the wall, but he didn't want to waste his precious mana intimidating her. Instead, he put a wisp of mana into a simple sound conjuration.

"Maybe," his voice whispered into her ear, "but I will make sure there is one less little vampire in the world before I go."

She whipped around, alarmed, and she flushed in embarrassment when she saw that Daelan was still sitting cross-legged on the floor, grinning. He winked at her and closed his eye. He was, of course, still watching her with his third eye, but she didn't need to know that.

Leadership is all in the details.

He chuckled to himself after she hurried out of the room.

Now that he was alone, he turned his attention to the tracking spell he had put on Marcus. He used the distance and direction to get a rough location on the map app on his phone.

Looks like he's going home.

He spent the next day converting as much electricity as he could to mana, buying a used motorcycle with most of his savings, watching Marcus' location, and thinking. Thinking about how to get rid of his vampire problem.

He wasn't doing it for humanity's sake. If he could have, he would have just walked away. He didn't think the family would let the killing of Jasmine's master go, though, so he had to teach them that revenge wasn't worth it.

He believed the best solution was simple: take out the head of the family. If the Aemilianus' were anything like the powerful families *his* family knew, once the movers and shakers were struggling to take over, everything else would be ignored, at least for a time. Enough time for him to start up again somewhere new.

The problem was that, even though Marcus considered himself fairly close to the family's head, Aisha Aemilianus, he didn't know where she lived and didn't see her often. He just received orders and carried them out.

So, how do I get Aisha to make an appearance?

He pondered for a couple of hours, but didn't come up with anything better than killing off as many local vampires as he could. Once enough blood flowed, the boss would probably get more involved. And if she didn't, he'd just keep killing. Either Aisha would show up, or the Aemilianus family would cease to exist in Oregon.

**

Three days later, Daelan was pleased. He had searched through the information the God-King sent him before he died and found a solution for his deteriorating body: an elixir that could remake his body. The ingredients were difficult to get, but the God-King had known where they could be found on Sicanthus, his home planet.

Now that he had a steady source of mana, it was just a matter of time before he had enough to create a portal home, at least when conditions for travel were good. After researching the stars, finding Sicanthus in relation to Earth, and doing the calculations, Daelan found that the astral tides would be favorable for a short time in three months. It was a little tight, but if he was diligent he should be able to accumulate enough mana to make the journey.

Daelan became even happier when he received a big delivery from Amazon. He'd been frustrated when making mana by how the electricity from the wall socket went back and forth, like waves that couldn't make up their mind which direction to go, instead of a steady flow like a river. A steady flow would be more efficient and require less of his attention.

A little research on his phone had solved the mystery.

Damn alternating current.

Fortunately, there was a solution. He ordered a power supply that created the steady power he wanted. He hoped it would make his mana generation faster, eliminating the risk of not having enough when the time came. He needed to get enough mana to stretch his core over the next few months, gradually increasing its capacity.

Daelan paused to think about how amazing the internet was. With it he could get almost anything he wanted—be it information, consumables, or hardware—easily and quickly.

The power supply delivery's timing was also good for his vampire hunt. He'd continued tracking Marcus' movements and was able to confirm a few of the locations the vampire had given him. It was enough for him to feel reasonably confident that the information he'd been given was solid.

He couldn't wait forever, because he was worried about someone noticing the changes in Marcus. Though his Father had been an expert in mind magic, Daelan was not. He had done his best, but he was pretty sure he had seriously compromised Marcus' memories, causing him to have partial amnesia at best, or personality alteration and psychosis at worst.

Someone would eventually realize that something was wrong, and that would lead back to this house, so it was time for him to leave and make his move on the other vampires.

Before he left, though, it was important to say goodbye. When he was done packing, he called Jasmine over.

"I am leaving, Jasmine. Are you going to miss me?" he asked with a mocking smile.

She rolled her eyes. "Yeah, it will be horrible not having to pretend that I like you."

Daelan nodded. "You did well keeping up appearances, and I appreciate that." Jasmine's eyes widened in surprise at his praise. "You will have no problems from me, as long as you do not cause me problems. Do you understand?"

She nodded reluctantly. "Don't blow your cover. Don't send the family after you."

"Exactly. Do that and we can both live long lives. Otherwise, I do not think I have to tell you what happens."

She shook her head stiffly.

"Good." He started to turn away, but, as if he remembered something, turned his head back and said, "Oh, and I suggest not hanging out with other vampires for the next few weeks."

She widened her eyes again, this time from fear. She opened her mouth to say something, but apparently changed her mind and said nothing. Instead, she just gave a brief nod.

I've trained her well. She would have made a good servant.

His favorites had always been the obedient ones that he could read like a book.

Chapter 16

Though Daelan planned on making the killings look like robberies gone awry, it wouldn't take long for the vampires to figure out that someone was after them, so it was important to not have any discernible patterns. It was bad enough that he would only be targeting vampires, as the list of targets was rather short. It would be worse if they knew beforehand what his *modus operandi* was.

To avoid falling into patterns even subconsciously, he decided to let random chance guide his actions, which was why he found himself following Ethel Ashworth to a hotel. The literal roll of the dice indicated that he should kill her first, and that he should do it outside. He'd thought about doing it immediately after she left her house, but, knowing that she was an escort and her late-night jaunt was probably a job, he decided to wait until after she was done.

He could say he was waiting to avoid having the john say something when she didn't show up, but that wasn't really why. What would he say? Hello, police officer, I made an appointment with a prostitute but she didn't show up?

No. The real reason was that Daelan wanted to get the money. A man had to eat after all, and, having quit his job at the Taint, Daelan needed a new source of funds.

Hopefully he'd get a new job soon. He'd had his first interview the day before and he thought it went pretty well. He'd knocked the coding questions out of the park, and he didn't think he'd put his foot in his mouth in any of the conversations. The interview with the other company was in two days.

When Daelan saw the attractive vampire step out of her car and walk inside, he chuckled. He wondered what her client would think if he knew that she was over a hundred years old.

While he waited, he pulled in nearby mana and cranked up the music on his earbuds.

An hour and a half later, she walked out. Daelan activated the camouflage and physical binding spells he had prepared beforehand. The purpose of the binding was to keep everything that was "Daelan" on him. He would not leave an iota of scent or DNA on the premises.

Prepared, he walked an intercept path to the vampire. She was taking out her keys when he summoned Quoz and took her head off with the ebon blade from behind. The head rolled on the ground and stopped a few feet away, eyes wide open in shock and dirt marring her face.

Blood spurted from her neck, and though it was easy for Daelan to avoid, her purse was already turning red from the grisly vampire bloodfall. Even though he reveled in the mana he was receiving from Quoz, he cursed inside about the purse. He decided to just leave the money.

With any luck, he would kill a few vampires in their homes.

**

Over the next week, Daelan went on a killing spree, eliminating nine more vampires. He was pleased with the results, having gained a great deal of mana and money. He also got a job from the first company he interviewed with, starting at the end of the month. All in all, it had been a good week.

Time to check in and see what Aisha is doing.

Daelan didn't have a line on the head of the vampire clan, of course. If he did, all this killing wouldn't be necessary. What he did have was Marcus.

Getting to Marcus took some time. He was at an estate on the Oregon coast south of Florence, but Daelan didn't mind taking the time to get out there. He enjoyed riding the used Kawasaki Ninja that he bought with his bouncer money.

The first few days he'd tried riding without a helmet, but eventually relented and got one. It wasn't a matter of safety. With his dexterity and reaction speed he could avoid most accidents, and he wasn't too worried about concussions or road rash. With his regenerative capabilities, he could fix all that.

No, what broke Daelan down was the bugs. A man could only take so many mosquitoes and flies to the face before he said, "Maybe a helmet isn't such a bad idea."

He laughed when he realized he got more attention from women with the helmet. He had a strong, fit body, but a "meh" face. With the black, tinted helmet he was a mystery man with a strong, fit body. When a convertible full of college coeds pulled alongside and playfully called out to him, the attractive brunette riding shotgun held the palm of her hand out with a phone number written in ink. Daelan chuckled, saluted them with a quick toot of the horn, and accelerated, putting the car far behind him.

After a two-and-a-half-hour ride, Daelan pulled off the road, a quarter mile from the estate. It looked like the kind of prettified fortress that celebrities had. Tall, rebar-reinforced concrete walls textured to look like stone, cameras every fifty feet covering every inch of the wall, and a line of trees on the inside for increased privacy told everyone who saw the place, "If you don't have an invitation, go away."

Daelan wasn't going to go away, but he wasn't going to intrude either, if he could help it. The truth was, he could have cast the scrying spell from anywhere now that he had Marcus' tracking spell as an anchor. The distance would have made the mana cost prohibitive though.

If he could reduce the distance further and get line-of-sight, it would lower the cost even further, but after waiting for two hours with no movement from Marcus, Daelan said "screw it" and decided to cast the spell, the cost be damned. He needed information even more than mana.

Once the connection was established, Daelan listened for a few minutes. Nothing happened besides mundane things— opening and closing a door, walking, murmuring "Hello", etc.— so he made the spell only activate when it detected enough power in the 300 - 3000 Hz range, much like a voice-activated recorder.

To save on mana costs, he still needed to stay in the area. Though the drain was minimal when the spell was in standby mode, as soon as it activated it would multiply if he was far away.

He briefly considered roughing it on the beach, but decided he could afford a few bucks for a cheap motel. He rode up to Florence and found a couple of dingy places with "Vacancy" neon signs lit on either side of Main street. Daelan couldn't tell much difference between one and the other, so he just pulled into the one on the right.

A bell chimed when Daelan walked through the office door, and he heard a television blaring in a dim room behind the counter. Through the beaded curtain that obscured the room drifted a man's voice. It was enthusiastically declaring the awesomeness of his Ginsu knives, which could be bought for the low, low price of…, before it was abruptly silenced. A meaty hand pushed through the beads, followed by an obese woman who looked like she'd seen enough of life and was ready to call it quits. She stubbed out a cigarette in an ashtray on the counter.

"What can I do for you, honey?" she asked tiredly.

"I would like a room for the night."

"Smoking or non?"

"Non."

Just then, the scrying spell activated.

"Master, thank you for contacting this unworthy servant. Do you…"

"Queen…"

"…want to…"

"…or…"

"…hear the…"

"…double?"

"…latest reports?"

Damn it. They would start talking at the same time.

Though he was more focused on the scrying spell than the woman, he'd picked up enough to know she was asking him about the bed. Annoyed, he just waved his hand at her and said, "Whatever."

"Of course I do," a mezzo-soprano voice came through.

The woman, looking peeved herself, once again interjected herself into the conversation.

"Andrew Philomon was…"

"Cash…"

"…killed yesterday…"

"…or…"

"…in his home…"

"…credit?"

"…by the chameleon."

Daelan glared at the woman and slapped a hundred-dollar bill on the counter so he could go back to listening to the conversation.

"Cameras picked him up, but, as always, we could not get any identifying images or marks. The alarm did not detect his entry. We're not sure how he entered. From the cameras we're pretty sure he entered a guest bedroom first, so presumably he entered through the window. The window was not, as far as we can tell, opened.

"No one has been killed today, at least as of the last hourly check-in."

Silence reigned for a few seconds, allowing Daelan to return his attention to the woman who glared at him as she held out a key.

"Where is change?" he growled.

"The room's $100," she sneered, her eyes daring him to contradict her.

Daelan was pissed, knowing she had jacked up the price. He didn't have the time to argue about it, though, so he grabbed the key and walked away. As he walked through the door to the outside he heard a woman say, "I'm disappointed that you have not solved this problem yourself, Marcus."

"I'm sorry, Master. I am a useless servant."

"It sounds like the Society. Have you met with the head of the local branch?"

"I have, and they insist it's not them."

"Hmph. And you believed those treacherous bastards?"

"No, I didn't. The mage didn't smell guilty, but she did have the stink of deception. I think they're either behind the murders or know something about them."

"Did you demand to interview their wizards?"

Marcus nervously answered, "I didn't think they would accede to my request."

"That's because you're weak," the feminine voice said coldly.

"Yes, Master."

"I will be there in two days. Prepare all of the evidence we have from the killings so I can review it when I arrive, and arrange a meeting with the Society."

"It shall be done, Master. I'll be sure to have the best of our local cattle for you, too."

"Mm. Until then."

Two days. Daelan smiled as he finished walking to his room's door and slipped the key into the lock. It would be tight, but it should be enough time to let him prepare a surprise.

**

That evening, in his motel room, Daelan prepared himself for his next step on the path to immortality: empowering his mana with a *dao* concept. Given how important this step was, he pulled out all the stops in preparation. That meant, in this case, lighting incense before sitting in the lotus position.

There was nothing mystical about the incense. He'd bought a pack of 10 sticks for $2.98 plus tax at Walmart. They were just for improving his concentration by covering the stink of weed and mildew.

And the incense smelled nice. Daelan was partial to lavender.

After settling into position on the multi-colored carpet whose main feature was hiding dirt well, Daelan closed his eye and entered a meditative state. After centuries of practice he did it with ease, letting his mind rest and simply observing thoughts as they passed by.

He breathed in the incense and was annoyed to note that he still smelled the marijuana. Sighing, he observed the feeling and let it pass. As he entered a deeper state, his muscles relaxed and his heart beat slowed.

Feeling that he was ready, he turned his attention to his mana core. It was a shifting and slowly rotating silvery ball with a mirror-like surface.

The mana was not, of course, metallic. That was simply how its pure nature manifested itself. It did not glow because that would be emitting energy, and therefore diminishing itself. It was not ebon-colored, because that would be absorbing external, lesser light. Instead, it rejected all externalities, pushing them back to where they came from.

His mana was unaspected, making it useful for casting any type of spell or powering any rune. He needed to condense it to increase his capacity and the power of his spells. The only way he knew for someone to condense mana was to give it an aspect.

It was like packing items with random shapes. Though cubes, spheres, pyramids, and toroids could coexist, the packing would be very inefficient, with significant gaps throughout. If all the items were turned into cubes, they would pack more easily and densely.

Mana was similar. Giving the mana an aspect would give it something in common, enabling Daelan to condense it and magnify its power.

It would also make it not as suitable for spells that did not match its aspect, but power always has a price.

Daelan had known for a long time what aspect he would choose. He had carefully considered it for over a century in Hell. He could have simply followed his Father's path of Earth and Fire but, much as he venerated the God-King, he knew his path had not been ideal.

It was not blasphemy. The God-King himself had regretted not knowing enough when he was young to pick a better path. He had, through persistence, intelligence, and luck, overcome his start and made his *dao* concept truly powerful and expansive, but it had taken a long time.

Daelan saw no reason not to take a direct path to the good stuff.

He envisioned two runes, side by side. "Motion" and "Stillness". Being opposite concepts, their runes were mirror images. Joining them together made a symmetrical rune pair.

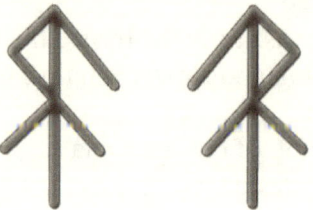

He fed mana to the runes and felt the concept resonate. Whether it was a mental or spiritual feeling or attunement with the universe itself, he could not have said. All he knew was that he felt the truth of it.

For a time he considered the concepts of "motion" and "stillness". He thought of all the forms of movement he knew of,

134

from the lowliest creeping snail, to the swift zephyrs over the roiling ocean, to starlight racing through the cold depths of space. Every form of movement had a form of stillness. Every snail dies. Every wind stills. Every beam of light is absorbed.

Following an intuition, Daelan rose and moved through a tai-chi-like kata that, through slow, controlled movements, encompassed both motion and stillness, the one transitioning to the other. He sank further into the concepts, his understanding of them deepening.

In a moment of epiphany he set the two runes to slowly spinning. He felt contentment when he saw the rune for "Motion", as the runes spun, turn into the rune for "Stillness", and back again. He also liked the spinning itself. It was motion, but it was also stillness in that it was static, never changing.

Daelan fed all of his mana into the runes, causing them to condense and solidify. If he had been more aware of his body, he would have smiled. The aspecting of his mana had gone exactly like he'd hoped.

**

Daelan rested in his room the next morning, tired after a long night of crafting items in preparation for the coming of the Aemilianus family's head. Even with his stamina, he was exhausted. Resisting the call of his bed, he checked his email.

Stupid spam, he thought with a growl.

He was about to close the browser when he saw one from Jasmine, with the subject "We need to talk" and dated a day and a half ago. He wished he could delete it like the spam, but knew that wasn't really an option.

Damn it.

He started up the burner phone app that allowed him to use different phone numbers. It called the app company, and the company's servers forwarded the call via a different number. It was like a VPN for voice calls.

While the line was ringing, he cast a quick spell to prevent sounds from escaping.

"Hello?" a sleepy voice answered.

"What's wrong, Jasmine?"

"Took you long enough to get back to me."

"Well, I'm here now. What do you want?"

"Marcus came back and asked about Master."

"He's dead, Jasmine, you don't have to keep calling him 'Master'."

"I thought he was just traveling," she said snidely.

Though her attitude pissed him off, Daelan chose to ignore it. "How did Marcus seem?"

"Stressed and angry. He kept demanding to know where Master was, and I kept telling him that he didn't tell us, that he just packed up and left. I'm not sure he believed me."

"Hmm. Good to know. Is there anything else?"

"I want to come with you."

Her request was both unexpected and unwelcome. "There's no way that's happening."

"Please," she said with as much genuine emotion as he'd ever heard from her. "They're eventually going to realize that something's wrong, and then I'm dead."

"So? Why should I care about that?" he said snidely, happy to take some of his ever-burning rage, that always burned a little higher when she was around, out on her.

Daelan could hear the anger and tension in her voice when she said, "You should care, because if I go down, I'll take you down with me. I'll tell them everything."

Damn it. He wanted to yell at her, threaten her, but that would be foolish. If she got to the point where she was going to die anyway, all his leverage disappeared. He either needed to kill her or take her with him.

He thought some more, and reluctantly said, "I'll take you on two conditions."

"What are they?"

"You have to tell whoever would look for you, besides the vampires, some story so they won't call the cops or anything."

"Okay. And?"

"And I'm not taking you with me permanently. I'll take you to another state and drop you off somewhere."

"At least three states away!"

Daelan wanted to reach through the phone and grab the vampire by the neck for the nerve of bargaining with him, when

136

she knew he wouldn't have any trouble killing her. He was tempted to risk the cops coming after him, but bit back the frustration and said, "Fine. Three states away."

"Deal. When can you come get me?"

"Soon. I have to take care of a few more vampires, and then we can leave."

"Okay. I'll be ready, but warn me before you come."

He ended the call without answering. He would warn her if he could. And if he couldn't? Tough.

He did have one last thought before preparing to sleep.

Once I take her out of town and no one's looking for her, there's nothing to stop me from killing her.

That was enough to cheer him up. The Daelan of 219 Hell-years ago would have balked at the thought, but a lot had changed since then. He thought about where he could dump the body as he brushed his teeth, got undressed, and set an alarm. Afterwards, he slept like a baby.

**

Come on, where are you, asshole?

Through the scrying spell Daelan had found out that Aisha, the head of the Aemilianus family, was scheduled to arrive at 4 pm, and here it was 5:06. Daelan had been on location since 2:15 in case she came early.

He was a hundred feet south of the vampire estate's driveway off the Oregon Coast Highway. Thick forests surrounded the roads, and he was sitting in a tree with good sightlines to the Highway on both the north and south.

He did not, unfortunately, know which direction the vampires would be coming from and didn't dare set up his ambush on the vampires' driveway, so he had been forced to set up two: one a hundred yards north and the other a hundred yards south. He had marked the trees where he had set up the traps, such that they could be seen from his position, but not by the vampires.

Daelan looked up at the sky when he heard a distant rumble of thunder. Dark gray clouds were moving in from the north.

Rain's coming.

At that moment, the southern sensor's rune plate pulsed. It had detected vampires. He didn't get too excited. It wasn't the first time he'd picked them up. There had been occasional traffic in and out of the estate.

The passive sensor was 400 yards to the south. Another engraved silver plate had a twin 300 yards to the south, whose sole purpose was to let him use his third eye as though he were there. He saw a small sedan with a driver and no passengers. Not a vampire.

The next car was a stretch limousine. The driver and two passengers in the back were vampires, and a human was riding shotgun. The driver and one of the passengers were female. The human had a mana core.

A mage. Crap.

Daelan was also bothered by the car itself. He had made the trap such that it could destroy a large car and everyone in it, but he hadn't considered an extra long car like the limousine. He could take out the mage and driver or the passengers, but not both.

It wasn't a hard call. The target was Aisha, not her bodyguards.

Passengers it is.

He grabbed the last silver rune plate he would need—the one paired with its twin in the trap mechanism. This one didn't have any sensory capabilities. Instead, it was made to transfer large amounts of mana efficiently.

While Daelan could have triggered the spell at a hundred yards, it would have been weak because of the distance multiplying the mana cost. The rune plates used the principle of similarity to make the two locations the same, magically speaking.

That is to say, Daelan could flood the trap with mana, and when he saw the rear half of the limo reach the correct position, that's exactly what he did.

Next to the rune plate was a large cake pan filled with nails, and covering both was a piece of camouflage cloth. Daelan used a powerful telekinesis spell, enhanced by his motion-aspected mana, to hurl the nails at supersonic speeds at the car. He felt the mage in the front start to create a shield, but it was too late. At most he would be able to protect himself and the driver, but they weren't in danger anyway.

The nails hit the side of the car and pierced through, creating a cacophony and clouds of sparks and smoke. Even from a distance, the sound was painful to Daelan. He could only imagine what it was like for the people in the front.

He was pretty sure it wasn't an issue for the ones in back.

The impact caused the limo's rear to spin into the middle of the road, preventing Daelan from seeing the results. He'd thought the nails would go all the way through the other side of the car, but they didn't.

Did I screw up? Ah, crap, it's probably armored.

He cast a scrying spell through the rune plates and sensed the massive holes in the far side of the car, looking for all the world like a gigantic shotgun had peppered it. Seeing the damage eased Daelan's worries. When he realized that the armor probably just caused the nails to bounce back into the passenger area for another pass, he chuckled grimly. He used the spell to look inside the passenger area. It was a puréed mess of blood, upholstery, tissue, metal, bone, and cloth.

Target eliminated.

The telekinesis spell had taken almost half his mana, but it was worth it. He saw the vampire and mage recover, with the mage quickly getting out of the limo. When he was out, he slammed the door shut and shouted, "Go, go!"

The driver nodded and trundled away in an ungainly way. The rear wheel was completely destroyed, even though it looked like it was a solid "run flat" tire. The nails had simply shredded it. Daelan wouldn't be surprised if the limo's frame was bent too.

Still, it limped its way to the estate. Daelan thought about taking out the driver, but didn't for two reasons: he was only after Aisha, and the mage clearly knew his location and was approaching.

Shit.

He cast a simple deflection telekinesis shield, threw the rune plates into his backpack, and jumped down to the ground. Almost immediately, he felt an impact on his shield that caused him to stumble. By the time he recovered and turned around, a fireball hit his shield, spreading out around it.

Though it caused the air around him to get hot, he just sneered.

As if they could hurt me with that crap.

Still, he put the tree between himself and the mage. He prepared his spell, and when it was ready, left his cover. The mage was forty yards away, so Daelan summoned Quoz in the form of a javelin.

'More people to kill? A mage even? How delightful.'

Ignoring the entity, Daelan threw the javelin at the mage. He didn't really intend to hurt him with the throw, it was more to give the mage something to worry about while he got in range for his real attack. He rushed forward, and at fifteen yards triggered the mental blast spell. It was the mental equivalent of the noise created by the nails hitting the car—a cacophony that disorients and incapacitates.

In his family's experience, few mages included mental protection in their shields.

The mage, a middle-aged man in an expensive italian suit, looked stunned and, after a moment, sank to his knees. Daelan re-summoned Quoz and put the mage out of his misery. It slipped through the man's shield like warm butter, and had an even easier time slicing through his neck.

Now that the immediate danger was past. Daelan looked up. Cars were approaching from both directions, and one had already arrived and stopped from the north. The driver, a young woman, was gawking open-mouthed.

Damn it.

Daelan cast his camouflage spell while running into the trees. He cursed again when he saw the woman pull out a phone and either take pictures or video of the scene.

While he would have liked to recover the other rune plates, it was time to go.

What a mess. Oh, well. At least I got Aisha.

While he ran to his bike, he listened to the scrying spell, which had been squawking at him for a while.

"...happened, Master?" Marcus asked.

"We were ambushed," a familiar soprano voice said. "He completely destroyed the back of the limousine. If I hadn't changed places with my driver, he would have killed me."

Damn it.

Chapter 17

Gabriel

The vampires were irate, which was enough to unnerve anyone, even the mages of the Society. Gabriel and his fellow mages were also frustrated, though, because the vampires refused to say much about what had happened, other than to make it clear that an attempt on the Aemilianus Family's head had been made.

The family head, a vampire that looked like Hedy Lamarr, was pissed and looking for blood, metaphorically speaking. At least so far.

"You and the Society had damn well better give me a better explanation than 'it wasn't us'!"

She was flanked by five other vampires, all men, on one side of a conference table. Three wizards were on the other. They were led by an austere but pretty woman who looked to be in her late twenties. Gabriel knew she was quite a bit older than that.

He was impressed by Eleanor's demeanor when she said in calm tones, "We can't give you a better explanation, because we weren't involved. If you told us more about what happened, perhaps we could help figure out who the culprit is."

An experienced wizard, Eleanor was chosen to lead the local branch of the Society as much for her composure as her magical abilities.

Still, even though her words were calm, he could see the tension in her face and shoulders. And if he could see it, he knew the vampires could. Their senses were notoriously powerful. They were said to even be able to smell someone's emotional state.

Gabriel nudged her leg under the table.

She glanced at him, frowned, and turned back to the vampires. "We have received an indication that an otherworlder has come to the Earth recently. We believe he may be behind the attacks on your family."

"An otherworlder? Seriously?" the vampire scoffed. "And how many 'otherworlders' have arrived so conveniently?" She emphasized her disdain with a sneer.

"Just one. We can give you a description if you…"

"That won't be necessary. Tell me, wizard," she said as she tossed a picture of a destroyed limousine onto the table. "How close would you have to be to do something like that to an armored limousine?"

Eleanor seemed taken aback. "I… I'm not sure I could do that."

Though he tried to keep it from his face, Gabriel couldn't believe what he was hearing.

Full points for honesty, sis, but this is not the right time!

He was pretty sure the vampires could sense their nervousness. If they believed they were weak, this negotiation could get bloody.

The comely vampire smiled condescendingly. "I suppose there exist some wizards who could do this?"

"Yes."

"How close would *they* need to be?"

"I'm not sure. Fairly close, I suppose."

Gabriel wanted to roll his eyes. *"I suppose?" There's no way it could have been done from far away.*

While in theory a powerful wizard could do it from a distance, they would have to have a year's worth of bones to pull it off. Not a year of their allotment of bones. A year of the *Society's* unearthed bones. And that was assuming they even could hold that much mana. It's not like the members of the Society had enough to test things like that.

"Well, let me tell you a bit more about the attempt on my life, since you seem so eager to know."

The vampire was smiling, but Gabriel didn't need a keen sense of smell to know that it held no friendliness, nor a whit of belief in Eleanor's words.

"We know there were at least two wizards," she continued. "We sensed magic usage at the ambush site and a position 100 yards away, near the estate. One of my men fought with the wizard by the estate, allowing me to escape."

Eleanor looked uncomfortable. "I can see why that…"

"I wasn't finished," she said harshly. "When we searched, we found an identical ambush site to the north of the estate. Apparently they didn't know which way I'd be coming, so they hedged their bets. So, two wizards, plus one manning another ambush site, makes…?" She paused, with a taunting look.

"Three wizards," Eleanor said unhappily. "We will, of course, need to verify…"

"Forget your verification!" the vampire shouted, the tips of fangs appearing.

Oh, shit.

Everyone in the room tensed, but the vampire took the time to collect herself and calm down. Still, the fire of rage burned in her eyes. She slammed a paper with a drawing of a man on the table.

"I demand that you deliver this wizard to us, alive!"

The three wizards looked at the picture. Eleanor glanced at Gabriel, unsure what to do.

Though it wasn't a perfect likeness, it was close enough to recognize the otherworlder. There was no way the vampires would believe them though.

The tension of the moment was disturbed by the opening of the door to the room. A wizard who looked to be a fit fifty-year-old strode in.

"Hello, Aisha. I hope you don't mind me listening to the conversation via my children while I drove here."

He attached a clairaudience spell to me? I didn't even sense it! Maybe it was on Eleanor…

As chagrined as Gabriel was about not noticing the spell, he was glad his father had come. His presence would deter the vampires' aggressiveness.

Aisha narrowed her eyes in wariness. "Duncan. I care far more about the murders of my family members and the attempt on my life. The treaties…" she said, looking meaningfully at the other wizards, "…only allow one wizard for every two vampires during negotiations."

Duncan nodded and looked at the man sitting at Eleanor's other side.

"Henry, would you mind stepping out?"

"Not at all."

"Thank you." The Region Archmagus stepped forward and looked down at the picture on the table.

"Before we continue, I'd like to show you something that I think you'll find enlightening."

"What is it?"

"The coming of the otherworlder that Eleanor spoke of."

"This again! I am tired…"

Duncan held up a placating hand. "Please. Trust me. You'll want to see this."

The vampire was still angry, but she crossed her arms and said, "Fine. Show me."

The Archmagus pulled out a small orb that looked like a miniature crystal ball and placed it on the table. Instead of rolling around, it stayed perfectly still. After the wizard backed away, a holographic cube, two feet on a side, appeared that looked exactly like the ramshackle room where the otherworlder appeared.

The events of that night played again, and when the otherworlder appeared through the portal, many people in the room drew in their breaths.

They could all tell that the man of the portrait and the otherworlder were one and the same.

"So," Duncan said. "Let's talk about how we can work together to find out what's going on."

Chapter 18

Daelan

Daelan tried to send a text to Jasmine while he was riding, but somewhere in the Bluetooth/voice-activated AI/app/cellular tech stack, things broke down, and Daelan wasn't about to stop to figure out what was going on. Speed was too important.

When he arrived at the mansion, he was relieved to see Jasmine's old, beat-up Volkswagen Cabriolet. It was rare for her to leave before it was time to hit the bars, but the way his day was going it wouldn't have surprised him to see it gone.

Unfortunately, leaving Jasmine here wasn't an option. She knew far too much about him.

He slammed the door open on the way in.

"Jasmine, you here?"

"Uungh." She weakly called out, "In theory."

Daelan barged into her room, without bothering to knock, and found the vampire lying in disarrayed bedding. Clothes and lingerie were strewn about the floor and chest of drawers. One particularly eye-catching bra was hanging on the mirror.

Daelan shook his head in disbelief. "Come on, Jasmine. It's almost 8 o'clock. What the hell are you doing in bed?"

She gave him a lascivious smile. "I had a very long night... and morning... and... no, I guess we stopped by noon."

"Don't care. If you aren't ready to leave in ten minutes, I'm leaving you behind."

Jasmine's eyes narrowed in anger. "You were supposed to warn me!"

"Yeah, because you totally would have answered your phone."

"I might have," she said with a pout.

"Whatever. Nine minutes and..." he made a show of looking at his phone, "...48 seconds." He left her room and closed the door.

Regardless of his threat, he had no intention of leaving her behind. He would just take her without her things if he had to. After all, she wouldn't need anything where she was going.

While he waited, Daelan texted Gus using one of his burner phone numbers. *'Hey, it's your favorite bouncer. If anyone comes asking for me, text me at this number and I'll deal with it.'*

After sending the message, he took a few minutes to go over the route he intended to take.

"You've got three minutes, Jasmine!"

"It's not enough time! I've got to pack my things!"

Figuring it was her own fault if she wasn't dressed yet, Daelan strode into her room again. He saw the vampire throwing clothes, a hair dryer, lipstick, makeup, and a hundred other things he didn't recognize into a large suitcase.

"You've got to be kidding."

She stopped and looked up at him, still leaning over the suitcase. "What?" she asked, clearly puzzled by his response.

"We're going on a motorcycle, Jasmine. How the hell do you plan on carrying that?"

"I can take my car."

"You mean the one that can do zero to sixty in, like, two days? And tops out at sixty-six? Not a chance. You can take your car, but I'm not waiting for you."

She pouted again. "Maybe I should just go by myself, then."

Daelan shrugged. "Suit yourself. Oh, by the way, I just killed all of Aisha Aemilianus' bodyguards a couple of hours ago, but she got away. See you later."

Daelan turned around and started to leave the room. He managed to keep from chuckling until he was facing away from the vampire.

"Wait!"

He stopped. "Yeah?"

"You suck."

"I think that's my line."

Jasmine rolled her eyes at his repartee.

She's just jealous that I got her so good.

"Fine. I won't take the suitcase, but I need something!"

"One second."

147

Feeling like an old man with creaky bones, Daelan leaned over and grabbed his backpack that held his rune plates and a couple changes of clothes. He took the clothes out, zipped it back up, and tossed it to Jasmine.

"You can fill that up, but do NOT take any of my stuff out. We'll buy another one on the way and split our stuff up."

She looked at the backpack in disbelief. "What am I supposed to do with this?"

"Throw all the gold and cash in that you can, and a change of clothes. You can buy new stuff when you get to your new town."

Jasmine glared at him, but did as he said.

It ended up taking another eleven minutes, but they did finally get on the road. Jasmine sat behind him and held onto his waist. She was helmetless, which caused more than one person to give him a disgusted look.

Once they were on the freeway, Jasmine turned her head and hugged herself snugly onto his back. Daelan knew she was likely motivated by staying out of the biting wind, but he still chuckled when he thought about how good she was at mimicking affection.

"What?" she asked.

Daelan didn't bother responding. She probably wouldn't hear him anyway.

He left town going east on Highway 22. He could have gotten to Idaho faster by going northeast on 5 to Portland, but he preferred the less heavily traveled road. There weren't as many towns or traffic, and it was surrounded by forests. He figured it shouldn't be hard to find somewhere to dump Jasmine's body.

He felt a little bad about killing her, but it wouldn't be the first time he'd killed a servant.

**

After an hour and a half of riding, Daelan pulled off. He'd been using a night vision spell to look for promising areas, and his third eye to look for places that didn't have residual auras, since that generally meant no one had passed by recently. He was patient. There was plenty of road and forest.

148

He came upon a dirt road—little more than a path, really—that was starting to be overgrown by trees and brush, and it didn't have a whisper of aura.

Perfect.

When he pulled onto the shoulder and started slowly working his bike onto the "road", Jasmine asked, "What are you doing?"

"Need to take a leak. We'll take a break for a minute and then head out again."

Daelan rode the bike about forty feet off the highway and used the kickstand. He frowned when it sank an inch into the dirt, but it stayed put there.

"Give me a second."

"Okay."

He walked to the treeline, unzipped, and did his business. When he was done, he turned back around and said, "Do you need a snack?"

Jasmine, who'd been looking bored, perked up and said, "I wouldn't turn it down."

Daelan held out his arm to her.

She made a face. "Ew. You didn't wash your hands! Can't I use your neck?"

Daelan snorted. "That's rich, coming from you. No, you can't use my neck. Just use the crook of my arm."

"Fine."

With a brilliant smile she took his arm and bit in, eagerly sucking in his blood. She quickly tensed and quivered in ecstasy.

"O-my-god! This is even better than before!"

"There's more mana than before."

She looked at him and grinned with a bloody smile. "Are you sure I can't stay with you?"

"Would you call me 'Master'?"

"Usually, Masters are the ones who feed, not the other way around, but for this I'll call you whatever you want."

He gently guided her head back to his arm. She did not resist, and eagerly took to licking the trail of leaking blood before biting down again.

As Daelan summoned Quoz, he thought, *Enjoy your last meal.*

He didn't let her suffer. Quoz smoothly penetrated her skull and fed on her as she started to collapse.

Daelan picked her up by the back of the neck, walked a few yards into the woods, and tossed the body deeper, the neck breaking from the rough handling. His eye paused on her broken body, limbs lying akimbo.

Goodbye, Jasmine.

As he walked back to the bike, he checked his phone. There was a text from Gus.

'*I like you, John, but I don't want any trouble, and I'm not gonna be a hero to save you.*'

He one-finger typed a message back. '*I'm not asking you to. Just don't volunteer any information, and tell me as soon as you can.*'

He sighed when he climbed back on the bike. *What a mess.*

**

That night, though Daelan's body was in a roach-infested motel, his mind was many years in the past, in a land of noxious fumes and quicksand.

His dream-self was dirty enough to blend in with the ground, so he simply lay on the baked dirt while a humanoid demon harvested one of its horrifying cousins. The jaundice-yellow man-demon took the bone sword it carried and hacked off one of the cattle-demon's limbs.

Daelan had taken to calling the misshapen and disgusting creatures of this plane "cattle-demons", because the man-demons treated them like livestock.

The wounded cattle-demon bleated in misery while juices oozed out of it and dribbled onto the sandy ground. The other cattle would no doubt have come to slurp it up, or perhaps even try to eat their neighbor, but they were too afraid of the man-demon, who was calmly chomping on the limb in front of its previous owner.

Though he felt an ever-present disgust for the demons, the scene did not affect Daelan much. He had seen its like too many times. It surprised him, though, when he realized that he felt a certain amount of pity for the cattle, that class of demon that tormented him during his early days in Hell.

He suspected that they started out as imps, small man-demons, and grew as they collected soul energy from the malignant spirits that arrived in Hell. When they were harvested, the man-demons took an arm, leg, a slab of flesh, or even a head if they happened to have more than one. When they healed, they replaced the hacked-off flesh with more limbs, new eyes or mouths, or sometimes new heads.

He believed the monstrosities he'd seen were once weak humanoid demons that had been harvested over and over again, turning them into disgusting wretches.

Though he hated them, he also felt pity, for they were pathetic creatures living a miserable life.

That wouldn't stop him from harvesting the demon himself, of course. But at least he would put it out of its misery.

Well, after making it wish for annihilation with every fiber of its being first, anyway, he thought with inner amusement. He did not take pleasure in torturing or killing the demons anymore. That fire had long since burned out. He wasn't sure when. Perhaps when he'd returned their pain a thousand-fold.

Now, he did it for survival. He still harbored dreams of leaving this wretched place, and for that he needed power.

After waiting for a couple of hours to make sure the man-demon was gone, Daelan grabbed the cattle by one of its throats. When the mewling thing scrabbled at him with its limbs he hacked them off, one by one, until he held a crying lump of meat.

"Hurt, wailer?" Daelan asked, using the demons' term for cattle-demons. "No worry. I free you from pain."

Daelan's command of the demonic language was rather lacking. Though they could communicate via telepathy, as far as he could tell they only did it when torturing people. He wasn't sure why.

He put up a sound nullifying spell around them to keep from drawing attention, and got down to business. He was just getting warmed up a half-hour later when he felt something push through the sound barrier behind him.

Daelan spun around quickly and saw the yellow man-demon seven feet away. Up close, he saw that the creature had fine scales and golden eyes with the horizontal orientation of a goat.

Oh crap.

He changed Quoz from a scalpel into a war scythe, but while he was moving into guard position the demon rushed up and grabbed him, pinning both arms to his body with crushing strength. Daelan felt his ribs creak as he struggled to breathe.

Desperate, he tried to move Quoz a little to cut the demon, while simultaneously hissing the words of power for a flamethrower spell. Agony erupted as fire spewed from his hand, immolating it. He just hoped he got the demon too.

The demon hissed and pulled his hand away, releasing Daelan on one side. It stared at its burned fingers, as if it couldn't believe what it was seeing. Daelan started incanting another flamethrower spell but never got the chance to finish it, because the demon brought his hand back in a fist and slammed it into Daelan's head, causing everything to go dark.

**

When he came to, he found himself in a cage, his hands tied together with rough hemp rope. His burnt hand was still oozing, but skin was starting to grow back over it. That was a mixed blessing, because it both itched and hurt. He hated the "pins and needles" feeling of healing.

Ignoring the discomfort, Daelan looked around. He was shocked to see that the cage was made of metal, which he had never seen before in Hell. Well, besides Quoz, and he wasn't convinced that Quoz was made out of metal.

The cage sat in the corner of a great hall, which was no less astonishing. The floor was slabs of light and dark stone, dressed into square tiles and arranged in a checkerboard pattern. The walls and ceiling were made of large slabs of the lighter stone. Daelan noted that the workmanship was surprisingly good.

A variety of man- and woman-demons were talking with a dark-gray demon sitting on a throne made of interlocking bones. Some of them, he who sat on the throne included, wore rough clothes.

A small demon in an adjacent corner cried out, "The wailer is *okuzuka*!" causing all of the demons to turn to him.

Damn it. They're calling me a "wailer". They think I'm cattle.

The chief demon said something, which caused four demons to bring his cage before the throne.

The gray demon, who looked like a hairless, muscular man, contemplated Daelan.

Daelan decided that if he wanted any chance of surviving this, diplomacy was called for. From what he'd seen of the humanoid demons, they were very big on hierarchy, and it was very simple: you were either a "Moaner", meaning the receiver of pain, or an "Impaler". It was obvious who the Impaler was. What he needed was a category change from "Wailer" (cattle) to "Moaner" (underling). He thought of what he could say to convince the demon in front of him and gnashed his teeth when he realized that his vocabulary was too limited to make any kind of meaningful argument.

All he could do was bow his head respectfully and say, "Impaler. I am Moaner."

This caused a stir amongst the demons. He wasn't sure if it was because he could speak demonic, or because he'd declared himself to be a Moaner.

The gray demon just looked at him for a few seconds, and then spoke.

"You *oyagala okunweereza*?"

Daelan was frustrated at how little he knew of Demonic. The good news was that the form of "you" the demon had used was for underlings, meaning that he had, at least for now, accepted his claim of "Moaner" status.

What can I say that will help? "I... want serve Impaler."

"Give me *omukono gwo*."

A frog-like demon came forth from the crowd and opened his cage. Daelan hesitantly walked out and was bidden to approach the gray demon.

Not knowing what he should do, he dropped to a knee when he was a few feet away. The gray demon stared at him expectantly.

What am I supposed to do?

The frog-demon, who had returned to the crowd, made gestures of extending his right arm. Daelan hesitantly mimicked the action. He was startled when the gray demon grabbed his wrist and pulled it closer with a strength that could not be denied, causing Daelan to fall forward.

He looked up to see what the demon was going to do, and was horrified when he saw the demon bring his hand to his mouth that was full of shark teeth. All he could see was that maw that was ready to rip and tear, and the cruel eyes above it. The vomit-green eyes stared at Daelan's face as his hand was brought ever closer, as if to see what his reaction would be.

At the last moment the demon's eyes shifted to the hand. It curled its hand around Daelan's, folding the fingers back except for the index finger. That one was brought inside the awful maw.

The demon looked him in the eyes again, as he brought his jaws together, snipping the finger off. Daelan was horrified as he watched it chew and swallow his flesh, but he froze his face in a stoic expression.

He had been through enough horrors that he could keep himself from reacting.

The demon looked satisfied at first, but grew increasingly agitated, as if expecting something more. Daelan saw the frog-demon gesticulating in the corner of his eye. It was pantomiming about something coming out of its throat.

Oh, if I want to be a Moaner, I have to moan.

Daelan bowed his head and moaned in pain, being careful to not go overboard, as that would make him a Wailer. When he looked up again, the demon seemed pleased.

Thank the Father.

He was in pain, horrified at watching the creature eat his finger, and afraid of being amongst so many demons, but he was still relieved. He would live another day, and he'd long since learned that was often the best you could do in Hell.

Chapter 19

Daelan sipped his drink in one of Cheyenne, Wyoming's hipster coffee shops while he listened to his client explain what he didn't like about the prototype website Daelan had put together for him.

"Okay, so if I am hearing you right, Mr. Peabody, you are not a fan of the color scheme. Do you not like the colors we picked, or is it how we're using them? You don't like the colors? Okay. Did you change your mind on wanting an ocean shore theme? No? Well, why don't we do this? I will ask our artistic director to get together with you to sort out the colors, and then I can put them in."

More sips as Daelan half-listened and half watched in amusement as a father tried to get his caffeine fix while wrangling two young children.

"Um-hmm. Yeah."

Once the client had wound down about the colors, Daelan asked, "Were there any other problems with the prototype?"

Daelan listened and took notes for another half hour. When they were done, he sent an IM to the artistic director and started working on the content changes the client had requested.

Daelan had seriously considered quitting the job when he was forced to go on the run, but decided not to. He still needed money.

He could steal it, and that would probably be faster, but he was trying to be different now that he was out of Hell. Sure, he didn't mind killing or robbing vampires and bad people, but he would prefer not to involve innocents.

Granted, his definitions of "bad" and "innocent" could get mighty flexible when needs arose, but if it took working with doofuses like Mr. Peabody to pay the bills, he could live with that. He shrugged and thought, *At least for the next few months until I leave, anyway.*

He just needed to expand the capacity of his core, gather enough mana, make sure the daughter of Joseph, his sibling, was okay, and avoid more problems. Though he hadn't decapitated the Aemilianus family like he wanted, hopefully he had scared them enough to back off. He was more than willing to let bygones be bygones.

He was worried they would seek revenge, though, and that they would be able to track him somehow. The thought bothered him. He much preferred to be the hunter than the prey.

It also bothered him that he didn't have a good understanding of what was possible with digital tracking. What was worse, no one else seemed to know either. Everyone he'd talked to was sure it was happening, but when it came to specifics the information got spotty fast. What's more, most people didn't seem to care.

They seemed to have a herd mentality—as long as they didn't stick out, they were protected by the millions of other people online. With terabytes of data, why would anyone care about theirs?

If Daelan was one of them he might feel the same way, but he had no way of knowing if the vampires could use such methods or not, and he wasn't willing to chance it.

He did some research and decided to implement a few counter-measures: dump his old phone and replace it with prepaid cell phones, pay in cash for in-person sales, always use a VPN on the internet, use a privacy-oriented browser, and use an email service that supported end-to-end encryption.

He didn't know if it was enough or not, but he hoped so.

To build up his cash reserves, Daelan had taken to selling one or two pieces of jewelry at a pawn shop in each city he passed through while using an illusion spell to change his appearance. He only dealt with places that didn't require ID, which was most of them. As long as the gold was legit, they didn't care.

Daelan shut down the laptop, got up, and stretched. He'd put in a solid eight hours, so it was time to move on to Ogallala, Nebraska and spend some time building up his mana reserves in the next motel room.

It was a slow way to make it to Imogen, Joseph's daughter in Florida, but he'd get there.

**

A few nights later, instead of hitting a pawn shop after work, Daelan visited a craft store. He'd been thinking about how to ameliorate the weakness of his aspected mana: the exaggerated cost of casting spells that did not involve *motion* or *stillness*. There were a variety of protection spells that he would like to run constantly, but the mana cost would be prohibitive.

He decided the best way to handle it would be to store unaspected mana in a way that would allow him to use it as needed. A staff was the traditional answer, but that would make him stick out like a sore thumb on Earth. A diamond ring would work, but he was familiar enough with American culture to know that it would look weird, especially if he put multiple large stones on it.

He decided to go with an arm cuff—a bracelet for his upper bicep. It would also look unusual to anyone who saw it, of course, but he planned on hiding it.

He took a small block of clay and began kneading it with a touch of water. Once it had softened, he started shaping it. Ten minutes later he looked at his creation and thought, *This looks like crap.*

While not literally true, it did look more like a child's version of a snake that had been coiled into a circle than the arm cuff he wanted.

Disgusted, he crumpled it into a ball and started again. After twenty more minutes of diligent effort he beheld his handiwork and, once again, growled while smashing the ugly thing.

It wasn't that he cared about how it looked. He planned to hide it, after all. If he had his druthers, no one besides him would ever see the blasted thing.

He did care about functionality, though, and his work didn't even meet that low bar. Part of the problem was his lack of skill, but an even bigger issue was the thinness of the coils. The arm cuff was designed to expand with his arm when needed and contract back into shape afterwards, hence the open spiral.

The clay didn't have the strength to retain its shape, forcing him to do the snake-like shape that was the worst of all worlds: thick and still unable to maintain its form.

I need something that I can build it on.

Daelan glanced at the room, and what he saw wasn't promising. He was not staying at places with bathrobes and minibars. He sought out the fifty-bucks-a-night dives, so he was pleased when he found a coffee pot that should do the trick. It was thicker than his upper arm, but it was close enough that he could wind the arm cuff a little tighter after he cast it in gold.

Having decided to go with a more "industrial" approach, Daelan grabbed a glass and used it as a rolling pin to flatten out the clay to a uniform thickness. Even though the clay would be supported this time, he decided to make it thicker than it had to be so he could embed the diamonds in the metal and not make them stick out so much.

Daelan used a utility knife to cut out a strip 1 cm wide that was long enough to do one and a quarter turns around the coffee pot. Once the strip was in place, Daelan smiled in relief.

Finally.

When he'd started, he'd expected to start making the silica mold the same night and finish the arm cuff in a couple of days. He realized now that he'd been wildly over-optimistic. He would probably only be able to start the silicone mold, and that was after he'd finished shaping the cuff, forming the settings for the three diamonds he planned to use, and adding the spell runes.

While he was disappointed, it was okay. He could be patient. He had, after all, two centuries of practice.

Chapter 20

Gabriel

Gabriel felt dirty. He didn't like what they'd done to the bartender who had worked with the otherworlder. The man had given John, or Daelan, or whatever his name was, up easily enough, so at least the interrogation mage hadn't had to use any of his techniques. Still, the Society couldn't afford to let him remember the questioning, so the interrogator had wiped it from his memory. Gabriel hoped that it hadn't damaged his mind too much. The mage said it wouldn't, but the bartender's slack-jawed look and trail of drool didn't give Gabriel much confidence.

He sighed and thought, *At least it's better than what the vampires would have done.*

He still couldn't believe that the Society was working with the evil scum-suckers. Though he knew they couldn't just let the otherworlder run around wreaking havoc, he didn't have a problem with the man taking out vampires. As far as Gabriel was concerned, he could destroy the whole lot of them with his blessing.

His father, though, was not as sanguine. Gabriel wasn't sure if he was more worried about the otherworlder or anxious to maintain a diplomatic relationship with the Aemilianus family. Whatever his reasons, he had fully supported the vampires in their efforts to track the man down, short of performing an expensive tracking spell.

Now negotiations were on to do the spell.

Gabriel looked at Eleanor, who was reading a book. "What do you think they're offering Dad?"

Eleanor responded without looking up. "No idea."

"Don't you think it's weird that we're working together like this? I mean, what do they have that we would even want?"

159

She sighed and closed the book before looking at her brother. "I don't know. But you know Dad. We'll end up benefiting."

Gabriel scowled. "Yeah, but... I'm not sure I want to benefit from anything they can give us. It's not like they're going to give us a bunch of mana bones."

Before his sister could respond, their Father swept out of the conference room, a tight smile the only indication of how the talks went. He was followed by Aisha Aemilianus, who was also smiling, and another vampire.

The Region Archmagus turned to his daughter and said, "Get a strike force ready to move out in two hours."

"What's going on?" she asked.

I'm going to cast the tracking spell. Then we," he said as he gestured at the head of the Aemilianus family, "will work together to take down the otherworlder."

Gabriel desperately wanted to talk with his father, but not with vampires in the room, so he stifled his many questions.

"Yes, Archmagus," his sister said as she bowed her head.

"Could we talk for a moment, uh, Archmagus?" Gabriel asked.

"Yes?" his father said with a raised eyebrow.

Gabriel glanced at the vampires. "Could we talk in private?"

His father gave him a reassuring smile and clapped him on the shoulder. "All your questions will be answered, but right now is the time to get ready."

Gabriel didn't like that answer, but he bowed his head and said, "Yes, Archmagus."

His father squeezed his shoulder affectionately before releasing him and leaving the room to make his own preparations. The vampires also left to do whatever the hell they would do. He didn't want to think too much about that.

Gabriel trusted his father, but he didn't like the situation. He glanced at his sister and shook his head.

He really hoped that when he did get answers to his questions, he would be okay with them.

Chapter 21

Daelan

Daelan was finally ready to finish the arm cuff. It had taken him almost a week to let the mold cure, pour in hot wax, and do multiple coats of a silica slurry around the wax until it formed a mold half an inch thick. He'd given the silica mold a couple of days to fully dry, so it could handle the heat of molten gold without cracking.

Before he could pour the gold, he had to remove the wax. Daelan took the white, gritty mold in his hands and whispered the words of power for a heat spell. He only fed it a trickle of mana because he wanted the temperature to rise gradually.

As the mold heated up, wax began to drip out of it and fall onto the cheap formica table. He kept adding more heat even after all the wax was gone. The ceramic shell had to be hardened so it could withstand the molten gold that was coming.

By the time he was finished, visible heat waves were rising from the mold and being close to it was beginning to be painful. He released the spell and let the mold start cooling. He didn't intend to let it cool much. If he poured the gold while it was still hot, there would be less thermal shock.

That's the theory, anyway.

Four minutes later, Daelan had a pool of molten gold sitting in a crucible. He carefully poured it into the warm silica mold. Hot air rose from a vent whose sole purpose was to give the air a way to escape and make room for the liquid. When the gold threatened to overflow, Daelan stopped pouring.

The gold quickly changed from a bright yellow liquid to a more muted solid. Daelan waited half an hour to let it cool, and then ran tap water over it. Satisfied that it was cool enough, he started carefully chipping away at the mold. He grew excited as the arm cuff slowly emerged.

Beautiful.

A jeweler probably would have disagreed, but Daelan wasn't concerned about how the arm cuff looked. He admired what it represented: power.

Time to add the diamonds.

Two hours later, the arm cuff sported three large, nearly perfect diamonds. They were embedded in such a way as to make them as unobtrusive as possible.

After taking a few moments to admire his creation, Daelan put it on.

He laughed after sitting down at the DC power generator and successfully shunting freshly created, unaspected mana into the diamonds. While he continued filling them, he thought about which of the arm cuff's protective spells he should run continuously.

Protection From Divination is top priority, he decided at last. After he left Salem he'd cast the spell every few hours to see if the vampires had created a magical link to him, and he'd been relieved when, each time, nothing was there.

It became a heavy mana drain after giving his mana an aspect, so as time went on and he got further down the road, he'd taken to casting it less and less often. He was surprised when he realized it had been almost 36 hours since he'd last checked.

Ah, well, with any luck I'll never be without it again, he thought as he fed some of the unaspected mana to the Protection From Divination spell form in the arm cuff. He admired how the runes took on a subtle glow, until he felt the spell cut off a magical link to something.

Oh shit.

Daelan sprang up and started throwing a few essentials into the backpack: DC power generator, silicone mold, and a dirty t-shirt and pair of underwear. He didn't bother with any of the tools, materials, or even the leftover gold in the crucible. As he zipped the backpack closed, he created a deflection shield around himself. He briefly considered adding shields that would protect his mind and soul, but cursed when he realized he didn't have enough unaspected mana to power it for long.

He'd have to use the mind and soul shields reactively. He didn't like it—you really want the shield up *before* someone tries to rip your soul or mind away—but there was no helping it.

He'd just put his leather jacket and backpack on when he heard a knock on the door. The door that was the only exit.

"Daelan Peregrinus, this is the police! Come out with your hands up!"

Daelan's fear and anger spiked. He knew that the police did not enslave or torture people, but he had zero confidence that he was actually dealing with the police.

Daelan used the arm cuff's mana to cast a clairvoyance spell. A man and woman in police uniforms stood on either side of the door, backs against the wall, and looked towards the door. The man held a shotgun, and the woman had a pistol and buck knife. A few more men and women were in the strip-mall-style motel's parking lot, most of them behind cars and looking at the door. None were in uniform, and a middle-aged man held a staff.

Daelan extended his magical senses to the two at the door.

Vampires.

He backed up to give himself some room as he thought. His ad-hoc planning was cut short when he saw the fake male police officer move in front of the door and prepare to kick it in.

With his *motion* mana and will, Daelan shot a circle of telekinetic force half a centimeter wide that burst through the door, taking a small piece of wood with it that punched through the vampire's forehead and erupted from the back of his head, spraying a gory mix of brain and blood into the parking lot.

A tenth of a second later, another circle blasted through the wall next to the woman, who was already reacting to the death of her companion. It pierced her back, breaking ribs and tearing the side of her heart before erupting from her chest. She looked down in shock and horror as blood poured from the grisly wound.

I have to get out of here!

All of Daelan's thoughts were centered on escape. He frantically looked at the ceiling and, with brute telekinetic force, ripped a man-sized section down. White powder hung in the air and dusted the room as the cheap drywall crumpled and dropped to the floor with a thud.

The hole in the ceiling revealed a joist and plywood. Daelan pushed the plywood with his mana, bursting it upwards and crashing it into the upstairs room that Daelan could now see through the hole.

A woman's scream pierced the air and added a painful melody to the cacophony. The noise almost caused Daelan to miss the slam of the motel room's door. The man with the staff walked in, a blue, shimmering shield surrounding him. The mage pointed the staff at Daelan as a ball of fire formed at the tip.

Daelan cursed as he telekinetically pushed himself up through the hole in the ceiling. In his hurry to escape he tore his clothes on the broken plywood and hit his head on the next ceiling.

Ow...

Before he could move on to the next step of his escape, an explosion rocked the room with a mighty "BOOM!", buckling the floor upwards and creating more holes. A spurt of flames leapt through the holes, battering Daelan with a blistering wind. He saw that his previous domicile was a charred wreck.

The woman, who had been screaming on the bed while hugging a pillow, had the misfortune of being over the center of the explosion. She was thrown to the side, slamming into a wall. Her screams cut off entirely, her voice as broken as the rest of her.

The hell? What happened to "keep things secret from the normies"?!

Daelan hadn't realized how far they were willing to go to kill him. He snarled, all inhibitions on violence as thoroughly incinerated as the bed he'd been planning to sleep in.

He was tempted to leave a telekinetic "bomb" in the room to mutilate whoever followed him, but he stifled the urge. As powerful as his mana was, it wasn't inexhaustible, and he needed it to escape. With a growl of frustration he hurried out to the walkway and ran next to the wall, using the floor to shield himself from the vampires and mages who were still outside.

Someone must have detected him because they yelled, "He's over there!"

Bullets flew and even hit his shield, but their low mass made them easy to deflect. Daelan snorted in disdain, but he knew he needed to get out of there before they pulled out more effective weapons.

164

And before I run out of mana..., he thought with a grimace. He dived over the railing and picked himself up, once again, with telekinesis. Before he could fly off into the night sky, though, a flash of light turned the night to day for a split second, and pain tore through his body as his muscles seized up.

A clap of thunder rocked what remained of his consciousness, the loud reverberations coming one after another as the echoes from buildings slammed his hearing over and over again.

Daelan dazedly looked over at the people in the parking lot. A man with a shotgun swiveled to point the gun at him, while another rushed towards him with a machete. A detached part of his mind noticed that they had unusually large canine teeth. Another, muffled part of his brain was screaming, *You have to get out of here!*

He stood up groggily, muscles twitching, and stumbled when he was pushed in the side.

Ow.

Though whatever it was hurt, he ignored it to deal with more important matters, like the vampire trying to cut his head off. He stretched out his hand and thought, *Get away.* The vampire flew through the air and crumpled the side of a car, but not before leaving his machete embedded in Daelan's shoulder.

The wizard with the staff walked out of his former motel room and started preparing another fireball.

Daelan did his best to take off into the air, but it ended up being more "falling and picking himself up telekinetically" than anything else.

He had enough presence of mind to gain altitude quickly to avoid buildings as he rocketed forward at four g's of acceleration, reaching 200 MPH in two and a half seconds. Though he quickly rose above the bugs, the buffeting of the air was annoying until he had enough presence of mind to *still* the air around him.

Daelan trembled as he thought about how close he had come to being captured or killed. It didn't help that he was hurt. His side was bleeding where he had been "pushed".

Must have been the shotgun.

He pulled the machete out of his shoulder and, after sterilizing it with a quick burst of heat to destroy his blood sample, dropped it to the ground, too dazed and in pain to care about where it landed.

Daelan took a few moments to restart his Protection From Divination spell. He needed it more than ever now that they had his blood. He was running now, wounded and looking for a place to hide, but he promised himself that soon he would be the hunter.

As Daelan flew, still dripping blood, he was tempted to find an open piece of land, use telekinesis to bury himself, and wait out the people chasing him. That's what he would have done in Hell.

It only took a few seconds to realize that was a stupid plan on Earth. He needed mana, and he wasn't going to get much in the ground. He needed electricity and privacy, which meant another motel.

Daelan had already left the greater Des Moines area behind, leaving him flying through the cold air over dark plains. Fortunately, all the lights Americans used made it easy to tell where the towns were. Daelan was down to twenty percent of his mana, so he couldn't run much further.

He picked the nearest lake of lights and landed a hundred yards away. While he walked towards the town, he thought about disguising himself with an illusion.

Don't have mana for that either, he thought unhappily. *Hopefully Podunk, Iowa doesn't have facial recognition.*

The first accommodations he came across was a Holiday Inn Express. Nothing fancy, but a couple of steps above the places where he'd been staying. Deciding to treat himself, he walked into the lobby with an illusion that covered his wounds.

Five minutes later he walked back out. The hotel required a credit card to stay. One thing people had been clear on was that credit card transactions could be tracked, making that a non-starter.

With a sigh, Daelan made his way to the run-down motel down the street with a flickering sign that advertised HBO and vacancies. He'd probably share the room with a family of cockroaches, but they would take his cash and give him electricity. It would do.

**

The next morning, after a long night of removing buckshot and shocking himself, he was sporting new scars and the arm cuff was mostly full. He'd put most of the mana in the cuff because maintaining the anti-divination spell was crucial.

He was embarrassed that he'd been tracked magically, but he took comfort in that it probably meant the vampires didn't have hooks into the technology surveillance network, or his anti-tracking measures were effective. Either was good news. He knew how to stop magical tracking, which meant he was a ghost now.

Hopefully.

He looked for motorcycles online on his phone while he ate eggs and sausages at a local diner. He was tired of only having his backpack to carry stuff, and he was looking for something with some storage. It looked like what he wanted was a "touring" bike, but they were expensive. He could buy a cheap car for the same price and be able to carry a hell of a lot more.

He was reluctant to go the car route—he'd enjoyed riding his motorcycle—but he was starting to resign himself to the idea when he found a used Honda Goldwing for sale in Des Moines for $16,000. It would make a significant dent in his cash reserves from web developer work and jewelry sales, but he could afford it.

Daelan convinced the seller to pick him up, and two hours later he was on the road with his new bike, his backpack stored in the saddlebags.

Time to put some distance between me and Des Moines.

Chapter 22

Two weeks later

Daelan rode into Fort Lauderdale, Florida, already sick of the place. He had the good fortune of arriving in the middle of "bike week". The good news was that he fit in, though his bike was rather plain compared to a lot of what he saw. The bad was that it took half an hour to ride a couple of blocks.

He failed to find a vacant room over the next couple of hours, so he gave up and went almost an hour north to West Palm Beach, where he found a motel and pulled off the road, grateful to be out of the mess. After settling into his new room with a surprisingly comfy bed that was a relief for his aching joints, he started looking up private investigators.

He had thought about how he was going to find Joseph's daughter, Imogen, and it seemed like private investigators were the way to go. He hadn't hired anyone before arriving, because this was firmly in the "pay with cash" category, as it was tied to a particular location.

He left messages with three different investigators and then settled down to make mana. He was tired of shocking himself, but knew it was necessary.

If he wanted to live, he had to pay the price.

**

"Hello, Mr. Santos? This is Chuck Bradford. I understand you need a private investigator?"

Good. I only had to wait a couple hours. "Yes. I need to find a relative," he said into the phone. "Do you do that sort of thing?"

"Absolutely. I've handled many missing persons jobs. What can you tell me about it?"

"She's not missing exactly. At least I don't think she is. I've been out of the country and haven't been able to look into what happened to her. My cousin, Joseph Santos, and his wife died a few years back, and I want to know what happened to their daughter."

"Joseph Santos… you mean the guy that was gunned down in his driveway?" the investigator asked, sounding surprised.

"Yeah. You remember it?"

"It was a famous case for a while. And, you know, being in the biz I keep tabs on things like that. I used to be a cop myself."

"I see." He paused and asked, "How much would it cost to find their daughter, Imogen?"

"It should be a relatively straightforward case, though it will take some time to go through records and such. I charge $100 per hour plus expenses, and for a case like this I require a three day retainer, or $2500."

"What happens if you find her in less than three days?"

"I'll return whatever portion of the retainer hasn't been used."

"Alright. Can I pay in cash?"

"Absolutely, though I must say, that's unusual these days."

Not wanting to talk about that, Daelan ignored the comment. "Where should we meet?"

After making arrangements, Daelan settled down to create mana again.

**

The next evening after he finished his day job, Daelan decided to expand his *dao*. It needed to be related to *motion* and *stillness*, and he had known from the beginning what it would be: *hot* and *cold*.

Unlike a lot of his roach motel rooms, the one he had at the moment was surprisingly nice. The carpet was in rough shape, but there were no noxious smells. He still set some lavender incense to burning (which he justified as being tradition at this point), sat down in the lotus position, and started meditating.

Once he was calm and relaxed, he started thinking about hot and cold. The warmth of sunshine. The cold of fall breezes. The heat of a fire. The cold of snow. The shared warmth of a companion. The cold of swimming in spring runoff.

In each case he thought about what was actually happening. The swimmer in melted-snow water is surrounded by sluggish, energyless water molecules. When the more energetic skin molecules collide with the water, some of the energy is transferred to the water, making the skin molecules slower and colder.

When sunlight hits the skin, it's absorbed by electrons, raising them to a higher energy state. That energy is transferred to the atom, and then the molecule, increasing its speed and making it hot.

Over and over again, he sought to improve his understanding and intuition of the nature of hot and cold. After a time he contemplated the runic representation of his *dao*: the runes for *motion* and *stillness*—mirror images of each other—joined and slowly spinning as a pair, the runes eternally turning into each other.

Daelan used his mana to form the runes for *hot* and *cold*, and attached *hot* to *motion*, and *cold* to *stillness*. *Hot* and *cold* were also mirror images of each other, so as the set of runes spun, *hot/motion* turned into *stillness/cold*, and vice versa.

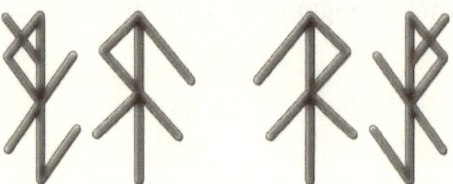

Beautiful.

Daelan opened his eye and rose to his feet. He calmly took a glass, filled it with tap water, and set it on the table. Using his third eye, he saw the heat of the water and, using his aspected mana, willed it to move to one side of the glass. At first it moved easily, but as the difference between the two sides grew, it resisted, forcing Daelan to use more will and mana.

As stingy as he was with mana, he didn't stint in this case. He wanted to see what he could do. He forced the heat to one side, the difference becoming a real strain where they met in the middle. As he forced the heat to separate into *hot* and *cold*, he felt the concept click and lock in his *dao*.

Wanting to see the result of what he'd done to the water, he ignored his third eye and concentrated on his normal vision. He laughed in delight when he saw ice and boiling water in the same glass. The next instant the glass shattered, spraying the boiling water and dropping the lump of ice on the table. Strangely, instead of melting like he expected, the ice grew a touch even though he had already released the mana.

He gingerly reached out to touch the ice, and it promptly froze his skin.

Abyss take it, that's cold!

He suddenly realized, when he took almost all the heat energy away from the water, he wasn't just turning it into ice, he was taking it close to absolute zero, which was -459°F. The ice grew because it froze the water vapor in the air.

Of course, that had taken a third of his mana. Power always has its price. Fortunately, with the further refining of his aspected mana, he could condense it even further. That was good, of course, but it meant he needed to spend more time creating mana by getting shocked. He sighed as he sat back down and got to work.

Chapter 23

"Mr. Santos, I know where Imogen is."

"Good. Where is she?

"She's had a rough time of it. No one took her in after her parents died, so she entered the foster system. In the last five years she's been with six families, and has racked up three charges of misdemeanor theft, one charge of marijuana possession, and one charge of assault. She's in a group home now."

"What's a group home?"

"It's where they send the hard cases, the kids that don't fit in with families and cause problems."

"That… doesn't sound good."

"It's not," the P.I. confirmed.

The line was silent for a few seconds as Daelan regretted not coming sooner. "Thank you for getting the information. If you text me the address, I'll consider your job done."

"Thank you, Mr. Santos. I have a couple hundred dollars left from your retainer…"

"Keep it."

"Alright. I'll send the address right away."

**

Daelan made an appointment to visit Imogen as soon as he could, which turned out to be two days away. Now he was fretting about what gift to give her.

He felt bad about the life she'd led since her parents died. He had assumed that one of her mother's relatives would take care of her. He knew it wasn't logical, but it felt like it was his fault, like he should have been here sooner.

What would a sixteen-year-old girl want?

Daelan didn't do a lot of shopping, and he hadn't set foot in a mall before now. It was a strange and uncomfortable environment for him, and the stores weren't helping him find anything. 90% of the stores were clothes, and he had no idea what she looked like now, or what kind of clothes she liked. He didn't know what she liked to do, though he did remember that she'd been into a boys' K-pop band. Maybe he should get something of theirs?

He ended up buying an assortment of things, hoping she would like at least one of them.

When the appointed day arrived, he gathered up the gifts in a gift bag and rode to the group home. It looked like a large community center, with calm, happy colors, but the high fence and the cameras told a different story. Not all of the cameras pointed outward.

He entered the lobby and saw a receptionist in the inner part of the building, doctor's office style.

"Hello. I'm here to see Imogen Santos."

"And your name is?"

"Daelan Peregrinus."

She looked at her computer, clicked on the mouse a few times, and looked up. They'll take you back in a few minutes, Mr. Peregrinus. In the meantime, could you fill out this form?"

She handed him a clipboard and a two-page form asking for background information, driver's license, occupation, relationship to the minor, criminal history, and health information.

What? Nowhere to put my bank account info?

The intrusiveness made him uneasy, but didn't know what to do about it short of simply breaking the girl out. He didn't consider that out of the question, but he sure as hell didn't want to do it before finding out how she would feel about it. In the meantime, he just hoped that his fake papers held up.

A few minutes later, a man unlocked a door and poked his head out. "Mr. Peregrinus? Imogen is ready to see you."

"I, uh, haven't finished the forms yet."

"That's okay. Just give them to the receptionist and you can finish them afterward."

"Okay."

The man took him to a nearby conference room with a small table and a few chairs and followed Daelan inside. Seated in one of the chairs was a young woman with bleached blonde hair with dark roots an inch long. She had a pixie cut, black eyeliner, a wifebeater shirt, faded green army pants, and battered black military boots.

The two sized each other up. Daelan saw the resemblance to the girl he'd seen when she was eleven, but she had definitely changed.

He was surprised by how confusing it was to see Imogen. Seeing her brought back the old him. The Daelan before the assassinations, the one that had a purpose and meaning in life. The one that could handle Hell.

At the same time, Imogen was very different. She was no longer a young, innocent girl. She looked wary, but was trying to hide it behind apathy. The clear markers of nervousness gave away the lie.

"Who the hell are you?" she asked, looking him in the eye.

"My name's Daelan. Daelan Peregrinus. I'm a friend of your Dad's."

"My Dad's dead."

Daelan nodded. "I know. I'm sorry it took so long for me to come. I came as soon as I could."

"Five years? Five *years*?" she asked, looking pissed. "Where the hell does it take five years to get here?"

Daelan frowned. "I… was a long way away. Like I said, I wish I could have come sooner." He turned to the man and said, "Could we, uh, talk more privately?"

He shook his head. "Sorry. No can do."

Daelan nodded in acknowledgement and turned back to Imogen. "I brought some gifts for you."

Imogen silently accepted the bag. She pulled out the wireless earbuds, which made her chuckle bitterly. The man said, "Sorry, Imogen," and held out his hand.

She handed the earbuds over and explained to Daelan, "They don't allow us to have any electronics."

"Oh. Sorry."

She shrugged and pulled the next item out: the skincare creams. She looked mildly intrigued, but set it on the table wordlessly. The next item was the hoodie.

"Awesome!" she said sarcastically. "A hoodie. In Florida. In the summer. I'm sure I'll be able to wear it all the time."

Daelan frowned, annoyed by her ingratitude and embarrassed by his useless gift. He didn't feel the heat much, so it was hard for him to tell when it was uncomfortably hot or cold for other people.

Last, she took out the candy. She sighed and handed it over to the man. "No sweets either."

"Sorry." *Was everything I brought crap?*

She looked at him. "It's alright. I appreciate the thought. Lord knows it's more than anyone else has done for me the last five years."

That mollified him somewhat. "What would you like me to bring next time?"

Her eyebrows raised. "There's going to be a next time?"

He was surprised by the question. *Does she not want me to come again?*

Looking at her, though, he understood. He saw the jadedness for what it was: hope that had been disappointed too many times. Though Daelan was sure what she had experienced was nothing like his time in Hell, he recognized a kindred spirit in Imogen. She knew pain and fear, and they'd hardened her.

So yes, he would visit again. Partly for his sibling's sake. Partly because it was what the God-King wanted. But mostly because she was like him, and he wished someone had helped him when he needed it.

He looked her in the eye and nodded. "Yeah."

She pursed her lips as if really looking at him for the first time. After a couple of seconds she said, "Shoes, women's size seven. Maybe some Converses or something. Black lipstick. Oh, and some tampons. Super-plus size." She quirked her lips at the last item.

What the hell are tampons? He thought about asking, but intuited she was messing with him and it would be a bad idea.

She burst out laughing. When she started to calm down, she asked in between laughter. "Were you... ha, ha... really... hee... going to get them?"

Daelan just shrugged. "Anything else you want?"

"Yeah," she said, getting more serious again. "Get me out of here. Take me to the park, or a movie, or freaking anything."

Daelan looked at the man. "Can I take her out?"

"No, not yet. You'd need to visit her a few more times, go through a background check, and have her permission, of course."

Daelan turned back to Imogen. "Alright, I'll work on it."

She looked at him as if trying to figure him out. "Who are you really?"

"I told you. I'm your father's friend."

"Prove it, because he never once said your name."

Daelan nodded. "We were close, but I lived a long way away. He told me about you and your mother often though."

"Oh, yeah? What did he say?"

"That he loved you. Loved to take you fishing."

Imogen snorted, looking angry. "You could have gotten that from the newspapers. We had just gotten back from fishing, asshole."

Daelan just nodded. "I know that you loved BTS. Your favorite was Suga. Your favorite food when you were a kid was pizza, but later on it became hot pot."

Imogen looked disconcerted. "How did you know that?"

"Your favorite class in school was science. You wanted to be a veterinarian."

"Every girl wants to be a veterinarian…" she muttered.

"Your favorite color was teal, your favorite sport is soccer, and your favorite teams were Real Madrid and Inter Miami FC. You had a poster of Cristiano Ronaldo in your room, next to BTS and Suga, of course."

"Alright! I get it! You know lots of stuff about me. Why didn't Dad ever talk about you?"

Daelan hesitated. "I'll tell you that, but can you wait until we're on our own?"

The man next to him stirred uneasily. "Mr. Peregrinus…"

Alarmed, Imogen held up her hand in a "stop" gesture and said, "It's fine! It's fine. I can wait."

The man frowned, but held his peace.

Daelan smiled at Imogen for giving him a small gesture of trust. "So, are you a Messi fan now that he's playing for Miami?" He didn't know jack about soccer, but had done a little research in preparation for the visit.

176

Imogen pursed her lips. "My feelings for Messi are complicated, but I'm coming around on him."

"Do you get to watch the games often?"

She frowned. "No! The guys say it's a sissy sport and don't let me watch."

"Maybe when we go out we can watch a game and get hot pot or something."

For the first time, her eyes lit up. "I'd... like that. She smiled and her eyes looked off in the distance, as if she was daydreaming. Daelan let her be and just watched with a small smile.

When she came to herself they continued the conversation, mostly talking about her. There was the unspoken promise of more about him later. When their hour was up, they got up and awkwardly looked at each other, unsure how to say goodbye. After a couple of seconds Imogen walked up to Daelan and gave him a hug, which he gently returned.

"Thank you for coming," she whispered.

He nodded, and was surprised to realize his eye was wet.

"You're welcome," he said thickly.

Before he left, he finished the forms and made another appointment for the soonest date he could.

**

That night he dreamed.

He dreamed of pain and misery, but this time, he was the giver.

"Come here, cattle. Stop running, stupid ."

The demon ran away, but not very quickly with its five legs that did not coordinate well. It only kept from tripping itself and falling through sheer desire and a wide base. Daelan walked up to it and chopped off one of the legs with Quoz, cutting through the muscle and gristle, and breaking bones.

The demon squealed in pain.

"You deserve. Sit down."

The miserable demon slumped down to the ground, resigned to its fate, expecting more limbs to be cut off. Instead, Daelan pulled out scalpels, hammers, and small clay pots with concoctions in them.

Over the next few hours, louder and louder squeals sounded through the dusty plains of Hell, until, at last, another demon desired nothing more than annihilation to escape the pain. Satisfied, Daelan returned with the leg and a few other cattle limbs from the harvest.

He turned them into a fat demon with rolls of skin called Thrush. Though he looked disgusting, Daelan knew the flab covered massive muscles.

"These are old!" he roared. "Why is your harvest never fresh?"

"I don't know," Daelan mumbled. "I came back soon as I could…"

"Lies!" Thrush grabbed a coiled bullwhip off a hook on the wall and, with one crack, wrapped it around Daelan's neck. The initial sting was quickly overshadowed by the choking. He tried to pull the whip off, but was jerked off his feet and into a sprawl when Thrush pulled on the whip.

"I told you what would happen if the harvest wasn't fresh again. You will feed the Impaler, Wailer."

Thrush's words sent a wave of terror through Daelan even as he choked on the floor. Not only was Thrush insulting him, he was relegating him to cattle. He thought about pulling out Quoz, but knew he would die today if he did. He wasn't strong enough yet.

He had to submit and live, no matter what it took.

Daelan moaned when his head was slammed into the stone by Thrush's foot. He wasn't sure if he was imagining it, but it felt like his skull was flexing, stressed to almost failing.

When the whip came off his neck, Daelan breathed in air gratefully.

"I no Wailer! Moaner!"

"I don't think so," Thrush said tauntingly. "I think you're a Wailer." His foot came off, only to be replaced by a knee. Thrush's corpulent face came into view. He grinned and asked himself, "What part shall I give to the Impaler? I think an eyeball."

Thrush dug into a pocket and pulled out a metal tool that looked like a small obstetrical forceps, one the right size to pull out an eye. Daelan looked at it in horror. He wanted to scream, but bit it back, knowing that it could only make his situation worse. He did let himself beg, though.

"Please!"

Thrush's grin only grew bigger and more malicious.

"Come on, Wailer! Wail for me!"

Daelan panicked as the forceps came closer, but other than hyperventilating he didn't make a sound as the demon forced his eyelids open and pushed the tool in around his eye, already forcing it partly out of the socket. He wanted to scream as he felt the connection straining and threatening to snap.

Then, as almost an afterthought, Thrush yanked it back and it was gone.

That son of a bitch! I'm going to kill them all...

Daelan consoled himself with such thoughts as he whimpered and watched the demon take the eye and put it in with the rest of the harvest.

He sat up and gingerly felt his eye socket. He knew it was gone, but he still had to touch it and verify that it really and truly was taken. He hung his head and choked down the sobs that wanted to come out.

Inside, he vowed revenge for what must have been the thousandth time. His day hadn't come yet, but it would. He would make them all pay.

Chapter 24

Gabriel

"Where do you think he gets his mana from, sis?"

Gabriel had asked the question that every mage who knew about the otherworlder was asking. They didn't think he was digging up his own mana bones, so where did it come from? Was it all mana that he had brought with him? If it wasn't either of those... he had another source. And that made him the most important person in the world.

Eleanor looked annoyed. "I don't know, Gabe. Other than how to find him, that's all they're talking about these days."

"Do they have any ideas about his source?"

"Yeah, but not many I would bet money on. The most popular is that he periodically goes back to wherever he came from, fills up, and returns."

Gabriel shuddered when he thought about the implications. Otherworlders were rare because it was difficult to make a portal to somewhere distant. If he could do it at will, from a place with abundant mana, then invasion was a very real possibility.

"That... would be scary."

Eleanor snorted. "You have a talent for understatement, dear brother."

"I take it we haven't made any progress finding him."

She shook her head. "No. They've been trying more indirect means, such as spells searching for otherworlders rather than him specifically, but that hasn't worked either. Dad said someone even suggested contacting the Elder Gods to see if they could pierce the shield."

Gabriel's eyes went wide. "Are they insane?!"

"I know. Dad and the others shut it down hard, but it just goes to show how much they want to find him."

The siblings stewed on their own thoughts until Duncan, their father, strode in. "Eleanor, we have a lead. Be ready to move out in an hour. Gabriel…" He frowned and seemed to be thinking about how to say something unpleasant.

"Dad, I want to go!"

"I understand, son, but the otherworlder is dangerous. You saw what happened last time."

"I saw what happened to vampires without shields."

Duncan frowned. "Yes, but you don't know what happened when he tried to kill Aisha Aemilianus, do you?"

"What happened?"

"He killed Lucas Walker after destroying two vampires and half of an armored limousine."

"Lucas? How? Wasn't he pretty skilled?"

Duncan nodded. "He was, and that's why I'm so hesitant. We couldn't tell exactly what he did, but he cast a spell that caused Lucas to collapse even though he had his shields up. And then the otherworlder chopped his head off with a sword that went through the shield like it wasn't even there."

Gabriel swallowed nervously after picturing the death of the mage. He was not put off, though. He was nothing if not stubborn. "I want to go anyway. I'm the most talented mage of my generation. You said so yourself, and that I'll follow in your steps."

"Right. Which is why I want to make sure you're safe."

"And when I'm the Region Archmagus or, fates willing, the Merlin, what will I tell the mages under me when they ask what role I played when the most important event of a generation happened? You want me to tell them I was hiding?"

His father stared at him, thinking. He sighed in defeat and said, "Boy, I'm not kidding when I say this thing—we don't even really know that it's a man—this 'Daelan' is dangerous. Are you sure you want to go?"

"I'm sure. Imagine what we can learn from him! If he really does have a new source of mana… how incredible that would be! Or if he could teach us new branches of magic!"

Duncan frowned. "Very well. Be ready to go in an hour."

Eleanor asked, "Where are we going, Dad?"

"Florida. A social worker did a background check on Daelan."

Chapter 25

Daelan

Today was a special day. After weeks of visits and a background check, it was the first—and unfortunately, probably also the last—time he could take Imogen out of the group home. Her eyes lit up when she saw him.

"Are you ready to go?"

"Are you kidding me? I've been looking forward to this for months!"

"I've only been visiting you for three weeks."

She looked embarrassed. "Yeah, um, sorry about that. I've been wanting to get out of there for a long time. I'm glad we can do something together, though."

Daelan shook his head while wearing a lopsided smile. "That's okay. I don't blame you for wanting to leave."

Though they'd grown closer over time, there was still the elephant in the room between them. Imogen still didn't really know who Daelan was, or how he knew her father. He knew that part of the reason she was looking forward to this outing was because he had promised her answers.

When he brought her to the Goldwing and got on, she laughed. "You have a bike?"

Daelan just smiled and nodded. "Put your foot there and then swing up behind me."

Daelan bought a passenger backrest to make it more comfortable for her. He'd also bought another helmet and installed an expensive set of communicators with noise cancellation, voice activation, and encryption into both of their helmets. They needed to talk, and he wanted to make sure it was private.

When they left the parking lot he took things slowly. He didn't want to scare her, and he wasn't used to riding with a passenger.

"Can you hear me?"

"Yeah. This is cool!"

"I'm glad you like it. When we turn, lean with me, okay?"

"Alright."

As they got used to riding with each other, he sped up a little and took them out to the freeway.

"Where are we going?" she asked.

"I said I'd take you to a Miami soccer game."

"You said we'd *watch* a game."

"Yeah, well, for your first time out I thought we'd do something special."

"We're going in person? Nice!"

Daelan knew it was time for him to tell Imogen how he knew her father, but he was reluctant. He wasn't sure how she would react.

"So… you said you were going to tell me how you knew my Dad."

Daelan sighed. "Yeah, I did. Listen, this is going to sound strange, but hear me out, okay?"

"Alright…?" she said uncertainly.

"Your dad was not a normal guy." Daelan thought about how to continue. *Damn it. I should have worked it out before coming.*

After a couple seconds of silence, Imogen laughed and said, "My dad? He was as basic as they come."

"No, he wasn't." He growled in frustration and said, "Let me try this again. A lot of things are real that you thought were make-believe. Magic, wizards, vampires, werewolves, all that stuff."

Imogen sounded pissed now. "What the hell are you talking about?"

"Like I said, I know this is hard to believe." He looked around for something he could use as a demonstration. "You see that palm tree next to the gas station?"

"Yeah?"

Without saying a word, Daelan used his mana to rip a frond off and pulled it towards them. It was expensive because of the distance, but convincing his "niece" was more important than the mana.

He kept the frond high to keep it out of traffic, but then let it slowly lower until it was next to Imogen as they flew down the road at 70 MPH.

"What the hell...?"

Daelan saw Imogen in his side mirror reach out and touch some of the leaves..

"What's going on, Daelan?"

"It's magic."

"Are you messing with me? Because I'm going to be really pissed if you are."

"I'm not. Look, we have a little time before the game because I was planning on getting hot pot. Why don't we stop somewhere, and I can answer your questions."

"Okay." Daelan telekinetically threw the frond to the side of the freeway. He didn't like seeing so many of the drivers and passengers in other cars staring at them, but it was whatever. He was confident they would come up with an explanation for what happened. They were just seeing things, or mistook a bird for a frond, or it was a fluke gust of wind.

He sped up and left the cars behind to avoid complications, and pulled off at the next exit. They stopped at a grocery store parking lot, parking in one of the far corners.

"So... magic," she said.

"Yeah."

"You can do, like, anything?"

He shook his head. "No, not anything. Doing stuff takes power, and I have a limited amount."

"But if you had more power you could do anything?"

"Well, not 'anything', but a lot of stuff," he admitted.

"Show me something."

"Like what?"

"Um... make me fly!"

Daelan gestured with his head at the other people in the parking lot. Imogen just looked at him with an impish smile. Daelan rolled his eye.

He considered her request. He needed almost all of the mana in his core and arm cuff to create a portal to Sicanthus in two days, but he decided it wouldn't hurt to blow some of it. He could make more in time, so why not?

184

He looked at her and said, "I could have made you fly on your own, but if I'm going to hide you, we'll have to do it together." He crouched down and bent forward. "Hop on."

Imogen gingerly got on his back, her arms around his neck.

"Not so tight, please," he said, struggling for air after he stood up and she got nervous. He gently squeezed the legs that he was holding. "I've got you."

She loosened her grip, only to immediately tighten it again when they rose into the air. When she realized what she'd done, she chuckled in embarrassment. "Sorry."

"No problem. You ready?"

"Yes!"

It was reported later that night that a mysterious sonic boom rocked nearby neighborhoods.

**

They talked more about magic and the mythical beings in the world while eating burgers and fries. They mutually held off talking about it during the game, as much or more because of the people around them than desire to watch the play.

On the way home, on the freeway again, Imogen asked, "So, why was my father special?"

Daelan explained about Darius, and how they were avatars. Imogen was skeptical, so Daelan reminded her about how he knew so many things about her.

"Wait, so you, like, saw me naked as a baby?"

"Um, yeah. Is that weird?"

"Yes!"

"Look. I'm not your father, but I'm a lot like him. You could think of me as your uncle."

"Trust me, you are very different from my father."

"Maybe, but mostly because we had very different experiences, and because he had intended to live a non-magical life."

"So, could he have done magic?"

"Probably, unless the ability was taken from him when he was created."

185

"No offense, but that sounds really weird. Like you were clones or something."

Daelan frowned and swerved around a car that was going slow. "We're not clones, but I admit that it's not a bad analogy. The main difference is that we could experience everything that the others experienced."

"Weird. So, if my dad could do magic, can I do it too?"

"Probably."

"Will you teach me?"

"Well…" Daelan didn't usually have a hard time telling people things they didn't want to hear. He made a way of life out of it in Hell. Here, though, with Imogen, he was dreading this part of the conversation.

"What's wrong?" she asked worriedly.

"I, uh, have to leave in a couple days."

"What? Just two days?"

"Yeah. My body is starting to fall apart on Earth, and I have to go somewhere else to fix it."

"Where?"

"Sicanthus. Where your dad and I came from."

"So… what does that mean for me?"

"It means you're going to have to stay in the group home. I'm sorry."

There was a hitch in her voice when she said, "It's okay. I'm used to being disappointed."

Damn it. He was used to being a hard ass, but it was a much different thing when you cared about the other person. "I've added your name to my bank account. When you're out you can use the money to get an apartment and get started in life."

"Thanks," she said dully.

"Look. I would think about taking you with me, but I have lots of powerful enemies. You're safer here than you would be with me." She didn't respond. "Imogen?"

"Yeah?"

"Are you okay?"

"Sure. I'm great."

Frustrated, he said, "Look, I'm sorry. I'm doing the best I can here. Assuming I'm still alive, I'll come back and check in with you."

"When?"

"I don't know."

"Yeah, well, forgive me if I don't hold my breath."

This fucking brat. I'm the one that's been tortured and probably going to die, and she's the one whining.

Daelan took a couple of seconds to keep from saying something he would regret. He reminded himself that she was a very young woman who hadn't been alive for hundreds of years or had the opportunity to see life from different perspectives.

"We still have a couple of days together," he said. "What would you like to do with them?"

"Why bother? You should probably just get rea…"

While she was speaking, a divination spell that detected danger started warning Daelan that something was wrong ahead.

Aw, crap. Not now.

Daelan did an illegal U-turn and headed away.

"What are you doing?" Imogen asked.

"Something's wrong. I'm going to take a different route to the group home."

She was silent for a few seconds. "What do you mean 'something's wrong'?"

"Hopefully it's no big deal, but it's possible my enemies have found me."

"What kinds of enemies?"

"Vampires and mages."

Daelan felt her arms tighten and a bit of a tremor.

Damn it.

The annoyance that he'd felt seconds ago washed away. He hated that she was afraid, and that she had reason to be. It had only been a few weeks, but he'd grown protective of her. It was a completely new feeling for him. It was like a side of himself that he hadn't even known existed woke up and made him feel strange things ever since he met Imogen in person.

He'd first noticed it a week ago, when she told him about some of the boys in the group home bullying her. He'd wanted to beat the crap out of them, and probably would have if Imogen hadn't talked him down.

He had mixed feelings about it. This desire to protect her was inconvenient as hell. *She* was inconvenient as hell, in a way that grated on him. He didn't like how taking care of her limited his freedom.

On the other hand, he felt alive in a way that he never had before. He had a reason to live beyond spiting his enemies, so he could come back and see her again and make sure she was okay. It felt good. Like he might do something that actually mattered. He didn't want to lose that.

"It's going to be okay."

She had clasped her arms around him again, her helmet against his back, and he felt her make a small nod.

After going west for a quarter mile he turned north to head towards the group home. It didn't take long for the danger spell to activate again, pointing towards the north-east, but it was changing direction, in real-time, to the north.

Whatever it was, it was adjusting to his movements.

He turned left again to head west, but the danger warning continued to sound. Daelan checked his Protection From Divination spell to make sure it was active. It was. He racked his brain to figure out how they were tracking him. Then he had an ugly thought.

"Imogen, has anything unusual happened in the group home?"

"Like what?"

"Have you seen anyone new?"

"Um, a nurse came in to draw blood from everyone to run some tests."

Oh, shit.

He was about to accelerate and get out of there, the police be damned, but at that instant the asphalt in front of him rose to make a three-foot-high wall. Daelan tried to brake and turn, but it was too close. He only managed to hit the wall at a 45° angle.

The rear of the bike lifted, throwing Imogen off. Daelan started to be thrown too, but his leg caught on the wall when the side of the bike slammed into it.

Damn it!

Though he was in pain, his primary concern was Imogen. He willed his mana to take her and cushion her fall. Once she was on the ground he let her roll a bit. It wouldn't kill her. He started taking stock of the situation. He cursed himself for not thinking to use his mana to avoid the wall, but he didn't have time for self-recriminations. He could kick himself later.

Shaking off the guilt, he found himself filled with other, more familiar emotions: fear and rage.

He got off the bike, his crushed leg painful even through the endorphins and adrenaline flooding his system. Didn't matter. That was something he would deal with later, too. Right now, all that mattered was escaping.

"Run, Imogen!" he yelled through their helmet radios.

He lifted himself with telekinesis above the wall, preparing to fly over and pick her up. Someone was trying to push him down magically, but it was just an annoyance. Daelan was at least as strong as they were, and he had the massive advantage of being closer. He looked with horror, though, when he saw asphalt grow around Imogen and enclose her in a gray tomb.

"*Daelan!*" she screamed through the radio as the asphalt closed around her.

'*No!*' Hoping that the radio would reach through the asphalt, he quickly said, "Don't worry, Imogen! I'm going to get you out of there!"

He thought about how to get her out, but every method had the same problem: it would take too long. Whoever was manipulating the asphalt would continue to work against him while their compatriots attacked. Unless they ran out of mana before he did, it was a losing strategy, and he had to assume they could call in reinforcements.

He had to kill them.

Decided, he turned away from Imogen and towards his enemies.

Daelan created a deflection shield, turned off the danger sense spell—it wasn't specific enough to be useful in battle—and opened his third eye, all in rapid sequence. Ten mana cores flared in his sight, rapidly moving to surround him and Imogen, along with twelve smoky existences he'd come to recognize as vampires who were coming straight at him.

Cowards.

Now that he knew what he was dealing with, he focused on his normal vision, summoned Quoz as a war scythe, and used his mana to speed up his body. He did not increase his strength

189

because that would have required his unaspected mana, and, frankly, because he didn't think he needed it. Between the sharpness of Quoz and the increased momentum that comes with speed, he expected to cut through them like tofu..

Daelan surprised the vampires by coming to them. He had no intention of letting them dictate the nature of the engagement, so he moved in a blur to the left-most vampire and casually sliced him in two outside the reach of the creature's claws. Its rib bones and spine slowed Quoz' passage, but not by much.

'*It appears that a plenteous feast awaiteth us,*' the entity crooned in delight.

Daelan saw a fireball approach in his peripheral vision, so with a thought he enhanced the deflection shield to include thermal dampening. He also took the time to whisper the words for a spell that would protect him from lightning bolts, as his *dao* was not advanced enough to handle them yet.

He was far from invulnerable, though an observer might have disagreed while watching him dash between vampires, dodge attacks, and duck under their arms, all while cutting off limbs, slicing them in half, and lopping off heads. Daelan knew that things were still dicey because every time his shields deflected a gunshot, blade, or magical attack, it drained his mana.

After Daelan took the head of a vampire who'd blasted him with buckshot, he realized he had just over 50% of the mana he'd had when he'd picked up Imogen at the group home.

I shouldn't have shown off to her. The supersonic flying while camouflaged had taken twenty percent of his mana.

It was too late to regret. All he could do was survive and kill, because failure wasn't an option.

Though he continued to hack apart the vampires, one that always seemed to avoid him was particularly annoying, pelting his shields with rapid-fire from two pistols. He managed to hit Daelan on every shot even though he held the guns sideways like a dumbass, gangster-style.

Congratulations, you've got my attention, Daelan thought as he darted over and bisected the vampire diagonally from ribcage to clavicle.

There were only a few vampires left, and all of them, except a roaring maniac with a machete, looked ready to bolt. Daelan rushed at the vampire, obscured from sight by two fireballs that hit his shields from different directions. Though his eyesight was ruined for the two seconds that the fire blazed around him, his *movement* sensor field showed him exactly where the vampire was.

Daelan threw Quoz towards a mage that was preparing to cast a spell and tackled the vampire, letting the fireballs' residue cook him. The two somersaulted once, and the vampire was fried by a lightning bolt that, once again, slid off his shield.

Daelan rose out of the somersault and threw the smoking and twitching vampire at the lightning mage, giving it some extra oomph with telekinesis. The mage crumpled around the vampire and was hurled with it into the side of a building. The mighty "boom" shook the edifice. For a moment the vampire and mage stayed there, in a ghastly embrace, until the vampire slid down. The mage followed, looking like a broken doll that a child had thrown away in disgust.

The two remaining vampires turned tail and fled. Daelan was about to set upon the mages, his *movement/stillness* mana down to 20%, when a voice called out. "Daelan! We seek a truce!"

Daelan paused and turned to the mage who had spoken, the one who had attacked him with a staff in Des Moines.

"Under what terms?" As he spoke he summoned Quoz, who was feeding on another mage. He didn't bother wiping the blood off the blade. He knew Quoz preferred it that way.

"We'd like to have a peaceful exchange of information."

"Peaceful?" Daelan snorted. "If this is what you call 'peace', then what the hell would war look like?" Though he despised demons, he'd give them this—they wouldn't bother lying to your face after trying to kill you, unlike this shameless bastard.

"See it from our perspective. You massacred the vampires and killed one of our own who had done nothing to you. You are an otherworlder, clearly dangerous and with unknown intentions. How would you react if you were us?"

"Oh, I don't know. I might have tried talking with me," Daelan said sarcastically. He noticed with his third eye that some of the mages' mana cores were dim but becoming brighter. When he turned to look at one of them, they were snorting something up their nose.

The hell?

When he realized that the mage was likely buying time for his allies to increase their mana, he was enraged.

He changed Quoz to a throwing knife and hurled it at the mage with the staff. After it left his hand he stopped its spinning and sped it up to supersonic speeds. With a boom it flew through the air, the entity cackling with glee.

Daelan prepared to send the knife from mage to mage, but was surprised to see the man with the staff slow the knife down and dodge it, though he was left with a cut on his cheek.

Daelan resummoned Quoz while being pelted with fireballs and projectiles. One of the mages tried to capture his feet with asphalt, but Daelan was already on the move, running towards the staff mage while throwing Quoz at him again. Daelan could more effectively push Quoz the closer he got, and he was throwing for center mass, so while the mage dodged again, Quoz pierced his chest, perhaps puncturing a lung.

While the mage prepared to counterattack, Daelan juked to the side and, summoning Quoz, sliced through the shield of a young man next to the wizard and stunned him with a blow to the head.

Daelan moved in a blur behind the young man and held the knife at his throat.

"Parlay!"

The staff mage, who was leaking blood and wheezing, said, "The last time we tried to do that, you attacked us."

"The other mages were taking in mana. That was a hostile action."

The wizard snorted and then grimaced in pain. Daelan saw a couple of the wizards moving surreptitiously to get behind him.

"Take another step and the boy dies!" he roared.

"Stay where you are!" the staff mage wheezed. Looking at Daelan he asked, "What do you want?"

Gesturing to the cocoon that Imogen was trapped in, he said, "I want the girl, and to be left alone."

"We can accept that if you teach us what you know."

Daelan snorted. "So you can use it against us? Forget it."

"What do you suggest then?"

"Like I said: we leave, everybody who's left goes on their merry way."

The wizard considered, but with a sad look at Daelan's hostage said, "I don't think we can accept that."

The young man quivered in reaction. "Hold still!" Daelan hissed. To the wizard, "Why can't both sides retreat?"

"Because you have many answers that we need."

Daelan was angry, frustrated, and low on mana. He kept looking for a way to break the deadlock and couldn't find one.

Damn it! I'm sorry, Imogen. I'll be back for you.

After grabbing the young man around the torso with his free arm, Daelan said to the wizard. "If you harm Imogen in any way, I'll kill you all. Especially do not mess with her mind. I'll know."

"Wait! We can…"

Daelan didn't hear the rest of the mage's words. He flew up into the sky with his captive. He needed to find shelter to regroup and come up with a way to get Imogen back.

Chapter 26

"What are you going to do with me?!" the young man asked.

"I'm going to drop your ass if you don't shut up," Daelan growled as he flew through the air. There was no chance of that happening of course, but the kid didn't need to know that. Daelan needed to think, and didn't want any distractions.

He activated the camouflage spell in the arm cuff, making sure to cover both of them, and thought about what to do.

Part of him wanted to ignore the whole thing, create mana 24/7 to have enough to make a portal in two days, and get out of here. *Once I fix my body, I can come back and rescue her,* he reasoned.

The other part knew he would regret it and feel like an asshole if he did.

Damn it! I could die if I miss this window.

The next one was in nine months. Who knew what his body would be like then? He may not even make it nine months.

But he remembered the little girl who sang "I'm a little teapot". The girl who was relying on him, and was in this mess because of him. He knew that if he left her now, he would hate himself more than he already did.

"Damn it," he muttered.

Half a minute later, they descended to the parking lot of the motel he'd been staying at.

"Come on, and don't get any stupid ideas."

Daelan dragged the mage to the door by the hand and fumbled with the key. It felt like it took forever to open the door, but Daelan knew it was only a second or two. He almost pushed the young wizard inside until he remembered that he had to be in contact with him at all times to "protect" him from divination.

He sighed and walked in, still holding the boy's hand. After closing the door, Daelan took a good look at the boy for the first time. The young mage was scared, and didn't have the experience to keep it hidden.

"How old are you?"

"N-nineteen."

"What's your name?"

"Gabriel. Gabriel Sheffield."

"Well, Gabriel, I'm going to be straight with you. I'd rather not kill you, but my back is against the wall, and I can't afford to deal with problems. Do you understand?"

Gabriel paled and said, "I-I think so."

"As long as you are cooperative and helpful, I'll keep you alive. Otherwise, it's easier for me to get rid of you, since I clearly can't trade you for Imogen."

"Y-yes, sir."

At least he has a brain. "Good. I'm going to take your mana, okay? That will make you less of a problem for me, so don't resist."

"Okay."

Daelan slammed his palm into the boy's stomach, causing him to double up and start coughing and gasping for air. He ignored the boy's misery and pulled on his mana. Gabriel did resist, but Daelan didn't hold it against him. It would take a disciplined wizard not to, as holding onto the mana was instinctual. Nevertheless, he used his mana to overwhelm the boy, made easier by his disoriented state. Within a couple of seconds he had the dregs of the boy's mana, leaving him empty.

"Sorry. It's easier if I get closer to your mana core."

Gabriel coughed a couple of times, still doubled over, and said, "It's okay," but he sounded bitter.

Daelan gathered the mana from the arm cuff that he needed to cast a truth-sensing spell. It was expensive, but less than what he would need to invade the boy's mind. Besides, he didn't want to do that to the kid if he didn't have to.

He whispered the words of power and felt the spell lock into place.

"What was that?" the young mage asked, while looking up at Daelan with a hungry look.

"Truth spell."

That only intensified the boy's look.

"Tell you what, kid. If you cooperate with me, I'll teach you the spell. What do you think?"

Daelan was amused to see the warring feelings on the boy's face. Either the kid was the best actor in the world, or he was painfully inexperienced in dealing with adversaries.

"I won't help you hurt the others."

Daelan shook his head. "I don't want to hurt them. I just want to get Imogen back."

If Gabriel had had his own truth-sensing spell, it would have been screeching right then. Fortunately, Gabriel didn't, and Daelan's face gave away nothing. He'd learned how to lie from the best.

Gabriel nodded slowly. "Okay. What do you want?"

"Do they know I'm staying at this motel?"

"Not that I know of."

Truth.

Daelan was relieved, as that would make his life significantly easier. He realized that staff-guy might know and not have told the boy, though, so he remained wary.

"Was that all of the mages and vampires in the area?"

"No. There were two mages at the foster group home and four vampires, in case you got past the ambush."

Truth. "How did you know where I was?"

"We had a tracking spell on Imogen."

Truth. "Where will they take Imogen?"

"I don't know."

The truth-sensing spell gave an ambivalent response. Not a lie, but not exactly the truth either.

Daelan intentionally made himself look angry. It didn't take much acting. "Bullshit. Tell me!"

The boy paled and quickly said, "I don't know!" When Daelan lifted his arm to backhand Gabriel, he stammered, "They'll probably take her to our local branch headquarters!"

Truth. Daelan slowly lowered his arm. "That's better. Where is the headquarters?"

"Homestead."

"Where's that?"

"A little south of Miami."

"Who is the mage with the staff?"

"If you mean the one you were talking to…"

"Of course I mean the one I was talking to!"

196

The boy looked obstinate. "There was more than one wizard with a staff, you know."

"Whatever. Who is he?"

"Duncan Sheffield."

Daelan's eyebrows rose. "Relative of yours?"

Gabriel grimaced and said, "My father."

Remembering how the man refused to exchange hostages and retreat, Daelan said, "Damn. That's cold."

Gabriel's expression darkened, but said nothing.

"How do you guys get mana?"

The boy's eyes perked up. "Mana bones. How do you do it?"

"None of your business. What are mana bones?" Daelan didn't think that any of his siblings had ever heard of such a thing.

Gabriel pulled out a jade box and carefully opened it, showing that it contained two delicate bones. Using his third eye Daelan saw that they did indeed have mana that very slowly dissipated into the air. He was fascinated. "What do you do with them?"

"We grind them up and, uh, usually we snort them."

"Up your nose?"

"Yeah. Sometimes we mix it into tea and drink it."

Though Daelan was fascinated, it also seemed a little disgusting. "How do you get the bone powder out of your nose?"

Perhaps sensing Daelan's disdain, Gabriel looked embarrassed. "We use a neti pot with salt water to wash it out."

Daelan had no idea what a "neti pot" was, but it didn't matter. The spell said Gabriel was telling the truth, and he understood the gist of what the boy was saying.

"What spells do Society mages use to detect people?"

Gabriel narrowed his eyes in anger and said nothing.

"Give me something, boy."

"I said I wouldn't give you anything you could use to hurt the others!"

Daelan was, in a perverse way, pleased to see the boy had a bit of backbone. Still, he wouldn't let him simply not answer. He growled, "Yeah, and I said I don't want to hurt them. I still don't. I'm not asking you about their defenses."

Gabriel stubbornly kept his mouth shut.

"Look, I can break your mind open like a nut and suck out everything I want, and all it would cost me is more time to recover my mana. For you, on the other hand, it would cost you memories and likely your sanity. I'm trying to be a nice guy here, but I'm okay with being an asshole too."

Gabriel looked like a scared young man trying to be brave. "How do I know you're telling the truth?"

"You don't, but by the time I prove it, it'll be too late." After giving him five seconds, Daelan said, "Last chance."

Getting no reaction, he started to accumulate unaspected mana. He used a minuscule part of it to make a glowing, blood-red ball of light approximately the size of a head.

"Alright! What do you want to know?!" he said in a screech.

Daelan stopped gathering mana, but didn't dispel the ball of light.

"What detection spells does the Society use?"

Gabriel said with gritted teeth, "There are a lot of them. You'll need to be more specific."

"How are intruders into your branch headquarters detected?"

The questioning went on for some time, but Daelan eventually got what he wanted. He was helped by Gabriel's naïveté. He was usually so truthful with his answers that it was easy to tell when he was dissembling. With a shiftier person some half-truths might have slipped by.

What else should I ask him? Oh, duh. "I get why the vampires are after me. Why is the Society hunting me?"

"My father made a deal with the vampires. I don't know what they offered him to get us to help."

The truth-sensing spell was ambivalent in the way that Daelan had learned meant Gabriel was holding something back..

"What aren't you telling me?" Daelan said with an eye narrowed with suspicion.

Gabriel looked guilty. "J-just that they also want to know where you get mana."

Truth, but he didn't really need the spell for that one. If they relied on "mana bones", of course they'd want a better way to get mana.

"Where do you get the mana bones?"

"I don't know. Somewhere in the Bermuda Triangle. The exact location is secret."

"What's the 'Bermuda Triangle'?"

"A region in the ocean to the east of Florida. A lot of ships get lost there."

"Is there an island or something in this 'Triangle'?"

"Yes, a few of them where they dig up the bones."

"Why do they have mana, when Earth has almost none?"

"Earth used to have mana. We dig up bones from when and where it was abundant."

Now that's interesting. "Why is there so little mana now?"

"We don't know…" When Daelan started raising his arm angrily, Gabriel held his one free arm out placatingly, "I wasn't done! We don't know why, we just know that it depends on the polarity of the Earth's magnetic field."

"What?" Daelan was perplexed, but the spell assured him that the boy was telling the truth, or at least what he thought was the truth.

"The Earth's magnetic field sometimes changes direction. Right now it comes out of the north pole and goes into the south pole, but there've been times in history when it switched, and came out of the south pole. During those times the Earth had lots of mana."

"And you don't know why it switches, or why it makes mana only in the one direction?"

"No."

"Huh." He considered that for a minute, but decided it didn't have any immediate relevance.

"What's that for?" Gabriel asked, gesturing at the DC power supply.

Aw, crap. "Never mind that."

Gabriel's eyes widened. "That's how you're getting mana! Can you turn electricity into mana?"

Daelan frowned. He didn't like that Gabriel had figured out a piece of the puzzle, but without the runes the information was useless. Fortunately, his tattoo was covered up by his leather jacket. "I ask the questions. How many mana bones does your group have?"

Gabriel shifted uncomfortably. "I'm not sure. I do know that the effort to find you has used up a lot of bones."

Daelan sensed he was telling the truth, but holding back a bit. "Do they have enough to fill up their cores?"

"Yes."

After getting the address of the branch headquarters and finding out what spells the Society's mages used, Daelan couldn't think of any urgent questions. He looked at the boy and said, "I appreciate you being cooperative, Gabriel. Like I promised, I'm not going to kill you, but I need to tie you up."

Gabriel nodded glumly, but looked up after a moment. "Wait! You said you would teach me the truth-sensing spell!"

"And I will. After I tie you up."

The boy grumbled, but cooperated. The two performed an awkward dance involving cutting strips of Gabe's clothing with Quoz while Daelan touched Gabe to maintain the divination shield over both of them. While working, Daelan considered whether he should actually teach the spell to the young man. He didn't mind going back on his word, but decided that honoring it might have benefits later, at essentially no cost to him. Might as well build a reputation for honesty and blow it at a critical moment. Besides, he knew how to beat the spell. What better way to fool someone than to have their own truth-sensing spell do it for you?

When he was done, the young mage was tied to the four corners of the bed, gagged, and blindfolded. Daelan had also removed his mana bones, phone, and a pendant on a leather thong around his neck.

Still maintaining contact the entire time, Daelan used Quoz to cut runes in the floor around the bed. It was another protection from divination spellform. Daelan ignored Quoz's whispers that he should simply give the young mage to it. If he had to, he would, but Gabriel might be useful yet.

Once the spell was in place, Daelan released a sigh and pulled his hand away from the boy.

Finally.

He needed to build up his mana, and then he would get Imogen. And if they'd hurt her... Quoz would feed well.

Chapter 27

Daelan ended up not going to rescue Imogen until the next night. He was sorely tempted to go earlier, but knew it was important to have as much mana as possible.

In that vein, instead of flying, he called a cab.

Man, I'm tired of losing bikes.

Fortunately, the driver, Hafez, was not a talkative type. When they were a couple of blocks away Daelan said, "You can drop me off at the corner." When the car rolled to a stop, he gave Hafez a $100 bill and slid out.

Just an hour ago, Daelan had confirmed Gabriel's guess that Imogen would be held at the local headquarters. His initial attempts to divine her location had been thwarted by a surprisingly good shield. He had ended up trying a soul-based divination that only worked for family members. He honestly hadn't been sure if it would work or not, and had been gratified when the connection was made.

As far as the universe was concerned, he and Imogen were family. It felt... good.

As he walked to the branch headquarters, camouflage spell running, he went over the defenses that Gabriel had outlined. It turned out that most of them were technological because mana was so expensive. The headquarters had all the usual locks, cameras, alarms, fence, etc., but no normie guards. That was also a mana thing. They didn't want to have to modify the guards' memories every time they saw something they shouldn't have.

There was one magical alarm, and the pendant Gabriel wore was one of the keys. It also served as an ID badge for the technological locks, but Daelan assumed that Gabriel's access had already been cut off.

They couldn't deactivate the magical side of the pendant so easily because, unlike the unique technological IDs, everyone had the same magical key. Gabriel explained that whenever a pendant was lost, the local chapters put the magical alarm in lockdown mode until the pendant was recovered, which usually didn't take long given that the pendants were also tracking anchors.

In lockdown mode, nobody could get through the alarm without it sounding, unless it was temporarily turned off.

All this meant that Gabriel's pendant probably wasn't useful to Daelan, so he hadn't bothered bringing it.

When Daelan turned the next corner he saw the Society's branch headquarters. It was surrounded by an old-fashioned wrought iron fence with spear-point tips. Ivy weaved its way through the ironwork, softening its image. A large Spanish-style mansion sat behind the fence. Several upward-pointing lights illuminated the orange terracotta, making it feel like a warm ember in the dark.

Daelan opened his third eye to see the magical alarm.

Damn.

He had hoped it would extend a few feet above the fence and stop, but there was a glistening dome covering the entire building and much of the yard. It might have even been a sphere extending into the ground.

Daelan telekinetically launched himself twenty feet into the air and flew above the fence and cameras to one of the property's rear corners. Once he was on the ground inside the fence line, he examined the barrier.

Daelan determined that he could drain its mana, but that would likely announce his presence just as effectively as the alarm itself. It was time for Plan B: waiting. Maintaining the camouflage spell would tax his unaspected mana, but there was no help for it.

Fortunately, it shouldn't take long for Gabriel's anti-divination spellform to run out of mana.

Though his father was clearly a ruthless bastard, Daelan was betting he wouldn't be able to resist sending someone to get his son once they knew where he was, even if he suspected it was a trap. Perhaps the father would even go himself. Either way, they'd have to turn off the magical barrier to let the mages through, and that would be Daelan's chance.

While he waited, he reestablished his connection with Imogen to fine-tune her location.

Other corner.

Daelan carefully walked to the other rear-corner of the house, putting himself only ten meters from the girl. He released the connection to save on mana and waited for something to happen.

Fifteen minutes later, he heard a door slam open and saw the magic barrier disappear.

Go time.

The next few minutes were anticlimactic. Daelan moved to the house, found a spot that wasn't covered by cameras, and released the camouflage spell. And then he waited some more. The barrier came back up, which was fine. He wanted the mages that were still here to feel secure, and for the mages who'd left to get far away.

After another fifteen minutes, he decided to make his move. He whispered the words of a spell that gave him a ghostly appearance, and walked through the wall. He saw Imogen sitting at a table, head resting on an open book, asleep, while the bed lay unused.

Sleep on, Imogen. We'll leave soon.

Daelan was on a clock, because he would run out of unaspected mana soon. He quietly cast a spell that gave him x-ray vision. He could still see objects, but they were ghostly. The mages' mana cores, on the other hand, blazed brightly.

There were nine of them. One in the library, one in the kitchen, two sleeping in bedrooms, and five talking in the main room.

Daelan stepped through one of the walls, entering an occupied bedroom. He released the ghost spell and replaced it with a silencing field created by his *stillness* mana. It had the dual benefit of making all of his actions quiet and preventing nearby mages from casting their spells.

He had learned from Gabriel that the Society mages knew nothing about runes, the *dao*, or aspected mana, which meant they could only cast spells by saying the words of power. No voice, no spell.

What followed was a massacre.

Daelan used Quoz to kill the two sleeping mages and the one in the library. He didn't bother walking through the walls or even camouflaging himself. He just maintained the x-ray vision and silence spells.

When only the group in the main room was left, he paused to consider how best to kill the mages. He thought about incinerating them with a fireball, as it would be a very efficient use of his aspected mana.

He decided not to, though, because the wizards might be able to create shields in time, and, well, it simply wasn't needed.

And it would be a shame to waste their lifeforce and whatever money they have in their pockets.

Quoz laughed. *'This was why I contracted with you, Daelan. You were a killer from the day you were born.'*

Daelan frowned. Father had been a killer, sure, but he had tried to be more than that. That was the whole point of the Sum of All Men project.

Quoz's opinion bothered him. Daelan knew he had been more than a killer when he was created, but he also knew his time in Hell had changed him.

Whatever I am, gazing at my navel isn't going to change it. Focus on the mission.

Daelan released the x-ray vision spell and used his aspected mana to increase his speed. What followed was a surreal, soundless sword dance amidst red curtains of blood. The mages' horrified faces grew ever paler as the dance progressed. The blood drained from their faces when they realized that their spells were useless, when they helplessly witnessed the horror of the gory scene before them, and finally, when they were bled like slaughtered pigs, blood cooling on the floor.

Daelan unsummoned Quoz and beheld what he had wrought.

Quoz was right. He was a killer. As he turned to walk to Imogen's room he thought, *But that's not all there is to me.*

Chapter 28

Eleanor

Eleanor's father was quiet as he drove. She was silent too, because she could tell how tightly wound he was. He'd aged years in the two days since her brother was taken, but he wasn't the kind of man that would talk about it.

Though she knew how dedicated her father was to the Society, even she'd been surprised when he refused the otherworlder's offer to exchange prisoners. Though she still loved her father, she looked at him differently now. How could she not, knowing that he considered his children to be expendable?

"You know this is likely a trap, right?" she asked carefully.

"Yes," he said grimly. "I know."

"Then why are we doing this?"

He took his eyes off the road to glare at her. "Because we have to get Gabe."

"It didn't seem like a high priority the other day," she said bitterly.

"I… I made a mistake. I didn't think Daelan would leave the girl."

"So you bet Gabe's life on it?"

"I said I made a mistake!" he roared, anger born from guilt and fear filling his voice.

She checked the tracking spell. "Take a left at the light." After a moment she asked, "So, are we just going to go straight in?"

"Do you have a better idea?"

"Not really." She went back and forth on whether she should say more or shut up. She decided to say what she was thinking. "We should have approached him peacefully."

Duncan glowered at the road. "Don't you remember what you told me about the mana at the portal site?"

Eleanor frowned. "It felt evil," she admitted.

"And then he goes and massacres a bunch of vampires…"

"Killing vampires doesn't exactly make you a bad guy, Dad."

"It does when it disturbs world peace! It took our ancestors a hundred years to get the vampires to agree to be parasites instead of killers!"

Eleanor knew that. What frustrated her was that even though she would have done things differently, she didn't really disagree with him.

The direction the tracking spell was pointing at was changing quickly now.

"Take a right at the next street. I think we're close."

A minute later they pulled into the parking lot of the "Traveler's Paradise" motel. They quickly determined which room held Gabriel and approached with their shields active.

"Let me go in first," Duncan whispered.

"You're not just going to walk in, are you?"

"Of course not." Saying that, he approached until he was 15 feet away and cast his own telekinesis spell that ripped the door off its hinges and blasted it into the room. It came to rest on the floor next to a bed where Gabriel lay spread-eagled, gagged, and blindfolded.

"Gabe!" she shouted.

"Hush!" her father commanded. He carefully walked in, staff pointed forward. He checked the closet and bathroom before deciding the room was safe.

Father and daughter walked into the bedroom.

Duncan said, "I'm sorry it took us so long to get you, Gabe. We'll…"

At that moment he stepped on the door, the back of which was covered in mana-empowered runes. Sensing their pendants, the spell activated, bursting the wood upwards in a spray of deadly shrapnel.

Duncan's last act was to push his daughter away. Though his shield was still active, much of the door was inside it. The wood shrapnel ripped through his body, embedding flesh, bone, and blood into the ceiling.

"*No!*" Eleanor screamed.

Horrified at the grisly scene, Eleanor was in shock. "He… he… he's gone, Gabe." She eventually realized that her brother was yelling through the gag and squirming. Like a robot, she pulled out a knife and cut the makeshift "rope" holding her brother.

He too broke down after removing the gag and blindfold.

"He...he told me he didn't want to hurt anyone!"

"And you believed him?" she asked bitterly.

"I..." He hung his head in shame. "I did. I thought he just wanted to get Imogen."

Staring at what was left of their father, Eleanor said, "We have to get him, Gabe. We have to get the otherworlder."

"We will, Ellie. I promise you."

Chapter 29

Daelan

Daelan hardly glanced at the blood-soaked corpses of his enemies before turning to find Imogen and wake her up. He paused, though, because he realized he couldn't take her back to the group home, so the two of them would have to survive the next nine months on the run. They were going to need money. Though she could help him toss the mansion faster, he didn't want her to see this.

He only gave himself eight minutes to look for money and valuables. He came away with a little over $3000 in cash and more gold and gems. The money was desperately needed because all of the remaining jewelry and most of the cash had been in the saddlebags of the Goldwing.

"Imogen," he said as he gently agitated her back. "It's time to wake up."

She groggily raised her head, then jerked it up and stared at him. "Daelan?!" she whispered. "You came for me!"

He smiled gently. "Of course I did. I couldn't leave my favorite niece with these assholes."

She looked like she wanted to cry but was holding it in as she said, "I was hoping you would, but after I waited a day, I figured you must have left..."

He shook his head softly. "No. It was my fault you got into this mess, and I wasn't going to leave you in it."

"What about your body falling apart?"

He grimaced. "We'll figure that out later. Come on."

He had to walk her through the main room to get to the front door, but he'd taken a moment to grab bedsheets and throw them over the bodies. He winced when he saw blood had soaked the sheets, making it clear what they were hiding.

"Is that...?"

"Yeah. Sorry you had to see that." She paused, looking at the covered bodies, so he grabbed her hand and said, "Come on."

She nodded wordlessly and followed him out.

When they were outside he crouched down and said, "Here, get on my back again." She climbed on and remembered to not choke him this time. "Ready?"

"Yeah."

Daelan crouched to leap into the air to jump into the air, perhaps subconsciously trying to act like a superhero for her. The effect was ruined when he groaned, his knees spiking with pain.

"Are you okay?"

"Yeah, fine," he muttered, and simply lifted himself with his *movement* mana.

They did not fly far. Though Daelan had plenty of aspected mana to fly with, he was critically low on the unaspected mana he needed for the protection from divination and camouflage enchantments, the only truly essential spells at the moment.

He took them to their new motel room, where he had already moved the DC power supply, and immediately started creating unaspected mana that he shoved into the arm cuff.

Imogen stared at him. "What are you doing? And why are we still holding hands?" Daelan had not let go since landing.

"Making mana, the stuff I use to power my spells. We're holding hands because I cast a spell that keeps the mages from knowing where we are. I have to touch you for it to work."

She took in his grimacing face. Though he was used to pain and the mana creation process, between being constantly shocked and his increasingly achy body, he looked uncomfortable.

"Are you sure you're okay?"

He nodded with a sardonic smile. "Yeah. Just a little sore."

She looked down at their still-linked hands. "We don't have to do this forever, do we?"

He shook his head. "No. As soon as I've built up some more mana, I'll make a piece of jewelry that will do the same thing."

Imogen's eyes were red, and she looked worn out, her chin resting on her knees as she sat on the bed. "Thanks for getting me out."

"You're welcome. I'm sorry I couldn't get there faster."

"No problem." She wiped her nose and looked over at Daelan. "So, what do we do now?"

Daelan sighed. "That's a good question. You can't go back to the group home..." He looked over and saw her teary smile. "...which I can see you're broken up about. The way I see it, you have two options."

"What are they?"

"Go into hiding under a new name. I have $13,000 in the bank. It's not a lot, but you could use it to start somewhere new. The other option is to come with me."

Imogen's eyebrows raised. "You would take me? What changed your mind?"

Daelan grimaced. "I feel bad for getting you into this mess. Also, I'd have nine months to get you ready before we could go."

"Nine months? I thought you were going to go today? With your body falling apart, why wouldn't you go sooner than that?"

"I can't. I can only make the portal at certain times, and the next one is nine months from now."

"I'm sorry," she whispered.

"No," he said, awkwardly putting his hand on her shoulder. "It's not your fault, it's mine, and it was my choice."

"Did you think about leaving?"

"No," he lied.

"Thanks."

He nodded. "Of course."

"So does this mean you'll teach me magic?"

"Yeah. If you're coming with me."

She was quiet for a minute. "Can you teach me something now?"

"Does that mean you've decided to stay with me?"

She shrugged. "I can stay here and be poor, or go with you and learn magic. It's not a hard choice."

"There's a good chance you'll die if you come with me."

"I could die if I stay and they find me."

"True. Alright, I'll teach you." Daelan looked at her contemplatively, wondering how he should begin. "How are you with science?"

Imogen shrugged. "Okay, I guess?"

"Tell me some of the different kinds of energy."

She looked at his apparatus and said, "Um, electricity?"

Daelan smiled. "That was an easy one. Give me some more."

"Kinetic?"

"Right. Keep going."

"Uh, gravity?"

"Not exactly, no. That's enough for now. Suffice it to say there are different types of energy, and some of them are higher order than others. The lowest order of energy is heat. Do you know what heat is?"

Imogen looked at him like she thought it was a weird question. "It's temperature, right?"

Daelan pursed his lips. *We have a lot of ground to cover.* "Close enough. The point I'm getting at is that heat is the lowest-order energy, which means that it isn't very good for converting to other forms of energy, but everything can convert to heat with 100% efficiency."

"So, if you convert electricity to heat...?"

Daelan nodded. "100% efficiency, which means every bit of it can become heat."

"Why is heat the worst kind of energy?"

Daelan chewed on his lip. "That's a good question, but the explanation requires more education. Let me say it like this: heat is the most random and least organized form, and therefore the worst."

"Random is bad?"

"Not 'bad' per se. What it is is the most common and least useful." Daelan could tell she wasn't getting it, so he decided to use an example. "Imagine I have a cardboard box, and I put 50 ping pong balls in the box and keep shaking it."

"Okay."

"At any given moment in time, where are those ping pong balls going to be?"

"They'll be spread out in the box."

"Right. We don't know exactly where they'll be, but they'll be spread out." He paused and asked, "Is it possible for all 50 balls to be on the left side of the box?"

"Well, if you tip the box..."

"Nope. No tipping, just shaking it. Can they all be on one side?"

"Probably not."

"Right," he said, giving her a nod of acknowledgement. "It *can* happen, but it is exceedingly unlikely. Heat is the ping pong balls all spread out. It's the most common and least interesting form. If all the ping pong balls were on one side, that would be unusual and even useful. Wherever there are differences, like a bunch of ping pong balls in one area and none in the other, you can use those differences. That's why when something is hot and something else is cold, we can use that difference to make things happen."

Imogen looked skeptical. "How could having all the ping pong balls on one side be useful?"

Daelan quirked his lips because he was pleased that she was asking questions and thinking about what he was saying.

"Okay, you got me. Ping pong balls aren't terribly useful, but that's because this is just an example. Still, let's say we wanted to move a tissue in the middle of the box. In the case where the ping pong balls are spread out, where is the tissue going to go?"

"No idea."

"Right. It will just move around randomly in the middle of the box. Now, same situation. Tissue in the middle of the box, but all the ping pong balls are on one side of the box. What will happen?"

"The tissue will be pushed to the empty side of the box."

"Right. It will move farther, and in a predictable direction, meaning that you can, in theory, do something with it. The side with all the ping pong balls is analogous to something hot. The empty side is something cold. Many useful machines, like power plants, do their thing by taking advantage of temperature differences."

"Hm. So heat is a crappy form of energy, but you can still do something with it where there are temperature differences." Imogen seemed thoughtful. "So what does this have to do with mana?"

"Mana is, in a way, the opposite of heat. It is the highest-order energy, and can transform into every other kind with 100% efficiency."

"Huh. That sounds kind of cool, but I don't really know what it means."

"That's alright. I'll help you learn over time. That, and a lot of other things you need to know."

She frowned. "That sounds an awful lot like school."

"Like homeschool anyway."

"Will I turn into a nerd?" Imogen asked with a smile.

Daelan shrugged. "You already look kind of dorky, so…"

"Rude!" Imogen said, surprised but still laughing.

Daelan chuckled, but then looked at her seriously. "Just remember what the goal is."

"What's the goal?"

"Power. Become powerful enough so the next time someone tries to take you, you can kick their balls up into their throat."

Imogen smirked. "I like the sound of that."

"I thought you might."

**

Imogen quickly learned that staying with Daelan wasn't as exciting as she thought it would be, because she was cooped up in the motel room. Even though he set up protection from divination runes like he had for Gabriel, she was confined to the bed. To go anywhere else she had to hold his hand.

That caused problems that neither one had foreseen.

"Daelan, I really need to go to the bathroom!"

"It's almost ready, just hold on a little longer."

"I *can't* hold on much longer!"

"Five minutes! Just give me five minutes."

Daelan had initially started working on an arm cuff for Imogen that could run the protection spell without her direct intervention, as long as someone fed it mana periodically. When he realized she needed something faster, he grabbed a ruby ring he'd taken from a mage and used his motion mana to carve the required runes.

He had to be careful because all sorts of bad things could happen if he wasn't precise. Almost anything could happen, from leaking mana to exploding. Perhaps even worse would be if the protection from divination worked, but had flaws. Imogen's protection from divination needed to be flawless.

He finished, injected some of his unaspected mana into the ruby, and handed it to her.

"Okay, it's ready. Here."

Imogen, who had her legs crossed and was hunched over, frantically put it on her right ring finger and dashed to the bathroom.

"Wait! Let me make sure…" he drifted off, realizing it was too late. He sighed and thought, *Hopefully the ring worked.*

**

Over the next few days Daelan really started hating this world full of records, IDs, and mass communication. His and Imogen's names and faces were all over the local news, him as the kidnapper and her as the kidnapped.

He had a spell that could change his face enough to be unrecognizable, and wigs and makeup would be good enough for Imogen as long as she was with someone that didn't look like him.

The real problem was identification. Daelan burned his driver's license and everything else that identified him as "Daelan Peregrinus" so he wouldn't be tempted to use them. Now he just had to figure out a way to replace them with a new identity, or somehow get along without one.

"Can't you get a new license from the guy you used before?" Imogen asked.

Daelan shook his head. "It would be too risky. The Society probably tracked him down after talking to my boss at the bar."

"So what do we do?"

Daelan frowned. "I'm not sure. For now, I'm going to change my appearance. Hopefully we'll think of something tomorrow."

"Is changing going to hurt?"

"Part of it is reshaping bones, moving them around, and all the tissue changes that go with that. What do you think?"

Imogen looked guilty. "Sorry. You wouldn't have to do this if you hadn't come for me."

His expression softened. "Don't worry about it. This is nothing. You have much worse to look forward to if you keep walking this path."

"Great," she said sarcastically. "I can't wait."

Daelan walked into the bathroom and looked into the mirror, analytically looking at his face and deciding what he wanted his new look to be. He used a picture of an average person on Instagram to be the basis for his new face. They wouldn't look like identical twins, but, if he did the job well, like brothers, perhaps.

He decided to create a new eye for himself, as people would surely be looking for a man with one eye. He hadn't before now because it was so expensive and he'd gotten used to just having one.

Once he cast the spell and started sculpting his face, he was careful to not make any sounds. He didn't want Imogen to know how much it hurt.

**

"I'm going out," he said the next night.

"Where are you going?"

"I just want some fresh air."

Imogen looked at him suspiciously. "You've never gone out for 'fresh air' before."

Daelan's long-practiced deception instincts prevented the frown that he felt like making. "Maybe I want to see how women I'm not related to react to the new face," he said with a grin. He now looked like he had some east asian genes, with black, almond shaped eyes, a narrow face, and black hair.

She stared at him for a few seconds. Daelan rolled his eyes and turned around, about to walk out.

"Why are you really going out?"

Damn it. Should have used a better lie.

He sighed, let the frown escape, and turned around. "I'm going to get ID."

"How?"

"You don't want to know."

"I don't want you to kill people, Uncle Daelan."

Daelan narrowed his eyes. "Do you have any better options? How exactly do you think I'm going to get revenge for your

215

parents, Imogen? Send sternly worded letters? I'm going to kill people."

She looked troubled, unsure of herself. "I know that, but I don't want you to kill people that didn't have anything to do with it."

"And when they send soldiers after us? What then? You realize they'll be people that had nothing to do with the assassinations, and are just following orders, right?"

"That's self-defense."

Daelan was frustrated. He both envied and despised her innocence and naïveté. "And when we do 'defend ourselves', what about the people who get caught in the crossfire? You know that's going to happen, right?"

"I... I don't know. But please, let's try to avoid killing people who don't deserve it."

Daelan sighed. "Fine. Help me come up with some ideas then."

**

The next night Daelan soared through the sky. He'd had to wait a day after they came up with a plan so he could put more unaspected mana into the arm cuff. The new plan required it.

When he arrived at the police station, he dropped onto the roof and used his x-ray vision spell to scout out the interior.

Bunch of desks and some people... holding cell... empty rooms... Lobby... shelves with boxes—bingo.

He was relieved to see that the evidence room was unmanned. They had hoped it would be since it was the middle of the night, but hadn't been sure.

Daelan walked to a spot above the evidence room and whispered the words to the ghostly form spell. When it took hold, he slipped through the roof and down into the room. His mana was being pulled out of the arm cuff in torrents, so he cut off the spell as quickly as he could, while leaving the camouflage spell active.

The room was filled with very practical and completely undecorated metal shelves that held a couple hundred cardboard boxes. The boxes were labeled with case numbers, but Daelan ignored them. Though the boxes had items he could use, there was much better nearby.

The room had four doors. One to the rest of the building, one to the drugs room, one to the guns room, and the last door, the one he'd come here for: the freezer room.

Inside the room that made even him feel a chill were more shelves and boxes. Daelan paused to look at them, wondering what stories they held.

He sensed that this room represented pain and misery, like an ever-changing monument to the dark heart of man.

Daelan did a slow circuit of the room, brushing the top of each box. He was looking for dust. Dust meant time. Years. Years of looking for a demon and not finding them. It meant a case that hadn't been touched in years, but couldn't be thrown away. It meant murder.

There were three boxes in a barely-lit corner that were covered in the cloak of time. The first held three plastic bags: one with a few hairs, another with some sort of fiber, and the third with a soiled pair of panties.

Ew. Rapist, he thought with disgust. Not what he was looking for, but if the others were no good, he could come back to it. He solemnly closed the box and put it back before opening the next.

He sifted through the plastic bags until he found what he was looking for—blood. It was dried and brown in the plastic sample jar, but it would do.

Jackpot.

He was displeased when he saw that there was more than one sample, but hopefully at least one of them had the blood of the perpetrator. He grabbed all the blood and hair samples and prepared to leave.

Daelan thought about looking through the last box, but decided to leave it. He could always come back if needed.

He was ready to start hunting.

**

"Did you get what you needed?" Imogen asked when Daelan walked in.

"Yeah," he said with a small smile. "It worked."

"When will you do the spell?"

"In just a moment."

Daelan pulled out the plastic jar of blood and unscrewed the cap.

"Is that what you're going to use as the link?"

"Yeah. There's a reason blood symbolizes life. Without it, we're dead. Our bodies desperately try to keep it, so it makes a good link. The blood and the body want to be restored to each other, even when the blood is this old."

"But, uh…" Imogen's face twisted up, as if she wanted to say something, but wasn't sure if she should. "Won't the blood be the victim's?"

Feeling stupid, Daelan muttered, "If the victim fought, it might be the murderer's, but yeah, you're probably right. Let's use the hair instead."

Hair was nowhere near as good as blood—hairs were meant to fall out and be discarded, after all—but they were still pretty good. And besides, unless the murderer happened to be a mage, it's not like the spell would be blocked by anything.

Daelan took one of the hairs and looked at Imogen. "Ready?"

She nodded while staring at the hair, looking extremely focused. He turned back to the hair and whispered the words of power while imbuing them with mana. The words, translated from runic speech, meant:

> Like to like, as father to son;
> Find your forebear, and ever be one.

It worked on the principle of sympathetic magic. The hair had been part of the person. The point of the spell was to reestablish that connection. It was not even a tracking spell, per se. Using the connection to find the person was just one, somewhat crude way it could be used. It could also be used to cast spells on them at a reduced cost, much like he did with the runic plates when he tried to kill Aisha Aemilianus.

Daelan was fortunate that he discovered and cut off the mages' magical connection to himself before their confrontation. If they had been able to cast spells on him directly while attacking him… He shuddered at the thought. The fight would probably have gone much differently.

When the incantation was done, pure mana from his arm cuff was drawn into one end of the hair and, as if it were the world's tiniest trumpet, pulsed out the other end and spread through the air, filling it with music that was only meant for one set of ears.

Go and find them, Daelan commanded. As if the mana were listening, it broke into tendrils that spread out through the city, seeking the head that bore the hair.

Hopefully it's not a hair from the victim.

Daelan hooked himself up to the DC power supply and turned on the power. It would probably take time to find the killer, and the arm cuff was getting low again. Sighing, he flipped the switch on, grimacing as the lights dimmed for a moment.

**

A connection was made an hour and a half later. It was weak, being made from hair—old hair at that—but it was plenty good enough for Daelan's purposes.

"I've got a connection," he told Imogen. "I'll see you later."

"Good luck!"

As Daelan flew through the night air, he wondered if the person he was tracking was the murderer, and if so, what they were like. He had met many murderers in Hell as spirits, but he was curious to see if it would be any different when they were alive.

After flying 60 miles, he came to the end of the trail in a quiet suburb. The homes were small and based on just two or three patterns. Slight variations in paint colors, the condition of their lawns, and the occasional basketball hoop or toys lying around were the only things that distinguished them from the outside.

The house that the hair drew him to looked disheveled. Paint was peeling, and the roof sagged here and there. The house looked like a middle-aged man who was way past his prime and had given up on ever looking good again. An old Mustang with rust spots sat in the driveway.

Daelan walked up to the door and rang the doorbell. He heard a few muffled noises, but then nothing, so he rang again.

"Whaddaya want?" a man yelled out.

For the second time in the same evening, Daelan felt foolish. He had not thought about what he would do if the man didn't come to the door.

"I want to speak with you."

"About what?"

Annoyed, Daelan said, "About repairing your roof."

"It doesn't need it. Go away!"

Sighing, Daelan sensed the locks and, using his *motion* mana, manipulated the pins and cylinder of the deadbolt such that it unlocked. He entered the house and closed the door behind himself, taking no great pains to be quiet.

A paunchy man who looked like he was in his sixties shuffled over with a drink in his hand, looking outraged. "Hey, what the hell do you think you're doing?"

"We need to talk, Mr. …"

"Miller. Why should I talk with you instead of calling the police?"

"Feel free, but when they come, I'm going to tell them that you're a murderer."

Daelan saw him react, but he recovered quickly. "I don't know who the hell you are, but that was cleared up a long time ago. I'm calling the police." He turned around and started walking away, so Daelan used his *motion* mana to pick up a chair from the kitchen table and slide it into the back of Mr. Miller's legs, causing him to fall back into the chair. He then slid the chair and man until they were before him.

"I'd like to talk with you first, Mr. Miller."

The man looked frightened. "H-how did you do that?"

Daelan smiled. "Magic." He made a mystical gesture as a joke while he cast a silence spell around them.

For a moment, the man was flummoxed. He recovered and sneered. "Yeah, right. Is this some prank?" He looked around. "Where are the cameras?" His expression changed, though, when he tried to stand up and was not able to. "Hey! Hey! You can't do this to me!"

Daelan ignored him while he tied him to the chair with rope he had bought, holding him through telekinesis while he worked.

Daelan frowned when he was done, because he was already tired of dealing with the man. He decided to cut to the chase by casting a silence sphere around them, followed by a spell that stimulated the man's pain nerves. It was a specialized spell from the branch of illusion magic that caused pain without actually damaging the body.

"OW! What the hell was that!"

"That was more magic," Daelan said with a grin. "The fun kind." Though he did not find torture fun, he found that making his victims think he enjoyed it caused them to break faster.

"What kind of bullshit is th...?"

Daelan restarted the spell, causing Mr. Miller to scream. He let it go a little longer, about a second, and then released it. Mr. Miller looked at him, horrified, while he panted.

"That is the lowest pain level. I can go higher. Would you like to try it?"

"No! No!" He panted some more while shaking his head. "Please... what do you want to talk about?"

Daelan smiled. "That's better. Let's talk about the murder. Tell me all about it."

"I didn't murder anyone!"

Daelan raised his hand, causing Mr. Miller to frantically shout, "I didn't do it, but I can tell you what happened! Okay? Then you'll see I didn't do it!"

Daelan said nothing, but lowered his hand and nodded at him to continue while silently whispering the incantation for a truth spell.

"It was a long time ago—fifteen years in August. My brother, Tom, was a lawyer, a hotshot defense attorney. He'd spent time as an ADA, and then went into private practice, defending scumbags. Said he knew all the prosecutors' tricks and how to fight against them. He got a lot of people off, and got rich off of them."

The spell indicated that everything Mr. Miller said was true, so Daelan let him keep going.

"Well, one day in August—I think it was the eleventh— someone broke into his office late at night and killed him. Shot him in the chest, arm, and head. The police never figured out who did it. Said there were a ton of people who had motives, from the criminals he put away to his clients who went to jail. There was no conclusive DNA evidence, so they had to drop it."

True, but deceptive.

Daelan had to struggle to not roll his eyes. Like he couldn't already tell that Mr. Miller wasn't telling him everything. He decided to not beat around the bush.

"Did you kill your brother?"

"No!"

False.

His fate was sealed, but Daelan decided to follow through to get the story, mostly out of curiosity.

"Why did you kill him?"

"I told you, I didn't!"

Daelan activated the pain spell and let it run for a couple of seconds.

"Stop lying to me."

"I'm not..." he struggled to get out as he panted, "...lying to you."

Without saying another word, Daelan reactivated the spell. Mr. Miller screamed.

When the spell ended and he recovered his breath, Mr. Miller yelled for help. Daelan let him, until he tired himself out.

"Are you done now? Have you been convinced that no one is going to come?"

"What do you want with me?" the man blubbered, tears and snot running down his face.

"I want the truth. You know you killed your brother. I know you killed him. Why did you do it?"

Mr. Miller was surprisingly resistant. He lasted ten more minutes before he broke. It turned out to be a sordid tale of resentment, love, and betrayal.

Tom was the athletic and popular brother, so Mr. Miller focused on his grades to get his parents' love and attention. It worked, sort of, but he always thought they loved Tom more. Mr. Miller became a corporate drone, married a kind woman, and they did the whole "house and white picket fence" thing. He finally felt like the more successful brother, since Tom didn't make as much as a prosecutor. When he became a defense attorney, though, that all changed. Over the next decade he bought a million dollar house, BMWs, Rolex watch, and tailored suits. His wife ended up working for Tom as an assistant. Mr.

Miller didn't love the arrangement, but they liked it, so he went along. Everything was great, until he found them *in flagrante delicto* one late "work night".

"You and your brother were identical twins?"

"Yes."

Hence why there was no incriminating DNA evidence. "Why didn't your wife say something?"

"She didn't want me to go to jail." He looked up with a bitter smile. "Said she loved me. I think she just wanted alimony and child support."

"Do you have kids?"

"Yeah."

Ambiguous truth.

Huh? What's that about? Oh. He's not sure if his kids are his or not.

Daelan had mixed feelings about Mr. Miller. Part of him thought he was pathetic, but part of him felt pity. Those were, he supposed, two sides of the same coin.

"Mr. Miller, you are a murderer, and are going to die tonight." The man just nodded, resigned to his fate. The only evidence of emotional impact was more tears streaming down his face. "You have a choice, though. I would like your help with something. It will not be painful, I just need to practice something. If you cooperate with me, not only will you die painlessly, I will make it pleasant for you."

Mr. Miller snorted. "And how would you do that?"

"It's just like the pain, except the opposite."

"And if I don't cooperate?"

"Then you are going to do a lot of screaming tonight."

"Gee, it's such a hard choice," he said bitterly.

"I'm glad you can see the sweet light of reason," Daelan said as he untied one of his arms. "I'm going to ask you to do some things, and I want you to try to not do them. And don't worry, I won't punish you if you succeed."

"O-okay…" he said hesitantly, clearly not sure if he could take the promise to not torture him at face value.

"Alright. Lick the palm of your hand."

"No?" he said, cringing a bit.

Daelan whispered an incantation and imbued his words with a tiny bit of power. *"Lick the palm of your hand."*

Mr. Miller opened his mouth and started to move his hand to it before he stopped and stammered, "N-no!"

"Good," Daelan praised. *Let's up the power a bit and try again.*

It was going to be a long but productive night, hopefully. It wasn't often you could practice mind-altering spells without worrying about damaging your subject.

**

The next morning, Daelan sighed as he looked at his new face in the mirror.

All that pain to look like this loser. Whatever. Freedom is more important than looks.

Though he'd never considered himself to be a vain person, he wasn't a big fan of "Mr. Miller's" receding hairline and premature wrinkles. The man had only been 47, but looked like he was 67. He stopped to consider if he didn't worry too much about looks in Hell because power was far more important to demons. When he was in charge, he could have looked like a literal toad and still had whatever demoness he wanted.

Disgusted at this weakness, he turned away from the mirror and resolved to not worry about it. He had things to do, after all. First and foremost among them? Get some wheels.

Buying his new ride was painful, both because he was short on cash and because he decided it was time to ditch the motorcycles. He kept losing them, and his enemies would probably be looking for a guy and a girl on a bike. For the sake of blending in, it was time to switch to a car.

The problem was, the only cars he could afford were pieces of crap. Though he'd slowly been filling up his Cayman Islands bank account with less-than-$10,000 deposits, there wouldn't be any more deposits for the foreseeable future, because he had to leave his web development job. It was tied to "Daelan Peregrinus", who was now wanted for kidnapping.

He ended up settling for an old, dinged-up Toyota Corolla, consoling himself that the only thing that mattered was that it ran.

After he drove it to the motel, he took Imogen to the local Department of Motor Vehicles. An hour and a half later they walked out with an ID for her, as one Marissa Miller, and left behind a worker who was missing a chunk of memory.

"We should celebrate!" Imogen said.

"What did you have in mind?"

"I heard there's a good salad bar nearby. Let's go check it out."

Daelan frowned. "Salad?" He turned to stare at her intensely, and in his best "hypnotist voice" he said, "You don't want salad, you want steak…"

Imogen's eyes went wide in alarm, as she had just witnessed what Daelan could make people do. "Hey! Don't do tha…" When she realized he was joking, she hit him in the shoulder. "Jerk. Don't scare me like that!"

Daelan just chuckled. "Alright, if you insist, we can eat rabbit food. Did you want to drive?" he asked with a grin, dangling the keys towards her.

"I… uh, would rather have some lessons first."

He nodded. "We'll work on that."

"When?"

"On the road. Now that we both have ID, we need to get out of here."

"Where will we go?"

"West. We'll get some distance from here, and then figure it out."

**

Daelan and Imogen got into a routine: a leisurely breakfast in the morning where they talked about magic, or K-pop, or whatever; traveling in the late-morning to early-afternoon while Imogen read textbooks or listened to music; then hard-core studying and mana generation in the evening. Daelan taught Imogen while he created mana.

225

He was teaching her how to open her third eye, which was the foundational step of becoming a mage. Imogen was becoming nervous, though she tried not to let it show, because she hadn't succeeded yet.

"It's only been a few days, Imogen. It would be weird if you had succeeded already."

"How long did it take you?"

Daelan mumbled something and looked away.

"What did you say? You have to speak up, old man," she teased.

Daelan sighed. "I said I did it on my first try." Seeing her crestfallen face, he hurried on. "But you shouldn't judge by me. The only reason I was able to do that was because I knew exactly how to do it and how it felt through my connection to my siblings. I had already experienced someone else doing it. You don't have that advantage."

"So what am I doing wrong?"

"I don't think that's the right way to look at it. It's not a matter of doing something 'just right', it's a way of looking at reality. It's discovering a sense that you've always had, but never recognized. What you need is an epiphany, and those mostly come to people who put in the work."

"Yeah, yeah," she muttered. "Do the work. Do the work," she said in an imitation of his voice.

Fortunately for the sanity of all involved, Imogen successfully opened her third eye four days later.

Chapter 30

As they sat in a truck stop diner one evening, waiting for their food, Imogen asked him, "So how come you aren't dating anyone?"

Daelan looked at her in disbelief. "You mean, 'Why am I not seeing anyone, with all the copious amounts of time I have between being on the run, teaching you, and keeping our protection from divination spells going?' Gee, I wonder why not."

Imogen made a face at him. "You haven't always been this busy though, right?"

"Eh," he said, tilting his hand back and forth in a gesture that meant "sort of". "Before I was on the run, I worked as a bouncer and was learning how to be a web developer. Oh, and I got my tattoo."

"When can I get one?"

"It's up to you. I've been holding off on bringing it up because it will be painful. Very painful," he emphasized, "Much worse than a regular tattoo, and getting shocked isn't fun either. But, realistically, you will need to get it sooner or later."

"I want to do it."

"You sure?"

"Yeah."

"All right. We'll get the supplies and probably do it in a few days."

Daelan was pleased that she didn't hesitate about getting the tattoo. It would mostly clean him out of cash again until his next payday, but he was glad to see that she was serious about her quest for power. It required determination, courage, and a touch of foolishness—a set of characteristics that, from what he'd seen, described Imogen pretty well.

**

Daelan was letting Imogen drive on a flat, dusty highway in Texas when white smoke started to rise from the edges of the hood.

He looked at it with concern and asked, "What did you do?"

"I didn't do anything! It's this piece of crap car, not my fault!"

"Maybe it will go away."

It did not go away. A minute later, a light appeared on the dashboard. They decided to pull over and look up what the light meant in the owner's manual. Fortunately for Daelan, they wrote the manual assuming the reader didn't know anything about cars, which, in his case, was pretty much accurate.

"It's the over-temperature light. Well, I guess it could be under-temperature too, but…"

"But, seeing as how it's 100 degrees outside, it's probably not warning us that the engine is getting too cold," Imogen snarked.

"Do you know what to do when the engine overheats?"

"No clue. The last town we passed isn't that far behind us. Maybe we should walk back and get it towed?"

"How much would that cost?"

"I'm not sure. I think a few hundred bucks."

"Ugh." *Everything on this damn planet costs money.*

He never thought he'd see the day, but he actually missed something about Hell. You didn't need money for anything. Just scare the crap out of the other demons, and they'd give you whatever you want.

He sighed and opened the passenger door. "Alright, let's walk to town."

They walked through the dusty heat until they saw a small collection of buildings and a sign that said, "Welcome to Flatonia! Population 1326."

"Man," she said. "Talk about Nowhere-ville."

It was 8:36 PM. Most of the homes were lit, but the businesses were not, except for a small diner.

Imogen frowned. "I'm going to take a wild guess and say a tow isn't happening tonight."

"Probably not," he agreed.

They stopped at the diner and got burgers, drinks, and directions to the only motel in town. Daelan was grateful when

228

he saw it had vacancies. He could handle sleeping out in the open if he had to, but he didn't want that for his niece.

He glanced at her and was pleased to see she wasn't phased by any of this.

Come to think of it, with a background like hers, she might already know what it's like to sleep in the open.

She was far harder to read than Gabriel. He'd been with her long enough to know that the emotion she showed on the surface wasn't necessarily what was going on inside. She wore a mask. He hoped someday she could take it off, at least when she wanted to.

**

"I have some good news and some bad news for you, Mr. Miller," the middle-aged mechanic with rough hands and grease-stained overalls said. Daelan waited for the line about choosing which one he wanted first, but it never came. Instead, the mechanic, whose sewn-on name tag said "Joe", continued, "The good news is that the engine overheating wasn't a big deal. You stopped before things got bad, so we just need to add some coolant and it will be fine."

"And the bad news?"

The mechanic chewed on his lip and said, "Let me show you the bad news." He walked over to Daelan's Corolla, which was parked over a pit in the garage. The pit gave access to the undercarriage without an expensive hydraulic jack system.

The mechanic opened the driver's door and sat down. Once Daelan squatted down next to him, the mechanic put his finger on a dark part of the dash.

"You see this?"

"See what?" There was nothing there.

The mechanic just grinned and said, "Watch." He grabbed something with his fingernails and pulled away a piece of dark plastic that matched the dashboard, revealing an unlit sensor light. When the mechanic turned the key halfway to start the electronics, the sensor light lit up.

"What does that mean?"

"It's the 'Check Engine' light. In this case, it means that one of your cylinders is misfiring."

Daelan thought about pretending he knew what that meant, since people on the internet seemed to think that mechanics were out to get customers, particularly those who were clueless. Daelan decided he would rather learn than stay ignorant, so he asked, "And what does that mean?"

"Misfiring means that one of your cylinders is either not firing or firing at the wrong time. In practical terms, it means that your car will have a lot less power, which is why when you were driving down the road at 70 MPH with the AC cranked up, the car overheated." He paused and asked, "I'm guessing that you bought this car not too long ago?"

Daelan nodded. "A few weeks ago."

"Well, I'm sorry to say that the seller did you dirty. They knew about the problem and put that piece of plastic on the dash to cover it up."

"What's it going to take to fix it?"

"If the seller had gotten it fixed when the problem started, it would have cost 400 bucks. Now that it's been going on for a while, things have gotten worse. Your catalytic converter is shot."

"How much does that cost?"

"$1800, Mr. Miller. Most of that is the cost of the new part, not labor, so before you ask, no, I can't lower the price."

Daelan grimaced. "So, it's $1800 and $400, for a total of $2200?"

The mechanic nodded. "That's right."

"I need to get the money. I'll be back soon."

"We'll be here!" Joe said.

**

As it turned out, the one bank in Flatonia was already closed on a Friday evening, and would not reopen until Monday.

Daelan asked Joe to give him some time to come up with the money. The mechanic took pity on him and told him he'd hold on to the car for a week for free. After that, he would have to charge him a storage fee.

"It looks like we're going to spend some quality time in glorious Flatonia, Imogen."

She looked around and said, "Gee, that's great."

"Think of all the time you'll have for studying."

She looked at him with narrowed eyes. "You've never worked in sales, have you?"

"Do you want to be strong, or not?" he asked seriously.

"Yes," she mumbled.

"Then stop whining."

"I'm just a kid," she said petulantly.

"So? Do you think the next vampire or mage you come across is going to care? Is that going to stop the next asphalt cage when it moves in to crush you?

"No."

"Tell you what. You don't have to do a damn thing. Watch TikTok, play games on your phone, do whatever the hell you want. I won't say a thing."

He turned away, angry for reasons that weren't entirely clear to him. Imogen grabbed his arm and said tearfully. "Please. Don't leave me."

Those four words instantly quenched his anger, and made him feel like an asshole. He turned back slowly, unsure what to say to fix things.

He looked at the girl who had her head down, but held on to his forearm firmly with both hands. He idly wondered if she would dig in with her fingernails if he tried to pull away.

"Hey," he said, while putting his free hand on the back of her head, gently rubbing it. "I'm not leaving you. I'll never leave you. You okay?"

She nodded her head quickly, still not looking up. Unsure of himself, Daelan moved in and hugged her with his one free arm. Imogen let go of his other arm and did her best to crush him with a hug while sobbing.

Daelan's actions were mostly based on memories of what Joseph and other siblings did with their children, because he didn't trust his own judgment. Having experienced parenting through them was not as comforting to Daelan as he would have liked, though, because he remembered how often they didn't feel

231

like they knew what they were doing. They frequently expressed self-doubt to their spouses and friends.

Still, it was better than nothing. Based on a memory of Joseph and Imogen, he hugged her with both arms, slowly caressed her head, and let her cry. Eventually she let go and looked at him with red eyes and a tear-streaked face. She wiped her hands, and when she was done, looked embarrassed.

"You okay?"

She nodded. "Sorry about that."

Daelan shook his head. "No need. I... grew up in a rough place where there weren't any kids, so I don't really know what I'm doing."

She nodded her head quickly, tears leaking out. She covered her face again, wiping her eyes. Afterward, she looked at him and said, "You haven't told me about your past."

Ugh. He frowned and said, "I will, just not right now, okay?"

"Alright."

Daelan looked her in the eyes and said, "You're the only family I have. You will always have a place with me if you want it, okay?"

"Yeah," she said quietly.

"I meant what I said, though. I'm not going to push you, because to get stronger, you have to really want it. Me pushing you is useless. Do you understand?"

"Yes."

"Okay."

They went to the hotel room, where Imogen was much more studious than usual. He stifled a sigh, sadly hoping that it was from her desire to learn and grow, but afraid that it came from fear of being left behind.

**

The next day, Daelan decided to broach a delicate topic. There'd been an elephant in the room between them from day one. First, it was Imogen not knowing who he was. Now she knew, and she knew that he was the only one left, but not much beyond that. Both of them, for reasons of their own, hadn't wanted to bring up the subject, but it was time for that to change.

232

"Imogen?"

"Huh?" she said as she looked up from her book on Newtonian mechanics.

"Do you mind if we talk about how your parents died?"

She looked guarded, but said, "Okay."

"What can you tell me about what happened?"

"Dad and I had just gotten back from a fishing trip. We were getting stuff out of the car, and Mom was there in the garage with us."

Her delivery was even and unemotional. It was clear she had told the story many times.

"A crazy guy walked up the driveway and asked Dad if he was 'Joseph Santos'. After Dad said he was, the guy pulled out a gun and started shooting. Dad tried to run at the guy, but fell down before he could reach him." She started crying, and all the emotion that had been missing came flooding in. "I ran like a coward."

"No, you did what your parents wanted you to do. I'm sure of that."

"Mom stayed and was shot too."

"She stayed to give you more time to get somewhere safe."

Daelan waited for her crying to stop, and then asked, "What was the name of the crazy guy?"

"David Wright."

Do you know what happened to him?"

Imogen nodded. "He's in a prison for crazy people in Tennessee."

"Why not Florida?"

"Dad was a U.S. District Court judge, so crazy-guy was tried in the federal system."

"Do you know the name of the prison he's in?"

She shook her head. "I don't remember. I'm sure you could look it up, but why do you want to know?"

Daelan chewed his lip. "I've told you that I'm the last of your dad's siblings, right?"

"Yeah."

"What I didn't tell you is that the others were all killed within a few minutes of each other."

"What?!"

233

Daelan nodded somberly. "Your dad wasn't randomly killed by a crazy guy. He was assassinated."

Imogen looked shocked. "All of them were killed the same day?"

"Yes."

"How many people?"

"54. 53 siblings and our Father."

"That doesn't sound like a coincidence."

"No," Daelan said quietly. "It doesn't. I want to meet Mr. Wright to see what I can find out about your parents' death."

"Why didn't they get you?"

"I was somewhere special. They either didn't know about me, didn't know how to get where I was, or thought I would never be able to get back."

"But now you are back."

"Yes," he said with a small smile, having recognized where her thoughts were turning.

"And you want revenge."

"Yes."

"I'm in," she said defiantly, as if to smother any objections he would raise.

He just smiled and said, "Of course you are."

Chapter 31

Gabriel

An attendant at The Eternal Society of Noble Wizards and Magical Studies' world headquarters in Bonn, Germany, entered the waiting room and said, "The Merlin will see you now."

Finally. Instead of voicing his frustration, Gabriel just nodded and said, "Thank you." He and his sister followed the man, who guided them through hallways and rooms that looked like they belonged in a museum, or perhaps even a palace in the days of European empire. The walls were adorned with art, the furniture was decorated with intricate inlays of wood, precious metals, and gemstones, and the floors featured classic parquet.

Gabriel noted the grandeur, but didn't pay much attention to it. All he cared about was the evil man that was out there, somewhere, sullying the Earth with his every breath.

When they paused before a large pair of wooden double doors, Gabriel straightened up and checked his outfit while the heavy doors opened. Satisfied, he followed his sister in.

The Merlin's office was surprisingly spartan, at least in terms of the signs of wealth elsewhere in the headquarters. There was very little furniture or art, besides a portrait of a woman and child. What there was, was mana. More than he'd ever felt before, other than when actively inhaling mana bone powder.

But this was just the mana in the ambient air. Gabriel was shocked and envious.

An elegant man in robes of deepest blue that were almost black stood up behind his desk and walked around it to greet them.

"Eleanor and Gabriel Santos, welcome. Please, be seated." He gestured to two chairs in front of his desk. After sitting down himself, he said, "I grieved when I heard about your father and the other mages. He was a great man. One that I wish I had known better. What can you tell me about what happened?"

"Thank you for seeing us, Merlin, and for your kind words."
Eleanor paused and collected herself. "It all started when the
otherworlder arrived about half a year ago…"

After she finished recounting the story, the Merlin appeared to
be deep in thought, with steepled fingers in front of his lips as he
looked at who knew what.

"It seems like the otherworlder cast a great number of spells.
Where did he get the mana? Is he stealing mana bones?"

"He took some from the Miami headquarters, yes," Eleanor
said, "But there are no other known incidents of him taking mana
bones. Evidence from my brother would suggest he didn't even
know what mana bones were before then."

"Really?" The Merlin's eyes focused on Gabriel. "Tell me
more."

Gabriel cleared his throat nervously and said, "Yes, when I
was captured, we spoke some. He asked me about mana bones
and acted like he'd never heard of them."

"What else did you talk about?"

Gabriel wasn't sure if his face went pale in fright or red in
embarrassment. Whichever it was, the Merlin waved away his
concerns. "Don't worry, Gabriel. I'm sure he threatened you, or
something. I just want to know more about the otherworlder."

Nodding his head in appreciation for his kindness, Gabriel
began recounting what he remembered. "We talked about why
my father wanted to capture him, where Imogen—the girl we
captured—would likely be held, and what kinds of spells Society
mages use."

Despite the Merlin's assurances, Gabriel still worried that he
would be blamed for telling Daelan so much, so he quickly
added, "I think I have a clue about how he was getting mana!"

"Really? How?"

If he had thought the Merlin's attention was intense before, he
hadn't even known the meaning of the word. He felt like a rabbit
in front of a hawk. He swallowed and said, "He had an electrical
power supply in his room. There was no reason for it being there
that I could think of other than being part of how he got mana."

The Merlin asked questions about the power supply and wrote
down notes on Gabriel's answers.

"Did you ever see him cultivate the mana?"

"No, I'm afraid not. He only did it when I was tied up and blindfolded."

"Pity. Is there anything else?"

"Yes. He taught me one of his spells, a spell for truth sensing."

"Have you tried it?"

"Yes, and it works, Merlin."

"Show me."

Gabriel felt pleased to show off to the Merlin as he said the words of power and felt the mana forming. Strangely, though, the leader of the Society grew pale as the spell progressed.

"Very impressive," he said after Gabriel finished, though it was obvious that he was thinking about something else.

Ambiguous truth.

"Do you have a likeness of the otherworlder?"

"Yes, sir," Eleanor responded. "This is a drawing that is a pretty good representation of what he looks like.

Truth.

"Mm," he said in acknowledgement as he stared at the picture. After a time, his eyes locked on the attendant. "Gather the council. We're going to have a meeting in an hour."

"An hour, Merlin? They may not..."

"IN AN HOUR!" his voice boomed in a way that Gabriel suspected was magically enhanced.

The man paled, said, "Yes, Merlin!" and fled the room.

Eleanor flinched when he turned his attention to her. "Don't worry, my dear. You did well in not killing the otherworlder. Now we need to capture him."

Truth.

He paused and looked at her consideringly. "I think you have a lot of potential. Both of you do," he said, nodding at Gabriel.

False.

"Just like your father. If you help us capture this 'Daelan', you will move up in the Society. Perhaps even take over your father's role as Archmagus. What do you think of that?"

Eleanor bowed her head and said, "It would be an honor, Merlin."

Ambiguous truth.

Sensing something off in her voice, the Merlin asked, "What is it, Eleanor?"

"It's just… it's… it's nothing, Merlin."

False.

"Ah," the Merlin said with a smile. "Let me guess. You want to kill the otherworlder."

"Yes," Eleanor hissed.

Truth.

"Don't worry. When we've gotten all the useful information from him, I'll give him to you, to do what you like with him."

Ambiguously false.

"Thank you, Merlin."

Gabriel was growing uneasy, uncomfortable with what the truth-sensing spell was telling him. He suspected that the Merlin had, in his excitement, forgotten that the spell was running.

"It's the least I can do, my dear, for helping us to capture someone with such valuable information. It's the kind of knowledge that can change… well, everything!"

Truth.

Chapter 32

Daelan

It took more than a week to get out of Flatonia—three days to get the money, five to get the new catalytic converter, and one day for the labor—but it finally happened. Daelan and Imogen were both happy to be on their way.

The tattoo artist with one-inch ear expanders and rainbow hair they were talking to was decidedly not happy, though.

"Dude, I can't put this… whatever it is… in her skin."

He was looking with disgust at a vial of chloroplatinic acid dissolved in distilled water that bore an unfortunate resemblance to urine.

"I assure you that the solution is safe. We'll also be happy to sign whatever waivers you want to absolve you of liabilities."

"It's not about liabilities, bro… okay, yes, it's about liabilities, but I also just wouldn't feel right about putting this in her. I have no idea what the hell this stuff is."

"It's a platinum solution that, when combined with another solution, will become this." Daelan showed the artist his tattoo. He made sure he was facing away from the tattoo store's camera when he showed it.

The artist's eyes widened when he saw the silver tattoo. "Damn, that's pretty cool."

"Thanks. This is the exact same solution I used to make it."

The man frowned. "No side effects?"

"No."

It took another half hour of convincing and signing waivers, but the man finally agreed to do the tattoo.

"Can I also get a normal tattoo while I'm here?" Imogen asked Daelan with her best "you wuv me, right?" smile.

Daelan quirked his lips. "Sure, as long as you pay for it."

She snorted. "Might as well just say 'no'."

"Okay. No."

"Jerk," she said with a smile.

**

Imogen gritted her way through the double tattoos—chloroplatinic acid, followed by the precipitating agent, sodium metabisulfite—like a champ. When they got back to the motel, though, she was having second thoughts about the last step.

"Couldn't we just leave the tattoo like this, Daelan?"

"We could, but then it would be useless."

"So, you can protect me from the heat?"

"Mostly."

"Mostly?! What does 'mostly' mean?"

"It means I'll take care of most of it. You might have a few burns, but they'll heal."

"Remember when I told you that you've obviously never worked in sales?"

"Yeah?"

"Yeah."

Daelan rolled his eyes. "Look, when you want to do it, let me know." He went to his twin bed and lay down, preparing to generate mana.

Thirty seconds after he attached the alligator clips to his arm and started shocking himself, Imogen said, "Okay, I'm ready."

Daelan exercised great restraint by only letting a small frown show while hurling imprecations at her inside his head. He grabbed her arm and prepared to purify the platinum and vent the waste gases. Knowing this would be painful for her, he took a moment to let the annoyance go and concentrate on what he was about to do.

"Remember, you have to consciously choose to not seize the mana. If you do, things will go poorly, okay?" She had been working on her control of mana ever since she opened her third eye, but it was one thing to do it in an exercise, and another when you were feeling pain.

"Yeah, I remember," she said as she lay on her bed, looking up at the ceiling while gritting her teeth.

"We haven't even started and you're already acting like I'm torturing you."

240

"This is scary, okay? I'm not you, Mr. Electrocute-Myself-Every-Night."

Poor kid really is scared. "It's alright, Imogen. It will hurt a little, but you'll be okay."

"Promise?"

"Promise."

Seeing that she had relaxed, he started the procedure. He pushed some of his *heat-motion/stillness-cold* mana into her arm and had it form spheres around the platinum molecules at the end of one of the runes. He caused the spheres to heat up inside, boiling away the waste liquids and separating the platinum from weakly attached sulfur compounds, while protecting the nearby flesh from the heat.

When the spheres' contents were boiled gases and pure platinum particles, he made the mana create holes in her skin to the outside air, whereupon the boiling gases escaped, momentarily burning her skin as it went.

"Oh, you *fucking* liar!" she yelled.

Daelan sighed. It was going to be a long night.

**

It took three days to finish the tattoo, because Imogen couldn't handle the pain. Daelan was disappointed to realize she was kind of a wimp, but then it occurred to him that maybe, just maybe, he had an unusual relationship with pain.

Either way, he wasn't going to call her a wimp… too often.

"This hurts, Daelan!"

Okay, she's really begging for it. Instead of telling her that her lack of fortitude shamed the God-King, her father, and her mother who pushed a watermelon out of her vagina, he said with only a hint of annoyance, "Then turn down the voltage."

"But then I don't get as much mana."

No shit.

He stuck to his decision to not push her. It was up to her to decide how much she wanted it.

"How do you do this?" she asked.

"I suffer."

She waited for ten seconds, perhaps expecting for him to expound on the thought.

"That's it? You suffer?"

"Yes. Did you think there was a secret to overcoming the pain?"

Imogen muttered, "I'd hoped there was…"

"There are ways to reduce it, but most of them would reduce or eliminate your ability to make mana. Of the ones that are left, none of them would reduce the discomfort much."

A minute later she asked. "You do this for hours. How do you do it?"

"I accept the pain. I don't resist it. Eventually you get used to it."

"That sounds horrible."

Daelan shrugged. "What will you do when you are old and in pain all the time, not just a few hours each day?"

"Take lots of drugs."

Daelan laughed while shaking his head.

**

The pair enjoyed using online reviews to find interesting food in every place they stopped. In Louisiana that usually meant cajun food. In Texas, beef barbecue and tex-mex. In Hot Springs, Arkansas, it was a Greek restaurant named "Santorini".

"So why are we here?" Daelan asked as he skimmed the menu.

"It has good ratings."

"Arkansas isn't really known for Greek food, is it?"

"Don't be so provincial," Imogen said primly. "I'm sure there's lots of culture in Arkansas."

Daelan raised an eyebrow. "Why do I get the feeling you just insulted me?"

"Maybe because you're having a rare moment of perspicaciousness?"

"Okay, now you're just messing with me."

Imogen grinned. "Maybe a little. I've been working on my vocabulary."

"Why?"

"I was thinking about how you support yourself as a web developer who can work anywhere. I want to be able to make money anywhere, too, so I thought maybe I could be a writer."

"Do they make much money?"

"Well…" she said, squirming a little, "… the big ones do!"

"So you plan on being a starving artist, eh?"

"Uncle Daelan would never let me starve, right?" she asked as she did her "cute little girl" act, hands clasped together, head tilted, smiling, and batting her eyes at him.

Daelan just snorted and asked, "How's your mana control coming?"

"Yesterday I levitated the ball, hand flat, for six seconds!"

"Not bad. When you get to a minute, let me know."

Daelan wasn't effusive with his praise, but he was proud of her. She was working hard and, just as importantly, willing to endure pain. He saw her sweating and gritting her teeth when she converted electricity to mana. She'd never converted longer than half an hour, but she was doing it without complaints.

"So am I your best student ever?"

He quirked the corners of his lips. "My only student ever. So I guess… yes. And my worst student ever."

"Jerk." She threw a wadded up napkin at him.

The restaurant had a TV playing in the background, which Daelan ignored until he heard his name.

"…grinus is a terrorist who has kidnapped a young woman, Imogen, or Jen Santos."

Daelan saw both of their faces on the screen. For him, it was the picture from his Oregon driver's license. For Imogen, it looked like a professional picture with a backdrop, where she was dressed up and smiling.

Oh crap.

"If you have information on their whereabouts, please call…"

Daelan leaned over to Imogen, handed her the car keys, and whispered. "We need to get out of here. Go to the bathroom, and then walk out to the car."

She looked confused. "What's going on?"

"I'll tell you later. Just go."

She nodded and slid out of the booth. She looked concerned, but followed his instructions.

When the waitress came around, she asked, "Do you need a few more minutes to decide what you want to order?"

Daelan looked apologetic and said, "I'm sorry, but my daughter has an upset stomach, so I think we're just going to leave."

"Oh! No problem, hon. Come back anytime."

"Thank you."

When Daelan got out to the car, he slid into the driver's seat and accepted the keys that Imogen handed to him.

"What's going on?" she asked again.

"Apparently I'm a terrorist and I kidnapped you. They had your picture on the TV."

"Oh, that's not good…"

Daelan snorted. "You think?"

"What are we going to do?"

"I can disguise myself, but it's much more difficult and expensive to do for you, so I'm afraid we're going to have to do a lot of takeout."

"Damn it."

"Language," he remonstrated calmly.

She looked at him with an expression that said she couldn't believe what she was hearing. "Seriously, Mr. Potty Mouth?"

He frowned. "I know I'm not a good example, but I'm trying to raise you the way your mom and dad would."

She looked at him with a mix of emotions. Finally she sank into her seat and stared forward at the windshield.

"That ship sailed a long time ago, Daelan."

He sighed softly and started the car.

I know, kiddo. I know.

Chapter 33

One week later they pulled into the parking lot of a motel in Nashville, Tennessee. They went straight into their routine: Daelan carried the DC power supply in and hooked it up, while Imogen threw herself on the bed that was deepest into the room and started looking on Google Maps for takeout.

Though their actions were the same as every other night, both of them were going through the motions, their thoughts on something else.

Nashville was the home of the Lois M DeBerry Special Needs Facility, where one David Wright resided in the maximum security wing. His attorneys had arranged a plea deal to avoid the death penalty, and instead serve a life sentence in a facility for the mentally disturbed. Imogen preferred to call his prison the "Arkham Asylum for the criminally insane".

No one disputed that David was insane. After killing Imogen's parents, he'd looked at her running away and sat down on the driveway, holding his head in his hands. That's how the cops had found him. He'd simply looked up at them, tears streaking down his face, and said, "I had to do it."

That's all anyone got out of him when they asked him about the murder. "I had to do it." Other than that he seemed like a disturbed child, despite being a 23-year-old man.

Daelan and Imogen had thought about trying to visit him the standard, legal way until the whole terrorist thing. In a way, Daelan was glad. He'd been uncomfortable with the idea of simply walking into the "Special Needs Facility" because he was afraid the Society, vampires, FBI, or some combination of all three would be surveilling it. The only reason he'd entertained the idea was because Imogen deserved to face her parents' killer if she wanted to.

Now it wasn't an option.

When it was getting close to the time to make his move, he looked at her and softly said, "You're not going to bed tonight?"

Imogen was sitting on her bed, arms hugging her scrunched up knees. She was watching videos that failed to bring a smile to her face.

"I don't think I could sleep."

Daelan just nodded in understanding. "I should be back soon."

"Okay."

When he left the room, the crisp night air woke him up. He could hear the raucous noise of bar bands and crowds of tipsy country music lovers in the distance. Their motel was on the other side of town. The poor, seedy side. So was the asylum.

Daelan camouflaged and lifted himself into the air. When he was well above electric lines and such, he flew towards the facility, careful not to go too fast. A sonic boom would be both stupid and pointless, given how close the asylum was. Even at a nice, sedate 50 MPH, he reached the facility in half a minute.

The prison complex was three hundred yards on each side. A third of that was parking lots and a large building that straddled the prison and outside world. Daelan assumed it was for visits or something. He didn't care about that portion of the facility. He cared about the razor wire fence and the buildings inside of it.

Floodlights lit up the inside and outside of the fence, and much of the inner grounds. There were no towers or guards armed with rifles ready to shoot to kill, but it was clear that they did not intend to let the inmates escape.

Daelan hovered over the center of the fenced-off area and began the tracking spell. He didn't have anything of Wright's—if he'd wanted a strong connection he could have brought Imogen, as the karma between them was thick—but he didn't think he'd need it. He was physically close, and he doubted anyone was magically protecting Wright, so all he fed the spell, besides mana, was a name and a mental picture of the man.

There.

Wright was in a building that looked like a giant bow tie from above. Daelan flew over and, after verifying the coast was clear with x-ray vision, dropped through the roof and ceiling into the sleeping man's cell.

He looked unkempt, with a scraggly beard and long, unmanaged hair. His skin was sallow, but his nails, strangely,

246

looked freshly manicured. They had a pink coat of polish and a different-colored kitten on each nail, each with its own pose.

David's eyes popped open, as if sensing him. If so, Daelan didn't know how, as he was camouflaged and silent.

"Who's there?" David asked nervously. "Are you here to take me away?"

Daelan released everything but his camouflage, and surrounded them both with a silence spell that would isolate them from the rest of the world.

"Do you want to be taken away?"

"I, uh... I think so? Maybe?"

"What's your name?"

"David."

"Do you know what year it is, David?"

"Um. 2012?"

"How old are you?"

"I was born in 1997, so, uh..." he started counting on his fingers. "Fifteen!" he exclaimed happily.

Seeing the sad condition of Mr. Wright's memories, Daelan decided it was pointless to talk with him about anything related to the murder. He wasn't surprised. He was sure the police had gone over it many times already.

"Do you mind if I touch your head, David?"

"Why?" he asked suspiciously, eyes darting to and fro. "I-I don't want you to touch me!"

Daelan sighed and used some unaspected mana to put the frail man to sleep. He released the silence spell, put his hands on David's head, opened his spiritual eye, and began the spell.

As callous as he was, he didn't like doing this. Though he was much better at mind spells than he was before he came to Earth, he was still not an expert. Still, it didn't take him long to realize that possible damage from his spell was the least of David's problems.

If a person's memories were a painting, showing the various scenes and stories of their life, broad swathes of David's painting had been scraped clean. Only it was done by someone who didn't give a damn about the painting, so it was done roughly, the canvas pierced through here and there.

Daelan felt pity for the man, but that didn't mean he wouldn't brutalize him even more, even if he used a far more delicate touch. He would, but out of necessity, not mercy.

Art historians had long known about scraped paintings. They even had a term for them: "palimpsest". Canvases were expensive, so it wasn't unusual to scrape a painting off of one and reuse it. Through fancy imaging techniques, one could "see" the original painting underneath the newer layers of paint.

That was much like David's mind. It was scraped and even tattered in places, but the original memories were still there if one had the skill to see them, especially since there weren't false memories in their place. In that regard, Daelan was glad that whoever did this to David hadn't used an ounce of subtlety. It would have made his job far more difficult.

Unlike, say, a fireball, the spell he was using was not a simple matter of saying the words of power, shoving in some mana, and sending it on its merry way. No, the spell's incantation was just the opening, a prelude to an improv performance that would put Miles Davis to shame.

Daelan started by getting an overall impression and seeing the depth and breadth of where the scraping had occurred, as well as its boundaries. The frayed memories at the edges of the mental wound were the closest things to what was removed, and would be needed to figure out what was taken.

He soaked in the faint traces of memory and tried to amplify them. It was a delicate process because he was tuning himself to the wavelengths of what remained, so his amplification had to be strong enough to do something, but gentle enough to not overpower what was there.

When the amplification was true, a gentle resonance arose between the wisps of memories and Daelan's reconstruction. He sought to strengthen the resonance by subtly adjusting pieces, like a game of hot-and-cold played over and over again, where the hints were faint whispers.

Slowly, he built up a fabric that felt true, or at least true enough. He would never know for sure how much of it was David's memories and how much was his own invention used to fill in the gaps.

He didn't try to recreate everything. That would have taken months, if not years. Instead, he got a general sense of what a memory was about and concentrated on the more interesting areas.

What emerged was a face. A smiling, seemingly open face that had probably fooled David, but Daelan saw the eyes for what they were—the cruel eyes of a betrayer. It was not much, but it was something. He now knew what his enemy looked like.

**

When Daelan walked into the room, Imogen was still hugging her knees on the bed. He didn't know if she just happened to be in the position again when he walked in, or if she hadn't moved the whole time he was gone.

"How did it go?" she asked, the faux calmness failing miserably to hide the maelstrom of emotions behind the words.

"It went well… I think." He'd decided to add the qualifier at the end to avoid getting her hopes too high. He did not, after all, know how accurate the face was.

"Did you kill him?"

Daelan paused. "No, I didn't."

"Why not?" she shouted, finally deigning to look at him with a furious face.

"Mostly for our sake. Although I was camouflaged, if someone reviews the tapes from the camera in his cell, they'll see something. I wanted to avoid attention, and avoid warning our enemy."

Daelan could have stopped there, but he felt it was important to say something more, for Imogen's sake.

"He was as much of a victim as you and your parents, you know," he said gently.

"Him?! My parents' murderer? How *dare* you call him a victim!"

Daelan thought about asking her to lower her voice, but instead cast a silence spell around them. The drain on his mana was worth it.

"Someone, a mage, messed with his mind. I don't think he wanted to kill your parents, and may not have even realized what he was doing. Someone destroyed his memories, to the point where he acted confused and thought he was in the year 2012."

"And you believed that bullshit act?" she scornfully asked.

He nodded slowly. "I do. I looked into his mind. It was a mess. But I was able to pull out something."

"What?"

"The face of your parents' real murderer. The one who made Mr. Wright shoot them. Do you want to see it?"

"Of course!" she said, with a fraught mix of emotions.

Daelan pulled out a piece of paper and a pencil, so he could transfer what was in his mind to something she, and the rest of the world, could use.

Chapter 34

Merlin

The Merlin was so tired of this godforsaken planet and its pathetic mana. Though Earthlings had done impressive things with technology, he just didn't feel like he could *breathe* here, which was why he so seldom left his office. With mana gathering arrays and a massive expenditure in mana bones, he had created an atmosphere in his 20' x 30' piece of heaven that allowed him to relax.

A tiny, rational part of his brain telling him that he would really, really miss his office was the only thing keeping him from destroying it in a fit of rage at the moment.

"What do you mean you won't help me?" he yelled at the face in the mirror. A face, it should be noted, that was not his own. "Have you not heard anything I've said?"

The man in the mirror narrowed his eyes in anger. He was in a bathrobe because the Merlin's timing had been poor. It was never a good idea to embarrass your superior, particularly when he had something the Merlin wanted so badly.

"I heard every word, Caius. Just like I heard every word the last twenty times you requested a transfer back to Sicanthus."

The Merlin forcibly calmed himself. "Have you heard me request a transfer, sir?"

The fit, middle-aged man snorted. "So you weren't going to ask for one?"

For the first time since carrying out his assignment five years ago, Caius had not intended to ask to return home. His previous pleas had made it very clear that General Horace had no intention of bringing him back.

"No, sir. I know that something needs to be done about Daelan before I return."

General Horace looked mildly surprised before returning to his skeptical expression. "So, why do you think this Daelan is one of the God-King's avatars?"

So much for "hearing every word", asshole. Caius was careful not to let his thoughts show on his face as he made his case. "At first it was just circumstantial evidence. Spells that match or are similar to what we learn in the army. For instance, he taught an Earthling our level 1 truth-sensing spell. I believe the spell he uses to prevent divinations is one of ours as well."

Caius' superior frowned. "Is that all? That's pretty thin."

"That was just the first evidence, sir. What really convinced me was that he sought out the Earth avatar's daughter, and when she was captured, he massacred a group of mages to get her back."

General Horace looked concerned for the first time. "Hmm. While it doesn't prove anything, I admit that it's enough to pursue it." He looked at Caius with an annoyed scowl. "Why did you capture the girl instead of the avatar?"

Caius frowned. "It was before I knew about him, sir. I learned of his existence after he killed the mages."

"What about the detector?" As part of Caius' original assassination mission, he'd been given a device that could detect people from Sicanthus, as an aid to identifying the Earth avatar.

Caius was hesitant. "It, uh, is not 100% conclusive, but it seems to indicate that Daelan is from Sicanthus."

General Horace narrowed his eyes in suspicion. "What do you mean by 'not 100% conclusive'?"

"It doesn't respond as strongly to Daelan's trace as it did to my target's, but I believe that's because it's been years since he's been on the homeworld."

"It's only been five years, Caius. That wouldn't be long enough to make much difference."

Fighting the temptation to grit his teeth, he said, "I know, sir. All I can say is that, assuming he is an avatar, there is clearly something different about him. Otherwise we would have known about him before now."

"Hmm." The general pondered the situation while rubbing his chin. "Here are your orders: capture this Daelan. Verify whether he is an avatar or not, and if there are any more. That is more important than killing him."

"Understood, sir. What about reinforcements?"

"When is the next astral conjunction?"

Caius frowned. "The next full conjunction is in nine months. There is a partial conjunction in two."

General Horace took on a thoughtful look. Finally he said, "I don't have the resources to create a portal during a partial conjunction. However, if you get hard proof that he is an avatar, I will get the resources from further up the chain. Failing that, I will send reinforcements during the full conjunction if you have not already captured him."

It wasn't what Caius had hoped for, but it was something. He inferred, though, that if he failed to capture the avatar on his own and had to rely on the general's reinforcements, it would detract a great deal from the credit he would receive. "Understood, sir."

Seeing his subordinate's disappointment, the general smirked. "Aren't you in charge of a group of mages? Use them."

"And after I capture him and verify he's an avatar, sir?"

The general chuckled, knowing the conversation would eventually reach this point. It always did. "After your success, we'll have you accompany the prisoner to Sicanthus."

"Thank you, sir."

After the communication mirror was shut down, the Merlin had his assistant contact a man they often used in matters that required technology. They paid him a great deal of money to be available 24/7. Forty-five minutes after talking to his assistant, Caius heard a knock on the office door.

As a matter of habit, he scried his visitors. It was his assistant, an elderly Archwizard with a mind like a steel trap, and a forty-something man with glasses, slacks, and a neatly trimmed beard.

"Enter."

"Greetings, Merlin," the consultant said as he bowed his head.

Caius appreciated the show of respect, but didn't acknowledge it. "We have a phone number for Daelan, correct?" he asked his assistant.

"Yes, Merlin. The one he used to contact his former employer."

"Is he," gesturing at the consultant, "familiar with the situation?"

"Yes, Merlin."

Caius wore a frown as he turned to the consultant. He was in the uncomfortable position of feeling superior to him, and everyone else on Earth, while needing him to get off this damn planet. "Can we trace the number?"

"Not directly. It is a number that goes to a company called "Secure Communications, Inc.". His actual number is held by the company."

"Can we get it from them?"

"We can," the consultant said hesitantly, "if we get a warrant, which would be easy to do with his status as a terrorist. The company's main selling point is their clients' privacy, though, and companies like that typically inform their clients when they receive a warrant. More subtlety may be called for."

"More subtlety? What did you have in mind?"

"We use the FBI, but in a more indirect manner, together with the phone company. They set up collection of the telephonic communications going in and out of Secure Communications, Inc., and then we call Daelan. They should be able to use the call timing and metadata to determine his actual phone number, and establish a trace from that."

"And he wouldn't be tipped off?"

"That's correct."

"Good. Make it happen."

Chapter 35

Daelan

"Yes, I see," Daelan said, speaking into his phone. "Thank you." He ended the call and looked at Imogen with a frown. "That's the third private investigator. They all agree that there isn't much chance of finding someone from just a drawing, even if it's a good one."

"So what do we do now?"

"I'm not sure." When he saw Imogen's despondent look, he comforted her. "Don't worry. We'll figure out something."

"Yeah."

Daelan thought about it for a few minutes.

"The problem is that there are too many people in the United States."

"We don't even know if he's in the U.S." Imogen said sourly. "Or if he's still on Earth."

Daelan nodded. "You're right. Let's assume he's on Earth, because if not, there's nothing we can do for now. So the problem remains—how do we narrow things down?"

Daelan could tell that Imogen was thinking hard about the problem, which made him happy. He wanted to find the killer, of course, but he also didn't want her falling into a mental abyss. He knew what that was like and wanted better for her.

After another couple of minutes, Imogen perked up. "We know he can do magic. If he's still on Earth, the Society probably knows about him."

Daelan nodded slowly, turning it over in his mind. "Unless he's laying low. Maybe even then. Good thinking, Jen."

"That's the first time you've called me that."

"Do you prefer 'Imogen'?"

She shrugged. "It doesn't matter to me."

He looked at her, trying to gauge what she really thought. He gave up after a few seconds, finding her inscrutable.

I had an easier time reading demons. Deciding it was best to move on, he asked, "So, how do we get information from the Society?"

They talked late into the night, kicking around ideas and making the beginnings of plans.

**

Daelan was eating a turkey-on-rye sandwich when a call came into his burner phone app.

"Yeah?"

"Daelan Peregrinus?"

Uh oh. It was a voice Daelan didn't recognize. "Who is this?"

"My name is Matthew Davis. I represent The Eternal Society of Noble Wizards and Magical Studies."

"That name is quite a mouthful. Have you guys ever thought of shortening it?" he asked while hurriedly putting his laptop away and gesturing to Imogen to do the same.

"Many times. As you might imagine, people who are hundreds of years old can grow pretty attached to things they're used to, so we remain The Eternal Society of Noble Wizards and Magical Studies."

Daelan chuckled. The call had him on edge, but it was not proceeding at all like he thought it would. He motioned to Imogen, who was wearing an expensive wig, that it was time to go.

"They say that progress in science happens one funeral at a time. Maybe it's the same with wizardry."

Matthew paused. "A joke some might call 'tactless' from one such as yourself, Mr. Peregrinus. Perhaps you're suggesting you've been trying to help the Society progress?"

"No," Daelan said as he pushed through the coffee shop's door and diverted some unaspected mana into his arm cuff's anti-eavesdropping spellform. "The way I see it, defending myself and freeing my kidnapped niece is plenty good enough justification for killing people."

"Certain rogue elements of the Society made mistakes, for which we apologize, Mr. Peregrinus. We'd like to enter into a

256

truce with you, and even talk about the possibility of reparations."

That's a surprise. Matthew and the Society were being surprisingly conciliatory. It was suspicious. "One moment, Matthew." He covered the phone's microphone and fake coughed, as if he was clearing his throat. He then whispered the words of power for a specialized truth-sensing spell, one that only required a voice. It would be expensive, but the arm cuff was full.

"What were you saying, Matthew?"

"We would like to enter into a truce with you, and perhaps talk about reparations."

False.

"From me to you, or you to me?"

"We recognize that we were the aggressors, so it would be from us to you."

"Should we meet? Do you know where I am?"

"No, we don't." *Ambiguous.* Daelan's blood ran cold, and he looked at Imogen and the environs in concern. "For an otherworlder, you have done remarkably well at hiding yourself." *Truth.* "Does the world you come from have technology like Earth's?"

Daelan mouthed "motel" to a worried-looking Imogen and started walking before answering Matthew's question. "No, it doesn't. Being here has been a real learning experience."

"I bet. Though I suppose you would have already known some things about Earth through your brother."

Daelan was about to respond when it hit him what Matthew had said. *Do they think I'm an avatar?* If so, he could be in real trouble. "What brother?"

"Your brother, Imogen's father. You said she is your niece, right?"

Damn it. It was stupid to call her that. "Why did you assume I was related to her father, and not her mother?"

"Hm, I'm not sure." *False.* "I guess I was being sexist. Are you related to her mother, then?"

"Yes." *By marriage.* He almost hoped they were able to cast a similar truth-sensing spell as his. He would love to see

257

Matthew's face when he saw that Daelan was telling the truth. He had only himself to blame for phrasing the question poorly.

"Well, as interesting as that is, why don't we talk about how and where we could meet?"

"Sure, but I get to pick the place."

"We anticipated that you would want that. It's natural that you would be distrustful after all that has happened. So, where would you like to meet?"

"I'll tell you later. Can I use the number you called from?"

"Yes."

Truth.

"First, though, tell me something. Did you find me through my phone?"

"What? No, I told you, we don't know where you are."

False.

Oh shit. The fact that the same denial went from "ambiguous" to "false" during the call told Daelan all he needed to know. Something had changed while they were talking.

"We'll talk later," he said before ending the call. He turned to Imogen, who was walking briskly to keep up with him. "We need to get out of here."

"What happened?"

"The Society found us somehow."

Imogen grew pale and hurried even more.

"How?"

"I'm not sure, but I think it's the phone." He walked up to a dumpster in the corner of a gas station parking lot and tossed it in.

"Should I get rid of mine too?"

The Society had found them when they called him, so he didn't think her phone was the problem, but he'd rather err on the side of burning it all down and making a clean start than bringing a problem with them.

"Yeah, toss it in."

Once both phones were in the dumpster, Daelan cast a spell that would start a conflagration when someone touched them.

"What did you do?" Imogen asked.

"Set a trap for our pursuers. When they try to take the phones, kaboom," he said with a malicious smile.

To his surprise, Imogen looked upset.

"What if someone innocent is the first person to touch them?"

"It's not guaranteed to get our enemies, but since there aren't any real downsides..." he shrugged.

"You can't kill innocent people!" she hissed quietly, trying to avoid drawing attention.

Clearly I can, he thought with annoyance. "Fine." He disabled the spell and reused the mana to cast a simple time-delay spell that would burn the contents of the dumpster in five minutes. "Let's go."

As they fast-walked, Daelan thought about their next move. The Society was using non-magical means to find them. It was time for them to do the same. He'd already talked to private investigators about finding the killer with his high-quality drawing. All of them said it was impossible.

But that just meant he was talking to the wrong people.

Chapter 36

Two weeks later

"Have you been checking your mirrors?" Daelan asked.

"Yes, Dad," Imogen said sarcastically, as she made a show of looking in the rearview and side mirrors. Unlike other teenagers learning how to drive, her lessons about "defensive driving" were more about how to spot tails and lose them than avoiding accidents.

"Have you seen any of the cars before?"

"Just a couple that have been with us the last few blocks." After stopping at the next light, she asked, "Where did you learn this stuff?"

Daelan scoffed. "Natural intelligence. It doesn't take a genius to know how to spot cars."

Imogen side-eyed him skeptically.

"YouTube may have helped…" he mumbled.

She chuckled, but didn't give him a hard time about it. She drove without incident to the motel they planned to stay at in Florence, Oregon, near the coast. More importantly, it was a few miles north of an enclave of vampires, who might know something about their mysterious assassin, or at least how they could find the Society.

After they checked into their room, Daelan looked at his email. He was surprised to see one with the subject "The distrustful mama who fed you lunch". It was from "g9273d@gmail.com". Frowning, he opened the email.

John/Daelan,

I need your help. I think I told you that my husband was looking for me and my son. He's taken Griffin. Please, I'm desperate. I don't know who to turn to because the police won't help. I'll give you $500 just to talk with me. Use the Signal app- 555-685-7928.

Jessica Hollis

The hell?

"What?" Imogen asked.

"I didn't say anything."

"You had a strange look."

"It's nothing," Daelan said. "A woman I met in Oregon emailed me asking for help. It's just a weird email."

"What does she want?"

"Her husband took her kid. She wants him back, I guess."

"How do you know her?"

"Why do you want to know?"

"I'm curious."

Daelan considered it a waste of time, but thought, *Eh, whatever.* He told her the story of their two encounters.

"Wait, so you *met* Griffin?"

"Yeah?"

"And you don't want to help her get him back?" Imogen was looking at him like he had two heads.

"Why would I? It has nothing to do with me."

"Daelan, don't you, I don't know, *feel* stuff?"

"I'm getting annoyed. Does that count? Of course I have feelings."

Imogen pursed her lips and spoke hesitantly. "I know you have feelings for me, but do you have feelings for other people?"

Daelan paused, not sure what she was looking for. "What do you mean?"

"What do you think about Griffin? Is he cute?"

He shrugged. "I guess."

"Wouldn't it be nice to see him back with his mom?"

"I don't know. We don't know the dad's side of the story."

"True, but did she seem like a bad person?"

"No."

"Did she seem like a good mom?"

"Yes."

"So...?"

Daelan sighed. "Why do you care about them, Imogen?"

Imogen had a look on her face that he didn't recognize. "Because that's what people do, Daelan. They care about each other, especially those who are smaller and weaker than us."

Daelan frowned. It wasn't like he didn't know what she was talking about. He had experienced his siblings, after all. It was just that two hundred years of Hell had burned that softness out of him.

In an ideal world, he could imagine being kind to other people. Maybe. But not when they were fighting for their lives. This was the time to annihilate their enemies.

"Imogen…" He thought about how to explain it to her. "We don't have the time to help everyone. We have to save ourselves, and then we can think about helping other people."

"I understand." She hesitated and said, "You've never talked about where you were before Earth, but sometimes you cry out in the night. Did you know that?"

"No," he said, vaguely ashamed of his weakness.

"I can tell wherever it was, it was a terrible place. I'm sure bad things happened to you. Did you…" She hesitated, but steeled herself and asked, "Did you sometimes have to do bad things too?"

Unwanted memories and feelings arose in response to the question. Daelan went stiff as he worked at shoving them back into the proverbial closet before slamming the door shut.

What the hell is this? he asked himself. *Why did her question bring up all this?* He wasn't sure why, after 200 years of dealing with Hell, it was giving him such problems now. *Maybe it's because I've been trying to put that life behind me. I don't want Imogen to see the old me.*

After half a minute, he looked at her and asked, "How did you know?"

Imogen once again had the expression he didn't recognize. "Sometimes, when you're having a nightmare, you say, 'I'm sorry.'" They both sat there for a time. Imogen finally said, "We're nice to people so when we have nightmares, we don't have to say 'sorry'."

Daelan thought about it. "Do you want me to help them?"

"I think you should at least talk to her and see what she has to say."

"Even if it delays going after your parents' murderer?"

She nodded. "If he's still on Earth, it will wait a little longer."

"Alright."

262

Later that night after he filled the arm cuff, added mana to his core, and, most importantly, had time for his feelings to settle, he called Griffin's mom through the app.

"Daelan?"

"Yes."

"Thank you for calling me." She sounded subdued. Depressed. "I know it was weird to reach out to you when I don't know anything about you, but I don't know who else to ask."

"Why did you think I could help you?"

She was silent for a few seconds. "I was married to my husband for twelve years. The men who worked for him... I, uh, had a similar feeling around you."

Daelan didn't say anything to that. He just nodded and moved on. "Where did you get my email address?"

"When I was looking through your phone, I sent it and your number to my phone. I tried calling you, but the number was disconnected."

"Tell me what happened."

"Does this mean you can help me?"

"We'll see."

Sounding a little hopeful, she said, "The police raided my home, said I had kidnapped my son, and took him away. They took him to his father, my ex-husband. That night, a couple of his men beat me up and told me they'd kill me if I tried to get Griffin back."

"Did you kidnap Griffin?"

She snorted. "Technically? Probably. I had primary custodianship, and he was only allowed supervised visitation because of domestic violence charges, but I still wasn't allowed to leave the state without the court's permission."

"So why did you?"

"Because my husband would eventually win. He always does. He has cops, prosecutors, and I'm pretty sure even some judges on his payroll. He offers them money, blackmails them with videos of one-night stands that he sets up, threatens them or their families. He does whatever it takes until he gets them. That's why he's never gone to jail."

"Why should I believe you?"

"I don't know, maybe because he's a famous scumbag!" she shouted. "Sorry. He, uh, wasn't famous when I married him. I didn't know who he was. Just... you can look it up."

"Okay. I'll do that and get back to you."

"Thank you, John. I mean Daelan. Whoever you are... thank you. Oh, and I'll give you, uh, $50,000 if you get Griffin back! No, $100,000!"

Daelan thought about snarkily asking her if she would threaten him too if he refused, but decided it would be cruel if she was telling the truth. Besides, he wanted the money. One thing still bothered him, though.

"How do you even have that kind of cash?"

"What, you don't think linguists can be independently wealthy?" she said ironically.

"Well, assuming you have the money, clearly you are, but..."

She laughed bitterly. "I'm not wealthy. I received a little over $600,000 in the divorce, a small fraction of my ex-husband's assets."

"I see. Let me think about it, and I'll get back to you."

A minute after he ended the call, pictures arrived through the app of Ms. Hollis in her underwear, from the front and back. There was nothing sexy about them. It showed her body covered with bruises. Some of them a deep bluish-purple. Others partially healed greens and yellows. It was a testimony of violence.

Though he sympathized, it proved nothing. He could and would do that to himself if that's what it took to get Imogen back.

He texted one of the private investigators he'd worked with previously.

"I'd like you to look up something for me..." When they were finished talking, he hung up and looked over at Imogen, who was generating mana. "Happy?

"No, this hurts like hell."

"Language."

Imogen looked at him in disbelief.

The next evening, the PI called.

"Unfortunately, the divorce proceedings are sealed, so I can't get anything there. There's enough on Ms. Hollis' ex-husband, though, to indicate he is a bad character. She took out a temporary restraining order on him shortly before the divorce. To be fair to him, that's not an unusual tactic to gain an advantage in divorces. Mr. Hollis was arrested once for witness intimidation and racketeering. Both the charges themselves and the fact they didn't go to trial is unusual.

"The racketeering charge suggests that he's part of a criminal organization, and the witness intimidation backs up what Ms. Hollis said about him threatening people to get his way. So, I guess the summary is that I have circumstantial evidence that backs up what Ms. Hollis told you, but no proof."

"Okay. If we were to continue, what would be the next steps?"

"I would hire a local PI to investigate. I think I've done all I can with public records, so it will take someone who has local contacts and can interview the people involved."

Daelan thought about it for a moment and said. "I think we'll end it here then. Just keep the rest of the retainer for the next time I call you."

"Will do. Thank you, Mr. Miller."

Daelan sighed and made his next call.

"Daelan?"

"Yeah."

When the line was silent for a couple of seconds, Ms. Hollis asked, "So... does your calling mean you want to help me?"

"I suppose so. Did a little digging, and it sounds like your ex-husband isn't a great guy."

She laughed bitterly. "That's putting it mildly."

"Do you know where Griffin is?"

"I believe so. He flew with his father to Paris a week ago, and I think they went to my husband's château. I've engaged investigators to verify that."

"Hm. I'll need a passport to fly there."

"You don't have a passport?" she asked frantically.

265

"No, but I can get one."

"That takes weeks, or even months!"

"I can likely get one faster. I'll need money upfront to pay for expenses though."

"How much money?"

Daelan considered the cost of obtaining passports, round-trip tickets for himself and Imogen to Paris, and lodging.

"$10,000."

"That's a lot," she said warily.

"It is. If it's too much for you, let me know."

She was silent for a few seconds, but finally said, defeated, "I'll do it. Just please, get Griffin."

"I will." After a pause, he said, "I still expect $100,000 when I bring him back."

"You'll get it." She laughed sadly and said, "Trust me, I wouldn't dream of crossing anyone who takes on my ex-husband and wins."

Daelan gave her wiring instructions for his account in the Cayman Islands and hung up.

A few minutes later, he received a text from Ms. Hollis.

"I want to go with you to France."

"Why?"

"I want to be with Griffin when you rescue him. He'll be terrified. Also, I speak French."

Daelan grunted in annoyance, though he had to admit it would be handy to have someone who spoke the language.

"It could be dangerous."

"I know. I'll up the expenses to $15,000. Just book flights for me too."

"Fine." He looked at Imogen, who was studying a chemistry textbook. "It looks like we're going to France."

"Nice! Can we see the Eiffel Tower?"

Daelan shrugged. "Sure. We, uh, will be taking Griffin's mom with us."

Imogen's eyebrows raised. "Really? What about using magic?"

"I'll tell her about it, probably. The Society wants to keep magic secret, but I don't care."

"Okay." She rushed up and gave him a hug, probably relieved to do something more exciting than driving or staying in a motel. "This will be so much fun!"

Daelan was surprised, but gently hugged her back. He was already glad he'd taken the job.

Chapter 37

Daelan had a couple of weeks to kill in Oregon before they got their new documents. He went to the closest State Department passport center and paid for expedited processing. He thought about giving the government worker a "mental nudge" to get the passports faster, but he and Imogen decided it wasn't worth doing to someone when Griffin should be okay.

Ms. Hollis hadn't been happy about the delay, but she accepted that it was the best that could be done.

Since he had some free time, Daelan decided it was time to upgrade his arm cuff. He did some investigating into how to buy the lead he'd need. He knew lead was frowned upon, so he thought he'd have to drive to a recycling shop or something and go to efforts to purify it, but was surprised to see he could get next day delivery for 99.9% pure ingots of lead from Amazon.

Sometimes he considered the conveniences of Earth to be their own kind of magic.

Spurred on by his success, he looked for graphite, a form of carbon he planned to use for the diamonds, and laughed in delight when he found next day delivery of 99.9% pure ingots of graphite as well.

Amazing.

He created a new Amazon account with a burner credit card and email address, and made the purchases.

Now that the ingredients for the arm cuff were on their way, there was one more thing he needed to do to prepare: upgrade his mana.

He already had his favorite lavender incense from Walmart, so he put a stick in a brazier and lit it with a thought and a wisp of mana.

"What are you doing, Daelan?"

"I'm getting ready to improve my *dao*, which enhances the power and usefulness of my mana."

"Wow," Imogen said, impressed. "When can I do that?"

"When you have a good enough understanding of how the universe works. That's why you study."

Daelan sat down on the floor and meditated. When his mind was prepared, he went over his existing *dao* of *heat-motion/stillness-cold*, envisioning the general concepts of motion and stillness, and then moving to heat and cold, which were the same concepts applied to large groups of molecules.

He refined the concept by picturing control of individual molecules. Instead of random heat that gave arbitrary amounts of energy to each molecule and let them bounce around as they may, Daelan controlled individual particles, giving them precise amounts of energy and setting them on a path of his choosing. The particles became squirrely because of the nature of quantum mechanics. They resisted being tied down to anything as mundane as a known direction and speed. Heisenberg's Uncertainty Principle meant he couldn't give them an exact energy or direction. Still, as he played with the air molecules between his hands, he found that he could give them direction, as long as he left them a measure of freedom.

When he insisted on a particular, precise direction, everything else became even more squirrely. He found the middle ground that let him shepherd the atoms without forcing anything too much.

As his understanding and intuitive feeling for the concept increased, he contemplated the spinning runes at the heart of his core: *heat-motion/stillness-cold*. The two sides were mirror images of each other, so as they spun, *heat-motion* became *stillness-cold*, and vice versa.

This time, instead of adding opposite, mirror-image runes, he added the same, symmetric rune to both sides: *particle*. Its nature was unity and wholeness at every level: molecule, atom, quark, string. It even worked conceptually at the macro level. Daelan was unified and one, resistant to division, making him a sort of meta-particle.

The rune fused with the *motion* and *stillness* runes. Instead of lining up with them as an extension, it was a modifier that fused into the runes, forming new ones. Daelan let the *heat* and *cold* runes go, as they were inferior to what was left behind: *particle motion/particle stillness*. The two-in-one runes were still mirror images of the other, following the yin-yang pattern of changing into each other as they spun.

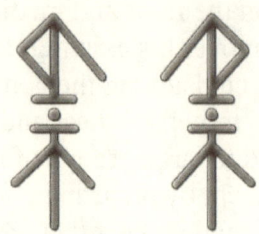

When he came out of his trance, it was two in the morning. Though he saw Imogen was asleep, he couldn't resist the temptation to try his new aspected mana. He accelerated electrons, creating arcs of electricity between his fingers. He grinned as he watched the beautiful display.

"Can you do that because of your *dao*?"

"Sorry I woke you."

"That's okay."

"I could have done this before, but only with a spell. Now I can do it with a thought, and it doesn't take as much mana."

"Cool. It didn't take very long."

Daelan didn't respond.

"When I do it, will it just be a few hours too?"

"No. I, uh, have some unique advantages. I've experienced my Father and many of my siblings establishing and building their *daos*, including the same concepts that I'm using, so it is far easier for me. It will take longer and be more difficult for you."

"That sucks. So unfair!"

"Life often is," he agreed.

"Sorry, Daelan," she said regretfully. "I know you had it much harder than I did."

"Don't worry about it, kiddo. Get some sleep."

The next day, when he received the lead and graphite ingots, he unwrapped them like a kid at Christmas. He was eager to get started, so he took an ingot of lead and looked at it appreciatively.

Imogen looked at him curiously. "What are you doing now?"

"Fusion," he said without looking at her.

"Um, isn't that dangerous?" she asked nervously.

Daelan grinned at her. "Not for me."

"Yeah, but what about *me*? And everyone else in a half-mile radius?"

Daelan rolled his eyes. "You know what I meant. I've got it under control."

"Should I have some lead shielding or something?"

Looking at the lead again, he said, "Nah. This isn't like hydrogen fusion. It takes in energy, it doesn't put it out. Besides, lead is toxic."

"Still…"

He sighed and said, "Fine, if it makes you feel better." He took one of the ingots and, using his *particle motion* mana, formed the soft metal into a thin sheet large enough to cover her. "Here. Wash up well in the shower afterwards, and wash your clothes."

"Thanks," she said as she hid on the other side of her bed and put the lead sheet on top.

He chuckled when he saw her eyes appear over the edge of the bed, watching him intently. He pulled out his pocket knife and cut off the last inch of the narrow ingot. He could have done it with his mana, but he needed as much as possible for what he was about to do.

Fortunately, his *particle motion/particle stillness* mana was perfect for the job.

Daelan suspended the lead in the air and heated it up until it was a glowing, liquid orb. He continued to heat it and added a barrier that reflected heat back into the sphere, both to not waste energy and to keep the room and nearby little girls from charring.

Now was when things started to get exciting.

Daelan used his mana to put one thousand pairs of lead atoms into spheres of power that both trapped and continued to heat them, bringing the atoms that were already at 2000 °F up to tens of thousands… hundreds of thousands… millions… and finally tens of millions of degrees fahrenheit, making them hotter than the core of the Sun. Though the energy density was incredible, the amount of mana required was surprisingly small, given that so few atoms were involved.

The entire time, the atoms tried to shed their heat, as everything does, by emitting photons across various wavelengths of light. Early on, most of it was in the infrared and visible light regions, but as they became increasingly hot they shifted towards ultraviolet, x-rays, and finally even gamma radiation. Because photons are particles, the spheres of power rejected them, bouncing them back inwards to be reabsorbed by the atoms.

In each of the spheres, the atoms bounced back and forth crazily, seeking to escape but unable to. Daelan had, in essence, made one thousand "poor man" particle accelerators. Where Earth scientists used huge tracks of magnets to propel particles to almost the speed of light and crash them into each other, Daelan confined the particles to a small region and let random chance give multiple opportunities to the atoms to collide. Eventually the atoms collided just right and with such incredible force that their nuclei merged and stayed together, forming, for the briefest moment, a super-heavy atom with 164 protons and 250 neutrons.

The nuclear forces were unable to hold such a ridiculously large nucleus together, making it unstable and incredibly radioactive. Within picoseconds it started shedding mass in the form of alpha radiation, beta radiation, and neutrons. The size of the nucleus dropped until it stabilized at 126 protons and 184 neutrons.

Though the nucleus was still ridiculously large, it was spherically symmetrical and "whole" in a way that the original fused atom had not been. The new atom was in the middle of the so-called "island of stability" that Earth scientists had predicted would exist, but never seen.

Much like the electron rings of noble gases are complete and whole and thus extremely stable, nuclei had similar "rings" which, when complete, made the nuclei symmetrically spherical and very stable.

Many scientists would have given their right arm to see what Daelan had done. A few fantasy enthusiasts would have too, because, for the first time, mithril existed on the Earth.

**

Daelan spent most of the night producing more mithril. It was a well-established process he had experienced through his siblings, but never done himself before. He vastly scaled up the production, creating hundreds of trillions of mithril atoms in each run. Unfortunately, that was still a paltry amount at human scale.

He siphoned off the radiation into its own sphere where it could sit in a soup of protons, neutrons, and electrons. The particles naturally formed new atoms, most of which were stable, some were not. The unstable atoms emitted radiation, continuing the process of creative destruction.

By three in the morning, Daelan had nearly exhausted his mana. He separated the mithril from the lead, and used the dregs of his mana to form the lead ingots into a thick sphere around the waste products.

Once he verified that the amount of radiation that leaked from the sphere was far lower than Earth's background radiation, he set it down with a tired sigh.

He was exhausted, sweaty, and ready for a shower and sleep. He felt bad when he saw that Imogen had fallen asleep on the floor, the lead sheet still on top of her. He leaned over painfully, removed the sheet, and gently put her into the bed.

"How did it go?" she asked tiredly.

"It went well."

"No new heads or limbs?"

He quirked his lips. "No."

"Good."

"Night."

"Mm," she said as she turned onto her side and fell asleep.

After showering, he looked at the ball of mithril he'd created. It was about the size of a marble, but very heavy for its size, about 50% heavier than lead.

It was a good start, but he needed quite a bit more. It was going to be a busy couple of weeks.

Chapter 38

Because the mithril fusion required massive amounts of mana, Daelan spent even more time electrocuting himself. Fortunately, his *particle motion dao* improved the efficiency of converting electricity to mana. He didn't have precise numbers, but he believed it had gone from eight to ten percent.

If generating mana has to suck, at least it sucks faster.

In the middle of a session, a text came in from Ms. Hollis.

"I want to stay with you."

Daelan frowned in confusion. "Why?"

"I don't like being alone with Griffin gone."

Having spent 200 years in Hell, it didn't take long for Daelan to take a confident stab at her motivation.

"...and you're worried I'll skip out on you."

"No!" Ten seconds later, a new message appeared. "Ok, maybe."

"😂"

"Lol. Somehow you never struck me as an emoji kind of guy."

"I have layers."

"And Shrek. Didn't see that one coming either."

"My niece said it was an important part of my cultural education. Also that I resembled him"

"You have a niece?"

"Surprised? I have a mom and dad too"

"The way your phone was so blank, I thought you'd dropped out of the sky." Daelan was surprised and wondered if she was onto him, when she texted, "JK"

"Imogen," he called out. "What does 'JK' mean?"

"'Just kidding'. Who are you talking to?" She got off her bed and moved behind his chair. "Oh my gosh, you're *flirting* with her?" She started laughing hysterically.

A new text came in. "Where are you from?"

Imogen calmed down long enough to read the text and gleefully said, "Tell her she can find out after the first date!"

Daelan rolled his eyes. "Right." He texted, "We're not going to bail on you. Why don't you just sit tight until it's time to fly?"

"Please. 😔 I wasn't kidding about my mental state. I'm going frantic without Griffin. It doesn't help that I'm worried my ex-husband will send somebody after me."

Daelan frowned and chewed his lip. "Fine." He thought about whether to give her their address or not. Even though the app they were using was supposed to have end-to-end encryption, he didn't trust it enough to do that. "Go to the BP gas station in Florence at eleven in the morning."

"Can't I come tonight?"

Daelan shook his head in annoyance and texted, "No." He needed time to practice his illusion spell so he could change his appearance back to what she was familiar with.

"Ugh, fine. See you at 11 AM then."

"Can't wait" He paused and, not sure if she would realize he was being sarcastic, added, "JK"

**

As Daelan and Imogen sat in a McDonald's with line of sight to the gas station, he asked her, "So, you're okay with this?"

She snorted while continuing to watch for Griffin's mom. "Isn't the right time to ask *before* you tell her it's okay to come?"

"Sorry."

"It's fine. I'm used to my caregivers not caring what I think."

Ouch. Daelan was angry. Why, he wasn't entirely sure. He took a few moments to calm down. When he realized that Imogen had tensed, apparently either sensing or anticipating his anger, he felt like a true asshole. "I'm sorry. I made a mistake. I'll try to do better."

Imogen nodded, but remained tense. He sighed, but knew he couldn't tell her to relax. That would either not work or actively make it worse.

He realized he had anger issues. It was necessary for survival in Hell, but was not what was needed with a 16-year-old girl who had a difficult past too. He had been on the internet enough to know that the usual advice would be "talk to a therapist". He would think about it if he thought it would work.

"Tell me about your childhood." Yeah, that would go really well, he thought with a snort.

"Is that her?"

Ms. Hollis had pulled up to the gas station's air pump in her BMW X5, gotten out, and was looking around. Although she was wearing oversized sunglasses, she used a hand as a sun visor. Her brown hair was in a ponytail, and she was dressed sensibly in jeans and a cream-colored shirt.

"Yeah, that's her."

"She's pretty."

"Eh," he said noncommittally.

She looked at him skeptically and laughed. He wasn't sure why, but he much preferred it to her being scared of him so he just went with it.

Daelan had picked the McDonald's because they could watch both the gas station and the road that she would be driving in on. They took a couple of minutes to look for people tailing her. When they were satisfied she was alone, they walked over. When she spotted Daelan, she hurried to them.

"I was starting to get worried."

She said it calmly, as if she was joking, but he could tell that she had legitimately been worried they would bail on her.

"We took a little time to make sure you weren't followed."

"Oh! Uh, good idea. Who's this?" she asked, glancing at Imogen.

"This is my niece, Jen."

"Your niece? Is she coming with us?"

"Yeah. I'm her guardian."

Her eyes widened in surprise, causing Daelan to chuckle.

Apparently she didn't see me as the parenting type either. Well, she's not wrong about that.

"Nice to meet you, Jen," she said, holding out her hand. "I'm Jessica."

"Hi."

"How do you like living with Daelan?"

"It's okay, though we're cooped up a lot."

"Well, we'll have to do something about that. Hopefully we can go shopping together while we're in France!"

"Could we try macarons?"

276

"Of course!"

Daelan could tell Ms. Hollis was trying to be nice to Imogen, which he appreciated. Still, he wanted to get out of the public eye.

"I hate to break this up, ladies, but we should get back."

"No problem. Where are the two of you staying?"

"The White Sands motel."

She pulled it up on her phone and made a face. "Could we, uh, stay somewhere else? Maybe... the, uh, River House Inn?"

"I'd prefer the motel."

"Why?"

"I like to use cash."

She scrutinized him, looking concerned. Whatever her doubts and fears were, she put them away and said, "I'll pay."

Daelan was about to shrug and accept when he thought about his recent conversation with Imogen. He turned to her and asked, "What do you think?"

Surprised, Imogen said, "That would be okay."

Daelan nodded, turned to Jessica and said, "Alright. We'll do it your way."

"Good!"

They split up, Daelan and Imogen to collect their things, and Jessica to get rooms. By the time they left the motel, Jessica had texted them a room number.

"I guess she has us rooming together still," Daelan said.

Imogen shrugged.

When they arrived and knocked on the room door, a smiling Jessica opened it and welcomed them in.

This is definitely nicer.

The couches, decor, TV... everything, in short, was a couple of notches better than what they were used to. There was a problem, though, that he couldn't put his finger on.

"Where are the beds?" Imogen asked.

That's it.

"In here." Jessica showed them an attached room with two queen-sized beds.

"Nice," Daelan approved. "Are you in one of the rooms next door?"

Jessica's face fell. "No. I, uh, was planning on staying with the two of you."

Daelan looked around to make sure he wasn't missing anything. "But there are only two beds."

"I thought I would sleep in here with Imogen, and you could have the main room."

"I sleep on the couch?" He wasn't super pleased about his demotion, but he'd slept on much worse before.

"The couch is a pull-out bed. I'll show you later."

Daelan shrugged. "Okay." He looked at Imogen. "Are you good with that?"

"Yeah."

"Great! Well, I think I'll go read in the bedroom, and we can go out this evening. I…" Her voice trailed off when Daelan held his hand up, gesturing for her to stop.

"If we're going to spend time together, there are some things you need to know."

Jessica's smile melted again, replaced by a nervous look. "And what would that be?"

Daelan sighed. "You're not going to believe me if I tell you, so let me just show you instead."

He held his hand up in cupping shape, fingers outspread, and slowly raised it as if he were struggling to raise something. At the same time, he lifted Imogen with his *particle motion* mana. She yelped when she started to rise, but quickly calmed down.

"What in the world…" Jessica breathed. "How are you doing that?"

Daelan just smiled, shrugged, and gestured to indicate she could approach Imogen. Jessica walked over, looking above Imogen's head and behind her. She ran her hands above and below her, looking for invisible wires.

She finally looked at Daelan and asked, "Why are you showing me a magic trick?"

"It's not a trick." He repeated his hand movement and lifted her as well.

"What are you doing?!"

"I'm preparing you to hear what you need to know."

He caused Jessica to approach Imogen and do a circle around her. Finally, he let the trembling woman and Imogen down.

"I apologize if I scared you."

"What's going on?"

"Magic is real, Ms. Hollis."

She spluttered. "That could have been magnets, or mirrors or something."

"Unless you're made out of iron, it's not magnets. We just got here. I didn't have a chance to set up mirrors." Seeing she was still skeptical, he said, "Tell me something I could do to prove to you that magic is real. If I can and it won't cause problems, I'll do it."

"Make a bird appear."

"Seriously? You want me to do a trick that fake magicians do to prove that magic exists?"

Jessica's face was bright red. "I was thinking of magicians, so…"

"Just give me something else."

"Tell me what I'm thinking."

Daelan frowned. "I could do that, but it would be dangerous for you. Give me something else."

"What's in my suitcase?"

"Ooh," Imogen said. "'What's in my pocket?' A classic."

"That will prove to you that magic is real?"

"It has to be specific. It can't be like, 'a dress', 'underwear'."

"Got it. Specific." He chuckled, wondering if she would regret her request. He drew unaspected mana from his arm cuff and invoked the words of power for a scrying spell that could see in the dark. "Let's see… you have a hairdryer."

"What model?"

"Dyson Supersonic."

"Lucky guess."

Daelan just smiled. "There's a pair of tennis shoes. Nike. White. Size… six."

Jessica frowned but said nothing.

"There's a light blue dress… or pajamas? Hard to tell with it folded up."

"Are there any decorations on the dress?"

Daelan nodded. "Pink flowers."

"What kind of flowers?"

He shrugged. "Beats me. There's a matching set of underwear. White. Lacy. Bra size is…"

She had been growing redder as he talked and finally burst out, "Alright! I believe you. Turn off the… whatever it is."

Daelan smiled. "Are you sure? It looked like there were some more interesting things in there."

She glared at him. "Yes, I'm sure. What the hell is going on, Daelan? Why are you doing this?"

"If we're going to live together, even for a short period of time, you're going to see things. I don't want to have to explain all of them."

She nodded her head slowly, clearly thinking. She pointed at Imogen. "Can she do magic?"

"Yep!" Imogen said happily.

Daelan gave Imogen a deadpan look. "Sort of."

"Jerk."

"Could you teach me how to do magic?" Jessica asked.

Daelan snorted. "Maybe, but I'm not going to."

"Why not?"

"Why should I?"

Jessica frowned, but didn't comment. "Are there other magicians?"

"You mean the real ones?" Daelan asked. "Yes, there are."

"Why doesn't anyone know about them?"

"They purposely keep magic hidden. Also, Earth is dreadfully low on mana, the stuff that powers spells."

Jessica slumped into a chair. "I just don't even know what to think."

Daelan nodded. "I understand. My advice? Take it in. Don't worry about it too much. It doesn't change much, other than giving you confidence that I can get Griffin back."

"Yeah," she said, looking brighter. "There is that."

Daelan chewed his lip and said, "There's something else."

"More?" she asked with widened eyes.

"Yeah. Though this…" he said, pointing at his face, "…is my true appearance, I'm currently using a different face." He dropped the illusion spell, becoming, once again, "Mr. Miller".

She looked at him for a while in shock. "It's, uh, still you?"

Daelan nodded. "It's still me."

280

Jessica looked bewildered. "I just… don't even know what to say." She went into the bedroom and closed the door behind her.

Daelan pulled out the DC power supply. "With that behind us, we can get started. You want to be up first, Imogen?"

She looked annoyed. "Sure, let's show her how you torture the little girl."

He just smiled and said, "Okay."

Chapter 39

Though Jessica turned out to be a low-maintenance person, after a few days she was ready to tear her hair out.

"Why don't you guys ever go out?"

Daelan looked at her, surprised at her naïveté. "Surely you've realized by now that there are people looking for us."

She frowned. "I'd hoped there was another explanation."

"Well, there isn't. We should be able to spend time outside soon, though."

"Oh?" she said hopefully. "What changed?"

"Jen is finally figuring out how to get mana from point A to point B without glitching every other second."

"Hey!" the offended teenager said while practicing her mana control.

Daelan just chuckled and picked up his gold arm cuff from the table where he'd been working on it, and held it out to Imogen. "Here."

She looked at him questioningly. "Isn't that yours?"

"It was, but I'll have my new one ready soon. Take it. I added an illusion spellform for you."

"So we could go outside again?"

"If your control is good enough."

Imogen rolled up her sleeve and put the jewelry on. Daelan had significantly tightened the spiral to fit her arm, so it fit snugly.

"The illusion spell form is the farthest one."

Imogen nodded and closed her eyes, concentrating. A couple of seconds later the bleached-blonde, pixie cut young woman in sweatpants and a t-shirt that said, "Remember when I asked your opinion? Yeah, me neither," disappeared, and in her place appeared a young woman with brown hair in a ponytail, a white blouse and jeans, wearing tasteful gold earrings.

Jessica's eyes went wide when she saw Imogen's disguise.

"She looks like… like…"

"You?" Daelan said. "I hope you don't mind. Either of you. Given that you're coming with us, I thought it made sense to have her look like a relative. And it made it easier for me to put the illusion together."

Imogen looked in a mirror, moving it back and forth to see different angles. She looked concerned, but finally smiled when she turned to Daelan.

"Sounds like a good excuse for checking Jessica out." She made air quotes and said, "Putting the illusion together."

He rolled his eyes. "I took a picture."

Imogen looked at herself in the mirror again, considering. "So, I can't change this image?"

"No."

"It's not the face," she said as she looked apologetically at Jessica. Turning back to Daelan, she said, "Always wearing the same clothes will be a problem."

He nodded. "If someone sees us often, yeah, but it should be good enough for casual use." He paused. "If you want something more flexible, you need to learn how to cast the spell."

"I know."

"Alright. If you show me that you can hold the image for half an hour without glitching, we'll go out tonight."

Nodding firmly, she sat down and concentrated. Though she had lasted a lot longer than Jessica, she really wanted to get out too.

**

After spending a couple of evenings out with Imogen and Jessica, Daelan decided to let them have a "girls' night". They wanted to do some window shopping, and he wanted to finish his new arm cuff. His and Imogen's passports were supposed to be ready soon, so his preparations would be the only thing holding them back.

Having laid out the necessary ingredients, he eyed the ingot of graphite that had gone untouched as of yet. Its time had come.

He broke off a piece and suspended it in the air. He was using the graphite ingot instead of charcoal because it was 99.9% pure carbon, but that last 0.1% and the air molecules surrounding it were still a problem. He wanted the diamonds in the cuff to be perfect, which meant removing all contaminants.

Daelan used his mana to create a containment sphere around the chunk, and removed all of the air inside it.

The next step was to liquify the carbon, an element that was notoriously hard to liquify, since it preferred to go straight from solid to gas. He wanted to liquify it for two reasons: to remove the remaining contaminants, and to create a uniform pressure throughout the carbon sample. That would allow a perfect crystal to form, without discontinuities, blemishes, or flaws.

Or at least that was the plan.

Daelan started heating the carbon and crushing it with the containment sphere. Unlike the lead, which required tens of millions of degrees to do its thing, forming diamonds required less than a thousandth of that temperature. Compared to the fusion he'd been doing the rest of the week, making diamonds felt like playing with an Easy Bake Oven.

Between the vacuum, the crushing pressure, and the heat, the carbon liquified, becoming a hot, glowing orb. He made ten containment cylinders in the shape of the diamonds he wanted, and filled them to the brim with liquefied carbon.

Feeling a touch of weariness and knowing he had quite a bit more ahead of him, Daelan paused to drink some water from a glass on the table. Hydrated, he continued onward, eager to see the results of his efforts.

He raised the temperature of the cylinder contents to 10,000 °F and increased the pressure. Daelan gave it a minute and then examined the lattice structure of the carbon. It was the tetrahedral matrix he desired. Smiling, he let his mana saturate the ten cylinders to look for any imperfections. There were a few. He added a little more heat to shake things so the atoms would move into place, and, when he was satisfied that everything was ready, froze the cylinders with *particle stillness* mana and brought them down to room temperature.

When he lowered the cylinders to the table and removed the containment mana, he was pleased to see ten perfectly clear diamonds. They were not terribly interesting looking. They had no facets to increase their brilliance, but that mattered little to Daelan. For storing mana, they would be unmatched.

Though he had enough mana to finish the job, he decided to rest before joining the diamonds and mithril. Instead, he took a pencil and a sheet of paper and started scribbling what spellforms he wanted to add to the arm cuff.

The point of the cuff's spellforms was to cast spells that would run constantly, and spells that either needed to be cast quickly or silently. Daelan started listing which ones he wanted by category.

Background spells: anti-divination, shield

Active spells: invisibility, truth-sensing, fool truth-sensing, telepathy, mental blast

He thought about adding a counterspell for disrupting other mages' magic, but his Father had found that it worked better if the spell was adapted to the magic you were trying to defeat.

The anti-divination and truth-sensing spells were the same ones he'd been using. Invisibility was an upgrade of his camouflage spell. "Fool truth-sensing" was exactly what it sounded like. No matter what you said, truth-sensing spells would say it was the truth.

Telepathy would be for communicating with others noiselessly, and mental blast was an attack that many mages would be defenseless against.

The shield spell would be his own invention, though it would be similar to what his Father and siblings had done in the past. It would be tailored to his particular *dao* and made to be energy-efficient.

Most shield spells were broken into two types: kinetic and energy. A particle shield could handle both. Daelan started writing what he wanted the shield to do. Once he had that figured out, he would translate it to runes and, hopefully, give it some symmetry to increase its power.

There were two key elements to shield spells: the trigger and the reaction. The trigger was the conditions that caused the spell to activate. You don't want to trigger on every gust of wind, or niece coming in for a hug, but you also don't want it to ignore darts and fireballs.

His Father had long used "energy density" to trigger his shields, making it a tried-and-true method. The idea was, if there was a region of energy density moving towards Daelan that exceeded a certain threshold, the shield would activate. That allowed Imogen hugs to get through, while stopping bullets that could easily have less total energy due to their lower mass.

The other half of the spell, the reaction, could also be implemented with various degrees of smartness. On one end was simply stopping whatever was coming in. That was the brute force approach, and required as much energy as whatever it was stopping.

A smarter approach was deflecting attacks, much like using a mundane shield to deflect a sword stroke instead of stopping it cold.

After spending a few hours putting together the details, he started working on the runes. When Imogen and Jessica came back, he had the following:

- *Sense Energy*
  - *From Self To 3E34 Planck Lengths Away*
- *If Energy Density > 5E13 Planck Energy Density*
  - *Create Mana Square*
    - *Turn From Self*
      - *Reflect*

The energy efficiency resulted from only running the energy sensing non-stop, and limiting it to a distance of about half a meter from his body. The energy intensive portion of the spell, the shield itself, only activated when needed.

It needed refinement and proper connections between the various phrases, but it had the heart of what he needed.

"What are you working on?" Imogen asked as she set two bags on the floor.

"Spells for the new arm cuff. How was the shopping?"

"It, uh, started out as window shopping…" she said with an embarrassed smile.

"And then it became shopping shopping?"

"Something like that."

Jessica paused taking clothes out of her own bag to say, "Well, I had a good time, and you needed some clothes. Speaking of… what do you have, Daelan? Like two pants and three shirts?"

"You forgot the one pair of underwear."

Jessica paled. "You're joking, right?" When Daelan just chuckled, she turned to Imogen. "He was joking, right?"

"Probably?"

Daelan looked seriously at Imogen. "Were you able to maintain the illusion?"

She looked guilty. "I lost it once, but it was only for a second."

"You need to get better."

"I know. I'll keep working on it."

"Good."

Jessica asked, "So, when can we go get my son?"

"We should have the passports in three days. That should give me enough time to finish my arm cuff and get some mana in it. Then we can go."

"Great! I'll book our flights!"

"You've already given us money for the flights, so why don't you help Imogen book them."

She shrugged. "Okay."

Daelan turned his attention back to the shield spell. If Jessica had asked why he was working so hard on it, he would have said it was because he wanted to reunite her with her son. It wouldn't have been a lie, but even more it was because he'd found he loved the act of creation. He wanted to make something beautiful with his own hands.

So much of his life had been focused on pain, destruction, and death. If he were to die today, he wouldn't leave anything behind except for a mountain of bodies and Imogen. Though that mountain was probably going to get bigger, he wanted to prove to himself, starting with the new arm cuff, that he wasn't just a destroyer.

**

"Do you have any bags to check in?" the airline ticketing agent, a middle-aged woman, asked.

"I don't, but she does," he said, nodding his head towards Jessica.

"If you could put your bag on the scale, ma'am…"

"Sure."

After they checked in and had their boarding passes, they headed to the security line. Jessica was unusually quiet, saying nothing and looking glassy-eyed as they shuffled forward in the line.

"You okay?" Daelan asked.

The question startled her out of her reverie. She gave a sad smile and said, "Yes. I was just thinking about Griffin."

Daelan nodded in what he hoped was a sympathetic manner. "He'll be okay."

Her look darkened. "I'm sure he is. Maybe too 'okay'. My ex-husband will pull out all the stops, and he has far more money than I do. I'm a little afraid Griffin won't want to come back with me."

Imogen side-hugged her and said, "Money doesn't make up for a mom."

Daelan said nothing. Having never had a mom, he had no idea.

**

That night, Daelan dreamed of his first lover, Trizna. She was beautiful and horrifying at the same time, with her heart-shaped face, shapely curves, patches of scaly skin, thick claws that could shred wood, and her penchant for pain, both giving and receiving. At the end of their lovemaking, she would leave with a smile and bruises all over her body, including around her neck. Daelan would look like he was the scratching post of a particularly energetic cat.

He didn't mind. It healed quickly.

Their relationship was not based on love, or even affection. She would much rather have been the consort of their Impaler or even a member of his harem, but she was disfavored. She took up with Daelan because she found him interesting. He knew she had trysts with other demons. He didn't care.

"Darling," she said while lying next to him, her mercurial eyes the color of lustrous silver at the moment, which meant she was in a good mood. "I have a toy we could play with."

"Eh?" Daelan said, breaking out of his post-coital thoughts. He smirked when he replayed in his mind what she had said. "And what would that be?"

"A whip. I've been practicing, and I can give even finer cuts than I can with my nails, and they have that little extra sting that's so delicious."

"Sounds lovely," he drawled. "Maybe later. I want you to do something for me."

"Oh? What is it?"

"I want you to get close to the demons who don't have a woman."

"Those losers? Why?"

"I want you to tease them, entrance them, and win them over to my side."

She looked at him. "To come over to your side, they're going to want a lot more than 'teasing'."

He gave her a flat stare. "Then give it to them."

Daelan thought he knew her fairly well—she didn't seem that complicated to him—but he couldn't tell what she was thinking at the moment. Her eyes became a stormy mix of silver and grey, her breathing quickened, and her cheeks had a slight flush.

Though she seemed a little excited, she also looked angry.

"You want me to become a loser too? A slut who will give herself to every almost-Wailer in the domain?"

Daelan didn't break eye contact. He just nodded. "That's what I want."

"Why?" she hissed. "Why should I do that for you?"

"You want to be with the Impaler, right?"

"Yes…" she said slowly.

"That's never going to happen. Unless I become the Impaler."

Her breath caught as she looked at him as if seeing him for the first time.

Daelan knew that this was the moment of truth. She would either be at his side, or he would have to kill her. He used some of his precious mana to feed a truth-sensing spellform he had carved in his ring, a small piece of metal that had taken him a year to earn.

She looked coy. "What if I decide I like one of them better than you?"

He quirked his lips. "Then I'll have to find you and beat you until you come back to me." He laughed inside when he saw her breathing getting faster.

"And if I succeed? What will you do for me?"

"Make you my consort. And…" Daelan paused before rolling on top of her, pressing his body into her while holding her wrists above her head. "…I'll practice with the whip until I can lash you so lightly that it almost tickles, or flay you until the skin comes off."

She shuddered with desire as she imagined what he had promised her. Her eyes were a bright silver. He looked deeply into them and asked, "So, will you do it?"

"Yes, my Impaler."

Truth.

**

Everyone was tired after the flight, so they stayed in a hotel in Paris that night and rented a car in the morning. Daelan and Imogen had never learned how to drive a stick shift, so Jessica became their chauffeur.

It took time to get out of the Parisian metropolis, but once they did, Daelan was surprised at how quickly the area became rural farmland. He had heard that the country was far more densely populated than the United States, so he'd been expecting more cities.

I guess it makes sense, considering all the wine and cheese they export.

As they traveled east, Jessica happily told them about the sites they passed, which family-owned stores had the most amazing fruit, and where the best bread was. She laughed as she told a story about a stinky cheese that she had tried on a dare. Daelan was mostly quiet throughout. He got the feeling she was mostly talking to not be alone with her thoughts, so he let her.

They stopped at a hotel fifty miles from the chateau. When they set their things down in their rooms, Daelan decided it was time to speak up.

"Imogen, could you give me and Jessica a minute?"

Imogen was surprised, but her expression quickly turned playful. "Of course!"

Daelan shook his head, but didn't say anything because he knew Imogen was just joking. When she left the suite, he turned to Jessica, who seemed nervous. "What outcome do you want from this?"

Her tastefully plucked brows furrowed in confusion. "What do you mean? I want Griffin."

"Sure," he said calmly. "But what about your ex-husband? What do you want to happen to him?"

Her eyes widened and she looked around, as if to see if anyone was listening. "Are you talking about killing him?" she asked in a soft voice.

"That's one possibility. I'm just asking, after you get Griffin, then what? Where are you going to live? How are you going to avoid your ex-husband? Should I do anything to him or his people to help you in your goals?"

She looked at him strangely. "You would do it, wouldn't you? Kill him, I mean."

Daelan nodded. "Yes."

"Why?"

He shrugged.

She carefully walked up to him, as if he were a dangerous animal that she didn't want to startle. "What was your childhood like, Daelan?"

It was Daelan's turn to be surprised. "Why do you ask?"

She paused and thought for a few moments. "Because if I ask someone to enter the lion's den and kill for me, the least I can do is get to know them. I don't know anything about you."

Daelan pursed his lips. "My childhood wasn't easy."

"Tell me about it."

"I was cut off from my family. And... I was in a place where people weren't kind."

"Like Imogen," she whispered, putting her hand on his cheek.

He started to nod, but stopped, not wanting to disturb her hand. "Yes." He felt shame, though, because he knew that was only part of his story. *Unlike Imogen, I became one of them.*

"I'm sorry. I'm sorry your parents didn't have someone they could send in to rescue you, Daelan. Thank you for being the man that Griffin needs."

She took her hand off his cheek, which he regretted, and began to unbutton her blouse.

"What are you doing?"

She shook her head. "It's not what you think. I want to show you something." Like the picture she'd sent him before, she showed him a torso covered with bruises. The larger ones were purple in the middle and turning yellow-green, while the smaller ones had lost all purple. He thought the bruises were amateurish. Random. There was no method to the madness.

The one interesting thing was a strange pattern of scabs on her stomach. They looked like crude, preschool level letters, only they were wrong somehow.

"Are those letters?"

"They're upside down and backwards, so I can read them from my perspective," she said sadly.

With that clue, he could read what would become a permanent scar. "Last chance"

"Last chance?"

"He was telling me that if I interfere with him or Griffin again, he would kill me."

"I see."

Jessica put her blouse back on and started buttoning it up. "If you get the chance, please kill him. But don't put yourself or Griffin at risk to do it."

He nodded slowly. "I understand."

She walked up to him again, less warily this time, and gave him a gentle hug. When she winced, he understood why, and felt bad.

"Thank you."

Chapter 40

Daelan waited an hour, until the winter evening was dark and chill.

"Have you bought our return tickets?" he asked Jessica.

"Yes, for tonight, like you asked."

"And they can be changed to tomorrow if we need?"

She sighed in exasperation, but her lips curled as she said, "Yes, Dad, I did it exactly like you said."

He patted her on the head. "Good job."

"I'd beat you up if I didn't want you in good health right now."

"Aw, you do care," he said, smiling. "Just not about me."

She looked at him, eyes moist. "Get Griffin for me, and you will be my hero for life."

He nodded. "Don't worry." He turned to Imogen, who was supposed to be studying but was just watching them. "See you soon."

Imogen looked concerned. "Be safe."

"Always."

Daelan activated the invisibility spell on his arm cuff and stepped out onto the balcony. He paused to appreciate the view—the lights of the town mirroring the stars in the sky, though the stars were far more delicate, like an almost invisible web with dewdrops that caught the light from below.

Shaking his head at his maudlin thoughts, he leapt onto the railing and, leaping again, hurled himself into the open air. He used his motion mana to accelerate, reaching hundreds of miles per hour in seconds.

He refrained from causing a sonic boom. The air resistance cost him more mana and, more importantly, it would be anything but discreet. Besides, the trip was already only six minutes.

Using invisibility, flight, and GPS, it was ridiculously easy to get on the chateau's grounds unseen. He simply lowered himself behind a row of hedge bushes next to the house. He didn't need the cover, given his invisibility spell would have been sufficient to keep him hidden, but he was happy to save the mana.

Once he was comfortable, he whispered the incantation for a scrying spell to scout the inside of the house. There was a moment of disorientation as his sight was split into two, but he was used to it and recovered quickly. He willed the disembodied view forward, through walls, as he scouted the house from his hideaway.

There he is.

He found Griffin playing with a firetruck while adults chatted nearby. He looked happy and healthy. Identity confirmed, Daelan released the scrying spell and used x-ray vision instead. Over the next couple of hours, Daelan periodically watched the goings-on in the house.

The boy spent time in the kitchen making cookies, judging by the cookie sheet in the oven, with a slightly hunched-over woman. Afterwards, he spent time with one of the men. Perhaps playing a board game? They spent an hour or two together before two of the women joined them—the hunched-over woman and someone else.

The boy went to bed at 9:45, but the adults did not, so Daelan continued waiting. While he waited, he thought about what to do with Jessica's ex-husband. He could, of course, kill him. He could even make it look like a natural death. It would be simplicity itself to stop a normie's heart until he was dead.

There were two problems: Jessica was nearby, and she would have Griffin. How to explain those things? He turned over the options in his mind.

By the time all the adults were asleep except for one man who, Daelan assumed, was guarding the house, it was 1:00 in the morning.

Daelan frowned. They would have to postpone their flight until later in the morning. He knew that was likely to be the case, but he'd hoped.

He reactivated the invisibility and calmly walked to the wall next to the master bedroom. After a final check with a scrying spell, he phased through the wall and saw the sleeping couple. Griffin's father was a fit man in his fifties, the gray hair at his temples and a couple of wrinkles his only visible concessions to age. Daelan ignored the woman in the bed, other than to cast a sleeping spell on her that, barring a major disturbance, would keep her asleep for the next few hours. He finished his preparations by turning off the invisibility, casting a sound isolation spell on the room, and turning on the lights.

The man opened his eyes and sat up. "Who the hell are you?"

"I'm the guy your ex-wife hired."

That caused a muted reaction that Daelan had a hard time reading. He suspected that Griffin's dad was a good poker player.

"So, why are we talking?"

"Because I need to decide what to do about you."

Even less of a reaction that time, though Daelan still wasn't surprised when he made a move. The man slithered out of bed, naked, and grabbed a pistol from his nightstand. Daelan let him.

"Feel better?"

The man laughed. "Yeah, I do. Now, tell me who the hell you are."

Daelan shook his head. "That isn't how this is going to go. I'm going to ask the questions and you're going to answer."

"Is that right?" he sneered. "It isn't hard to ID a corpse." Three booms erupted from the pistol, expelling hot lead at near supersonic speeds at Daelan. To the man's shock, though, the bullets stopped in front of Daelan and dropped to the ground with a clatter. "What the..." he muttered in disbelief.

"Are you done now?" Daelan asked. "The ringing in your ears is going to make it harder to talk."

Ignoring Daelan's words, the man stared at the gun and, with a desperate look, pointed it at Daelan again and fired bullet after bullet until the gun dry-fired.

Five more bullets clattered noisily on the limestone floor.

"Tell me about your relationship with your ex-wife."

"What?" The man looked around and saw the woman in the bed, unmoving. "You killed her?"

"No. She'll wake up in the morning. If you don't start giving me some answers, you won't be joining her."

He put the gun on the nightstand, sat on the bed, and ran a hand through his hair, clearly trying to make sense of what was going on.

"What did you ask?"

"Your relationship with your ex-wife."

"What do you want to know?"

"Why do you beat her up?"

"What the hell kind of question is that?"

"Last chance. Answer, now."

"Because she doesn't listen, okay? She didn't do what I asked, and I had to get through to her! There, you satisfied?"

Not by a long shot. "Griffin seemed happy tonight."

"Is that a question?" he asked angrily.

"Why was he okay with being away from his mom?"

"He's a kid. Give him attention, treats, and toys, and he'll be fine."

"What did you tell him about his mom?"

"I avoided the topic."

Daelan questioned him about his business activities. It turned out some were legit, but most were fronts for criminal activity. He asked the man about his family and childhood. He wasn't sure what he was looking for.

Sympathy, I guess.

He was looking for a reason to not kill him, and so far wasn't finding anything convincing.

"Do you love your son?"

The naked man stood up and looked indignant. "Of course I do!"

Daelan stifled a laugh at the ridiculous sight. Glowering, the man sat back down. Getting serious again, Daelan looked at him for a few seconds and asked his last question.

"Then why haven't you shown him how to be a good man?"

Griffin's father gaped, at a loss on how to respond. Daelan walked over to a small desk in the room and looked through the drawers until he found a piece of paper and a fancy pen.

"Write a letter, explaining why you're ceding all parental rights to Jessica."

He sneered. "It's 'Jessica' now, huh? Let me guess, you're doing this because you're sleeping with her. I ain't gonna sleep with you, but I can give you triple whatever she's paying."

Daelan just said, "Sit your ass down and write the letter."

"And if I don't?"

"Then you die."

The man smiled. "You don't want to kill me. It will cause you problems. It will cause *them* problems."

Daelan chuckled. "I'd rather not kill you, but trust me, I'll be happy to do it if I have to." He paused and said, "Oh, and I can make it look completely natural." He invaded the man's body with his *stillness* mana and used it to still his heart.

The man panicked, as breathing did him no good. After a few seconds he grabbed the desk to keep from falling and shouted, "Please!"

Daelan released his heart, causing the man to gasp in relief.

"What the fuck was that?!"

"That's how you're going to die unless I get a really good letter."

The man looked at Daelan like he was a monster.

"Fine! Fine. You win."

The man sat down and started writing. When Daelan was satisfied with his efforts, he tucked the letter away and said, "Okay, time to go back to bed."

The man was hesitant. "So, that's it? You go away and we never see each other again?"

"That's right. As long as you leave Jessica and Griffin alone."

The man put his arms out in a "stop" gesture. "I will leave them alone forever, I promise, as long as it keeps you the hell away from me."

He gingerly got back into bed, watching Daelan the entire time. When his head was on the pillow, he asked, "Now what?"

"Now you sleep," he said as he cast the sleep spell. When he was fully under, Daelan's eyes took on a malicious look as he stilled the man's heart. "Enjoy Hell."

**

When Daelan returned to their hotel room's balcony and entered the room holding a sleeping Griffin, Jessica rushed up and grabbed her son.

"Griffin!"

She cried for a time, holding him such that his head rested on her shoulder. Daelan released the sleeping spell to allow him to wake up.

"Mom? Where am I?"

"We're in France, honey, but we'll be going home soon."

"Where are Dad and Grandma?"

"They're, uh…" She looked at Daelan questioningly. He dragged his thumb across his neck in the universal "killed" sign. "We'll talk about your Dad later, Griff. I'm so happy to see you! Mommy missed you."

"Mom, you're getting me wet."

"I'm sorry, sweetie."

She reluctantly set him down, still tearful but smiling. She turned to Daelan and mouthed. "Thank you."

He nodded and handed her the letter written by her ex. As she read, her eyes grew bigger in shock. She looked at him and asked, "How?"

"We can talk about it later. There's another copy at the chateau."

She looked at him for a moment and nodded, turning her attention back to Griffin, who was exploring the hotel suite.

He looked at his mom and asked, "Did you bring Teddy?"

Jessica went and pulled out a well-loved bear from her things and held it up. "Of course! We can't leave Teddy behind, right?"

"Right," he agreed with satisfaction.

As mother and child talked, Daelan turned to Imogen, who was looking at the scene with a wistful smile.

"I'm sorry you're not getting many opportunities to see France."

"That's okay. I hope to live a long time. I'll see everything I want, eventually."

Her answer surprised Daelan. He curled his lips and nodded at her.

You're right.

**

When they landed and got to baggage collection, things became awkward. Jessica and Griffin had checked in luggage, Daelan and Imogen had not.

"What are your plans now?" Daelan asked. "Do you need a ride somewhere?"

Jessica smiled for a reason he couldn't divine. "No, I can get an Uber. Thank you, Daelan. For everything." She looked down at Griffin. "Say goodbye to Daelan, Griffin."

"That's not Daelan," Griffin said suspiciously. "Daelan has hair and is missing an eye."

"You're right," Jessica said. "I meant to say that he's Daelan's friend. Can you say goodbye?"

Griffin looked at his mom. "Are you friends with Daelan now? You thought he might be a bad guy before."

"That was before. Daelan is a good guy."

Daelan snorted, but didn't otherwise respond.

Griffin stood on the edge of the baggage carousel. "Bye, Daelan's friend!"

"Bye, Griffin." He turned to Imogen. "Let's go."

Imogen hugged Jessica and followed Daelan towards their car. "So, what now?"

"Now, we go twist some vampires' arms."

"Um, why are we doing that again?"

"To see if they know who the assassin is, or where we can find the Society." He looked at her and asked, "Nervous?"

"Well, yeah! Vampires and wizards! Who wouldn't be scared?"

"They're nothing compared to what we'll face in the future."

"Really?"

"Really. Are you having second thoughts?"

"No!" she said, but her voice hitched.

He looked at her, thinking. "How would you like to begin weapons training?"

"Seriously?" she said excitedly.

He sighed. "Yes, seriously."

"That would be great! What weapons?"

"That will depend on you. We'll figure out which ones are best for you. And don't worry, by the time we're done, you won't be trapped in the room with them, they'll be trapped with you."

299

Chapter 41

The next night, Daelan disconnected himself from the DC power supply, looked over at Imogen, who was studying, and said, "I'll be back soon, okay?"

She frowned. "Be careful."

"I will." He paused and said, "We have to chase the leads we have if we want to find your parents' killer."

"I know. Just… be careful."

He nodded and tried to give her a comforting smile. He understood her worry. Until now they'd been dealing with criminals and mages, who were scary enough. Vampires, even if they weren't necessarily as objectively dangerous, held a special place in the psyche of the people of Earth. They were the monster under the bed, the bump in the night.

"I will," he repeated, and walked out into the cool night air.

After making sure no one was watching him, he turned invisible and flew up into the sky. He traveled at a sedate pace, feeling mellow for some reason.

Maybe it's all the second-hand smoke, Daelan thought with a chuckle. It seemed like every city in Oregon smelled like weed, but Portland reeked.

It didn't take long for Daelan to reach his goal, a dingy apartment complex with open dumpsters, graffiti, and cigarette butts strewn around the parking lot. He lit on the ground, and started searching for the vampire's domicile, building 3 apartment 2D according to Marcus.

When he found it, he was surprised to see a cheery doormat with "Home, Sweet Home" on it, and what looked like a half-basket that was flat on back, hanging on the door a little below eye level. The basket held yellow daisies. When he looked at it closer, Daelan realized that the basket was actually a small planter with soil in it.

The hell…?

Daelan double checked the address on the door and in his notes from his interrogation of Marcus, to make sure he had the right place.

Mentally shrugging, he phased through the door. If he didn't find any vampires, he would just leave.

The inside of the apartment was more or less what Daelan expected from the outside. Clean and tidy, scented candles, pictures of a couple in cute frames that had hearts on them. Daelan found himself both disgusted at the uselessness of it all, and vaguely envious when he compared it to the motels he and Imogen stayed at.

Daelan took a moment to scry the two rooms beyond the small front room. They were a small bathroom, and a bedroom with a sleeping couple that looked to be in their early twenties. Frowning, feeling sure he must be at the wrong place, he silently entered the room and opened his third eye.

To his surprise, the woman was a vampire.

Daelan put a sleeping spell on the man, and, once he was satisfied the man was out, nudged the woman awake.

"What...?" she said sleepily, turning to the man. When Daelan nudged her back, she startled awake and sat up at a speed that was hard to follow. "Who are you?!"

"Quiet," Daelan said, annoyed. He knew hers was a natural reaction, but that didn't mean he liked it. "I put a sleeping spell on your man, but if you agitate him too much, he might wake up."

The young woman looked scared. "What do you want?"

"Information. I know you're a vampire. I just want the answer to a couple of questions, and then I'll leave, and hopefully we'll never see each other again."

When Daelan declared her to be a vampire, she became even more terrified. "A-are you the chameleon?"

Daelan's brows furrowed in confusion. "The what?"

"The one who killed vampires a couple months ago."

"Oh. Yeah, I suppose that's me."

"P-please don't kill me," she pleaded, her trembling visible.

"I won't, as long as you answer my questions."

She nodded her head, still trembling, so Daelan brought out the hand-drawn picture of the assassin he had made after visiting the gunman who killed Imogen's parents. "Do you recognize this man?"

301

She shook her head quickly. "N-no... I could, uh, ask other people in my family if they..."

Daelan cut her off. "We'll come back to that. Next question: where is the local branch headquarters of the Society?"

The vampire looked relieved to get a question she could answer. "It's a mansion next to the Sandy River!" She didn't know the address, but she pulled up a map app on her phone and showed him where it was.

Daelan nodded thoughtfully. "Thanks. I just want one more thing. Tell the head of your family, Aisha, that I'd like to talk with her about a truce."

"Uh, I can't really talk with her..."

Daelan rolled his eyes, "Just tell whoever you can talk to that 'the Chameleon' would like to talk with her, okay? And give her this phone number." He gave her one of his burner phone numbers. "I'll wait for her call at 3 PM, the next three days."

Having been tracked through a phone before, Daelan wanted to minimize the danger by keeping the battery out, except for a five minute window at 3 PM. Daelan and Imogen would immediately move position after each call window.

The young vampire nodded nervously. "Alright..."

Daelan quirked his lips and turned invisible before turning around to leave. He stifled a chuckle when she squeaked in fright. He liked fear. Fear meant safety.

**

The next day, Daelan received a call on his burner phone at 3:00 and 42 seconds.

"Hello?"

"Daelan?" The feminine voice sounded tense.

Daelan looked around, suddenly wishing he was somewhere more private than a restaurant booth in downtown Portland. Fortunately, at three in the afternoon there were very few people. "Yeah, it's me."

"Why did you ask to speak with me? And why should I speak with you after you tried to kill me?"

Daelan drawled, "I was kind of hoping we could let bygones be bygones."

Aisha Aemilianus, the head of the Aemilianus vampire family, huffed in aggravation. "You kill a couple dozen of us, and I'm just supposed to let that go?"

"That seems like a better deal than me killing more of you."

In an angry but controlled voice, she asked, "So what do you propose?"

"Exactly what I said. Let bygones be bygones. I don't go after you. You don't go after me."

"That's it?"

"Well..." he said with a half-smile, "I would like some information too.'

"What information?"

"The name of a mage."

"Why do you want it?" she asked.

Daelan said nothing.

The woman snorted and said, "Send me the picture, and if we can help, we'll discuss the price."

Daelan frowned, but it was to be expected. "Alright." He texted her the picture. Seconds later he heard laughter.

"Oh, this is delicious!"

"I take it you know him?"

"You could say that," she said. He could practically hear her sneer. "I assume you plan on causing him problems?"

"You could say that."

"Then I'll give you the information for free. His name is Caius, and he's the Merlin of the Society of Mages."

"What's a 'Merlin'?"

"It's the title of the supreme leader of the organization."

Huh. Must have pulled that off with Sicanthian magic or something. "Where can I find him?"

"Bonn, Germany." She gave him the information he needed to find the Society's headquarters.

After he finished writing it down, Daelan said, "So, do we have an agreement to stop hunting each other?"

Daelan grew uncomfortable as he waited for an answer.

"Yes, we have a deal." Before he could respond, she said, "Good hunting... as long as you're after the Society," and hung up.

He thought about what she had told him as he and Imogen left the restaurant and tossed the phone in one of the city's trash cans. Getting the assassin might be trickier than he'd thought.

**

"So, I have good news and bad news," Daelan said after they got back to the motel.

Imogen frowned. "What's the good news?"

"The vampires are no longer after us." Daelan paused and added, "Probably."

Imogen looked at him worriedly. "Probably?"

He shrugged. "We agreed to stop going after each other, but I'm still going to lock the door."

Imogen bit her lip as she considered that. "And the bad news?"

"The bad news is that your parents' assassin is high up in the Society."

Her face tensed with anger. "Them again? How high is he?"

Daelan frowned. "Really high. He's the head of the organization."

Imogen collapsed onto the bed. "Well, that's just great."

"It makes it tougher, but we can still get him."

"You really think so?"

Daelan nodded. "I do. The mages here are, honestly, kind of weak. And even though the assassin is from my homeworld, I still know more than he does."

"How do you know?"

He smirked. "The God-King never gave out his most prized secrets. Except to me."

Imogen considered that after sitting up. "So, what are our next steps?"

"Good question. I think we should get away from everything for a while so we can stop traveling and focus on training instead. I want you to be able to defend yourself against mages and vampires. That should still give us enough time to kill the assassin before we leave Earth in eight months."

"Where do you want to go to 'get it away from it all'?"

"I don't know." Daelan opened up his laptop. "Why don't you help me find somewhere?"

**

It took a few days, but Daelan and Imogen eventually decided to go to the Alaskan wilderness for the next half a year. It was springtime, so they would be there for the sunniest part of the year.

Once the decision was made, Daelan did a lot of research on "living off the grid". They were going somewhere they would likely not see another soul—the northern foothills of the "Gates of the Arctic" national park—so they had to bring everything they would need to survive on their own.

Let's see... cabin, outhouse, and well plans; concrete; lumber; nails; tools; windows; doors; shingles; mattresses; blankets; solar panels; inverter; batteries; wood-burning stove and chimney; water pump; ...

It seemed to Daelan that as he went further down the rabbit hole, the list of things they needed multiplied. The solar panels, inverter, and batteries alone were $41,000. The cabin, outhouse, and well materials were $45,000, and shipping for everything to one of the northern Alaska ports was around $10,000, leaving them with just $4,000 of their Jessica Hollis money and the $19,000 or so that Daelan had left from web development and pawning jewelry all over the country. They would need that money for food and miscellaneous supplies.

Daelan sighed. *Well, at least I felt rich for a few days.* He looked up from his work and saw Imogen eating a burger and fries. "Slow down," he told the hungry teenager. "Chew your food. Make it last."

Imogen just gave him a puzzled look, wondering what brought that on.

**

Daelan and Imogen flew up to Alaska weeks later, when supplies they had ordered started coming in. The solar panels from China were first. They paid someone to transport the pallets a few miles out of town to the side of the road.

The truck driver looked concerned when he saw the site, or lack thereof. "You sure you just want it here at the side of the road?"

Daelan nodded. "I'm sure. Someone else will be coming to pick us up shortly."

Shrugging, the man used the truck-mounted forklift to offload the pallets. Done in a few minutes, he nodded at the pair and said, "Take care," before driving back to town.

Daelan and Imogen admired the rugged landscape while they waited a few minutes to make sure the truck driver was gone. He enjoyed looking at the thick forest on the inland side of the road, with the hemlocks, cedars, and spruces he'd read about while preparing to come up, and the wind-tossed waves of the ocean on the coastal side.

He grinned at Imogen. "This is something else, eh? What do you think?" he asked as he gestured at their surroundings.

Imogen did not look nearly as chipper. Her arms were crossed and she looked like she was trying to hide in her jacket. "I think I'm cold."

"Then I suggest putting your coat on," he said dryly.

It took a few minutes to get geared up—she resisted when he told her to put on her wind-resistant balaclava, but relented when he took her on a quick flight without one. When they were ready, she climbed on his back and they took to the air, followed shortly by the three pallets.

"Isn't it beautiful?" he asked as they moved inland.

"Mmm."

"You may not be convinced now, but I think you'll grow to like this place. We'll be able to relax, work on our skills, and not worry about anyone finding us." *And when we're ready,* he thought, *we'll go hunting.*

Chapter 42

Merlin

The Merlin was uneasy, and had been ever since finding out about the possible avatar. He spent a lot of time talking with technology consultants, thinking about how to break through the anti-divination spell, and looking over his shoulder. It had made his time on Earth go from "suffocating" to "hellish".

He needed to go home, and was willing to do just about anything to make it happen. Even sell years of his life.

"You have the level 3 tracking spell?" he asked the woman in the communication mirror. Her red hair was pinned up in an elaborate up-do, and her shoulders were covered in a toga.

"I do," she said with a self-satisfied smile. "Are you ready to enter into the contract?"

He hesitated, feeling like he was making a deal with the devil. "I am."

"Very well." She gestured to a man who came into view. He spoke words that created glowing bands of mana that gathered in both realms. Caius quailed when he saw that on his side they looked like bonds, while on the Senator's side they looked like reins. "You agree to serve me without reservations of any kind for 50 years. If you die before you're able to do so, the burden will be borne by your firstborn. In exchange, I shall give you the army's level 3 tracking spell. Do you agree?"

Caius' self-control was sorely tested by the rage boiling in his chest. He tightly controlled his voice, but there was no keeping the edge of anger out of it. "You never said anything about including my son in the contract." His son was only seven years old, and Caius would be damned before he let him be forced to serve the Senator, or anyone else.

The Senator lifted a delicate eyebrow. "Well, now I have. I have no guarantee that you will ever return to Sicanthus, which would make you useless to us. Your son is merely a guarantee that we will get something from our investment."

He took a few breaths and said, "Fine. I agree to the contract." *I'll make sure to get back and serve the time myself.*

"Then seal it with your blood."

Caius cut the palm of his hand and put his hand on the communication mirror, creating a bloody partial handprint that quickly disappeared into the glass. The bands grabbed him, but not his flesh. They sunk in and bound his very soul.

What have I done?

"Relax," the Senator said. "It's only fifty years. And you might not even have to serve it!" she said with a laugh.

Caius narrowed his eyes in anger. He would never let his son serve her. He would deal with Daelan, return to Sicanthus, do his time, and… well, he would see. It would depend on how they dealt with him. He was not as powerful as the Senator, but a mistreated dog could still bite.

The final ribbon of mana did not bind his spirit. It was his reward. The glowing slip entered his head and filled him with the knowledge of the spell.

Excellent.

It required a great deal of mana. Enough to take a year of mana bones to power, less if he took more from the Society.

Caius thought it was fair. If he wouldn't have enough mana to cast spells over the next year, then neither would they.

Chapter 43

Daelan: 6 months later

Daelan smiled inwardly when he saw the beads of sweat collecting on Imogen's forehead, and her stance that was a mix of leaning forward as if into a coming wave, while simultaneously hunching her shoulders and making herself small. It was all a sign of her nervous anticipation.

"Ready?"

"Ready."

He lifted the 12-gauge shotgun and pulled the trigger, hurling a non-lethal bean bag at the young woman. He noted that her flinch reaction was diminishing.

Good.

He did his best to stop himself from wincing at the pain in his shoulder from the recoil. Walking was painful enough, shooting was even worse, but he didn't want Imogen to know that. She didn't need the guilt.

He shot four more bean bags at her. Each one hit the passive shield from her arm cuff and, depending on where they hit it, veered off to the side or rebounded and dropped to the ground.

Daelan used his more-than-human speed to load four more rounds. "You better hurry!"

Imogen was nervously speaking the words of power for another shield, and he was proud to see that she didn't pause when he shot the next four rounds. She had barely finished the spell when her arm cuff's shield failed on the third shot. A new shield that glowed a soft blue in the view of his third eye appeared, surrounding her in what looked like a soft cocoon.

A little too soft, he grumped to himself. Still, she had protected herself from all the bean bags for the first time, so he called out, "Good!" Her shield would gain more solidity with practice, concentration, and will.

She excitedly said, "Thanks!" but shrieked when she saw him pull out two metal batons the size of daggers, rush up at the speed of a vampire, and start "stabbing" the shield. This was a new element in their combat role play, one that had taken her by surprise.

"Defend yourself!" he roared, the pain he was feeling in his joints adding a touch of verisimilitude to the pretend rage.

She whipped the staff she was holding at him, forcing him to parry with one of the batons.

"Good! The best defense…"

"…is a good offense," she stated flatly, obviously tired of repeating the mantra.

"Especially when you can't parry worth crap," Daelan finished.

Instead of replying, Imogen focused on the battle, and even managed to touch Daelan with her staff after a minute when she telekinetically pushed one of his batons aside.

"Good! That's the way to do it. Use your weapons and magic together."

"Thanks," she said while panting. She had long since learned that all-out fighting was an extreme form of anaerobic exercise.

"Five minutes rest, and then we'll go again."

"But I succeeded that time!" she complained.

"You don't practice until you get it right. You practice until you can't get it wrong."

Imogen frowned, but tiredly nodded before sitting down.

He was pleased with her progress. She was in much better physical condition. Her mana control had improved by leaps and bounds. She was proficient, barely, with a quarterstaff. The main thing she needed to improve was her casting speed and using all of her skills together.

Daelan wasn't worried about attacks from vampires anymore, but he still used them as Imogen's pretend antagonists because he wanted her to be able to handle opponents that were stronger and faster than normal humans.

While he waited for her to recover, Daelan sat down to rest his weary bones. A few minutes later, he asked, "Are you ready?"

"Ugh," she groaned. "I guess."

He gingerly stood up and picked up the shotgun. "Alright, let's do it again."

**

The next morning, Daelan sat on a chair that was just the rough-hewn end of a log, and hooked himself up to the unconditioned output of their solar panels. It was a little dicey to put 10kW of power into his body, but it was good for practicing mana control. He found that burning the hell out of his arm when he messed up did wonders for his concentration.

Imogen made a face when she saw what he was doing. "I don't know why you do that. Why not just hook up to the batteries?"

Daelan grinned at her. "Because I'm not a wimp, unlike some people."

The teenager rolled her eyes. "Right. And unlike some people, I didn't almost burn off my tattoo the other day."

Daelan looked away and grumbled, refusing to look her in the eye. *She just had to go and bring that up.*

Imogen smiled at her guardian and mercifully did not push the issue. She knew he was doing it to stretch his mana core, to get stronger because their enemies were legion. That didn't mean she didn't think he was being stupid, just that she understood it.

"How are your experiments going?"

Daelan grimaced. "Not well. The silicon and sulfur supplements don't seem to do anything other than make my mouth taste like gritty, rotten eggs."

Imogen laughed. "Oh, they do more than that!"

Daelan's cheeks colored from embarrassment. The sulfur supplement had had a decidedly unwholesome effect on his flatulence. Imogen had taken to calling his farts "cabin clearers".

Seeing his embarrassment, she decided to change the topic. "Can I ask you a question about thermodynamics?"

Daelan spat out, "Sure," but most of his focus was on handling the ten kilowatts of electricity entering his body.

She frowned and looked concerned. "Shouldn't you, uh, turn it off while talking?"

"I'll be fine."

"Riiiiigght," she said in a sarcastic drawl. She shrugged her shoulders and said, "Fine. I just want to know what entropy is."

Daelan sighed, switched the power feed to charge up the batteries, and unhooked himself. This was going to take some time. He very pointedly did not look at or acknowledge Imogen's grin.

"What's your understanding of entropy?"

She grimaced. "Isn't it, like, disorder or randomness, or something?"

Daelan nodded. "Yes, but that's looking at the trees, and not the forest." He started to explain how everything behaves like it wants to be at the lowest-energy state it can. Balls roll down hills and come to rest. When ovens are turned off they cool down until they're the same temperature as the rest of the house. He went on to explain that low-energy states are disordered.

"Remember the ping-pong balls in the box?"

"Yeah. When you shake the box, the ping-pong balls are all over the place."

"Right. While shaking the box, could they all go to one side of the box, even for a moment?"

"Technically yes," she said, "but they won't."

"Why not?"

"Because…" she stopped to think. "Because that would be a higher-energy state?"

"Yes, but that's not why. It's because disordered states are much more probable." They talked some more, going back and forth, and before he knew it, an hour had passed. "You little scamp. You just didn't want to study."

"Guilty as charged," she said with a smile, "But I still learned a lot!"

"Good." He paused and said, "We're getting low on meat. Why don't you go get us some?"

Her eyes widened. "By myself? Really?"

He nodded. "Yeah. Unless you're not up to it." He raised a questioning eyebrow.

"No! No. I, uh, I can do it."

"You sure?"

"Yeah." She started gathering her rifle and outdoor gear and, when she was ready, gave him a nervous but happy look. "See you soon!"

Daelan just nodded while taking in as much electricity as he could handle. "Good luck."

When she'd been gone a few minutes, he switched the power back over to the batteries and prepared to go out. He wondered how she would do on her own. He intended to trail her and make sure she was okay. He wanted her to learn independence, but he wanted her to have a safety net when she did.

**

"Mm, this is so good!" Imogen said as she bit into the mule deer steak that evening.

"Meat that you hunt usually is. It's like the camping multiplier."

"What's the 'camping multiplier'?"

"Anything that you eat while you're camping tastes five times better than it would at home."

"Then how come your stew usually tastes like, uh…" She paused as she saw his glare. "...you're right, it makes your stew taste, um, decent."

"You know what would make the food even tastier?" he asked as he maintained his laser-focused glare.

"What?"

"Cooking it yourself. That stacks another 3x multiplier, at least."

"Uh, that's okay, your stew is great!" she said, trying to recover the situation.

"No, no, I insist. It's an important survival skill."

"Ugh. Me and my big mouth," Imogen grumbled.

Daelan chuckled as he worked on cutting off another piece of venison. "We'll be leaving Alaska soon."

"How come?"

Daelan's eyebrows raised. "I thought you'd be happy to hear that."

She looked conflicted. "I am. Sort of. It would be nice to get back to civilization, but I've grown to like it here."

"Here" was about as far from civilization as they could get. They were staying in the northern foothills of the "Gates of the Arctic" national park in Alaska, far from any coastal cities or Inuit towns.

They didn't have much, but it was enough. They had spent most of the $100,000 they received from Jessica to buy and ship the solar panels, lumber, and supplies they had needed to a northern Alaskan port. They'd carried it all the rest of the way themselves via flying and telekinesis.

Daelan had wanted to get away from the cameras, the police, and everything else, and just enjoy some peace and quiet while he trained Imogen.

"I'm glad you've grown to like it, but summer is coming to a close, and it's going to become cold and dark. We could handle the cold if we had to, but dark means not much electricity."

They were so far north that for a very brief time around the summer solstice, the sun never set. It was strange to experience, but great for their electricity production. In the winter that would all be reversed, to the point where the sun would not even rise around the winter solstice.

"Yeah, I get it. Wouldn't be fun to be here during the polar night anyway."

Daelan frowned, not eager to bring up the other reason for leaving. "Also, we only have two months before I have to leave Earth to try and reforge my deteriorating body. I don't want to put off killing the Merlin until the last moment." Daelan had told Imogen what he had found out, that the leader of the Society was the person behind her parents' deaths. "We don't know how long it will take, so we should give ourselves some time."

Imogen looked troubled. "I understand."

"Anyway, we don't need to leave right away. We still have enough sun, and a month should be enough to take care of the Merlin. We'll stay for one more month."

"Alright. Thanks, Daelan."

"You're welcome."

In the evening, like they did most evenings these days, they talked. Not about cultivation or getting stronger, or anything like that. They told stories, mostly about themselves. Daelan had gradually opened up to Imogen about his life in Hell, though he left out the worst stuff. He might tell her about that stuff someday, when she was ready.

Hell, I'm not sure I'm *ready for that yet.*

She opened up more to him about her time in the foster system. She also shared happier memories about her family. Daelan hadn't experienced that much of her father's life, so he wasn't familiar with most of them.

This whole "relationship" thing was new to him, and he found that he liked it a lot. He hadn't realized how lonely he was until he was with someone else that he could trust and open up to. Although they had an "uncle/niece" relationship, they were the kind of uncle and niece that could talk about deep stuff, knowing the other person would understand, or at least not judge.

At the thought, Daelan flinched a bit, because while he hoped Imogen would understand some of the darker things he did, he wasn't sure she would, and he wasn't willing to find out.

Anyway, she has enough baggage of her own without dealing with my crap.

The uglier parts of his past could stay there, as far as he was concerned.

**

That night, Daelan dreamed.

He was in a storage room with his small but growing band of conspirators, sitting on a chair, while the others stood facing him. It was a motley bunch of "losers", as Trizna described them, that Daelan couldn't trust at all. Each meeting started with a declaration of loyalty while Daelan had his truth-sensing spell running. It had caught two liars so far. It remained to be seen how many it would catch tonight.

"Impaler," Trizna said, addressing him formally, "We have brought three recruits to see if they meet with your approval."

"Seriously?" the largest of the three, a hulking brute, said while gesturing at Daelan. "You really follow this pathetic Moaner?"

Some of the demons were amused, curious to see how Daelan would handle such blatant disrespect. Others, like Trizna, were angry. "You knew we follow Daelan!"

The demon laughed. "I knew you said that, but I couldn't believe it. No wonder you came to me, Trizna. I bet you can't even tell when he impales you."

She hissed and pulled at her black leather belt, which uncoiled and turned into a braided whip. She was about to strike the demon when Daelan said, "Stop."

He stood up from his chair and approached the leering demon. Speaking to his followers, he said, "None of you have seen how I feed. While I do eat demon flesh, that isn't how I grow strong. I think Idiot here..."

"My name is Rennoc," he growled.

"I don't care. You're 'Idiot' now."

The other demons laughed, and laughed even harder when they saw that Idiot couldn't move and couldn't be heard, though he was clearly struggling and shouting.

"As I was saying, none of you have seen me feed. The way I feed is to turn a Moaner into a Wailer and make him yearn for death. Make him crave annihilation. Make him desire an end to the pain so badly that he will do anything, even open his *anima*. And then I consume it. That is how I feed. That is the source of my strength."

The demons looked fascinated and horrified. Their eyes only grew wider when Daelan gestured, causing Idiot to collapse to the ground.

"Feeding usually takes a day. Idiot doesn't look particularly tough, though, so it might only be half a day, who knows? Each of you will attend to your duties for the soon-to-be-former Impaler, and when you are able, come here to observe."

One small demon carefully asked, "Will you teach us how to feed on *anima* as well?"

Daelan quirked his lips. "When I am the Impaler, as a reward to you who followed me, I will teach you how to feed."

That caused the demons to smile.

Daelan pointed at the two other recruits to the cause. "You two, tie him up." They hurried to obey, finding strong cords and cinching them tightly.

When they were done, Daelan smiled and said, "You all have the privilege of witnessing my perfected technique for breaking demons. I consider it a work of art."

316

He took out a well-used scalpel—Quoz was too sharp for this task—and started carefully cutting into one of Idiot's big toes. The other demons, and even Idiot himself, looked surprised. Daelan laughed inwardly because he could practically hear what they were thinking.

What are you going to do? Tickle him to death?

Daelan just kept working, carefully flaying flesh. Though they couldn't hear him, they could see that Idiot was whimpering. The other demons looked disgusted. One of them even said, "It's just your foot, Wailer," before spitting on him.

The demons eventually saw what appeared to be a small, delicate web emerge. Daelan held it up as far as it would stretch so they could see.

"These are his nerves, the source of pleasure and pain. When they are encased in flesh, it takes a great deal to cause them pain. In the open air, however," he said with a malicious grin, "the slightest breeze is agonizing."

Daelan demonstrated by gently blowing on the web, which caused Idiot to howl and arch his back in agony.

"The nerves can't live outside the body forever. Fortunately, demons are tough, so they and their nerves can last four days, more or less. So the good news is, you only have to last four days, Idiot, to keep me from eating your anima. Maybe even three if you're lucky. Of course, no demon has lasted longer than 26 hours, so..." he trailed off with a grin. Idiot looked horrified.

Daelan resumed working, and the demons occasionally went in and out. They were both fascinated and intimidated by the process. They had thought themselves connoisseurs of pain, only to find out they were children compared to the human. Though Idiot was not strong enough to have a woman of his own, he was, or at least had been, a Moaner. He could handle pain, but the would-be Impaler had broken him in less than an hour.

Daelan extended the silence sphere to the room, so they could get the full effect of what Idiot was going through.

He alternated between threatening Daelan and pleading with him. After that, it was just pleading and offering him anything and everything to let him go. Then it was anything and everything to be killed. After an hour, he no longer spoke, he only screamed and wept. Each of the demons could see Idiot's face—the face of suffering so intense that the proud demon didn't care how he was degrading himself.

An hour and forty minutes in, he entered seizures and fell into a semi-catatonic state. His eyes were open, but did not see. He only existed in a world of suffering, suffering with no end, and no limit.

Daelan had extracted Idiot's nerves up to his thigh.

"Couldn't you kill him now?" one of the demons asked uncertainly.

Daelan shook his head. "No. He craves death, but not annihilation. Not yet, anyway." Daelan looked at the demon and smiled.

Gotta make them think I enjoy it. That's half the battle in breaking them.

Daelan continued. His victim broke—mind, body, and soul—at seven hours and thirteen minutes. He set the web of nerves down, causing a fresh round of twitching, and reaped the demon's life with Quoz, his ebon blade.

The demons, who interacted with spirits often, saw Idiot's anima be drawn in and consumed by the blade. The anima which they had previously thought indestructible,

"Impaler!" "Impaler!" "Impaler!" they whispered, each round growing in strength. The light of devotion and fear was in their eyes. They believed that Daelan could not only become the new Impaler, he could also teach them how to reach new heights of power.

Chapter 44

Merlin

Caius was not a jovial man by nature, and the last six months had been nothing but misery for him. Life without mana was not a life worth living as far as he was concerned.

Yes, he had used the Society's wealth to indulge in other… distractions, but that was all they were. Distractions.

He was well aware that the members of the Society avoided him these days. He didn't care. In fact, he welcomed it. The Earth mages were pathetic gadflies that could do nothing more useful than complain about the lack of mana bones, as if he wasn't going without too.

Today, though, Caius smiled, because the day had finally come. They had enough mana bones to power the tracking spell and take Daelan down.

While others made the final travel arrangements, he entertained himself by envisioning how he would take his frustrations out on the avatar. He sighed when his imagination got carried away.

Can't do that. I have to keep him alive.

Killing the avatar would be a disaster. Caius had to bring Daelan to Sicanthus alive and more or less whole. That still gave him a great deal of leeway, fortunately.

He looked to his second in command, a man who looked forty years old but was more like two hundred.

"Is everything ready?"

"Yes, sir. Our fifty best mages are ready to go with a double combat supply of mana bones."

"Alright. Let's begin."

Chapter 45

Imogen

"Good!" Daelan said, as Imogen parried his weapons with both ends of her quarterstaff, even at the speed of a vampire.

With a thought, a cocoon of power formed around her. She immediately went on the attack, trusting in her shield to protect her. Within seconds she knocked aside his "daggers" with telekinesis and paused the staff by his head, grinning.

"Not bad," he praised. "You are now fully qualified to handle at least one vampire…" Her grin grew wider. "...as long as it just got out of bed and hasn't had its morning coffee." Now it was Daelan's turn to smile. As much as he ever did, anyway. His grins were getting bigger and more natural over time, but he was still nowhere near being "expressive".

"You jerk," she said, with a storm in her eyes and a smile on her face. "Would it kill you to say, 'You're awesome, Imogen! Great job!' without adding anything else, for once?"

He took on a thoughtful look, holding his chin with one hand and looking into the distance. "You know, it just might."

Imogen shook her head and chuckled, knowing that this was, for Daelan, high praise. Praise that she had earned with hard, and often painful work. She was particularly proud of achieving her *motion/stillness dao* a week earlier.

Daelan had told her about the benefits of having a *dao*, but he hadn't told her about the—for lack of a better term—the spiritual aspect of it. The connectedness she felt, as if she was, in a small way, connected to the universe. It had comforted her, though she wasn't sure she could articulate why.

She knew she had abandonment issues. She didn't blame her parents for leaving her, of course, but the fact remained that she *was* left. There was a deep, primal part of her that feared it happening again. Though those fears were less with Daelan than they had been earlier in their relationship, they had not gone away.

The *dao* felt like connection to an ineffable *something* that would never leave her or be taken away.

Both she and Daelan wanted to deepen their *dao*, but for different reasons. For him, it was more like a tool. An advantage. For her, it was... she didn't know how to put it into words. Security. Trust. Daelan often talked about his Father, and yes, she always heard the capitalized "F" when he said it. The larger-than-life God-King.

If Daelan was her father figure, then perhaps the *dao* was her God-King.

Their practice done for the day, they gathered their equipment and returned to the cabin. They were both solemn, as it was their last day here. She would miss this place.

"I have a gift for you," Daelan said, breaking into her thoughts.

"Hmm? What is it?"

He held out a ring that at first she thought was silver or platinum, but then she noticed it had a slightly greyish cast to it. Her eyes widened as she realized what it was. "Mithril? Seriously?"

Daelan smiled and nodded. "Yeah. It, uh, I thought you would want to use it for a long time, so I decided to make it the best I could." He glanced away, seeming embarrassed. "It's a storage ring. You can put things in an extra-planar space, like I do with Quoz. I made it out of mithril so the mana costs would be as low as possible."

She put it on the ring finger of her right hand. It was a perfect fit. She admired it for a few seconds before excitedly threading her mana into the start of the script. She gasped when she felt the space make itself available to her. She didn't have exact measurements, but it felt like it was a cube, about three meters per side. She put her favorite quarterstaff in to try it out, and released the space.

"This ring is fire, Daelan! Thank you!" she said as she hugged him. She had been wondering how she would carry her quarterstaff around. She didn't want to look like a weirdo, but she also didn't want to be without a weapon.

"You're welcome," he said with a gratified smile. "Make sure to take some knives and stuff too. In fact, why don't you grab all this stuff, especially the power supply. I think you get to be the pack mule, since I can only carry Quoz in mine."

"Ah," she said, laughing, "Now we see the *real* reason for the ring."

"Yep. So you can finally start pulling your weight around here."

"Thank you," she said as she hugged him again.

He hugged her back and gently kissed her on the top of her head. "You're welcome." He released her and said, "Get some rest. In the morning we'll top off our mana and head for Bonn."

She felt the tingle of goosebumps all over. She honestly couldn't have said whether it was from excitement or fear. Probably both. She wanted to confront her parents' killer—the real killer who set up the madman.

It had taken her time, but she had gradually come to understand and pity the gunman who shot her mom and dad. He was just as much a victim as her, trapped in a broken mind by the Merlin. Though she was terrified, she looked forward to getting justice for all four of them.

She discreetly watched Daelan as he gingerly got into his bed, and smiled sadly. Though he tried to hide it, she knew that he suffered.

She was grateful to him. The last eight months had, in some ways, been the best time of her life. It wasn't that it was truly better than it had been with her parents. It wasn't. Back then, though, she didn't understand how good she had it. Now, having had all that stripped away, she understood how precious family was; how good it was having someone who cared about you and took care of you.

Thank you, Daelan.

Chapter 46

Daelan

"ARRRRRNNN! ARRRRRNNN! ARRRRRNNN! ARRRRRNNN!...."

The harsh klaxon of their perimeter alarm woke Daelan up instantly, though his brain was still trying to catch up with the situation. When he realized that the alarm wasn't the one for large lifeforms, rather the one for large lifeforms with mana, he paled.

Oh shit... "Imogen! Get up!"

"I'm up! I'm up!" she said as she sat up in bed and rubbed her eyes. "What's wrong?"

"We need to get out of here! Now!"

"Okay. I'll grab..."

"No time. Use camouflage and exit right after me. Run to the hills."

Looking scared and dressed in her flannel pajamas, she said, "O-okay."

Frowning, he said, "Put your shoes and coat on, but that's it. Do you have the ring?"

"Yes."

"Good. I'm going out. Follow me as soon as you can."

She nodded from the floor as she was putting on shoes.

He ran out in his thermal underwear. The cold, boggy ground was wet and uncomfortable, but he ignored it. He moved away from the cabin so if he was targeted, Imogen wouldn't be caught in the crossfire. He opened his third eye and saw two clusters of mages flying towards them from opposite directions.

Damn it! How did they find us? He knew he didn't have time for questions like that, so he focused on the here and now. His natural inclination was to become invisible and fly away, but he couldn't leave Imogen like that. Instead, he grimaced and prepared to let them know exactly where he was while he cursed himself as an idiot.

Ignoring his more pragmatic side, he created a white-hot fireball and launched it at one of the groups. It was a beacon that drew every eye in the dim, pre-dawn light. A few seconds later, after muttering a few words of power, he launched another at the second group. He was not surprised when they dodged the fireballs, and chuckled when he heard cries of alarm when the balls veered suddenly towards the nearest mages.

Though both were hit, only one burned to a crisp and had his corpse drop to the ground. The other plowed through, protected by a shield spell.

Daelan created his own telekinetic shield, and a secondary one through his arm cuff that protected him from mental and soul-based attacks. He didn't know if the Society mages knew how to attack the soul or mind, but he certainly wasn't going to risk it.

Daelan took a moment to look for Imogen. He was pleased to see her, or rather her mana core, loping towards the mountain foothills.

Good girl.

He turned back to the Society mages and saw that roughly half were continuing to approach by air, with the other half hanging back on the ground, probably to conserve mana. Daelan frowned, because he'd much rather they all came together. He briefly considered taking to the air to attack the mages held in reserve and draw them in, but decided against it. If they fought in the air, Imogen was more likely to be caught in the crossfire.

"I hope you appreciate the things I do for you," he growled to himself, eying the multitude of fireballs that, collectively, formed two walls of fire that were getting ready to crush him in the middle.

It was too late for him to dodge all of the attacks, so he made the best of a bad situation by sprinting towards one of the walls, doing his best to run at maximum speed despite the pain in his knees. He would have to tank the one set of fireballs, but at least the other ones in would miss.

While he ran he summoned Quoz as a war scythe that he held in one hand, and used pure thought and his *particle motion* mana

324

to create a plasma whip—a thin, glowing cylinder of superheated plasma contained by telekinesis that could move according to his whims. It was, essentially, a long, flexible lightsaber.

The fireballs were pushed to the side by Daelan's shield, which maintained the air inside at a constant, cool temperature. An outside observer would think they had done nothing to him, but Daelan knew they had caused his shield to drain 15% of his mana.

Despite the loss, Daelan was pleased to see the widened eyes of the mages who did not expect to see him so close. He launched himself up into the air and swung the war scythe at one of the mages, bisecting his head from crown to neck as if cutting a ripe melon. The weapon was momentarily stuck in the man's torso, but instead of levering it out—an awkward proposition in mid-air—he simply let go and resummoned it, thus maintaining his forward momentum.

Daelan simultaneously grabbed a flying mage with the plasma whip, but was disappointed to see it take hold of a sphere around the mage instead of the woman herself. Though the sphere contracted from the pressure, the glowing plasma was stopped a full foot from the woman, who looked nervous.

She should. Her mana must be dropping like a rock.

He used the whip to fling her around, knocking her into nearby mages, spoiling their flight and spells. Within a few seconds, the shield dissipated, allowing the whip to constrict around her. In moments, the smoking upper and lower parts of her body fell to the ground.

The nearby mages looked horrified, but resumed attacking Daelan after a brief pause.

What followed over the next couple of minutes was a deadly exchange of destructive force between the two groups, mediated by their mana levels. It was a race to see who could drain the other side's mana first. Though Daelan tried attacks that might evade the mages' defenses, such as mind attacks, he was stymied. The mages were being cautious.

There were two wildcards in the fight. One of them was Quoz. It could cut through the mages' shields almost as if they weren't there, and feed Daelan a portion of the mana it recovered from their lifeforce and soul. Though the mana did not make up for what he was losing, it extended Daelan's ability to fight.

I might pull this out if I can kill the mages a little faster.

Each kill was a huge boost for him, both because of the injection of mana from Quoz and because he lost mana a little slower, given there were fewer attacks his shield had to absorb. Once he gained mana as quickly as he lost it, the mages were dead meat.

The other wildcard, unfortunately, was the mages held in reserve.

Both victory and escape would be a win for Daelan. Victory was killing all of them or getting them to retreat. Escape meant draining most of their mana so they couldn't chase and overtake him. Keeping mages in reserve worked against both of those goals.

His overtaxed mind briefly considered whether he could escape by flying invisibly, but concluded it was unlikely. They had, after all, found him here, and that had nothing to do with their sight or distance.

The Merlin is from Sicanthus. He must have a higher-level divination spell.

Daelan knew higher-level anti-divination spells than the one he had been using, but didn't have enough unaspected mana to use them, so it was conquer or die. He realized that the problem was even worse when he saw a mage fly over to the reserve and be replaced by one of the waiting mages. With his third eye, he saw the mage who had quit the field pull mana into his core from something in his hand. Likely a diamond or some other crystal that contained mana.

Ah, crap.

If he let them restore their mana, he was a dead man.

Though he couldn't escape through invisibility, he could use it as a tactical weapon. He turned himself invisible and flew over to the reserve group with the recovering mage. He was about to take the man out with Quoz when the mages reacted and pushed him away telekinetically.

They can see through my invisibility. This is just getting better and better.

He turned off the invisibility to save mana, and engaged the reserve with fireballs, trying to draw them into the fight. They refused, simply avoiding the fireballs when they could, or soaking them up with their shields. Though that did drain their mana, it did nothing to lessen the attacks coming at him, so Daelan reluctantly disengaged and focused on the mages attacking him.

Right before turning away from the reserve, he saw a familiar face.

The assassin. That asshole.

He was tempted to re-engage with the reserve to try to kill the man behind the deaths of Imogen's parents, but knew it was foolish. If he wanted to kill him, he had to be smart and win this battle.

Seeing that he could not get the reserves to approach, Daelan decided it was time to spring his trap. He reached into his pocket, found a square piece of engraved aluminum, and injected a sliver of mana into it. It was paired with another piece of engraved aluminum buried in the ground nearby, which was connected to five large, perfect diamonds and a silver loop that formed a circle one hundred meters in diameter around the cabin. The loop was engraved with lightning generation spells and a targeting system that sought out large lifeforms that didn't have an artifact that identified them as a "friendly"—one like the engraved bear claw on a leather thong around Daelan's neck.

The staccato booms of thunder rolled through the land and echoed from the nearby hills as lightning strikes hit the fighting mages. Most of the time, the lightning spread out around the mage, as if an invisible umbrella protected them from molten metal. Occasionally, though, the lightning pierced through and incinerated the mage, turning their body into a charred husk.

Daelan took advantage of the lightning by flying around and killing as many as he could while they were distracted. After all, it was a shame to waste their mana.

All too soon, though, the lightning ended and the thunder stilled. Ten mages were left, and all of them fled to the reserves. Every one of the mages in the reserves, all twenty-five of them, flew up to meet Daelan and engage him, while the ten pulled out mana crystals.

Damn it.

Daelan shot multiple fireballs at the recharging mages, trying to finish them off, but others interposed themselves and soaked up the damage.

Daelan went cold with fear. He knew that if he didn't turn things around, he was a dead man.

Chapter 47

Imogen

Though she knew Daelan would want her to flee as far as she could, she couldn't help but stay to watch a half-mile away behind the ridgeline of one of the hills. She trembled as she saw Daelan take hit after hit, terrified that his shield would give out. Time after time, though, it held, and he continued to wreak havoc among the mages.

She was shocked at the brutality of the fight. People were fine until their defenses failed, and then some cruel death instantly followed. Beheading. Incineration. Perforated by rocks. One mage was even impaled by another mage's sword when Daelan, presumably, hurled him into his comrade.

She was glad, of course, that Daelan was killing the mages, but couldn't help but cringe at how he did it. She forced herself to watch and told herself, *This is what mage battles are. You have to get used to this.*

Her hopes rose when she saw the lightning storm. She knew he had put together some defense, but didn't know the details. She was shocked by the power of it. He had made it very clear that she should never go without her bear claw necklace, and now she knew why.

I wonder why he didn't use it earlier, when there were more mages?

When Imogen saw the reserve mages fly up to engage Daelan while the nearly-incinerated ones recharged, she despaired. She was tempted to go back down and enter the fight, but she knew that was stupid. She wasn't a good enough mage to make a difference, and would only cause problems for Daelan.

She didn't know if God existed or not, but she offered fervent prayers and a multitude of deals if he got Daelan out of this.

God, if you save Daelan, I'll give half my money to charity from now on. Please.

Her pleas became more hopeless, though, as she saw the mages continue to rotate in and out of the fight. Their numbers still diminished—there were 28 mages total now—but they were dying at a slower and slower rate, and Daelan's attacks were fewer and farther between, as if he was conserving his mana.

He tried to fly away but was always pulled back by the mages. After one attempt a reserve mage shouted, "His shield is down!"

Daelan was telekinetically slammed down into the ground, and a nearby rock moved a few feet to bash his head, causing him to go limp.

No! What do I do?

They placed manacles on his wrists and removed his arm cuff and necklace. They didn't seem sure about what to do about Quoz. One of the mages tried to pick the war scythe up, but it didn't budge. Eventually they gave up and left it there.

A couple of mages flew around the area, presumably looking for her. She hid and had camouflage turned on. Eventually they gave up and returned to the group. Imogen watched forlornly as the mages lifted the unconscious Daelan and flew eastward.

What do I do?

A part of her thought about the Cayman Island bank account. With the money and her magic, she could take care of herself now. She could go anywhere she wanted and start fresh. She didn't have any particular skills, but with her magic she should be able to do *something*.

She felt ashamed at the thought. Daelan had taken her in, cared for her, and taught her. Everything she had was because of him. Leaving him the moment he needed her would be cowardly.

And... I don't want to lose anyone else.

The thought of being alone again was, in its own way, more frightening than the mages. She didn't know if she could handle losing someone again, or get close to someone new if she did.

There was also the guilt that had been eating away at her for years. The guilt from running away and leaving her parents behind to die. She knew that she had done what her parents wanted, and they would have been glad that she had gotten away, but the guilt didn't listen to reason. It just told her that she was a coward who only thought of herself. It said that if she had run at the gunman, maybe she could have knocked his aim off, and together they could have overpowered him.

She didn't think about it too often anymore. Sixteen-year-old Imogen knew that ten-year-old her couldn't be expected to do anything but run away. Still, being older and stronger now, she wished she could go back to that day and have another shot at it, but that was never going to happen.

At some level she intuited that this was her second chance. Her way to prove to herself that, if she could have, she would have saved her parents. Her chance for redemption.

I'm so sorry, Mom and Dad, she sniffled. *I'm sorry I couldn't save you.* Looking towards where the mages had flown away, she whispered, "Hold on, Daelan. I'm coming."

**

Imogen followed the mages at a distance. A fleet of helicopters waited for them a few miles away. They were painted a variety of colors and had different logos. Daelan was loaded into a red, four-person helicopter.

Imogen thought about disabling the other helicopters while they were in the air, but quickly thought better of it. She wasn't sure she could stop one of the rotors, even the small ones at the end of the tail. And even if she could, she would have to be really close. Bad idea.

A more practical solution would be to throw rocks at the rotors. Even if it worked, though, what would she do when the mages got out of the helicopters and chased her?

Better just follow them for now.

They made their way south over the mountains of the "Gates of the Arctic" national park. The view was beautiful, but it was cold. She only had her pajamas and heavy coat, and the wind was freezing. She pulled the hood over her head and pulled the drawstring tight. It was an improvement, but her nose still felt like it was going to freeze and break off.

Needing a distraction, she pulled out her Starlink-enabled phone and looked at the GPS map.

Looks like we're going to Fairbanks.

It made sense. There were no large cities in Alaska, but Fairbanks was one of the bigger ones, and boasted an international airport.

While flying, Imogen tried using her magic to keep from getting hypothermia, or perhaps even frostbite. She thought about trying to warm the air or something, since she knew that was an aspect of *motion*. *Heat* was not yet a direct part of her dao, though, so it would be more difficult and inefficient than it would be for Daelan. She decided to keep it simple. She simply slowed down the air around her, at least from her perspective of a person flying through the air. She supposed that would mean the air was moving faster, but whatever. It made her a lot less cold, which was all she cared about at the moment. She wasn't comfortable, but she would survive.

After half an hour, they left the mountains behind. A half hour after that, Imogen saw a small city and the airport, which was almost as big as the rest of the city. It was a good thing, because her mana was down to 25%

Better land.

Planes were taxiing to take off, and she saw another one coming in. She needed to get on the ground before anyone saw her. It would suck to walk the rest of the way, but it had to be done.

**

"Ma'am, I really need your help!" Imogen tearfully said to the ticket agent. "They took my dad to get the surgery he needs, but they didn't tell me where they were taking him!"

The agent, a forty-something-year-old woman, frowned but her eyes were soft and looked at the girl sympathetically. "Did they fly on United, honey?"

"I-I don't know. They just said they were going to fly him to the hospital."

"What's your dad's name?"

What was his fake name? "Uh, George Miller."

The agent eyed her for a second, but looked down and started tapping away at her keyboard. "No, it doesn't look like a George

Miller has or is going to fly with us today." She looked up, sympathetic again. I'm sorry, sweetie."

"Please!" Imogen cried out while thinking about her parents' deaths to stimulate more tears. "I have to know what happened to him!"

The agent frowned again, sighed, and said, "Okay, but I need to see some kind of ID first."

Imogen gave her a driver's license with her picture that identified her as "Marissa Miller".

The agent looked at it, handed it back, and got on a landline phone. "Tom? Hi, this is Cynthia. I have a young lady here who needs to find her father, George Miller. Says some people flew with him today to take him to a hospital, but she doesn't know where they went. Is there some way we can find out for her?"

The woman listened for a while, making occasional "mm-hm's" and "okays". She looked at Imogen, hand covering the lower half of the phone. "What does your father look like?"

"Brown hair. Brown eyes. Receding hairline. Kind of pudgy. Oh, and he was wearing his long johns and was unconscious!"

The agent relayed the information, listened some more, and said, "Thank you, Tom. Let me know when you find out." She turned to Imogen and said, "He's going to find out what happened, honey. In the meanwhile, can I have you step to the side so I can help these other people?"

"Uh, sure. Thank you!"

"You're welcome." Turning to the next person, an older man, she asked, "How can I help you?"

Imogen waited and, after hearing her stomach growl, got some food. She had forgotten that she hadn't eaten anything yet.

She paced as she waited for the information. She knew the Society's headquarters were in Bonn, Germany—Daelan having gotten the information from the vampires—but didn't know if they were taking Daelan there or not. She had to be sure.

A half hour later, the agent called out to Imogen. "Marissa, honey, can I talk with you?" Imogen hurried over, and the agent leaned over the counter as if to give her secret information.

"We found your dad. He was taken on a private plane. They're flying to Bonn, Germany, and refueling in Montreal,

Quebec. The plane's tail number is D-C621. That's all I can give you, honey."

"That's great!" she said as she wiped her tears with her coat. "Can you, uh, help me get a ticket to Bonn?"

The agent smiled. "Of course."

Chapter 48

Daelan

Daelan was not the kind of guy who hit the "snooze" button on his alarm. Once he woke up, sleep time was over, so it was a strange experience for him to come to gradually, as if his thoughts were muffled by layers of blankets that were pulled off slowly, one by one.

He couldn't move his body. He was tied to something. A... chair. A wooden chair with armrests. He was tied with thick cords. Although his body was significantly stronger than the average human, he still could not free himself with his strength, and with his deterioration, it hurt to even try.

The brain fog had mostly lifted when a man walked in wearing opulent robes and rings with precious stones. What most caught his attention, though, were his eyes. The eyes were an unusually light green, which, despite their hue, managed to appear flat and dull. They were the eyes of a killer.

The assassin from Sicanthus.

The thought shook off the last of the brain fog.

"I'm glad you're finally awake. I've been looking forward to this. Let's get started, shall we?"

"Who are you?" Daelan asked, feigning ignorance.

The man looked at him with a superior smile. "I am known on Earth as the Merlin, the leader of The Eternal Society of Noble Wizards and Magical Studies, but since you are a fellow Sicanthian, you can call me Caius."

"Sicanthian? What are you talking about?"

Though Daelan was still not at his best at the moment, he was an excellent liar when he needed to be. The trick was to take on a role, much like an actor, and become that person. At the moment he was a self-taught mage from Earth.

The man sneered. "Come now, avatar. The time for games is up. We both know who you are."

"You might, but I have no idea what you're on about."

Caius' eyes narrowed in anger. "If you insist on playing games, then fine. I'll just drag the answers out of you."

While Caius was talking, Daelan tried to use his mana, only to find he had none. He remembered running out of mana, getting slammed to the ground, and getting hit in the head. Of course he didn't have any mana.

He tried to use his arm cuff, but it was gone too. He could use the mana invested in his dao runes if he was desperate enough, but causing a break in his connection with the universe would forever cripple him. He would only take such a step if that was the only way to survive.

"Is this because I can use magic? What are you going to do to me?" he asked with a worried look.

"Well, this can go a few ways. If you tell me what I want to know, I will treat you well, with food, drinks, women—whatever you want. I will have to take you to Sicanthus to my higher ups, and then it will be up to them what happens to you, but until that time I will provide you with any comfort you could desire."

"That doesn't sound too bad."

Caius smiled. "The second option, if you're not fully cooperative but I'm feeling merciful, is to use my poison as a narcotic that I have found very effective when questioning people."

"I'm not into drugs, but that doesn't sound too bad either as long as you don't OD me."

"The last option, Daelan, is pain. Lots and lots of pain."

"Um, I would rather not have pain."

Caius grinned. "A rational response. So you will answer my questions?"

Daelan nodded. "Sure. I just have to tell you the truth?"

"That's right. Let's start with an easy one. What's your name?"

"George Miller."

Caius' eyes narrowed. "I have a truth spell running, and it says you're lying."

Damn. Daelan opened his third eye and saw a familiar mana spellform. Caius wasn't bluffing. Daelan wasn't surprised about the truth-sensing spell, but had hoped he wouldn't have to deal with one. He knew how to fool it with another spell, but… no mana.

Daelan thought about it and decided that ambiguity was his best bet. It wasn't a great strategy, but lying was almost as bad as telling the truth if the assassin could tell it was a lie. Better not to say anything at all.

The mage became angry when Daelan didn't talk. After repeating the question a few times, he tried others.

"Where were you before you came to Earth?"

Daelan ignored him.

What does your tattoo do? Is it part of how you get mana? How did you make the silvery tattoo?"

No response.

"What do the runes in the tattoo mean?"

When Daelan continued ignoring him, Caius switched to, "How did you learn the truth-sensing spell that you taught Gabriel?"

After Caius tired of his obstinance, he shook his head mock-sadly.

"This buys you nothing, you know. You're going to Sicanthus in two days, even if you say nothing." He pulled out Daelan's arm cuff. "Remember this?"

"Of course. It's mine."

Caius looked at it admiringly. "This is, by far, the most expensive thing I've ever held in my hands. Made of mithril. It has runes I've never seen before or heard of. Some people would sell a kingdom for this. Do you know what happened when I showed it to you while you were drugged up?"

Though Daelan was dismayed to hear that he had talked and didn't remember it, he still rolled his eyes at the theatrics. "What happened?"

"You told me all about it. How you made it. What spells you used. And…" he looked at Daelan meaningfully, "…where you got those spells."

Daelan shrugged. "A man will say anything when he's drugged."

Caius smiled at him condescendingly. "Whatever. You know. I know. You know I know." He shrugged, stood up, and walked towards the door. "Two days, avatar."

337

Have I really been out that long? The astral conjunction was supposed to happen in two months. Though he didn't want to say anything, he still asked, "What happens in two days?"

Caius stopped, hand on the doorknob, and looked at him with a grin. "Lesser conjunction. Once I showed the general the arm cuff and told them what you said, he got the Empire moving. Enjoy your time."

There was good news and bad news. The good news is that Daelan hadn't been unconscious for two months. The bad news was that the Empire must want him very badly indeed. It would take orders of magnitude more mana to create a portal during a lesser conjunction than it would when he planned to do it in a couple of months. That kind of mana was, granted, a drop in the bucket for the Empire, but the Empire was big. For any given entity inside it, even a general, that would be a shit-ton of mana.

They must believe I'm an avatar. If I don't escape, I'm fucked.

His racing thoughts were interrupted by Caius' words to someone outside the room. "As promised, you can do what you want with him, just don't kill him or damage his brain."

A familiar, tense voice said, "No problem."

Caius nodded and exited. Gabriel, the young mage he had kidnapped, entered the room, and a woman followed after him. They both looked like they were grieving and pissed, and then confused. Gabriel turned towards the door and said, "This isn't Daelan! He looks completely different."

The Merlin snorted. "It's him. Trust me."

The young mage turned towards Daelan again. His sister's gaze had never left.

"Are you Daelan?"

Daelan shrugged.

"You killed my dad, you son-of-a-bitch!"

Daelan's eyebrows raised. "The guy who wouldn't exchange you for Imogen? He actually came for you, eh? I'm kind of surprised."

With an enraged shout, Gabriel hit Daelan in the stomach. He coughed a couple of times and said, "Not a bad punch, kid." He would normally shake the punch off, but in his weakened state it hurt.

Gabriel sneered. "I was just 'draining your mana'. It helps to get close to the core, after all."

Daelan gave him a pained smile. "Lucky for you then, I don't have any."

Gabriel pretended to think about it and said, "I think I'll make sure for myself." He turned to the woman. "What do you think, sis?"

She nodded. "Definitely make sure."

Gabriel shrugged his shoulders with a "What can I do?" look. "Sorry, Daelan. You heard her. We have to make sure."

Daelan nodded. "I get it. Security is important."

Daelan suffered through the next hour. Eventually the young mage tired himself out.

Though he was in pain, Daelan's thoughts were on just two things: "Is Imogen okay?" and "How do I get out of here?"

**

That night, Daelan dreamed.

He dreamed of blood and fire, death and destruction. And wailing. Many proud demons became wailers that day, and food to be consumed by Daelan and his followers.

Many of the most elevated demons in the previous warlord's regime were raised up on poles, where anyone could stroll and admire them, flay their flesh and extract their nerves, or simply amuse themselves by blowing on the exposed web of nerves, causing the demons to howl.

Though they were still intimidated by the former warlord, they even took to torturing him after Daelan exposed his nerves up to his chest. Only the demon's massive vitality kept him from dying. He still wouldn't last more than a day or two.

It should be enough to break him.

He had to admit that the demon was a tough old bastard. It had taken six hours of increasingly hideous pain before he even whimpered. Ten before he howled. Now the demons, to their delight, saw him weeping and begging for death, his pride completely gone.

Daelan watched the scene before him and anticipated the bounteous harvest of anima he would soon enjoy. His followers

339

thought they would receive as well, fools that they were. He would let them partake in the future…perhaps. He would not give away his secrets so easily. The God-King himself hadn't given the knowledge to anyone besides Daelan.

"When are you going to declare me your consort, Impaler?" Trizna, his loyal seducer asked as she sat at his feet.

Daelan sneered. "Never."

"What?" she said, outraged. "You promised me!"

"So what? Do you honestly think I would make a whore that pleasured most of my followers my consort? Please. I would be a laughingstock. Be grateful that you're in my harem."

"But I…"

"One more word," Daelan said coldly, "and I will put you up on a pole myself."

Though she looked angry, she was quiet. It was good enough. If she behaved and accepted her new role, he would reward her later. Though she disgusted him, she had been a loyal and useful servant.

Daelan surveyed the crowd and saw a demoness that was shrinking in the corner, trying to attract as little attention as possible. That didn't keep a couple of demons from taunting and propositioning her. Though she was horrified by what had happened to her consort and her new, nonexistent position in Daelan's regime, she still dismissed the demons with a sneer.

Good. Now let's see if she's as smart as she is proud.

He glanced at Trizna and said, "Bring me Gilara."

She stared at him angrily. "Why?"

Daelan just stared at her, impassive but waiting. Trizna paled and hurried off to the demoness. As Gilara walked towards him, staring and head held high, Daelan considered how he would bend her to his will and conquer her. Though he was doing it for political reasons—taking the former warlord's consort as his own would solidify his rule—he found that he was excited by the idea.

He sighed, knowing that his time in Hell had changed him. Though the demons still horrified and disgusted him, he knew that he had become more like them than he cared to admit.

Oh, well, he thought as he leered at the beautiful demoness— because the first rule of breaking someone was making them think you enjoyed it— *I might as well take what pleasure from it I can. Who knows when I will get out of here and get revenge?*

Chapter 49

Imogen

Imogen was exhausted when she finally arrived at the Cologne-Bonn airport. It took four flights and 25 hours to get there, and she was ready to drop. She had done very little traveling before meeting Daelan, but had since learned that she could not sleep on flights. Like, ever. In a hard plastic chair in the airport, sure. But there was something about being in the air, she just couldn't do it.

She was coherent enough to get a taxi to a cheap hotel, book herself in—thankfully, the man at the front desk spoke English—and crash for ten hours.

She awoke, groggy and hungry, around midnight. Her GPS maps app indicated there wasn't much open, so she took the DC power supply out of her mithril storage ring and set it up. She needed to be at her best today, and that meant being full of mana. Grimacing, she hooked herself up and got to work.

**

The Society headquarters was outside the city proper, by an animal preserve to the south. It was surrounded by a ten foot high stone wall with a wrought-iron gate manned by two guards. The top of the wall was decorated with triangular pyramids that were adorned with the image of Medusa's head. It creeped Imogen out, especially because the eyes looked weird, until she realized they were cameras.

Weird freaking mages…

Already camouflaged, she lifted herself up in the air to see the rest of the grounds. It was about four acres in size and included four buildings. People walked between the buildings, sat on benches, wrote, and talked with others. It looked like a college campus where there was only faculty, no students, with buildings that had been around since the Enlightenment.

It'll be a shame to tear this place up. I wonder which building Daelan is in?

Though the vampires had given them the location of the Society's headquarters, Imogen still had to find her uncle. She thought long and hard about how she could figure out where they were holding him, and came up with nothing. All of her plans were cringy to begin with—fly around and look in windows, camouflage herself and follow somebody through a door—and that was before taking into consideration the spherical barrier that she saw with her third eye. It looked like what Daelan had described from the Miami branch, so she hoped it was just an alarm and not a mage-zapper.

She finally decided that it didn't matter if she didn't know where he was. She wasn't strong enough to take on the entire Society, or knowledgeable enough to sneak him out. The best she could do was create a distraction and hope he could take advantage of it.

It frustrated and scared her to feel so helpless. Though she had learned and grown so much, she was still a tiny fish in a big pond.

She looked one more time over the headquarters, irrationally thinking that maybe one more look would let her see Daelan. Sighing, she turned away.

I'll do my best, Daelan. I hope you can take it the rest of the way.

**

That night, Imogen came back to the headquarters with her core and arm cuff full of mana, and her ring stuffed with everything she owned, along with some key supplies for causing havoc. There were still two guards stationed at the gate and a couple of people talking on the grounds, but otherwise everything was quiet.

She was so nervous that she was trembling. She turned to her go-to's for whenever she was scared: humor and denial.

Have fun storming the castle... she thought to herself in Billy Crystal's voice. She sighed. *What the heck are you doing here, Imogen? You're not ready for this. No one's ready for this.*

She grimaced and tried to psych herself up. *You're just creating a distraction. Daelan will do the rest. And when it gets to be too much, you just run away.*

Unfortunately, she also thought of one of Daelan's favorite sayings: "No plan survives contact with the enemy."

Still, she had to do it if she ever wanted to see Daelan again. If she ever wanted to have a smidgen of self-respect again. She was *not* a coward, damn it, and she *would* have saved her parents if she could have. This was her chance to prove it.

She slowly flew up into the air, a couple hundred feet above the headquarters. Ignoring the chill breeze of the night air, she pulled out of her storage ring a molotov cocktail—an opened bottle of "Weingeist" that contained 96% ethyl alcohol, and a rag stuffed into the bottle's neck.

Here goes nothing...

She drifted down until she was just ten feet above the alarm barrier and lit the rag with a simple application of her *motion* mana. Holding her breath, though she couldn't have said why, she dove down.

Didn't fry! she thought as she passed through the barrier unharmed. *Good start.*

She threw the molotov cocktail at one of the buildings' windows, adding a little oomph to it with telekinesis, but was disappointed to see it fail to break through the window. Instead, the bottle broke and covered the window and nearby stone with fire.

Dang it!

A couple of people shouted in alarm, but Imogen ignored them for the moment other than making sure her shield was active. She took out one of the fishing sinkers she'd brought, a ball of lead a centimeter across, and threw it at the window with a great deal of telekinetic force. The window flexed and had numerous cracks that looked like a spider web, but did not break.

Great. Bulletproof glass. Now what?

She rose through the air and watched what was going on while trying to think of what to do. She started to realize that it

344

might not matter if she didn't throw the cocktails inside the buildings. She was getting a pretty big reaction anyway. Seeing that, she dove to the gables of one of the buildings that hid her from the growing crowd of people, and pulled out two more cocktails. After lighting them, she threw them at two more buildings.

Once again, the fires caused more shouting. The flames were put out quickly, and a few wizards rose in the air to see what was going on.

Oh crap!

Trembling, she pulled out more sinkers. She could see four mages in the air: two with shields activated and two without. The shields did not look as solid as those of the mages who had taken Daelan. One of the mages without a shield turned slowly in the air and saw her on the roof. Just as he opened his mouth in alarm and started moving his arm, Imogen telekinetically hurled the sinker into his chest. The mage looked shocked and, after trying to say something and failing, fell to the ground.

She felt like she was in a surreal dream, seeing the body of a person she had killed fall in her peripheral vision, as she started hurling more and more sinkers. She was surprised when even the mages with shields were wounded or even killed.

Is this really happening? Why are they so… weak?

Though the mages were getting hurt badly, she couldn't stay where she was. She flew in the air and hid behind trees outside the campus to break visual contact, and then flew to a different location where she could attack more mages.

She continued to use these hit-and-run tactics until some of the mages used a spell to see through her camouflage. At that point there was no hiding, and she fled for her life.

Hurry, Daelan!

Chapter 50

Daelan

Daelan was worried.

He'd been waiting for an opportunity to escape but hadn't seen one yet. Time was running short, so he was considering making a move regardless.

Quoz was his ace in the hole and the reason he would get out of here. The mages didn't know that he didn't need mana to summon it, nor that when he killed, he received mana. If he could consume the soul of one mage, he liked his chances of getting out.

The problem was that he was always guarded by at least two mages, and they were always alert. It didn't help that he recognized their faces from the group that attacked him in Alaska, meaning they were probably the Society's elite and knew the kind of speed and power he could wield. Their knowledge made them wary.

Relax... he tried to project into their minds, though he had no ESP powers. *I'm just a harmless little bunny...*

He sighed. Judging by their faces, his attempts at spontaneous telepathy were not bearing fruit.

Daelan perked up when he heard shouting, and his excitement only grew when he heard people running in the building. He kept his face impassive, though, not wanting to draw attention.

"We're being attacked! Everyone to their positions!"

The two men guarding him looked at each other worriedly. The younger man asked, "What do we do?"

The older mage, who had a crooked nose and looked like he knew his way around a fight, said, "Our job is here. You know what the Merlin said."

Daelan wondered what was going on. *Could it be Imogen?* He hadn't held out any hopes that she would come to save him. She

346

was still very young and new to her powers, and not, frankly, up to taking on the Society.

The younger mage nodded but didn't look happy. They returned to guarding Daelan, though the younger mage looked agitated. When they heard screams from outside, the mage looked at the older guard, who grimaced and said, "Fine. Go."

The young mage nodded and ran out the door.

The older mage growled, "Don't even think of trying anything."

Daelan smiled, and then winced. The Society had continued to beat him up over the last day, and his body wasn't in the best condition at the best of times these days.

"I wouldn't dream of it," he said, as he summoned Quoz in the form of a small knife and started working at the rope binding his hands behind the chair. He stifled a grimace when he accidentally got his hand with the knife, but was surprised when he realized he wasn't cut. '*You can choose to not cut things, Quoz?*'

'*Of course, wantwit.*'

'*Huh. Can't believe I didn't know that after all these years.*'

Though Quoz did not cut his skin, the rope parted easily, releasing his hands in seconds. Releasing his feet, unfortunately, would be harder to hide. He had Quoz transform into a throwing knife while he asked, "What do you think is going on?"

The mage narrowed his eyes. "I don't know, but it doesn't concern either of us. The others will take care of it."

"Okay."

Everything was in place to kill the mage and take his mana, but Daelan wanted to minimize the chances of failure. He only had one shot at this. He thought about using the commotion to get the guard to look at the door, but decided to just keep it simple. He waited until the mage blinked and then hurled Quoz. It slid through the mage's shield as if it wasn't there and sank into his chest.

Sweet, sweet mana.

Daelan was sorely tempted to recall Quoz so he could free his legs, but he had to make sure the mage was dead and that he got as much mana as possible, so he worked at the knot by hand instead. He wasn't finished freeing himself when the flow of mana stopped, so he recalled the entity and sliced the rope apart.

Though his body hurt like hell, he didn't think about it as he rose, dagger in hand and mana in his core. He was too joyous to worry about something as trivial as some aches and pains. He might be in the middle of the Society's headquarters, but as far as he was concerned, he was already free.

The door was locked, but a swipe with Quoz to cut the latch took care of that. He moved into the hall and saw a male mage running towards him. When the mage saw Daelan, he stopped with wide eyes, preparing to shout. Daelan threw Quoz, using his telekinesis to guide the knife and stop it directly under the mage's chin, letting it prick his neck and drain a bit of lifeforce.

"Shut up, or you die now."

The mage looked terrified, but said nothing.

"Smart man. Where is the exit?"

"T-that way." The mage pointed in Daelan's direction, where he had been running towards.

"And where is the Merlin?"

The mage started shaking his head, and then stopped when he felt the prick of the knife. "I don't know."

Daelan moved Quoz incrementally forward, causing the mage to shriek while doing his best to point behind himself without moving, "I don't know! But his office is that way!"

Daelan nodded. "Thanks." He shoved the knife up into the man's brain stem and started to move forward, towards the Merlin's office. He paused when he thought about the situation. *If it's Imogen, she might need my help.*

Daelan was torn. He so badly wanted to kill those who had trapped him in Hell and destroyed everything he had sacrificed for. He wanted to rip them apart and send their souls to Hell.

But, Imogen.

Damn it.

He turned around and ran through the hall, starting to feel every single one of the pains in his body. Still, he ran as fast as he could. He would worry about his body later.

Chapter 51

Imogen

"Shoot, shoot, shoot..." Imogen whispered to herself as she dodged as many fireballs, projectiles, and lightning bolts as she could, which unfortunately was not all of them. She now regretted every complaint she had ever made about Daelan's shield training. It was the only thing keeping her alive right now.

At the rate she was going through her mana, though, it was only going to protect her for a couple more minutes.

What do I do?

She had lost most of the mages that had been chasing her—at one point there had been eleven—but the three that were still on her tail refused to be shaken off. She was over a wooded, uninhabited area, so she decided to fly between the trees. Maybe she could get them to crash or something. *I mean, it works in the movies...* At the very least it would be harder for them to attack her.

When she saw a round-ish, twenty foot long break in the canopy, she dove, praying that she wouldn't hit any branches.

"Ahh!" she cried out when one particularly knobby one appeared and hit her on the arm. "Damn it!" She glanced out of habit to see if Daelan was around to reprimand her. When she realized what she was doing, she laughed bitterly. *Girl, you need to get your head in the game.*

The forest was old-growth oak and beech trees with very little brush, so she flew just a couple of feet off the ground to avoid as many branches as possible. Fallen leaves flew up behind her because of the wind of her passage, making it unfortunately easy for the other mages to see where she had gone.

When she realized what the leaves were doing, she despaired. *At least they're not hitting me with anything.* That would buy her a few more minutes of flying.

Her mind raced, trying to find a way to escape, when she saw a leaning tree that looked like it would fall if it weren't caught on the branches of another one. She had been veering back and forth, trying to cause the mages to crash with no success, so she veered in the tree's direction. When she passed it, she gave it a hard enough pull to dislodge the tree, careful not to do any bodily motions that would tip the mages off about what she was doing.

They would hear and see the tree eventually, of course, but she hoped by then it would be too late to avoid it.

That was about a half-minute worth of mana for flying. I hope it was worth it.

She was rewarded with yells and cursing from behind. When she had the time to sneak a glimpse, she did. Just two mages, a young man and a woman, were chasing her, and they looked pissed.

Yes!

A few moments later she was clipped by a hurled rock, which dissipated more of her mana and altered her trajectory to the point that her side slammed into a tree, breaking her shield.

"Ow! Damn it..." she cried as she collected herself and started rising to her feet. "Have to get out of here..."

"The only place you're going is with us, you little harpy," a young man's voice said. The two mages landed on the ground twenty feet away and started approaching her cautiously.

Imogen rose despite the pain, leaning against a tree for support. Her breathing rasped painfully. She suspected she had broken ribs.

I'm out of mana. What do I do? Coming up with nothing, she asked herself, *What would Daelan do?* She laughed painfully when she thought, *He would throw Quoz at them and reap their mana.* It was not, unfortunately, useful advice for her situation.

"What's that?" the woman asked, pointing at the golden arm cuff that was exposed by her torn shirt.

The arm cuff! It still has mana!

It was unaspected mana that would not shield or fly her as well as her own, but it would do in a pinch. She lifted herself into the air until she was slammed back down to the ground.

"She still has mana!"

The two mages both launched fireballs at her. Imogen, being pinned to the ground, was terrified. Her training paid off, though, as she raced through the words of the spell in record time, forming the field just in time to keep from being cooked.

She started looking for a rock to throw at them when she heard a familiar voice.

"It's alright, Imogen."

"Daelan?" She looked up and saw her mentor. She was so happy and relieved that she almost didn't notice the mages. The woman's bisected body was dribbling out blood, most of it already soaking into the rich forest soil. The young man was scowling as he probed a lump on his head with his fingers. Daelan's ebon blade was at his throat. "You got out!"

He smiled gently and nodded. "Thanks to you. Are you okay?".

She grimaced. "Sort of? I think I have some broken ribs."

"Don't worry. I'll get you taken care of." Daelan turned his attention to the mage at his feet and sighed. "You shouldn't have gotten involved, Gabriel."

"Why? Feeling guilty after murdering my father?" Gabriel snarled.

Daelan shook his head. "No, I..." He stopped and thought about it for a second, and realized he did feel... something. Maybe it was guilt. Having lost his father himself, Daelan felt bad for taking away Gabriel's. It made no sense. He had killed several people today and didn't feel bad about it. Why feel sorry for Gabriel just because of his dad? He scowled and said, "Maybe."

Imogen looked between the two of them. "What's going on, Daelan?"

"This is the guy I kidnapped when they took you. I set a trap that killed his dad when he came to get Gabriel."

"Oh," She looked at Gabriel with sympathy and said, "Sorry."

"You can take your 'sorry' and shove it up your..."

Daelan kicked him in the head hard enough to stun the young man. "Do *not* finish that sentence," he growled. Frowning, he looked at Imogen. "What do you think we should do with him?"

It only took a second before she said, "Let him go."

Though he had been half-expecting it, he was still flummoxed. "Why? I killed her," he pointed at the other mage. "Why spare him?"

She looked at him sadly. "Not everything can be reasoned with logic, Daelan. There's been enough death today."

He didn't like it, but wasn't eager to kill the young man either, so he just said, "Fine," and leaned down towards the mage. "We can do this the hard way, or you can suck in your stomach."

Gabriel looked defiant. "Just do it," he said, not sucking in his stomach at all.

Rolling his eyes, Daelan gently put his palm on Gabriel's stomach and pressed inwards, forcing his way as gently as he could to the mage's mana core. He tried to take Gabriel's mana, but the mage resisted. Daelan growled, "I'm trying to be nice about this kid, but I will kill you if you don't let me take it."

Gabriel looked even angrier, but turned his head away. When Daelan tried again, he was able to pull the mana to himself. He stood up and said, "Alright, get out of here."

The mage warily got up and looked like he was about to spit at Daelan before thinking better of it. "I'm going to kill you," he said, before turning around to walk away.

"Join the club," Daelan muttered. Once Gabriel had walked far enough that he wasn't concerned about him, Daelan turned to Imogen. "How bad are your ribs?"

The thought of riding piggyback on Daelan caused her ribs to throb painfully. "Bad enough that I'm not sure I can ride on your back like we used to do."

"Just lie down in a comfortable position, and I'll take it from there."

She did as she was told, grimacing in pain the entire way. Any kind of movement hurt. Hell, breathing hurt, but she still got down.

Daelan got by her side and lifted her telekinetically, somehow making it as gentle as a bed. "Are you ready?"

"Yeah, but are you sure you have enough mana for this?" She knew that distance increased the cost of magic, and she really didn't want to fall out of the air.

Daelan looked at her, thinking of all the mages he had killed that day. "Don't worry. I've got plenty."

Chapter 52

Daelan

Daelan was in turmoil. He was pissed, and sad, and proud, and concerned, and outraged, and…

He was not used to this mix of emotions. He was plenty familiar with all of the emotions and feeling them strongly, but generally just *one at a time*. Feeling all of them at once was exhausting.

He looked down at Imogen, and despite his anger at the mages, the emotion that dominated was how proud he was of her. She had shown a great deal of courage, courage that he didn't know she'd had. *You did well, kid.*

He often felt at a loss with Imogen. None of the lessons he learned in Hell applied. One of his greatest fears was reacting to her the way he would have with his minions whenever she gave him teenage attitude.

What would Joseph have done?

He remembered times when Joseph was proud of her and later regretted not telling her that.

"I'm proud of you, Imogen. You did good."

She looked up at him, eyes wide. Once she got over the shock, she looked pleased, then playful. "Did it hurt to say?"

His brows furrowed as he asked, "Why would it have hurt?"

She smiled with only a bit of a wince as she said, "Oh, I don't know. Maybe because you had to form your mouth in strange and unfamiliar ways. Use muscles that have never been used before to get those words out."

He rolled his eyes. "Har, har."

She looked up at him with a sincere expression. "Thank you, Uncle Daelan. You have no idea how glad I am that you got out."

"Me too. Tomorrow they were going to take me to Sicanthus, the home of the God-King's empire."

Her eyes got wide again. "Tomorrow? I thought they couldn't make a portal for a couple of months, when the planets aligned or something!"

"Apparently they were so eager to take me in that they were willing to use a shit-ton of mana to do it."

"Language, Daelan," she said with a smirk.

He shook his head and chuckled.

"So what do we do now?" she asked.

"I'll make sure you're taken care of, and then I'm going back."

"Back?!" She coughed a couple of times after yelling and winced in pain. "Why?"

"Because they've seen my tattoo, and it's only a matter of time before they learn how to make it themselves and use it."

"So?"

"So that will make it easy for the empire to invade Earth."

"Oh, crap..."

"Yeah," he nodded.

"Thousands of mages full of mana..." she whispered to herself. "Wait, doesn't the Empire already have the runes? I mean, your dad was the ruler and all."

"He was, but out of caution he didn't give away all his secrets. Runes were one of them. And no, if they come, it won't be thousands of mages, rather *hundreds* of thousands who are trained to fight together."

She absorbed that for a time. "People will figure out what they're doing and shut off the electricity."

Daelan nodded. "Probably, but how much damage will they do in the meantime? Better to keep them from coming at all."

"Yeah."

"So, where do you want me to take you?"

Imogen frowned and said, "Anywhere with an outlet."

He raised his eyebrows. He looked at her face. She looked... resolute. *She's grown.* He nodded slowly and said, "Okay."

**

After healing Imogen and setting her up in a motel, Daelan made his way to the Society's headquarters and got into the campus easily. He was not concerned about the physical protections and the cameras. Between his invisibility spell and being able to phase past walls, they were minor inconveniences. The only real problem was the magical alarm.

He waited for a mage to pass through to see what happened. When he saw the mage pause until the alarm was disabled, causing it to disappear, he nodded.

Just like in Miami.

He would have said that they were foolish to stick to their usual protocol, but if they hadn't, he would have passed even more easily with one of the slain mages' necklaces. Since he didn't have his mana cuff, he flew to the closest cover, a tree, and hid behind it. He turned off his invisibility, as it was unneeded and was a significant drain on his mana.

Now all he had to do was wait. He would have been concerned about the mages finding him—they were patrolling the campus vigorously after the attack—if any of them had the third eye, but none of them did.

Besides the Merlin, I suppose.

Since he was a good hundred yards away, when Daelan saw the next mage approach he flew invisibly at near-supersonic speeds to get through the disabled alarm in time. He had to use his stillness mana to keep his passage from making noise or creating a breeze. As soon as he made it, he flew to one of the gabled roofs where he couldn't be seen. The exact spot, as it turned out, that Imogen had used. Once there, he turned off his invisibility again, caught his breath, and used an x-ray vision spell to scout the headquarters.

Mithril, like bone, would show up very easily, especially if they left the mana in it.

There it is.

It was in a nearby building, the one he had been held in. It was next to a person with much denser mana than anyone on Earth he'd seen before. It was someone who had a *dao* and knew how to condense their mana.

Merlin.

None of the Earth mages knew about daos. The only person it could be was Merlin, the Sicanthian assassin.

How convenient that he and the arm cuff are in the same place, he thought with a dark smile. They were in a different building, but that was easily remedied by invisibly flying to the roof of the right one.

While he spoke the words of power for the phasing spell that would allow him to pass through the roof and walls, he saw that the Merlin had picked up the arm cuff and was standing next to an artifact full of mana. Concerned, he finished the spell and drifted towards them as he descended.

What's going on?

Daelan paused before descending into the room because he saw a mana barrier. He examined it more closely with his third eye, though, and saw that it was a simple silence spell, presumably to prevent eavesdroppers.

Daelan descended into the room and saw the Merlin talking with a man via a communication artifact. They were speaking in Sicanthian, the language of the God-King's empire.

"...ave good news and bad news, sir."

The man on the screen, who wore the uniform of a general in the Sicanthian army, frowned. "I don't like the sound of that. What happened?"

"We, uh, unfortunately lost the avatar, general, but we will..."

"You lost the avatar?" the general asked in a voice that could have chilled dry ice.

"Y-yes, sir, but I found him once. I'll find him again."

You don't have to worry, assassin. I'll find you, Daelan thought grimly. He had been making his preparations while listening, including turning off the phasing spell and starting a silence spell with a thought using his *stillness* mana. Since invisibility was not part of his *dao*, the mana costs were chewing through the mana in his core, but it was necessary to maintain for now. He looked at his mithril arm cuff longingly. *I can't wait to have you back.*

"Hmph. So what's the good news?"

The Merlin smiled with a look of relief, presumably glad to have made it through the worst part of the meeting.

"I found out how the avatar has been getting mana. He..."

The general didn't get to hear the secret to Daelan's mana generation, because the Merlin's head fell to the ground, followed shortly by the rest of his body. Daelan released the invisibility spell and unsummoned Quoz, revealing himself to the general.

"General," Daelan said with a slight nod that would be an appropriate gesture of respect from the God-King to one of his underlings.

The Sicanthian's eyes narrowed, and Daelan thought he saw a flash of fear in the man's eyes. *If so, he smothered it very quickly.*

The general spoke slowly. "I take it that you are the avatar."

Daelan nodded. "I am."

"How did you escape the purge?"

Daelan adopted a serene expression and said nothing.

"You don't look like the God-King," the general continued.

Daelan snorted. "If you knew anything about the avatars, you would know that very few of us looked like him. Anyway, this is not my true appearance."

The general considered the man in front of him. "I take it you want to talk. What do you wish to say?"

At least he's not a complete imbecile. "What is your name?"

"General Horace."

"Is this communication being recorded, General?" He knew it was. The God-King had created the communication mirrors, or at least their progenitors, and established the protocols of the military.

"It is."

Daelan smiled. "Then you have a choice to make, General Horace, because I am a true avatar of the God-King, and intend to take back what is mine. And…" he said as he snapped his fingers and used mana and a magic security code to turn off the recording, "…the device will show that we will have talked for a period of time, unrecorded, after I announced myself."

The general looked alarmed at the announcement, and fiddled with the device at his end to confirm whether it was true or not.

He looked paler when he finished and returned to the conversation. "How did you do that?"

Daelan looked at him gravely. "I am, for all intents and purposes, the God-King." While that was not strictly true, of course, Daelan considered it to be close enough. He had a cloned soul, a similar personality, and, particularly relevant for this discussion, the passwords for the backdoors that Darius had put into key pieces of his empire's infrastructure. "You have three choices. You can tell your masters everything and try to convince them that you remain loyal, but you and I both know that they will never trust you again. Your career is over at this moment if you go that route. The second choice is to erase all evidence of our conversation and tell them that it turned out there was no avatar, in the hopes that you can get them to not look too closely into it. That could work as long as you are competent and convincing."

Daelan paused here and let the general chew on what he'd said.

"And the third choice?"

Daelan smiled predatorily. "You work for me. I am coming to Sicanthus, General. You and everyone else will have to pick a side. I suggest you pick mine, because I will prevail." He paused and said, "And because I have excellent blackmail material."

The general had a pretty decent poker face, but there was no hiding the flash of fear. "What blackmail material?"

"Do you really think you can erase all the evidence of this chat? When I come to Sicanthus, I will bring a recording of this conversation with me. I can, of course, make alterations to the recording if needed."

The general looked angry. "Well, you're certainly as ruthless as the God-King anyway."

Daelan chuckled. "Thank you. So, what do you say?"

The general chewed on his cheek while he looked at Daelan. He sighed and said, "It seems I don't really have a choice."

Daelan nodded. "I'm glad you understand."

"What do you want from me?"

"For now, I want you to collect some materials…" Daelan listed off the materials he would need to reforge his body and fix the deterioration from leaving Hell. He was careful to mix the required ingredients with others, to throw the general off track if he tried to figure out what Daelan intended to do with them.

"It will be difficult to get all these materials discreetly. How quickly do you need them?"

"I will require them in two months. Be as discreet as you can."

The general nodded. "It shall be done, God-King."

"Good." Daelan looked cold. "Don't disappoint me, General."

"I won't, Your Majesty."

Daelan favored him with a smile. "Serve me well, and I will reward you beyond your dreams when I ascend to the throne."

"Thank you, Your Majesty."

Daelan ended the conversation. He considered what had happened as he put on his mithril arm cuff. He wasn't sure he wanted to be the God-King, but if he wanted revenge, there wasn't really another option. He had known that for a while, but had avoided thinking about it.

It was long past time to acknowledge the reality of the situation. Daelan had to ascend to the throne and kill his enemies, or die.

Chapter 53

Two months later

Daelan walked out of his thatched cabin a different man. He had just changed back to his original face and form, because he had no desire to live a second longer as "George Miller" than he had to, even if changing back had been painful as hell.

He walked through fine sand that let his feet sink in until they were almost buried with every step. The heat of the sand was relaxing for him, like a warm blanket.

Which probably means it's painfully hot for Imogen. Oh well. She'll live.

Daelan lowered himself onto a beach lounge chair gingerly, wincing at the never-ceasing pain. He reached into the cooler, pulled out a cold beer, popped the top off, and took a swig.

This is nice, he thought as he listened to the crashing of the waves and breathed in the clean air seasoned with a touch of salt.

He watched Imogen bodysurf a wave in and stand up before running aground on the wet sand. She walked out of the water and towards the other lounge chair, turning it into a run as she got closer and her feet got drier. When she plopped down into the chair she grimaced and brushed the sand off her feet.

"Stupid hot sand." She glanced at him and asked, "How come it never bothers you?"

Daelan shrugged. Though he was in the closest thing he'd found to paradise and had enjoyed traveling the last two months and taking it easy, he was feeling a little melancholy. He still trained Imogen, but at a slower tempo. They both needed the break. Imogen for the last ten months, and him for the last 200 years.

"Have you had fun?" he asked her.

She smiled. "Yeah."

"Good." On a whim, he pulled out his phone and got ready to take a selfie of the two of them, the arthritis in his elbow flaring as he extended his arm out. "Say 'hi' to Rob, Imogen." Imogen smiled and waved at the camera. He emailed the photo to the Calvary Hill Men's Shelter with the text, "Rob, It's not Tahiti and she isn't my girlfriend and no one is fanning me, but I'm at the beach and life is good. Wish you were here. John."

"What was that about?"

"Just saying 'hi' to a friend."

She shrugged, put on her sunglasses, and lay back on the lounge chair to soak up the sun.

"You don't have to go, you know."

She turned her head to look at him and scowled. "We've talked about this before. I want to stay with you."

"I know. It's just that I think you would be safer here."

"It's not safe anywhere, Daelan. Your enemies could try to capture me to get at you. Besides, how would I make money? With my booming writing career?"

Daelan smiled. "Just think of all the great material you're getting. Make my character handsome, okay?"

She looked at him and slowly shook her head.

"Handsome is asking for too much, eh?"

"I'm staying with you."

Daelan chewed his lip. "You sure?"

"Yeah."

"Alright."

**

The next day, they gathered by the cabin. It was nearly time. Though they could probably make a portal anytime over the next couple of hours, there was a window of a few minutes that was most propitious.

Both of them were dressed in leather sandals and rather expensive clothes that did not look expensive, because they were made of organic hemp. Daelan wanted them to be able to pass as locals when they got to rural Sicanthus, and while these clothes weren't perfect, they would suffice.

Neither one was wearing a backpack, because Daelan had made a mithril storage ring for himself, so Imogen wouldn't be the only "pack mule".

362

"Are you sure you've got everything?"

Imogen rolled her eyes. "Yes, I'm sure. It's not like it's hard to check a two-room cabin."

Daelan curled his lips. "I suppose you're right." He watched the waves as the seconds counted down. Eventually his phone beeped to tell him it was time. "Are you ready?"

Imogen looked nervous, but her voice was steady. "As I'll ever be."

Daelan nodded and started speaking the words of power while drawing on the mana in the mithril arm cuff. Its ten large, perfect diamonds could hold a massive amount of mana—far more than was needed for the portal. Still, he said the words as precisely and applied his will with as much clarity as he could, so there would be no problems. It did not take a lot of error in an interplanetary portal spell to have a really bad day.

The spell went off with no hitches, and they saw a grassy knoll on the other side.

We're really doing this. Part of Daelan was afraid. They were going into the belly of the beast, after all, but if he wanted to live there was no other choice.

And he did want to live. Before, he would have been fine dying if it meant killing his enemies. He looked at Imogen, who smiled at him with trust, and knew that revenge wasn't enough now. He wanted to live, to protect her and the other families left behind by his siblings.

Daelan held his hand out to Imogen. "Let's go."

Thank You!

Thank you for reading "Daelan the Damned"! I hope that some part of it has resonated with you.

I would be truly grateful if you would leave a review or rating of the book. Amazon being what it is, your feedback has a massive effect on how many people see it.

www.ingramcontent.com/pod-product-compliance
Lightning Source LLC
Chambersburg PA
CBHW051943240626
47153CB00005B/1604